never going to happen

who watches the watchers?

ANDERS TELLER

Topham

PUBLISHING

To Cass,
whose unfailing support is a constant inspiration

"The one pervading evil of democracy is the tyranny of the majority, or rather of that party, not always the majority, that succeeds, by force or fraud, in carrying elections."
– Lord Acton, *History of Freedom and Other Essays* (1907)

"Power always sincerely, conscientiously, de très bon foi, *believes itself right. Power always thinks it has a great soul and vast views, beyond the comprehension of the weak.*
– John Adams, in a letter to Thomas Jefferson (1816)

"The best love is unexpected."
– Anon

Foreword

On 23 June 2016 the people of the United Kingdom voted in a referendum to leave the European Union, which the nation had joined in 1973. The vote was carried by 51.9 per cent to 48 per cent of the eligible electorate on a turnout of 72 per cent. A two-year period of negotiation leading up to withdrawal started the following March.

On November 8 2016 the people of the United States voted in Donald J Trump as their forty-fifth President. He won the election by 304 electoral votes to 227, although the 65.8 million popular votes cast for his opponent, Hillary Clinton, amounted to 2.9 million more than those cast for him.

These are facts. The rest of this story is fiction.

Chapter 1

White coats, green scrubs, grey walls. Long corridor, tall windows. The bustle of visitors in uncoordinated outdoor clothes, peering around for direction signs to the ward they want. The ping of lifts arriving and leaving. A cluster of hard hospital chairs against the wall. His left leg stretched out in front of him, captive from the knee down in its complex metal and fabric splints. A dull but incessant ache.

A nurse in light blue uniform apologising. "We're finding it hard to recruit porters these days." A quick smile. "Hang on – there must be somebody who can take you downstairs."

So he waited. He didn't have much option. Finally she was back with a wheelchair and man in his early twenties to push it. "Good luck." An encouraging smile. "You'll be fine. Just give it time."

Down to the thronging foyer, then the porter parked him at the end of a row of plastic seats. "You should be all right here." And he was gone.

So this was what it was like to be an invalid, consigned to the mercy of strangers. Up in the ward, the constant attention had been a distraction from his compromised state, but here among the fit and the walking wounded he felt helpless.

Where was Jan? She'd said she would be here when they discharged him, but there was no sign of her. His mobile phone was packed away in his bag, and he was in no mood to wrestle with that. So he watched the world go by, and counted the seconds between each pulse of pain from his leg.

Suddenly she materialised, crisply dressed as though ready for a business meeting. Her dark shoulder-length hair bounced on her shoulders in that familiar way.

"Ready?" A forced brightness.

He glanced up at her. "As I'll ever be." He attempted to pull his crutches on board while she fiddled at the back of the chair, trying to release the handbrake. Finally they were heading out through the main doors and into fresh air – the first he'd experienced for what seemed like a lifetime.

"Thank god for that," she muttered. "I hate hospitals."

"You're not the only one."

As she trundled him over to the short-term car park, every bump seemed to jar his whole body. She was talking as she pushed. "If you're wondering why I was late, I couldn't risk hanging around. If I'd left the car and waited for you, it would have been clamped by the time we got back to it."

"Don't worry about it."

It was soon clear that he couldn't get into the front passenger seat; the leg brace was too bulky, and he could only partly bend his knee. The solution turned out to be sitting across the back seat, half-leaning against the door pillar.

He would have preferred to be returning to their terraced house in Winchester. Although Storton was only twenty-five minutes away down narrow country lanes, the village felt like another world. But she'd kept insisting that this would be better. "Think about it, Tom – where would you sleep if you were in Winchester? How would you cope with the stairs?" In the end he'd given in.

Centuries-old buildings fronted the village's main street, but Jan continued to the outskirts, slowing as they approached a large nineteenth-century house. It was partly hidden behind a thick hedge and was flanked by similar properties. As they pulled into the short driveway Tom noticed a black multi-purpose vehicle parked opposite. It was out of character with its rustic surroundings, and its dark-tinted windows gave it the slightly sinister air of something from a spy movie.

He forgot it as he wrestled with his crutches at the front door. "I suppose I'll get used to these in time."

A little awkwardly she said, "Welcome to your new home."

Temporary home, he reminded himself. He didn't want to live here permanently, in Jan's parents' former home. When her father had died a couple of months before his accident, they'd talked about keeping this house and renting it out, and she'd had the place renovated while he was in hospital. Now it was to be the scene of his convalescence.

He attempted a cheerful smile as she led him to the lounge. It was a relief to flop down. She slid a footstool over to support his leg, and he glanced around at the improvements she'd had done on the property. He knew she'd had a new bathroom and kitchen fitted, and the place appeared to have been redecorated throughout.

"The refurbishment job you've done on this house is amazing."

"It was good timing. The workmen only finished last week."

"It's like a show home."

She followed his gaze. "Just a bit of judicious updating, and it was transformed. The work cost less than you might think. It's a pity my father couldn't have lived to see the potential of the place."

"It's a nice nest-egg for you, inheriting this house."

She shrugged. "It's too big for us, of course. Once you're properly on your feet again we'll need to rent it out."

"We can use the money. I won't be bringing in much for a while." He gave her a guilty look.

"I can't exactly blame you for that." It should have been a reassuring comment, but was there a hint of reproach in it?

* * *

When they'd first got together three years ago, Tom had thought of Jan as his soul mate: lively personality, quirky sense of humour, always on his wavelength. She was also good looking – tall and slim, with dark silky hair, high cheekbones and penetrating blue-green eyes. They'd met at a conference, and with almost unseemly speed they'd moved in together. And for more than two years they'd lived a happy life in their little house in Winchester.

Gradually, though, something had changed, and the cause was more than just the accident. Officially they were still living that same happy life, yet an edginess had entered their relationship. Then the accident had put everything on hold. During his long months in hospital they'd seemed to strike a tacit agreement to rewind to an earlier time. He wasn't convinced. Perhaps the veneer of goodwill had worn too thin.

She cooked him a pasta, which she presented in the lounge on a tray:

his first home-cooked food for many months. She said, "Don't get too excited – I won't be providing room service every day."

He attempted a smile.

Apparently she wasn't planning on joining him. "I had a heavy business lunch," she explained. "I couldn't eat another thing."

Had he offended her? It occurred to him that he should have expressed more interest in her life. He'd been too focused on his own situation. He now said, "How are things with you? I should have asked you before."

She gave a small sigh. "Fine, thanks. We're overstretched, but what's new in that?" Her job in finance took her to London's Docklands every day – an hour-long train journey from Winchester, plus local travel in London. She'd taken a day off to collect him from the hospital. He should have shown more gratitude.

"I'm glad all's well."

She'd made up a single bed for him in a small room adjoining the lounge. "Dennis from next door helped me carry it downstairs." She led him round the corner to a ground-floor shower room. "Convenient, isn't it? You can see why I thought this was such a good idea."

She watched as he unpacked his overnight bag on the bed, fumbling awkwardly with his crutches. She stepped forward, wanting to help him, but he recoiled. "Best if I learn how to do this kind of thing on my own."

So she leaned against the wall instead. "I've got you set up with my parents' doctor here in Storton," she said. "I thought it would be crazy for you to have to trek all the way to the surgery in Winchester every time you need something."

"Thank you."

"I'll take you to see him next week. I've made an appointment."

He straightened and looked directly at her. "Thanks for everything you've done here. You've really put yourself out."

She waved away the compliment. "You're welcome."

He sat down awkwardly on the bed. "So what's the latest on the accident?"

Chapter 2

The accident: a mystery as yet unexplained. One evening earlier in the year he'd taken it into his head to get into his car and drive out into the country – destination unknown. On the way back from wherever he went, he'd hit a tree and turned his car over in a ditch, and it was several hours before a passing motorist had discovered him.

This was what he'd been told, though he had absolutely no memory of it. One minute he was watching TV at home, the next minute he was lying in a hospital bed, barely able to move, and people were saying it was nine days later.

Jan asked, "You still don't remember anything about it? No change now that you're out in the world again?"

"No, it's a complete blank. I don't remember anything from the entire week leading up to the accident." He'd worked this out over a period of weeks. Lying in that hospital bed, he'd had plenty of time for such reflection.

"Maybe it's just as well. It must have been a horrible experience."

"All the same, I want to remember. Have the police told you anything more?"

She shook her head. "They haven't been in touch for weeks now.

"But they still think no else was involved?"

"Not as far as I know. It was a one-car accident. Nobody knows the cause, and obviously you don't remember it yourself. Maybe you swerved off the road to avoid a fox or something."

It was a logical explanation, yet somehow it didn't ring true. Tom prided himself on his good driving. That kind of mistake seemed completely out of character. He said, "At least they don't think I was drunk."

"No, the blood-alcohol test was unequivocal."

"And still no sign of my phone?"

"Sorry, no. Oh, and I meant to tell you – the computer store confirmed that there's no chance of repairing your old laptop. They didn't even think they could recover any data from it."

"Great." He paused a moment to take this on board. "And have you had any more thoughts about why I was on the Twyford road? Where was I going? Or was I coming back? Last time I asked, no one seemed clear about that."

"The police said you were coming back from the Twyford direction, but I have absolutely no idea why."

"So I definitely didn't tell you where I was going?"

"I wasn't at home, don't forget. I stayed over in London that night. You never said anything about going out when I left home that morning."

"Do we know someone who lives in that area? I can't think of anyone."

She shook her head. "It's as much a mystery to me as it is to you."

* * *

The first night in the village proved a long one. The hospital had been like a machine – sometimes busy, sometimes quiet, always ticking over. He'd grown used to the constant background hum, to the soft steps of the night staff, even to the occasional burst of excitement over some medical emergency.

By contrast, his room in the village was utterly silent. He couldn't settle. Also the bed was uncomfortable. It was modern, but the slatted headboard was hard, and the yielding mattress felt alien. He finally fell asleep through sheer exhaustion from the events of the day.

When he woke at nine thirty Jan had long since left for London. He dressed slowly and carefully. The shower room mirror was too low for his six-foot frame; he had to stoop slightly to shave. He studied his reflection thoughtfully. He looked fitter than he felt, and that eager expression, often commented on by friends, was back in place in spite of everything. His light brown hair seemed too short; the over-enthusiastic hospital hairdresser had seen to that.

He made his way to the kitchen. Carrying a mug whilst on crutches proved impossible, so he sat awkwardly on a stool at the breakfast bar to tackle coffee and toast.

When he'd finished he swung his way through to the lounge and over to the window, and gazed absently out into the house's unexciting gravelled drive. Just visible through the gateway was the black vehicle with darkened windows that he'd seen yesterday. It seemed odd that it should be parked there when every house in this stretch of road seemed to have ample parking space in its own driveway.

He dismissed the thought and took up position on the sofa. He had some calls to make. The first was to his friend Bernard, who had left a cryptic text message for him, saying he had news to report. Tom announced, "I'm out! I'm at the village."

"Good for you."

"What's this news you've got for me?"

"I've got a job driving – and guess where. At Carswells!"

"You're having a joke."

"Deadly serious. It's part-time. I choose my days and hours, I use my own car, and the pay's not bad."

Both men had been managers at Carswells, a courier company outside Southampton. Bernard was much older than Tom, and had retired several years ago, but had complained to Tom on numerous occasions since then that he was bored.

Tom said, "Don't you find it a bit demeaning, taking orders from people you were once in charge of?"

Bernard sounded indignant. "Not at all. I hardly see them. I just get a call or a text with instructions for the day."

"Well, good for you."

"You should give it a try yourself when you're back on your feet – that's assuming you don't find something else to occupy your mind."

"Huh. I'll keep it in mind."

His next call was to Malcolm Drew, a friend from his student days. He and Malcolm had done media studies at college together. Afterwards, Tom had found a job on a local newspaper, but when it closed down he'd switched to the management world.

Malcolm had stuck with journalism, and was now an assistant editor on a high-profile news website, *Seismic Scene* – one that had transcended the ephemerality of so much on the internet, gaining a solid status and reputation in the realms of news reporting. Some regarded it as a mainstream challenger to the *Huffington Post*.

Tom said, "I thought I should square things with you about that article. I've just come out of hospital."

"Do I presume you're recovering from your argument with the tree?"

"Little by little."

"So are we back on track with the article?"

This was not what Tom wanted to hear. He said, "I thought I'd missed the boat with that after all this time." What he meant was that he was hoping he'd missed it.

"Not at all. It's just as much a hot topic now as it was then. More so, if anything."

Tom thought back to his last encounter with Malcolm, not long before the accident. Malcolm had come down from London to spend the weekend with him and Jan. On the first night the two of them had ended up in a long session at the pub, and as the evening wore on, Tom had become increasingly vocal on a single subject: Britain's looming exit from the European Union.

In the end, Malcolm had turned to him with a glint in his eye. "Seeing as you're so fired up on this subject, why don't you write a keynote article for us? 'Brexit – an everyman's viewpoint'. Something like that."

Tom had demurred. "I'm out of practice. I haven't written for the media for years."

"Once a journo, always a journo."

"But I don't know anything about Brexit."

"You obviously have views, though. You'll bring a fresh take and an enquiring mind. What more could we ask? And it'll give you some pocket money while you're in between jobs."

Tom wasn't so sure. Like many people, he'd been stunned when, just over six months earlier, the referendum had resulted in a narrow margin in favour of Britain leaving the EU. But his views, as Malcolm characterised them, mainly concerned the disorganised and fractious debate that had immediately erupted over the terms of departure, threatening to blight exit negotiations before they even started. When it came to the merits of leaving or staying in the union, his thoughts were much vaguer.

As they'd stumbled out of the pub, Tom had merely told Malcolm he would think about it, but the next day Malcolm had emailed him with a briefing note, plus leads to follow up, a proposed fee and a deadline. Suddenly the project had become a reality.

He now said, "You do realise a lot of what I know is at least four months out of date?"

"All the better. You'll come to the subject without too much prejudice."

"But why now?"

"Why now?" Malcolm paused before answering. "Because Brexit is in the news every day, yet no one is standing back and seeing the big picture. Everyone's wrapped up in procedure. More of us need to ask again why we're doing this at all."

"And you think I'm the right person for this?"

"You have a good analytical mind. You'll be able to get your head round the issues and explain them in a balanced way." He warmed to his subject. "I'm imagining something with a bit of input from selected talking heads on both sides. I can give you contacts."

"Have a heart! I'm still on crutches. I'm not exactly mobile. I'm still getting my bearings. I don't want to over-promise on this ..."

"But you can talk on the phone? You can type?"

"Well, I suppose I could take another run at it – but don't rush me. I need to get back into my stride."

"Completion in a month's time?"

"I think it'll take longer than that."

"It gives us something to aim for." It was a neat bit of manipulation, but Tom wasn't quick enough to protest.

He ended the call with a sense of disbelief. He knew he'd been railroaded, but that wasn't the foremost thought in his mind. He was reflecting on the strange fact that he'd talked about the subject with such passion in the first place. He seemed to be finding a political instinct he'd never recognised before.

Chapter 3

The sound of the front door buzzer burst through Tom's thoughts. Several shapeless days had passed since his return from the hospital, and he was beginning to suffer from cabin fever. He swung his way through to the hall and pulled open the door. Any variation from his normal routine seemed welcome.

A woman in her twenties was standing there, holding a brown leather case under her arm. Her light-coloured hair was pulled back in a bunch, and she was wearing a shapely tan business jacket and skirt. She gave him a bright smile, holding out her hand. "Tom Anthony? Emily Sanders. I'm sorry I'm a bit early." A glance at her watch. "It seemed pointless hanging around waiting for the appointed hour."

He adjusted his crutches. "Sorry – you're a bit early for what?"

"For the insurance run-through. It *is* today, isn't it?" She frowned. "Yes, of course it is. Wednesday at ten. When were you expecting me?" She had a slightly husky voice, and he now noticed a faint Lancashire accent.

"I wasn't. Who set this up?"

Now she was looking puzzled. "My boss. I thought he talked to you, or sent you an email? He must have."

He shook his head. "News to me." He forced a smile. "Maybe he did. Poor memory seems to be one of the after-effects of my accident. Come on in." He hopped aside on his crutches and waved her past. "Go straight on through that way. I was just making coffee."

She put her case down on the kitchen table and turned to the counter. "I can finish doing this if you like."

"Thanks."

He sat down on one of the kitchen stools and watched her. She was attractive, though her turnout was somewhat severe. She kept reaching round to lift her ponytail off her collar, as if she was unused to it. He said, "Remind me why you're here."

"The insurance company requires someone to come and see you in person, to confirm the extent of your injuries."

"This is about my personal accident insurance, is it? Not my car insurance?"

"Yes, of course."

"It's just that my car insurance has been slow to pay out as well. I've been waiting for months for them to resolve this."

"Sorry to hear that." She gave him a chagrined smile.

"But I would have thought the hospital could have told you everything you need to know."

"You know what these companies are like."

She carried the coffees through to the lounge and they sat down opposite each other. She opened her case and pulled out a thin file of paperwork, then glanced around. "This place is nice. It's more modern than I expected from the outside."

"My partner had the house redecorated and refitted while I was in hospital. It belonged to her late father."

She nodded, then glanced down at her notes. "It says here that you're thirty-six." She looked up again as if genuinely surprised. "You're older than you look."

"What – you think I'm an impostor? Someone from rent-a-victim, maybe? Hired to cheat the insurance company?" He accompanied this with a smile.

"Sorry, no, of course not." She spread her hands towards him, perhaps implying that the contradiction was self-evident.

He shrugged. "Story of my life. People seem to think I'm younger than I am. They're inclined to assume I'll be a pushover."

"I wouldn't be complaining if it were me."

He smiled politely at this. "I treat it as an asset. People underestimate me, then I surprise them."

She smiled back at him. "I can imagine you do."

She explained that she needed to talk him through a checklist. Most of her questions were elementary, and many simply required one-word answers. Then at one point she said, "Do you have your hospital discharge paperwork handy?"

He raised his eyebrows. "I don't know. I have some medical notes that they gave me. Is that what you mean?"

She nodded, and he struggled to his feet and hopped through to his bedroom, returning with a thin sheaf of printed pages. "Will these do?"

She took them from him and leafed through them for a moment. He sat down and watched. "I just need to copy this page," she said, pulling out her phone and pointing it at one of the documents.

She resumed her questions. It took her only a few minutes to reach the final topic, which involved his memory loss. He explained that he remembered nothing about the accident itself, or the week leading up to it. Part-way through his account she held up her hand. "Do you mind if I video this part? They like to keep this kind of thing for their records."

"Really? I've never heard of anything like that."

"It's optional. You don't have to do it if you don't want to."

He shrugged. "Doesn't matter to me. Go ahead."

She lifted her phone again and held it towards him as he spoke. For a second time he explained his memory loss. She seemed very focused on this aspect, and quizzed him extensively on the sequence of events before and after the crash. What was the last thing he remembered? (A theatre visit the previous weekend.) What was the first new memory he had? (The taste of hospital coffee.) Had he managed to recover any of his missing memories during the months since the accident? (No.)

She moved on to ask what kind of treatment he was receiving, and how much hope he'd been offered of an eventual recovery of his memory. He told her, "No one will say for sure that I'll ever remember any more than I do now."

As she was gathering her belongings together he glanced at the notes she'd photographed. They were open on a page describing his memory loss. Key phrases jumped out at him: "Traumatic retrograde amnesia" and "No clear prognosis for recovery".

It was only as he was waving her away at the front door that he was struck by the fact that she hadn't been using a tablet computer, which seemed the *de facto* norm for such questionnaires. She'd been working purely from paper forms, which she hadn't actually showed him, and she hadn't asked him to sign anything. She hadn't even left him any

contact details. It was probably unimportant, but at least he should
have asked.

* * *

The chance to find out more about his memory loss came two days
later, when Jan had arranged for him to see the village doctor. She
skipped her day at the office in order to ferry him to and from the
appointment.

The surgery was based in the doctor's own house, a sprawling inter-
war property at the other end of the village. Jan dropped him outside,
then drove off to do some shopping at the tiny village store. He swung
himself through the portico into a square hallway like a sitting room,
where he was greeted by middle-aged woman behind a desk.

"Have a seat," she told him. "The doctor shouldn't be long."

There were easy chairs arranged against the walls. He struggled into
the highest he could find. The environment felt more like a hotel lounge
than the waiting room of a doctor's surgery. No other patients were in
evidence. He said to the receptionist, "Just the one doctor?"

"Yes, this is a single-doctor practice. We're a dying breed."

"Not surprising in a small village like this, I suppose."

"Dr Melcombe works in private practice three days a week. I just
come in for two mornings."

A door opened and a man leaned round. "Tom? Come on through."

The doctor sat down behind a desk and waved Tom to the patients'
upright chair. He was a good-looking man, probably somewhere in his
forties, with brushed-back sandy hair and a slightly reddish
complexion. Tom sat down obediently, cursing as one of his crutches
clattered to the floor.

"Don't worry about that," the doctor said. "How's the leg?"

"It hurts sometimes."

"But nothing drastic?"

"No, I think the medications are keeping things under control."

"Sounds as though everything is progressing normally." He gave a
tight smile. "You'll need to go back to the hospital for periodic check-

ups on the leg. They've done a remarkable job on you. Just treat me as your local fallback."

"So can you help me with my memory problems?"

"I can try."

"I can't remember anything at all from the week leading up to the accident. It's a total blank."

"This sometimes happens with traumatic episodes like yours. I'm sure you've had all this explained to you."

"So will I ever remember anything?"

"It's perfectly possible." He gave Tom a penetrating look. "You definitely don't remember anything at all just prior to the crash? Absolutely nothing?" It felt like a test he had to pass.

He shook his head emphatically, yet his mind immediately flashed back to white coats in the hospital, and to the ordeal of an MRI scan: lying on his back inside that great drum, and staying motionless for endless minutes while a strange array of noises assailed him – hums, whirrs, buzzes, clicks. Until this moment, that experience had completely disappeared from his memory.

"Actually there *are* things I vaguely remember from after the accident. A scan that I had, for instance."

The doctor was watching him closely. "But nothing from before?"

He shook his head. "A complete blank."

"You can't always hurry these things." The doctor leaned back. "Give it time."

* * *

Jan drove him back to the house. As they approached the gateway Tom noticed the black car with tinted windows, which was back once again in its position nearly opposite. He said, "Do you know whose car that is?"

"No idea. The woman who lives there doesn't have a car."

"It's a strange place to park."

Climbing out of the car, Tom swung his way back to the gateway on his crutches and looked across the street at the car. Was that a slight movement inside? On an impulse he started to cross the road towards it, thinking he would knock on the window and ask why it was there. As he approached, the engine started and the car pulled abruptly away. He swivelled in surprise and watched as it disappeared.

He turned with a shrug and headed indoors. He told Jan, "I'd like to go over to the house in Winchester some time, just to check it, and maybe to pick up a few bits and pieces."

"I've been going down every week or two since I moved up here, and in between times I've made arrangements to keep things ticking over. I've told you all this."

"All the same, I'd like to catch up with things for myself."

"Mary from next door is watering the plants every week. And our mail is being redirected here."

"You make it sound as if we're never going back. You don't really want to live here permanently in this house, do you?"

"Of course not. It's far too remote from everything."

He wondered if he was convinced by this. He said, "I would have thought you'd have picked Chris to do the watering." Christine lived across the road from the house in Winchester.

She gave him a strange look. "Christine doesn't need to be involved in everything we get up to." She turned on her heel before he could reply, and went off to work at the kitchen table.

What had she meant? Jan had never been entirely comfortable with Chris, but that dismissive tone seemed to take her dislike to a new level.

His relationship with Jan had started in what he'd thought of as a one-night stand – a single night that had extended to three years. Admittedly, it had taken a knock after that first intense weekend when he'd discovered that she was married – something she'd neglected to mention in the rush to her bedroom. He'd always kept his own life simple and clear-cut. Stealing another man's wife had not been part of the plan.

However, by that stage his involvement with her had been so all-consuming that he'd been prepared to adjust his philosophy. Before long she'd agreed to move into his house with him, and for most of the time since then he hadn't regretted it. She had already been heading for a divorce, and once that went through, the relationship had settled into one of sunny good nature on both sides.

Yet he couldn't ignore her recent edginess. Could their neighbour Christine have something to do with it?

Chapter 4

"Headington."

The abrupt response took Tom by surprise. He'd just dialled the number for one of the names supplied by Malcolm Drew as potential contacts for his Brexit article, but he hadn't expected an answer.

Marcus Headington was chair of a vigorous and growing think tank and campaigning organisation informed by a single objective: to head off Britain's exit from the EU. Malcolm wanted Tom to talk to a range of people with this kind of influence and test out their thinking at first hand. What Tom had originally envisaged as a piece of top-of-the-head comment had grown considerably in scope.

He'd met Headington once, shortly before his accident, but his memory of the encounter was vague. Still, this seemed a good place to start the research. He said, "Tom Anthony here. We met a few months ago, and we were going to schedule a chat about Brexit for an article I'm writing for *Seismic Scene*, the news website."

"Oh. Sorry, I thought you were someone else calling back." Headington paused, evidently flustered and perhaps about to end the call; but politeness won the day. "Who did you say you were?"

Rejoicing inwardly, Tom said, "Tom Anthony. I was hoping you could give me some informed input from the Remain camp for a news article."

There was a pause, then Headington said, "I think I remember your name. But didn't you cover this ground with me before?"

Surprised, Tom said, "We were going to schedule a proper conversation, but then I was in a car smash, so it never happened."

"I'm sorry to hear that."

"I'm trying to pick up the pieces. I want push the article to completion. I'm hoping you'll give me a few minutes more of your time to pass on your latest thinking."

"Of course. Have a word with my personal assistant or our press officer." He gave a slightly weary chuckle. "I should warn you, these days I tend to be booked up for weeks ahead."

This wasn't what Tom wanted to hear. He said, "But I'm already talking to you now. Could we not just pencil in a slot? A few minutes one evening, perhaps?"

Tom could almost hear Headington weighing up his options. He wanted to end the conversation, but he was reluctant to pass up the possibility of exposure for his cause. Unexpectedly, he said, "Look, you could drop in this Wednesday evening if you like. I happen to know that a meeting has just been cancelled, so I'll be free for a while. Do you know our campaign headquarters in Kensington?"

A personal visit was definitely not what Tom had in mind, but this seemed much too good an opportunity to miss.

"I'll find the place."

"About six-thirty PM, if that suits you."

*   *   *

Jan was unimpressed. "Are you really fit for a trip to London yet? All that stress could set back your recovery."

She was staring at him with a surprisingly scolding look. It transformed her undeniable attractiveness into something very different. In their early days, her chameleon-like changes had intrigued him, but latterly he'd found them increasingly unnerving.

He said, "I think a trip will do me good. The sooner I start to take control of my life, the sooner I'll get better physically."

She assented dubiously. "You're too nice, Tom. It's always been your downfall. You need to learn when to tell people no."

He shrugged. "I thought I could come into London with you on the train."

"I suppose that would make sense."

"The appointment isn't until the evening, so maybe I could wait around in your office or something?"

Immediately she was resistant. "I don't think that would work. They don't like spouses and partners hanging around there. I've told you that before."

She had, though he'd never understood the reasoning. Sitting in a reception area couldn't do any harm, could it? Besides, Jan was quite a high flyer. Surely she must have some influence with her employers? However, it didn't seem like something to argue about.

"I wonder if I could wait in the flat, then?"

"What about the stairs? You'd never manage them in a million years."

"Yeah, you're right. I never thought of that."

The tiny one-bedroom flat was on the top floor of an apartment block in that amorphous area of south London between Vauxhall and Brixton. Jan's brother had lived there, then when he'd moved to New York two years ago she'd taken over the tenancy from him. It gave her somewhere to stay in London when she was obliged to work late. With their two salaries coming in, this had just about been affordable, though if Tom remained jobless for long they might have to rethink it.

He said, "Well, I can wait in a lounge at one of the big hotels – that place at Victoria, for instance."

"Will you be OK travelling back to Winchester on your own?"

"I'll manage."

* * *

The journey to London went as planned. Jan took him with her in the car to Winchester, then found him an aisle seat in the train and helped him with his crutches. She buried herself in her laptop computer for most of the hour-long journey, while Tom spent much of the time calming the angry stabs of protest from his leg. It sapped his energy.

The Stay and Prosper campaign had its headquarters in a solid Georgian terrace in Kensington. Although it was early evening when the taxi dropped him outside the front door, a receptionist was still on duty. She buzzed him in and directed him to a large high-ceilinged waiting room. He lowered himself painstakingly into a modern easy chair, and one of his crutches thudded to the floor. He left it there.

Minutes passed, but there was no sign of Headington. Tom picked up a newspaper from the coffee table and scanned the front page. Monck Chervil, an American pharmaceuticals giant, had announced plans for multi-billion dollar investment in Europe, with the lion's share of new money coming to the UK. He speed-read the piece. It appeared that the deal would create several thousand jobs over the next two or three years, mostly in South Wales and the East Midlands – places where they were very much wanted.

He replaced the newspaper and picked up a pamphlet that turned out to have been published by the Stay and Prosper campaign itself. His eye was drawn to the row of asterisks in the headline.

Brexit Means B*******: Three Things You Should Know

1: Brexit does NOT mean Brexit

Actually Brexit means a mayfly's mating dance. Or the shavings left over from a carving made out of American maple. Or the fastener on my wife's purse.

*Do you see what we're getting at? Merely repeating the mantra "Brexit means Brexit" does not make it more true. It was meaningless in the first place. Technically it is called a tautology, but we call it b*******.*

2: The British public did NOT vote to leave

"The British public voted to leave." How often have you heard that? It's not true. To be precise, 37.4 per cent of the registered electorate voted Leave – a little over ONE THIRD. But 62.6 per cent either voted Remain or didn't vote at all. "Britain" didn't vote to leave. It was just some of the people who live here.

3: We will NOT better off if we leave the EU

After the Brexit vote, the pound dropped in value against other key currencies, which made our exports more attractive. Meanwhile, we're STILL IN THE EUROPEAN UNION! So until 2019 we have the best of both worlds. No economist knows what will happen after Brexit. Don't trust anyone who says they do.

Are we clearer now?

Chapter 5

A door was thrust open and Marcus Headington strode purposefully across the room, smiling apologetically.

"Tom, is it? Nice to see you again. I'm so sorry for the delay. I was held up in my last meeting. Thanks for taking the time to stop by." He held out a hand in greeting, and Tom struggled to his feet. As he did so, Headington stooped and handed him the crutch that had fallen.

Headington was the chair of an international engineering group – noted for his charismatic personality and his track record of turning round unsuccessful businesses. He was a well-built man in his fifties with sleeked-back light-coloured hair and a large, squarish face showing just the beginnings of a double chin. It was an attractive, reassuring face, familiar from television and the media. And immediately Tom was convinced that they had indeed met before.

"I see you've read our latest bit of propaganda," Headington said, glancing down at the pamphlet.

"Yes – very witty."

"Do you think so? My second-in-command says it's too brash. He's worried that people might find it patronising. We're not sure whether or not we'll actually circulate it."

"But all this stuff must be on the internet already, surely?"

"Of course, but it's a question of context and tone of voice. We want to win hearts and minds without giving offence. What comes out of this office must be persuasive, but also true, verifiable and non-aggressive. These are our key tenets."

Tom nodded respectfully, and Headington glanced at his injured leg. "Let's go and find somewhere more comfortable for you to sit."

He led the way across the room and held open a door for a moment, gesturing past it. "You might be interested to see our research operation."

Tom glimpsed ten or a dozen non-matching wooden desks, some with black computer monitors on them. A woman in her twenties was seated at one of them, leaning forward and studying something on her screen. The other positions were empty.

"Most of our people are volunteers at this stage," Headington said. "More of them will be coming in later this evening. Once we get our donations better organised, we'll be taking on more paid staff." He pointed to an alcove set in the far wall, where there were hints of computer cabinets on metallic shelves. "We have an integrated IT network with our own web server, so all our operational and research data is pooled centrally."

"Impressive."

"We mean business in every sense. Upstairs there's another room like this for our media and outreach department."

He steered Tom towards another door at the far side of the room. It opened into a small wood-panelled office.

He made a show of shuffling an upright chair into position for Tom in front of an antique desk, then took his crutches and leaned them carefully against the wall. When both men were seated he leaned back in his office chair.

"So, Tom, you probably know as much about Brexit as the next man or woman. What exactly do you want to hear about it from me?"

*   *   *

Tom took out his phone, tapped a couple of icons, and held it towards Headington, indicating that he'd set it to voice record mode. Headington nodded his assent.

There was a long moment's silence as they weighed each other up, then Tom asked, "Will we actually leave?" He accompanied this with a bland smile.

"Ah, now there's a question. Will Britain leave the EU in the end?" He fixed Tom with a stare. "To be honest, I have no idea."

"That seems a strange comment from someone in your shoes."

"I'm only being realistic. Leaving seems such a stupid thing to do that you would imagine rational people would eventually put a stop to it. But when did reason prevail in the world of politics?"

Tom resolved not to be taken in by the sweeping assumptions behind this comment. He needed to press Headington to justify it. "There are two sides to the argument," he said. "Plenty of people could give you a lot of sound reasons for leaving the EU."

"No doubt they could."

He waited, but Headington added nothing. He asked, "What does your instinct tell you?"

Headington relaxed slightly. "It tells me we won't leave in the end. Things will change. The EU we stay in won't be quite the same one we contemplated leaving. Maybe we'll go into a transitional period, and it will last forever. The bottom line is that basically, we'll stay." He gestured round the office. "I wouldn't have taken this job on if I didn't believe in that possibility. I'm not interested in fools' errands."

"Not many people seem to agree with you."

"You'd be surprised."

Tom thought back to the web trawling he'd done in the hotel lounge that morning. "The latest polls say people are resigned to leaving."

"That's because they've been bludgeoned into submission. They're tired of uncertainty. They've heard 'Brexit means Brexit' so often that they've started to think it was handed down on tablets of stone. Wait till they realise it wasn't."

He fell silent for a moment, then continued, "Do you remember the referendum wording? I do. 'Should the United Kingdom remain a member of the European Union or leave the European Union?' Did you ever hear anything so simplistic?"

"At least people were given a nice clear choice."

"But a choice of what? What terms? What deal? What timetable? Nobody asked those fundamental questions." He snorted impatiently. "How can you change a nation's history on the basis of sixteen words? The referendum should have been advisory. In fact it *was* advisory. Legally speaking the result was never binding. The Government simply chose to interpret it as such."

"I didn't know that."

"Look it up. It's all documented on the internet. Or better yet, take one of our discussion papers with you when you go." He gave a short smile. "Excellent reading on the train."

*   *   *

Finally Tom paused the recording. "I'm sorry to interrupt the flow, but could I ask you about something else?"

"Oh yes?"

"It's about my car accident – " He gestured towards his leg. "Afterwards I suffered traumatic memory loss. I don't remember the incident at all, or the days leading up to it. I'm trying to work out what I was doing at the time, and how it happened."

"And … ?"

"You and I spoke during that week. I wondered if you could recall it? I don't remember the circumstances, and I hoped you could help me."

Headington made a show of thinking back. "I think we must have spoken at our inaugural anti-Brexit conference in the Queen Elizabeth Hall. Were you there?"

Immediately a strong memory of the auditorium rushed into Tom's mind – of muted, air-conditioned hubbub, of subdued excitement among delegates, and of a conversation snatched with Headington in a corridor between sessions, with several of his minders and associates hovering in attendance.

He said, "Yes, you're right! I phoned you a day or two before, and asked to speak to you, and you suggested a quick chat during that conference. You emailed me a delegate pass."

"That sounds about right, yes."

"I'm sure it is! Do you know what we talked about?"

Headington shook his head with a regretful smile. "Brexit, I would imagine. You can hardly expect me to remember all the conversations I've had on that subject."

"No, of course not. I just wondered if there was anything especially memorable about our conversation?"

Headington was shaking his head again, but another memory had already flashed into Tom's mind. It involved not Headington himself, but one of his helpers. He said, "Bradwell. Do you know someone of that name?" Suddenly this seemed important.

"Neil Bradwell? He was one of our first paid employees. A very fervent young man – just the kind of person we wanted on board. He must have been with me at that conference. Maybe you talked to him?"

Tom sensed a qualification. "But?"

"Oh, it's just that we had to let him go a few months back. A shame."

"Why was that, if you don't mind me asking?"

"Differences of opinion. It ended up in a shouting match with my associate, Victor Rudge. We couldn't go on like that."

Memories were sparking in Tom's brain. Bradwell had pulled him aside at the end of the encounter. "We should talk," he'd said quietly. "There are things you won't pick up from Marcus – things you need to know."

What things? Tom had no idea, but felt intrigued to find out. He now said, "Do you know how I could get hold of him?"

"Not a clue, sorry.

There was a discreet knock at a side door, and a middle-aged woman leaned round. "Five minutes to your next phone call, Marcus."

"Thanks, Sue." He turned back to Tom. "I need to get on. No rest for the wicked." Then he called after her, "Sue, before you go, do we still have a record of how to contact Neil Bradwell?"

"Possibly. I could look it up for you tomorrow."

He turned back to Tom. "Sue will email you if we have anything."

On the way across to the door, Headington asked, "Who have you talked to in the Leave camp? I assume you're trying to paint a balanced picture?"

Surprised, Tom said, "I haven't set anything up yet."

"Have a word with Kenneth Moir. You'll get some sense from him, not just muddled thinking and empty-headed slogans. Mention my name when you talk to him. I'll get Sue to give you his contact details when she emails you about Bradwell."

Back in the foyer, Tom marvelled at Headington's apparent even-handedness. He was almost enjoying this.

That was when something heavy slammed into one of the front windows, and the lower panes collapsed to the floor in a jangling crash.

Chapter 6

A high-pitched electronic alarm immediately started screeching. Tom stood frozen in place for a moment, then Marcus Headington came striding back into the foyer. "What the hell was *that*?"

Almost simultaneously footsteps sounded on the staircase, and a male figure in dark clothing hurried down. "Bloody hell, Marcus, are we under attack?"

"Looks like it. Over there."

All eyes turned to the window. Not far from it lay a wine bottle with a short trail of paper or fabric extending from its neck. Headington said, "Jesus, it's a petrol bomb. Stay clear!"

Tom hopped precariously back a pace on his crutches, staring fixedly at the bottle. Nothing happened. It seemed inert. He said, "It's not burning. Maybe they forgot to set light to it."

Other doors opened, other voices gave cries of consternation. Finally the newcomer from upstairs stepped towards the bottle. He was a slim man of around fifty with short-cropped dark hair and a hint of designer stubble. "Looks as if it might be a dud," he commented, peering at it.

"Stay clear, Victor," Headington advised. "It might be a trick of some sort."

"I don't see why we should be intimidated by something like this."

"Let's not take any chances. In any case, the police will need to examine it. We mustn't interfere."

Headington looked round. His PA Sue was standing behind him, and two or three other people had gathered at the foot of the stairs. The broken window was immediately next to the main entrance, and glass shards had scattered in front of the doorway. Speaking loudly and firmly, he said, "As a precaution, everyone stay away from the front door. Please move to the back of the building NOW, and go outside into the yard."

Hesitantly people started shuffling out. Headington watched them as he lifted his phone and tapped out 999. Reluctantly, Tom swung after the others on his crutches.

The patio light cast an unnatural pallor over the small group, whose indignant chatter gradually rose in volume. The dampness of an early dew gave a sheen to the faces, and the summer air had an unseasonable crispness. Headington said to Tom, "I'm sorry about this. I'm afraid it comes with the territory."

"Are you saying this kind of thing has happened before?"

"Well, not an actual attack, but yes, we've had death threats on several occasions. Mostly it's hot air, but we can't afford to be complacent."

"You mean people would actually contemplate killing you just because you want to overturn Brexit?"

The man from upstairs, who had so far said nothing, responded, "Surely you're not surprised? And there's always been a violent fringe behind the Far Right. They thought things were going their way when the Leave vote came in, and they'll do whatever it takes to prevent what they see as backsliding."

Headington said, "I should have introduced you. Tom, this is Victor Rudge, vice-chair of the Stay and Prosper group. Victor, Tom Anthony. He's writing an article about us."

Rudge nodded without smiling or offering to shake hands. "I'm going to see if I can turn that bloody noise off."

Headington said, "I'd better go in too. I'll need to talk to the police."

* * *

The aftermath seemed to go on much longer than the incident merited, but the police were clearly taking no chances. They talked to everyone in the building, and called in an explosives expert to examine the bottle.

During the long wait, Headington rejoined the people huddled in the yard, and in between phone calls he held court, chatting to his team and keeping the mood light. During a pause in the conversation Tom asked him, "What do you think of that story in the press today – the announcement of a big UK investment by Monck Chervil? It's good news for a post-Brexit Britain, isn't it? It shows confidence that the country will still be a good place to do business in after we leave."

"That's certainly the spin that's being put on it by the Leave camp." Headington smiled briefly. "Hey, I'm not going to knock it. This country needs all the investment it can get. But it's just an isolated instance. It might bring three thousand jobs to the UK, but do you know how many jobs will disappear to the Continent because of Brexit? It'll be many times that number. Many times."

Victor Rudge, who was just finishing a phone call, leaned into the conversation. "And do you know how much our beloved Government has promised this company by way of sweeteners and inducements to locate themselves here? It's a scandal. Someone in high places thinks that because we're leaving the EU, we can invent our own rules about competitive intervention."

"We don't know that's what happened here," Headington said.

"Of course we do. Just wait and see."

Finally Headington was summoned indoors by the police, and returned a few minutes later with the news that the building had been declared safe, and the bottle had been removed. "It was filled with some kind of resin," he said as Tom prepared once again to take his leave. "That's why it didn't break. And there was a message taped to the outside."

"What did it say?"

Headington hesitated. "I'm not sure if I should tell you, but I can't see what harm it will do. It said, 'Brexit means Brexit,' and then underneath that it said 'The next one will be real.'"

Tom looked at him searchingly. "Do you think there *will* be a next one?"

"I don't know. Clearly we've got to tighten up our security, and start working more closely with the police." He shook his head reflectively. "This is the kind of world that the referendum ushered in."

Tom said, "There will always be zealots and hard-liners. You can't blame the referendum for that, surely?"

"No, but the Leave vote made them feel empowered. The same thing happened after the American election with the resurgence of the Far Right over there."

Tom nodded his goodbyes and made his way out into the street to hail a taxi. It was only as he was approaching Waterloo station that he realised he had a scoop on his hands. He'd just been party to a bomb threat. He'd witnessed the process from start to finish. It was so many years since he'd been a journalist that he no longer had a journalist's instinct for news. He silently cursed himself for failing to take a single photograph on his phone.

Nevertheless, he could write up the event for Malcolm's website, using a few choice quotes from his interview with Headington to flesh it out. The rest of the press would undoubtedly report it, but he would have the inside story.

Once on the train, he opened his laptop and started typing.

Chapter 7

On Thursday morning Tom had his first opportunity to visit the house in Winchester.

The day started with a pre-arranged set of appointments at the hospital in Southampton. Jan offered to take him, but he suggested asking Bernard, who jumped at the idea.

Bernard was something of a father figure to Tom, though he would probably have laughed at the idea. Tom admired his charm and unflappability, and he treated Tom like the son he'd never had. He was now in his early seventies, but still had a full head of tight greying hair, and always seemed to radiate energy and good cheer.

The hospital visit seemed endless, involving consultations in three separate departments, but Bernard sat patiently through it all. As they finally drove away, Tom asked him, "Would you mind going back via Winchester? I could drop in at my house."

"You're the boss."

He experienced a wave of nostalgia as they pulled into the narrow street of neat terraced houses. No parking was allowed on either side of the road, so Bernard dropped him at the door, then headed off in search of somewhere else to leave the car.

The house had a musty smell, but was tidy and in good order, and as Jan had promised, the houseplants had been watered regularly, and seemed to be thriving. After a few minutes Bernard announced his arrival with a discreet knock.

Hobbling around on his crutches, Tom opened drawers and cupboards at random. Bernard, standing to one side, said, "What are you looking for, if I might be so bold as to ask?"

"I don't really know. I'm trying to work out what I was doing during the week before the accident. I don't remember anything about it. I'm looking for clues."

Giving up on the ground floor, he asked Bernard to help him up the stairs.

Bernard looked at Tom's crutches and compromised leg. "No way," he said. "Tell me where to look and what to look for, and I'll do it for you."

There was nothing to be gained by arguing. Tom said, "Maybe notes or files that I've left lying around." He gave it some more thought. "Stuff I might have been working on just before the accident."

So Bernard clattered around for a while upstairs, opening drawers and ferreting around in cupboards. Tom contemplated the ancient telephone answering machine on the sideboard. The previous owners of the house had left it behind, and on a whim Tom had connected it to the landline and got it working. Jan always protested inability to operate it, and had never paid it any attention, but he could see that its message bank was full. Idly he pressed the playback button and stood listening to the messages.

Most of them were cold sales calls, some of which were aborted with no message. But then came a strange call in which both sides of the conversation had been recorded – a capability he'd never been able to exploit on purpose, only by mistake. The caller's voice was tense and low.

Caller: "*There are things you don't know about the Remain campaign – things they'd rather you didn't find out.*"
Tom: "*Who is this? What do you mean?*"
Caller: "*I just want to be sure I'll be putting the information in the right hands. You seem like a man of integrity, but I need to know for sure.*"
Tom: "*I hope so. What's this about?*"
[*A pause.*]
Caller: "*Shit! I've got to go. I'll contact you again.*"
[*Clunk of the call being disconnected.*]

What the hell was *that* all about? Could the caller be that man Bradwell from the Brexit conference? Tom couldn't be sure. He didn't recognise the voice, but he'd only exchanged a few words with Bradwell, and that was months ago. In any case, the quality of the recording was poor.

Bernard's footsteps sounded on the stairs. "Nothing doing up there, I'm afraid."

"It was just a thought." Tom beckoned to him. "Have a listen to this." He rewound the tape and played the message again.

Bernard frowned. "What's this all about?"

"I haven't the faintest idea. I told you I'd lost my memory of the accident. This call must have come in during that week."

"So you don't know this guy?"

"I don't remember a single thing about that conversation. It might as well be someone else on that call."

He'd seen enough. He told Bernard he was ready to leave, and Bernard went off to fetch the car. Tom wandered outside to wait in the tiny front garden, half-sitting on the low brick wall.

A woman's voice called, "Hello, Tom. How are you doing?"

He looked up to see his neighbour Christine from across the street. She was hovering in her own little front garden, two houses along. She sounded diffident, and made no attempt to come over.

He waved to her awkwardly with one of the crutches. Her dark hair had that familiar look – loosely gathered and dangling down her back.

"Getting there," he called back. "I might be able to graduate to a walking stick in a few weeks' time. How about you?"

"I'm fine."

She was about to go inside. He felt unaccountably disappointed.

Christine's role in Tom's life was difficult to define. She'd been living across the street with her husband when he bought his house ten years before. They'd hit it off immediately, and when he split up with his then-girlfriend, he found himself drawn more and more into her company.

Back then Tom was still a journalist, and sometimes worked from home. He would catch sight of her in the street and find some reason to go out and greet her, and their chats in the garden gradually progressed to coffees in the kitchen. He sensed that her relationship with her husband was less than ideal, and she seemed to draw comfort from his undemanding friendship.

Then her husband moved out. Apparently it was the cue they were both waiting for. Mutual consolation quickly escalated into unexpected passion. For a few weeks the affair seemed full of promise, but Christine was uneasy. She still held out hopes of a reconciliation with her husband, and in the meantime she was reluctant to give mixed signals to her small daughter.

It came to an abrupt end when Tom switched from journalism to management, and found himself out at work all day. Christine took the opportunity to draw a line under the episode, and for a while they avoided each other altogether. Finally, though, they drifted back into the casual friendship they'd known before. Her husband hadn't come back, and Tom was relieved not to have lost a valued confidante. When Jan moved in with him a few years back, he tried to draw her into their little circle, though Jan seemed less than enthusiastic.

Quickly he called to Christine, "I've missed being around here. The village where Jan's parents lived is very quiet. Nothing ever seems to happen there. I just hope I won't have to be there long."

"You'll be coming back here then?"

"Of course. We're only staying away until I can handle the stairs properly."

"I see." There was a strange detachment in her tone. "And you're saying Jan will be coming back with you?"

"Of course. What makes you ask that?"

She shrugged. "If you don't want to talk about it, that's fine." She started to turn. "Well, see you then."

Something was wrong here. He called, "Christine, have I offended you in some way?"

She looked round, but at that moment Bernard drew up in the car, blocking his view. He hopped out through the narrow gateway, peering after her, but she had already disappeared into her house.

Chapter 8

The following morning Tom received a call from an unexpected quarter.

"It's Felix here. Can you spare me a minute?"

The show of humility was unconvincing. Felix wouldn't respect the social niceties unless he wanted something. What did he want today?

Felix Schaefer (he pronounced it to rhyme with "wafer") was chief executive of the company that had employed Tom until he'd been made redundant a month before his accident. Felix had grown up in east London, the child of immigrant parents, and graduated from doing pizza deliveries on a moped to running his own van delivery business. Then he moved the eighty-odd miles south-west to Southampton, where he acquired a tiny delivery company called Carswell Couriers.

From that starting point, through a combination of toughness and vision, he'd built the company into a flourishing nationwide concern. Dozens of small Carswell vans were now based in every major town and city, doing anything from local deliveries to hundred-mile dashes with urgently-needed spare parts. A medical division delivered organs for transplant to hospitals where they were needed, and a home shopping operation delivered purchases to consumers on the same day they bought them.

Tom answered, "What's up, Felix?"

Uncharacteristically, Felix hesitated. "How's the leg?"

"It's on the mend, thanks. But it's a slow process."

"Hell of a thing, that accident of yours. Did they ever find out what caused it?" His accent was a curious mixture of east London and middle-class English, with a smattering of something middle European thrown in.

"No, and my memory has blocked it out. That's what the medics are telling me."

"Bloody hell." Felix paused to reflect on that. "Maybe it's just as well."

Tom waited. Apparently weighing his words, Felix said, "I don't know if you were aware, but the sale of our international division never went through."

It had been a contentious issue. Felix had stripped out various management layers from his business in a bid to make the international division look more cost-effective to a would-be buyer. Tom had worked on domestic operations, not international, but his job had been lost in a wave of collateral damage.

He said, "Yes, I heard something."

"The buyers backed out. Uncertain times. They weren't ready to commit. A shame, but you have to be philosophical."

"So …"

Felix switched into confidential mode. "The reason I'm calling has nothing to do with that. Since you left us, I've had no one in the coordination role."

Many of Carswell's branches were in reality independent companies. They simply traded under the Carswell umbrella. Part of Tom's job had involved keeping them committed to the network. He waited expectantly.

"We've got a problem with one of the members," Felix said. "Up in Lincolnshire. They're disputing our terms of service – all kinds of crap. I've tried talking to them myself, but …" He tailed off. "I know what I'm like. I've heard it enough times from other people. I'm a bull in a china shop, I don't listen to what I'm being told, bla fucking bla."

Tom waited.

"It pains me to admit it, but I need someone with your light touch to go and see these people and talk things through in person. And you know the business backwards, so you're the ideal person." He hesitated again. "Would you consider it?"

*   *   *

Half an hour later, Tom was still unsure how to respond to Felix's request. He didn't know whether to feel flattered at being invited to help out, or resentful that he was expected to come running back to his old job at the snap of Felix's fingers.

Either way, his first instinct was to say no. He'd enjoyed working for Felix, but the man had been a demanding boss – constantly expecting status updates, never satisfied. In some ways Tom was relieved to be free of him. Could this request be a prelude to an invitation to him to return to the company full-time? Would he want that?

Yet the idea of turning down a challenge offended him. His adage was "Never say no". The main problem would be travelling all the way north to Lincolnshire in his present compromised state. The distance had to be a couple of hundred miles.

Then a solution occurred to him. He could ask Bernard Weatherley to chauffeur him. If he wasn't doing courier work, he would probably welcome the trip – and Felix could pay for it.

Bernard, as expected, was delighted at the idea. "Gardening just isn't me," he grumbled when Tom phoned him. "Put me on the road and give me a destination, and you'll take five years off my age."

Felix sounded pleased when Tom called him back. "Just say nice things to these people in Lincolnshire. I've tried being nasty, and for once it hasn't worked."

"I'll do what I can."

Felix said, "I realise now that you had a real knack with these negotiations. I didn't give you the credit you deserved."

Tom waited.

"I'll be frank with you, Tom, I worried at first about giving you that coordination job. You can come over as a bit naïve sometimes, if you don't mind me saying so. A bit literal."

Tom decided he'd better not rise to this.

"But you had it all under control, didn't you? You knew how to listen to both sides of an argument, and come up with something in the middle."

As the conversation came to an end, Tom asked on a whim, "How is Brexit playing for you, given that the sale fell through?"

"We'll still be far better off coming out of Europe. Bollocks to the bureaucrats!"

"I won't ask which side you're on, then."

"I'm a Leave supporter, and I'm not afraid to say so. Red tape, irrelevant laws, interference and bullying from Brussels – who needs it? We'll do far better on our own."

"But surely Brexit kiboshed the sale of your international operation? I'd have thought you'd be up in arms about that."

"I won't deny it – some of our international clients have been shitting themselves, worrying about the tariffs and customs delays they think they'll be up against after we leave."

"So?"

"There's no gain without pain. This kind of thing is just a short-term setback. The continental business will perk up in a few years' time. Watch this space."

* * *

An email pinged in on Tom's laptop: a message from Sue, Marcus Headington's personal assistant. As promised, she'd sent him both mobile and landline phone numbers for Kenneth Moir, the eminent pro-Leave campaigner, along with a mobile number for Neil Bradwell, the man he'd talked to at the Stay and Prosper conference last winter. She'd added a note saying, "He moved home while he was working for us, but we never got a note of his new address."

It was Bradwell's number that particularly interested him. He wanted to know if this man had been the caller in that strange phone conversation he'd recorded. He couldn't swear to it, but the gist of the caller's comments seemed to echo what Bradwell had told him at the conference: something was amiss in the Remain campaign. He felt increasingly convinced that unravelling this would help to unlock more of his missing memories from the week of the accident.

He tapped out the number on his phone. A voice announced, "You have dialled an incorrect number. Please try again." He tried again.

Same result.

Chapter 9

"Can't say I've ever been to Sleaford before." Bernard tried to peer past the long stream of stationary cars in front of them. "And at this rate I won't be going there today."

The journey north from Winchester had gone smoothly up to this point, but now they were stuck in a long traffic jam just north of Oxford.

"It's a market town," Tom said. "I read up on it. Gateway to the Fenlands, some people call it. There were a lot of RAF bases in the area during the war."

Their progress was slowed again on an hour-long two-way stretch from Northampton to Stamford. Finally they were scything through the green flatness of the Lincolnshire landscape. The journey had taken well over four hours.

The Carswell depot was on the edge of the town. It was actually called Dingle Deliveries – a quaint name for what seemed a professional and well-run business. The essence of its dispute with Carswells was simple enough. As Dan Hollis, the chief executive, explained, "Under our deal with Felix, we have to paint two thirds of our vans in Carswell colours. We've found that it doesn't sit well with some of our other customers."

Tom said, "You must have signed an agreement with Felix when you joined as a member. You must have accepted Carswell's terms."

"All the same." Hollis stared impassively at him.

"OK, so what proportion would suit you? Fifty-five per cent?"

Hollis glanced at his colleagues, then back at Tom. "How about fifty?"

"I think I can swing that." He avoided a slightly sceptical look from Bernard, and pressed on. "Felix is a pragmatist. Tell me something positive that I can give him, and he'll see sense. But don't tell any other Carswell members that we changed your terms, or you'll cause a mass revolt."

Hollis suggested a late lunch, and drove the party through Sleaford's pretty central area and out to a country pub. "This is a popular town these days," Hollis commented as they pulled into the pub car park. "They're building a lot of new housing to absorb the growth. Not everyone is happy about it, but we are. More business all round."

They sat in the sun at a picnic table in the pub garden. Tom managed to perch on the end of the bench. In due course the conversation turned to Brexit. He said, "I understand there was a strong Leave vote here in the referendum."

"Very strong," Hollis agreed, "but over in Boston it was even stronger. That's half an hour east of here. There's a big immigrant population there – Poles, mostly, and very hard workers. The agricultural community couldn't exist without them, but some people don't like the foreign-language signs springing up all over the place. You can't help seeing their point. There's not a great deal of assimilation going on."

"So you voted to leave the EU?"

"Not at all. I wanted to stay in. All I'm saying is that I can see both sides of the argument."

They continued to chat amiably. Sandwiches arrived; a second round of drinks was ordered. When they finally stood up to leave, Bernard put a hand on Tom's shoulder and said quietly, "I know this will sound feeble, but how would you feel about making an overnight of it? I must be getting old, but I can't face another four or five hours on the road this afternoon."

"I wish I could do some of the driving for you."

"Don't worry – that's what I'm here for."

Tom turned to Hollis. "We've decided to stop overnight here and head off in the morning. Can you recommend somewhere with a bit more character than a motel?"

* * *

After checking into a hotel in the town that evening, Tom and Bernard wandered a few doors down the street to another pub. As they waited for their pie and chips, Tom said, "I don't think I've ever asked you where you stood on coming out of the EU."

Bernard toyed with his knife and fork. "I'll be frank with you. I voted to leave, but I wish now that I hadn't?"

"So why did you?"

He shrugged. "I was caught up in the notion that we needed to be in charge, we needed to cut all the Brussels red tape, and we shouldn't have to defer to European courts and European rules and regulations. I should have known better. I should have thought about Marie." His wife was French-born, though she'd lived most of her life in Britain. "It was an impetuous vote. I never thought the Leave side would win."

"A lot of people didn't think that."

Bernard leaned forward. "What I hate most is all the xenophobia that's come out since the Leave vote – all this hatred of immigrants. The vote seems to have brought out the worst side of humanity. And as for this area – " he glanced round the pub – "it seems to have been one of the worst affected. Immigrants have driven the agricultural economy here, yet some people just want to wish them away. Talk about ingratitude."

A loud voice suddenly said, "What would you know about it, mate? Who gave you the right to come poncing in here, making judgements on things you don't understand?" A heavily-built man of around thirty was leaning over from a table behind them. He had a buzz-cut and was wearing gold studs in both ears.

Bernard twisted round. "No offence intended."

"No, of course not." The man's tone oozed sarcasm. "You wouldn't be defending these people if it was your jobs they were taking, your houses they were living in, your women they were shacking up with."

"What's to stop you going for those jobs yourself, if you don't mind me asking?"

Tom glanced at Bernard in surprise. He seemed to be provoking this man. It was a hitherto unknown side to his character.

The man glared at Bernard, and a blond woman at his side was also frowning. The man said, "What – at the rates they work for? We couldn't live like that. They're driving down wage levels for everyone. They've been a total disaster for this area, yet until now no one has lifted a finger to stop it. The Leave vote is the best thing that's happened here for decades."

Bernard said, "I suppose you're entitled to your opinion."

"It's not an opinion, mate, it's a fact. People like you have been ignoring what's been going on here for years. Well, the boot's on the other foot now."

"I'm very happy for you."

The man glared at Bernard. "Are you trying to be funny?"

"Not funny at all."

The tension hanging over their tables had risen palpably. For a moment the two men simply stared at each other, then Tom reached over and tugged at Bernard's arm, forcing him to face away from the man. Quietly he said, "Leave it, Bernard. There are no winners here."

Bernard shrugged himself away from Tom, mouthing, "Pillock." Tom wasn't sure if the man had seen this. There was a long moment's silence, then the man turned away and started talking to his companion.

Bernard said, "I don't know about you, but I'm having another pint."

Chapter 10

It was after eleven thirty when they finally decanted themselves into the street. Bernard said blearily, "Which way is the hotel?"

"It's along there."

They set off at a meandering pace, with Bernard taking the lead. The street was very quiet. Tom was now adept with his crutches, and was putting some of his weight on his damaged leg. He kept pace with Bernard easily enough.

Abruptly two figures emerged from a narrow opening and confronted them, both wearing dark clothing and hoodies. One stepped forward, muttering, "Pillock, you reckon?" and thrust Bernard fiercely by the shoulders. He staggered back, shocked.

Tom managed to steady him and shouted, "What's the matter with you? Pick on someone your own age!"

"Oh yeah?" The figure stepped forward and thrust at Bernard again. Bernard stumbled backwards against Tom, who couldn't keep his balance this time. He pitched over and fell clumsily on to the narrow pavement. His crutches clattered to the ground beside him. Looking upward, he saw the figure approaching Bernard a third time, and this time he delivered not a thrust but a fierce punch in Bernard's midriff.

Bernard sank to his knees with a muffled grunt. It looked like game over, but the assailant hadn't finished yet. He lifted his foot and shoved Bernard over on his side.

Tom struggled into a sitting position and started trying to get up, but the other figure stepped round Bernard and shoved him back down. "Best stay put, mate," he muttered.

The first man now stood over Bernard, looking down at him. "Not so cocky down there, are you?" he said. Then he kicked him hard. And again. And again.

Tom leaned up, crying out, "For Christ's sake, you'll kill him!"

The other man now kicked Tom – not hard, but hard enough to knock him flat again. Pain shot through his body from his damaged leg, engulfing him. Finally the first man stepped back. The two of them looked at each other, and one of them said, "I think he got the point." They turned and slid back into the shadows, not hurrying.

* * *

Bernard was unconscious when Tom struggled over to him, and he was still unconscious over an hour later, after they'd both been delivered by ambulance to the accident and emergency unit at a hospital in Lincoln, some miles away. A nurse who might have been Polish asked Tom what happened.

"He upset some people by defending immigration, and they decided to teach him a lesson."

She nodded and gave him a meaningful look, but said nothing. He asked if Bernard would be all right.

"He is in a coma. We do not know yet what injuries he has sustained. We are doing everything we can for him."

It was not the answer he expected or hoped for. Bernard had come here to do him a favour, and this was his reward.

Tom himself had suffered grazes and bruising, but to his surprise he was told there had been no damage to his injured leg, even though it was still aching relentlessly. After being attended to he sat in the waiting room, drinking coffee from a machine and keeping an eye out for news about Bernard. Occasionally he slipped into a doze, but he woke up every time he slumped over.

After a very long night there had still been no development. Bernard remained unconscious, and there was no prognosis for when he might wake up. Reluctantly, Tom phoned Bernard's wife Marie, who told him the hospital had already contacted her. She had booked herself into a hotel in Lincoln, and was about to leave home for the railway station. She must have been rattled, yet managed to remain impressively calm.

A policeman came to interview Tom, who recounted what he knew, describing the encounter in the pub and the argument about immigrants. He said he was convinced that one of the assailants was the same man. "But I don't suppose there's any proof."

He was asked if he could identify the man. "At least then we'll know who is in the frame for this." He agreed to go to the police station once Marie had arrived, and look at some photographs.

The policeman lingered for a moment. "I shouldn't say this, but that man doesn't speak for the people in this area. He's just a bad penny. You always get them. The community here are decent and well-intentioned, and the immigrant population is well settled. Even people who oppose immigration wouldn't do what was done to you. This is a good area to live in. I'd hate you to get the wrong idea."

"It's all right. I understand."

He was sitting in the hospital café some time after lunch when he spotted Marie scanning the tables for him – a slight woman, still attractive in her late sixties, and dressed smartly in spite of the circumstances. He waved her over.

"He is comfortable," she said with irony. "But that's what they always say, isn't it?" After nearly a lifetime spent in England her French accent was slight, but still detectable.

"He's a tough old bugger," Tom said. "I'm sure he'll be all right."

"But he's not as young as he used to be, or as fit as he thinks he is."

A policeman arrived to take Tom to the police station, and there he was shown an array of mug shots of known troublemakers. He had no difficulty picking out the man from the pub.

"We know him," Tom was told. "Nasty bit of work. We'll be checking CCTV and looking for other evidence. We may need you here again if we find any."

Back at the hospital, Tom suggested that he and Marie should share a taxi to Sleaford, so that she could pick up Bernard's car and drive it back to her hotel in Lincoln. On the way, she said, "How are you, Tom? You've been in the wars as well."

"On the mend," he told her. "As you can see."

"Bernard has always had a soft spot for you."

"I hope I haven't taken unfair advantage of him."

"Of course not. He makes his own decisions."

The idea of starting out on a solo train journey all the way to Hampshire in the early evening held little appeal. Instead, he booked himself in for a second night at the original hotel in Sleaford. He barely had time to undress before falling into a deep sleep.

Chapter 11

There would be a kind of poetic justice, Tom reflected, if he could confront Kenneth Moir, the noted Brexit advocate and target interview subject, just days after a Brexit supporter had put Bernard Weatherley in hospital. Not that he could blame Moir for what had happened, of course; but it would make him feel better to raise the point with him – to remind Moir of the more extreme outcomes of the referendum vote.

The morning after his return from Sleaford he checked his email for the contact details that Headington's PA had sent him. After only a moment's hesitation he phoned Moir's number.

Unsurprisingly the call went to voicemail, and he left a message. To his amazement, only minutes later his phone buzzed and a confident voice said, "Moir here. How can I help you?"

He repeated his pitch about the article he would be writing. "I wondered if I could spend a few minutes chatting over Brexit issues with you – progress to date, your feelings about the negotiations in Brussels and the British Government's stance, and your vision for the future of Britain outside the EU."

"Nothing ambitious then?" Moir gave a resonant laugh. "Well, I hope you can speed-write, because I'll need to speed-speak to cover all that."

"Just the basics would be great. We could do it on the phone if you like."

"I prefer to see the whites of a man's eyes when he's interviewing me." He suggested meeting at an office where he often worked in Millbank, on the north bank of the Thames in central London. "And you say you're in some sort of hurry over this. You want to do it this week?"

"Well, if you're free."

"Hang on." A pause. "I'll be there this Thursday after lunch. How would that suit you? I can give you twenty minutes."

"Absolutely perfect."

* * *

After travelling alone from Sleaford back to Winchester, Tom felt ready enough to undertake another train journey to London. This time Jan's protests were more muted; she could see there was no dissuading him. As last time, she helped him as far as Waterloo, from where he took a taxi to Millbank.

The office where Moir worked was in a large, faceless building thrown up during the 1960s. Tom was directed to a suite on the ninth floor, with sweeping views across the Thames and over south London. A receptionist pointed him to a small waiting room. "He shouldn't be long."

He'd researched Moir, a former member of parliament who had lost his seat in the last election. He was now a non-executive director of various companies. He had no formal role in guiding the UK out of the European Union, but had been an energetic pro-Leave campaigner in the run-up to the referendum, and was now a go-to name when the media wanted comment on the subject. He usually offered a better-balanced view than those of his more strident fellow-travellers.

"So you've been talking to Marcus," he said as he bustled in, holding out his hand to Tom. "Very sound thinker. It's just a pity he's so blinkered on this subject. He's got a lot of respect in industry, but he'll see it draining steadily away if he persists in his vainglorious attempt to rewrite history."

Moir was a tall man in his sixties with a large, earnest face and fleshy worry lines round his eyes and on his forehead. His curly black hair was shot with grey, matching his dark pin-stripe suit, and he breathed heavily through his nose. He spoke with a very light Scottish accent.

Tom said, "So you think Marcus is on a hiding to nothing?"

"We're leaving the EU. That's all there is to it. The public voted. The die is cast."

"But only thirty-seven per cent of voters chose to leave."

"Oh, you're going to start quoting statistics, are you? Look, the Leave side won. They got more votes that the Remainers. No one on either side disputes that. End of subject."

Tom could see it would be fruitless to pursue this line of argument. As they sat down in easy chairs next to Moir's desk, he said, "Leaving aside the figures, will it really be in Britain's interest to leave the EU?"

It was the cue Moir wanted. He embarked on what sounded like his standard denunciation of red tape and Brussels bureaucracy. Leaving would staunch the flow of funds to the EU, he said; it would free the British Government to make its own laws; it would open the nation up to more international trade. "Just ask the fishing industry if they like following the EU's constraints, and letting EU countries deplete our fish stocks. Ask people who can't find work if they enjoy seeing all those jobs go to European nationals."

This sounded like an opening for Tom. He said, "My friend Bernard knows that only too well. He was defending immigration in a pub the other day, and he got beaten up for his pains. He's still in a coma."

Moir gave him a sympathetic look. "I'm sorry to hear that. There are always extremists in any society. But you can't generalise from specific cases. Unrestrained EU immigration has opened the door to a lot of this, and something needs to be done to control it."

"But leaving the EU will have no effect on immigration from the rest of the world. It won't stop terrorism – home-grown or imported."

"What about all the terrorist cells operating in European capitals? And what about the extreme Right? That has strong roots in mainland Europe. Brexit won't cure all our ills, but we might as well start somewhere."

"But it's the extreme Right who are celebrating Brexit most loudly. Are you saying you defend them? I'm sure my friend would love you for that."

Moir sat back. "I thought you were planning on writing an even-handed article? You're beginning to sound as if you just want to pick a fight." He shook his head reproachfully. "Look, of *course* I don't defend extremists of any complexion. I can't be responsible for what they think about Brexit. Immigration from *all* quarters needs to be controlled. The British Government will be working on that."

He'd made his point; there was no need to antagonise the man. Trying another tack, Tom said, "What about the politics of all this? The EU was meant to bind European nations together, and prevent any future wars. Now we're opting out. A lot of Europeans already dislike us – they think we're stand-offish and arrogant. How will leaving help that cause?"

"We've spent forty-odd years deferring to Europe. Britain implements their rules more rigorously than any other member-state, and we're one of the biggest net contributors to their budget. But what thanks do we get? No, we need to be able to hold our heads up. It's clear that they won't let us do that while we're in their club, so now we're going to be free to do it on our own. It's all about gaining their respect."

"In other words, we take back control?" He was parroting the Leave slogan.

"You can mock it if you like, but that's what it amounts to, yes."

Tom said nothing. Moir looked at him for a moment, then pointed to the phone he was using to record the conversation. "Look, can I speak off the record?"

Tom nodded and paused the recording.

Moir said, "You won't hear many people make this argument, but think about the last war. It was the Allies against Germany. So who do you think came out victorious?"

Aware that he was being drawn into a trap, Tom said, "The Allies, obviously."

"And now look at the balance of power in Europe today. Who's setting the pace? Who's making the rules? Basically, who's in charge?"

He simply shrugged, and Moir said, "You don't want to answer, but the fact is that it's Germany. They may have lost the war, but they've well and truly won the peace. And we've simply rolled over and let them. It's time we stood up for ourselves."

Tom led the conversation back to safer ground, and they continued for a while longer. As a parting shot, Tom asked him, "What about the next generation? The polls showed that the majority of young people wanted to stay in the EU, but the minimum age for voting in the referendum was eighteen. If sixteen-year-olds had been allowed to vote, we wouldn't be leaving."

"You want to entrust our future to people with so little life experience?" Moir shook his head sadly. "It was misguided optimism that got us into the EU in the first place. Now the challenge is for practical people to steer us out again." He stood up. "Don't forget, the young generation of today will be the older generation of tomorrow. And they'll be thanking us for securing their future for them."

Chapter 12

A puzzling phone call came in on the landline from Tom's personal accident insurance company next morning.

"We're just going over your claim documents," the woman said, "and there seems to be a mistake in the name. We've got Thomas as your first name and Anthony as your middle name, but no surname."

Tom sighed. It wasn't the first time this had happened and it wouldn't be the last. Patiently he said, "Anthony is my surname. Someone must have typed it in the wrong field. It happens all the time."

There was a pause while the caller took this in, then she said, "OK, I can see where we've gone wrong. Sorry about this."

"No problem."

On a whim, Tom said, "By the way, do I ever get to see the video?"

"Sorry, video? What do you mean?"

"The video your agent took when she came here the other day."

The caller seemed perplexed. "When exactly was this?"

He thought back. "Two or three weeks ago. I can't tell you for sure."

"Did the agent give you a name?"

"Yes, Emily Sanders."

A pause, then: "We don't have an Emily Sanders on our books. Are you sure that was the name? Did she leave you a D700 form?"

"She didn't leave me anything, but she took a load of details from me, and she shot some video. She said it was normal procedure."

"Video? Definitely not. That's not part of our system at all. Did you receive a confirmation letter or email from us before the visit?"

"Not that I know of."

Another pause. "I'll have to look into this, but it doesn't sound like anyone from our company."

"I don't want to delay the insurance payment. It's been a very long wait already."

"I'm sure we'll sort it out."

As he put the phone down, he was reminded that the woman called Emily had given him no proof that she represented the insurers. She'd followed a script from a form, apparently noting down the answers he gave her, but she hadn't showed it to him at the end of the session. He'd found it odd at the time that she'd left no contact details.

When Jan returned from work that evening, he said, "That insurance assessor who came to see me the other day – did she contact you beforehand to set up the meeting? She said I was supposed to be expecting her, but it was the first I'd heard about it."

"Nobody contacted me. I did think it was odd when you told me about it."

"The insurers rang today, and they say they've never heard of her."

"Typical administrative balls-up, by the sound of it."

"I suppose so."

He leaned on the breakfast bar, watching her prepare their supper. Her dark hair brushed her shoulders as she worked, and her face assumed a familiar look of deep concentration. He'd always found it strangely appealing.

After a while he said, "I should do more of the housework. I can cook. I'm not incapable."

She turned to him. "It's good of you, but I don't want to come home and find you collapsed on the kitchen floor."

"Preferably not."

"Well then."

"And I should be looking for another job. The fee for that website article won't keep me going very long."

"But your redundancy money should keep you going for a while, and the insurance pay-outs will help as well."

"I suppose so."

"Then there's the big one."

"I'll believe that when I see it."

Not long after he'd got together with Jan, she'd offered him the benefit of her financial knowledge to invest thousands of pounds of his savings through her firm in an obscure but promising stock. She'd said her instincts told her it would pay out in a big way, and he'd trusted her judgement. In fact, the value of the shares had fallen steadily since then.

She said, "Don't be so cynical. I'm told there could be some movement on that stock pretty soon."

"I'm not holding my breath."

They watched TV together later – something they'd done in the old days in Winchester, but not so much in recent times. As she straightened the cushions at the end of the evening he felt an unfamiliar wave of fondness. Suddenly nervous, he said, "I could probably manage the stairs these days. I could have a shot at sleeping in the bedroom."

Sleeping with Jan was what he meant. There'd been no physical contact between them in the weeks since he'd come out of hospital. The prospect of sex had seemed both painful and impracticable – and in any case it had been off the agenda for a good while before the accident. Turning the clock back now would be a big leap.

She gave him an uneasy smile. "Let's not push things, Tom. Give yourself a chance to recover properly. You're not ready … and nor am I."

* * *

In the morning Bernard's wife Marie phoned with good news. "He's completely recovered consciousness, and they say I can take him home in a couple of days' time."

"That's wonderful."

"He told me to ask you when is the next trip?"

Tom smiled to himself. He'd kept in touch with Marie over recent days, but up to now her reports had been cautious. This was a major step forward.

As soon as he'd ended the call his phone buzzed again. It was Malcolm Drew, his friend on the news website.

"How's the article going?"

"I'm getting there, but I'm out of practice."

"I know you'll come up with a good result."

"So what can I do for you?"

"It's an opportunity for you, really. We're running a round-table session on internet news reporting next week. Our founder, Diane Draper, is very hot on issues of probity and integrity. We'll be thrashing around ideas about fake news and how to avoid being accused of spreading it. That kind of thing. I thought it would help you get your feet back under the table."

"Sounds good to me. This is in London, is it?"

"Yes, at our office in Shepherd's Bush. You're all right to travel now, are you?"

"I'll be there. Tell me the time and place."

He put the phone down with a sense of relief. The prospect of writing the article had been weighing heavily on him, but this choreographed reintroduction to journalism promised to lighten the load.

* * *

Tom was still brooding on his accident. He was a safe, attentive driver. He'd been proud of his previously blemish-free record. What kind of drastic failure of attention could have allowed him to drive off the road and into a ditch, even though no other vehicle had been involved? It contradicted everything he knew about himself.

He was also still baffled that he had lost all memory of it – and of the entire preceding week. How could that happen? He was increasingly convinced it harboured mysteries that he needed to unlock.

Among them was the question of what he'd discussed with that man Neil Bradwell, whom he'd met at Marcus Headington's Brexit conference. Had Bradwell really been the mysterious caller in that recorded conversation?

He scrolled through his contact list to find the number that Headington's assistant Sue had given him. Last time he'd tried it, the number was unobtainable.

It was still unobtainable today.

Perhaps Sue really had written it down wrongly. She'd never replied when he sent her a message asking her to check it, so he still didn't know the truth of it. He opened his email app and sent a message asking her again. Within seconds an automatic out-of-office reply pinged in, telling him she was away until next week. Frustrated, he read through her message, which offered two other email addresses to try and a phone number to ring. For want of a better idea he rang the number.

"Stay and Prosper campaign, Emily speaking. How can I help?"

It was a warm voice, husky and appealing – and it sounded familiar. Where from? It didn't take him long to work it out. She reminded him of the woman who had interviewed him for the insurance company. Perhaps he was being ultra-sensitive after his conversation with the insurance company, but it had made him suspicious. This woman had the same first name, and he thought he'd even picked up a trace of that distinctive Lancashire accent. But how could she be the same person?

He said, "It's Tom Anthony here. I was trying to reach Sue, but she's away. She left this number to call."

There was a moment's silence, then the voice said a little tersely, "I'll need to transfer you. Hold on."

Quickly he said, "Don't I know you? Your voice seems familiar."

"I don't think so." There was a clunk, and she was gone. He waited several seconds, then a different woman's voice said, "Hello? I understand you wanted to contact Sue. I'm afraid she's away today."

In other circumstances he would have felt frustrated by this, but he was still intrigued by the previous voice. He said, "Can you tell me who I was just talking to? It was Emily someone."

"Emily, yes. She's on our research team. What was it you were calling about?"

"What's her surname, please?"

"We just use first names for our volunteers. She would need to tell you that herself."

"Can you reconnect me, then?"

"I'm sorry, she's just gone out."

"Oh." He paused for a moment, definitely frustrated now, then explained the original purpose of his call. The new woman said, "I'm sorry, I'm not authorised to give out details from our personnel records. You'll need to speak to Sue when she's back in the office next week."

He was going round in circles. Fighting an impulse to hang up without even responding, and said meekly, "Thanks, I'll do that."

He wondered about that voice. Could it really have been the Emily who had visited him in Hampshire? It was possible that she worked for the insurance company and also volunteered for the Stay and Prosper campaign – but surely that would be quite a coincidence?

If he wanted to follow this up, he would need to speak again to the Emily at Stay and Prosper – assuming she would speak to *him*. It was a task for another day.

Chapter 13

Three days later, Tom had a smaller leg brace, a walking stick, and a hire car with automatic transmission.

He'd come close to an argument with Jan over the car. She was convinced that he wasn't ready to drive yet, and had told him he would be a risk to himself and everyone he encountered. "What will happen if you get into difficulties and can't go for help?"

"What difficulties? I don't see the problem."

"And think of the cost! You'll be spending all that money even though you don't really need a car at all."

"I need the independence."

In the end she'd reluctantly conceded the argument, and dropped him off at the rental company on the way back from his latest hospital visit. Arriving home triumphantly in a modest Ford, he said, "See? Back in one piece against all odds."

"Just so long as you're taking it easy."

He felt buoyed up. He said, "If I can do this, I bet I can handle the stairs in Winchester. In theory we could go back home tomorrow. We don't have to keep on living here."

Fleetingly the look on her face suggested alarm. "Not yet surely?"

He was puzzled. "Why not, if I'm up to it?"

She seemed to gather her emotions. "I don't think you should rush this."

"I just want to get back on my feet – literally."

"I know." She nodded rapidly. "But why not take things one step at a time? Let your injuries settle down properly."

Her reluctance was baffling. He said, "My injuries will settle down just as quickly in Winchester as here. Surely being here is just extending an unreal situation? Besides, the longer we stay here, the longer it will take you to get any paying tenants in this place."

"Let's not worry about that." She hesitated, then attempted a guilty smile that didn't quite work. "Let's see how things look at the end of the month."

He managed to hold his peace. There was no rush to return to Winchester, and given how helpful Jan had been in moving here in the first place, it would have felt churlish to press her to return before she was ready.

* * *

The following afternoon he decided to take advantage of his new-found independence. He'd been wondering since the accident why he'd been driving along the road where it had happened. Perhaps if he actually went there, memories of the incident would come back to him.

He noticed as he reversed into the street that the black car with tinted windows was nowhere in sight, and it occurred to him that he hadn't seen it there for some time. Its visits would probably remain one of life's small unsolved mysteries.

He drove into Winchester, then made his way out to the Twyford road. It passed under the M3, then turned south towards the village of Twyford. To the left, green fields stretched away in a gentle ascent towards Twyford Down, which years before had become the focus of a *cause célèbre*. Environmental protesters had hoped to prevent the motorway from being extended through it. In the end their efforts had failed, but their point had been made.

It was a modest country road with little traffic, and in the afternoon sun the surroundings looked rustic and benign. He'd been given an exact map location for the incident, so he drove slowly, trying to find it. The road was lined on one side by a hedge and on the other by trees and bushes. Eventually he felt he'd found the place, but there was no sign of a ditch. He pulled the car on to the narrow grass verge and climbed out.

The ground immediately beyond the verge sloped down slightly and then levelled out again, merging into a field. He leaned against the car, wondering if he'd found the right place. Then, a few cars' lengths away, he spotted a gash on a tree. That must be the spot.

If so, the reports of the accident had been misleading. His car couldn't have ended up in a ditch because there wasn't one. It must have struck the tree at an oblique angle, then continued down the shallow slope and overturned in the field – presumably out of sight of passers-by, which would explain why it had taken so long for someone to report the incident.

This realisation pleased him. If there was no ditch, it was hardly surprising that he didn't remember one. It was a small victory.

With slightly mawkish curiosity he limped over to the tree and examined the gash. It still told the story of a violent impact, but already it had been dulled by weathering. Beside the tree he could see a hint of vehicle tracks leading down towards the field, though they were more or less grassed over.

He looked around. What had happened to cause him to veer off the road? Could someone have forced him off it through reckless overtaking? It was possible, though he had no recollection of such a thing. Or maybe he'd been spooked by the sudden appearance of another car. There was no concealed turn in the vicinity, but a few yards further on, a farm gate on the opposite side of the road provided access to a field, and there was a pull-in area just in front of it. Another vehicle could have been parked there, and could have shot out in front of him. But this was all conjecture; he didn't actually remember anything.

He returned to the car, still wondering where he'd been going – or rather, where he'd been returning from. Nothing came to him. He was sure he didn't know anyone who lived in this area.

He drove slowly through Twyford, an up-market period village, and continued into the countryside beyond it. Still he had no hint of what had happened on that day. He carried on until he was entering the fringes of the Southampton conurbation. He decided to join the M27 motorway and return to the M3 that way.

At some point on the journey, he noticed an "Alternative Route" sign. These had always intrigued him. Most of the time they were meaningless, but their hour of glory came when traffic was diverted from some bigger road – perhaps during road works or a busy public event, or following a serious accident. For a brief period they had a function, showing drivers how to rejoin their original route.

What if he'd been using the Twyford road as a diversion? What if he hadn't been returning from a location in that immediate vicinity after all, but from somewhere further away?

* * *

His return journey took him back through Winchester, and on a whim he turned off and drove to his terraced house. He parked in his familiar slot in the next street, limped back to the house and let himself in. It still smelled musty, but the plants looked healthy enough.

Warily he tested his performance on the stairs. Taking them one at a time, he found it easy enough to reach the upper floor, and he made his way to his cramped home office. Paperwork from before the accident was still scattered over the surface of the desk, and his eye was drawn to two words written in pencil with a circle drawn round them: "Arundel services". What was that about?

He returned to the lounge, and through the window he spotted Chris across the road. She was dressed casually and was pruning the growth in her tiny front garden. This might be an opportunity to make his peace with her. He grabbed his walking stick and opened the front door.

She looked up on hearing him. "Hello Tom. I see you're a bit more mobile now." Her tone was cool, but at least not hostile.

He crossed over to her. "I'm getting there, but I have to wear this thing for a while longer yet."

"The time will fly." She gave him a perfunctory smile.

Moderately encouraged, he said, "I don't suppose a cup of tea would be on the cards?"

She looked uneasy for a moment, then gave him a nod of acquiescence. "If you like. Come in."

He followed her through to her kitchen and clattered a chair out from the table. She switched on the kettle and turned to him as he sat down, giving him a measured look.

"I hope you won't mind me saying this, Tom, but I'm wondering what the hell I'm supposed to think. One minute you're all over me, the next minute you're telling me you don't want to see me again, then you come out of hospital acting as if none of this had happened. Now here you are, sitting in my kitchen. It's a different story every time. What's going on? Is this some kind of game?" She leaned back on the edge of the counter.

"No, of course not. When did I tell you I didn't want to see you? What did I mean? Why would I not want to see you?"

She shrugged and said nothing for a moment, then, "I thought, you know, after what happened …" She tailed off with a sigh. "I don't know what I thought, to be honest. I shouldn't have thought anything, should I?"

"What do you mean? What did happen?"

She gave an empty laugh. "It's no good sounding like someone who's lost their memory."

"But I *have* lost my memory. Didn't anybody tell you? It was down to the accident. I don't remember it at all, or what led up to it. Didn't Jan mention this?"

She looked at him incredulously. "No! She just said you'd broken your leg, and you were unconscious for nine days."

"Well, I also lost my memory of the whole thing."

She was still staring at him in amazement. "So have you got your memory back now?"

"No, not at all. I don't remember any more about the accident now than I did that night."

"What else don't you remember?"

"What don't I remember?" He attempted a smile, but then realised she was in no mood for levity. "The whole week leading up to the accident is pretty much a blank."

She nodded slowly, as if in dawning awareness. She said, "After your accident I did ask Jan if I should drop in to visit you, but she thought there would be no point – you were unconscious. And then of course I found your email."

"What email?"

"The one where you said you didn't want to see me."

The conversation seemed to be going round in circles. He said, "I don't know about any email. When did I send it?"

"I don't know – just before your accident, I suppose."

"So how come you still wanted to come and see me in hospital after receiving it?"

She gave him an indignant look. "I don't know! Why are you going on about it?"

"I just want to understand the logic."

She screwed up her eyes in thought. "OK, I'd arranged to visit my mum for a week, just after your accident. While I was with her I didn't check my email very carefully. When I came back, I found your message in my spam folder. It must have been there for a week."

"Fair enough."

"I'm glad we've got that straight." She gave him an empty smile.

"But I definitely don't remember sending it. Do you still have it now?"

"No, I deleted it, sorry." An ironic look. "I was annoyed."

He tried to absorb the meaning of all this as he watched her make the tea. When she turned round and placed the two mugs on the table, he asked her gently, "Why did I not want to see you again?"

She sat down slowly and gave him a long look.

"Why do you think?"

Chapter 14

Before he could draw breath there was a brisk knock at the front door. Glancing round, Christine said, "Oh, shit. I completely forgot David was coming round. We're supposed to be discussing Joanna. He wants to take her off on holiday somewhere."

"But we haven't finished talking."

"It'll have to be some other time. I'm sorry, Tom."

He followed her to the front door, saying "Can we pick this up soon? I'm really struggling to understand what's been happening."

She looked over her shoulder at him. "Come over next time you're in Winchester. You know where to find me." She pulled the door open.

David, her estranged husband, nodded as Tom made his way out. "I'm glad to see Chris is still giving succour to the wounded and the needy." He tilted his head towards Tom's injured leg, but it didn't disguise the fact that his words were meant as a provocation. They'd vaguely known each other when he was still living in the street, and he'd never liked Tom. Perhaps he now had some inkling that Tom had once stepped into his shoes.

Christine nodded almost imperceptibly to him as he passed her.

Back over the road in his own front room, he tried to unpick the conversation they'd just had. She'd clearly been implying that something intimate had passed between them around the time of his accident, but if it was true, he simply didn't remember it.

Had it? The idea was disturbing. He'd always thought of himself as principled, and the notion simply went against the grain. But in the months before the accident he knew he'd let his guard down. He'd given Chris oblique insights into their strained relations. More than oblique hints, in fact; he'd more or less spelled out their situation. As ever, she'd provided a ready listening ear. Had one thing led to another? Had their long-abandoned involvement flared up again?

He wanted to unravel this mystery immediately, but he couldn't just lurk here in his house, waiting for David to leave. He might stay for hours. In any case, Tom had the sense that she didn't want a repeat visit today. The answer would have to wait.

He glanced around, checking that he'd left everything in good order, and his eye fell on the answering machine. He wandered over and replayed the messages recorded on it.

The strange call about the Remain campaign came round, and as he listened to it again he was reminded of his suspicion that the caller might be Neil Bradwell, the man he'd met at Marcus Headington's conference. Was it him? The jury was still out.

Bradwell's words certainly fitted this explanation. He launched into the conversation as if the two men already knew each other, and told Tom he presented himself as "a man of integrity". If they hadn't met before, what made him think that?

He decided not to delete the message. Instead, he opened the machine, took out the tape cassette and put it in his pocket.

* * *

Jan was already home from work when he arrived back, and told him she'd been convinced that he must have driven the hire car into another tree. "I know there's no hands-free in that car, but I've been texting you. You could have called me to say you were running late."

"I'm sorry, I wasn't checking my phone. I should have told you I was stopping off in Winchester. It was just a last-minute thing."

She said, "I know you're looking forward to going back there to live, but I don't see why you have to keep visiting the place." She paused. "I suppose you couldn't resist the chance to catch up with dear Christine?" She loaded the "dear" with irony.

Uneasily he said, "Not at all."

"I bet she was there, though."

"I said hello when I saw her."

"There you are then!"

"But that wasn't why I went."

She looked at him dubiously, and he glared back, suddenly irritated. As far as he was aware, Jan had no knowledge of his distant involvement with Christine. He was reminded that she sometimes seemed resentful at any inclination on his part to speak to other women.

He said, "You can't run my life for me, Jan. I have to recover from all this on my own terms. I need to reconnect with how I was before the accident."

"So did you reconnect? Is that working?"

"I'm not sure."

She seemed unconvinced. He said, "I'm sorry if you were worried about me, but please let me deal with all this in my own way."

She cooked a stir-fry dish for their evening meal, and seemed to have mellowed by the time they sat down together. She said, "I'm sorry if I seem to keep carping all the time. I have your best interests at heart."

"I know you do."

"You need to take care of yourself."

Later, when he'd retired to his makeshift bedroom, there was a light tap on the door and she peered round. "I bet you forgot to take your pills with you today."

She was right. He raised his arms contritely. "I seem to have lived to tell the tale."

"That's not the point. You need those medications to get better. Dr Melcombe was very emphatic about that. It's part of the healing process."

"I know. It's stupid of me."

"Well all right. Just be sure there's no backsliding. OK?"

*　*　*

Next morning Tom received a phone call from Victor Rudge, the strategist and second-in-command at the Stay and Prosper campaign. "We met on the night of that petrol bomb incident," Rudge said. His voice held quiet menace; it put Tom in mind of a teacher on the point of handing down poor marks or a punishment.

Cautiously he said, "I remember you, yes."

"That was an interesting piece you wrote about the bomb scare for that news website."

Was Rudge about to reproach him for exploiting his inside knowledge or quoting Headington out of context? Perhaps Tom had lost his feel for acceptable journalistic practice. He said, "I hope it was useful."

"The world needs to know the kind of thing that's going on behind the scenes in the Brexit debate."

No reproach, then. He said, "Did the police find out who was responsible for the attack?"

Rudge hesitated. "They have a pretty good idea, but there's no proof, so no action has been taken."

"It must be unnerving."

Rudge said nothing to this, and instead said, "I don't suppose you get to London very often, do you? I was hoping to catch you for a quiet word."

"What about?"

"This and that. I want to be sure we conveyed the right message when you talked to Marcus the other day."

Tom was thinking fast. "As it happens, I'll be in London the day after tomorrow. I could see you in the late afternoon if that suits you."

"Around four would work for me."

As Tom disconnected he glanced out through the window. A movement had caught his eye: a car pulling away from the property opposite. It looked very much like the big multi-purpose vehicle with tinted windows. He hadn't seen it for a while, but evidently it was back.

Chapter 15

"I'm sorry, Mr Rudge has had to go out." The woman at the Stay and Prosper reception desk gave Tom an apologetic smile.

Tom's first solo journey to London had started well. He'd reached the *Seismic Scene* offices in Shepherd's Bush in good time, and the round-table session on journalistic ethics and practice had proved usefully informative. But it stretched right through lunch and into the afternoon, and before he knew it he was running late for his meeting with Victor Rudge. He'd rushed out in a panic to grab a cab to Kensington, but now he was being told his haste had been in vain.

He said, "And he's not coming back?"

"I don't think so, no."

"Did he leave a message for me?"

"No message."

He stood there for a moment, uncertain whether to feel frustrated or philosophical. Should he try to negotiate a new appointment with the receptionist. No – too complicated. Mark it down to experience.

He was about to turn and leave when he had an idea. He'd intended to check the phone number he'd been given for the elusive Neil Bradwell, and Marcus Headington's PA Sue could probably do it for him now.

He said, "Is Sue in?"

"I'm sorry, no, she left just before you got here."

"Oh. Fair enough." Then another thought struck him. "What about Emily? Is she working this evening?"

"I'm not sure. I can check."

She pressed a button on her console and talked into her headset, then turned to him. "I'm afraid Emily isn't here either." Another smile. "We're not doing very well for you, are we?"

"Is she due in tonight?"

She spoke into her headset again. "They think she's coming in, but they don't know when."

"Maybe I could wait for a while?"

She smiled and pointed to an old leather sofa set against the front wall – just under the window that had been shattered by the fake petrol bomb. It looked like something from a gentlemen's club. "Make yourself comfortable. But you might have to wait a long time. There are no set working hours for the volunteers."

So he sat reading the newspaper and checking messages on his phone. An hour slowly ticked by. Various other people were buzzed in at the front door, either singly or in pairs, and disappeared into the inner sanctum. Eventually the receptionist asked, "Do you want me to give Emily a call, and see if she's actually on the way?"

The last thing he wanted to do was deflect her. Quickly he said, "No, no thank you. I'll give her a bit longer, then if she doesn't turn up I'll leave it for another time."

He turned over the newspaper and scanned it for stories he hadn't already read or dismissed. He would give her five more minutes.

Four of those five minutes had passed when the front door was buzzed open again and a young woman walked in. It was the same Emily. In jeans and a casual jacket she looked younger, and her hair was loose, not tied in a bunch, but it was definitely her.

She walked past him without looking round and went over to the reception desk. The woman behind it said, "Visitor for you," and pointed at Tom.

She turned, looked at him in obvious dismay, and said, "Oh. What are you doing here?"

Standing up, he said, "I was going to ask you the same question."

"I work here in the evenings. I'm on the Stay and Prosper research rota."

"And the insurance company?"

"What about it?"

"You said you worked there."

She looked at him for a moment without answering, then said, "Did you specially track me down here?"

"No, I was due to see Victor Rudge, but I missed him."

"Oh. Right."

"But since I'm here, maybe you could tell me what's going on. Do you work for that insurance company or not?"

Her look of dismay deepened. She glanced around, as if seeking help from some invisible third party. None was forthcoming. She turned back to him and said bitterly, "I *knew* this would happen."

"Knew what would happen?"

She looked around again, this time perhaps checking whether anyone was listening. There was no one in sight apart from the receptionist. Lowering her voice, she said, "There's a pub at the end of the street. You should be able to walk there – it's hardly any distance. We could talk there if you like."

"OK, great."

"Give me ten minutes. I'll meet you there."

He gave her a sceptical look. "How do I know you'll turn up?"

She shrugged. "I will. I just don't want to be seen walking out of here with you. It would look peculiar."

So he made his way slowly down the street to the Victorian corner pub, and sat waiting at a table by the window.

* * *

After twenty minutes he was ready to give up, but then he saw her peering around the pub, looking for him. He waved, and she nodded. She went over to the bar to buy a drink, then joined him carrying a glass of white wine.

"Sorry I took so long. I got caught up in something." She looked at him warily.

He said, "Thanks for talking to me."

"I probably owe you."

He waited for her to settle, then said, "So what's the situation with the insurance company?"

"I don't work for them. I think you got that. But I did once work for some insurers, doing assessments. I know how the system works."

"You don't seem very keen to defend yourself."

"I won't gain anything by lying about it."

"So what was it all about?"

She looked around furtively. "If I tell you, will you promise not to say I did? Could you say you found out from your real insurers or something?"

"Why should I?"

She shrugged. "No reason. I'm asking you as a favour."

To avoid answering, he said, "You seem to be fessing up without much of a fight."

"The whole thing made me uncomfortable. It seemed so devious."

"I won't argue with that."

She continued to look disconsolately at him. After a moment he said, "So who put you up to this?"

"It was a guy at Stay and Prosper. Martin Frankl, his name is. He's one of the permanent staff. He knew I used to work in insurance, and he thought that would give me a good cover story."

"Was he asking on his own behalf, or on behalf of Stay and Prosper?"

"He didn't tell me that."

"So what was the objective?"

She lifted her hands helplessly. "I have absolutely no idea."

Chapter 16

She seemed sincere. She gave no impression of holding anything back. Tom said, "What exactly were you told to do?"

"Martin gave me a list of questions to ask you. To be honest, most of them would have been normal questions for a real insurance company." She thought back. "I suppose one of the key things he seemed interested in was your memory loss. He was very keen to know if I thought it was genuine."

"Huh! Why would he care about that?"

"No idea."

"So what did you tell him?"

"I told him yes, a hundred per cent." She seemed eager to impress him on this point.

"What about my real insurance company? Wouldn't they have disowned your interview eventually? Then I would have known the whole thing was a sham."

"Not necessarily. You wouldn't have raised it with them, and they wouldn't have raised it with you. The pay-out would have gone ahead, and everyone would have been happy." She paused. "But obviously that didn't work out. You realised something was wrong."

It all sounded plausible. The only reason he'd stumbled on the truth was because the insurers had called him about the error over his surname.

Then he thought of another objection. "How did Martin Frankl know the insurers hadn't already paid out? Normally they would have settled months ago, and your visit wouldn't have made sense. How did you know there was a delay?"

She gave him an unhappy look. "Martin found out who the insurers were. Don't ask me how. Then he got me to call them up. I knew the routine, so I was able to check on your claim status. They told me it was still pending."

He was running out of questions. He said, "Who is this guy Frankl? Is he German?"

"No, he's as British as they come. He might have German ancestry somewhere in the past, but I would guess it was a long time in the past."

"Wasn't he worried that I might eventually show up here and bump into you? He probably knew I was researching an article on Brexit. Didn't it occur to him that I might ask for an interview with Marcus?"

She shrugged. "Who knows how that man thinks?" Then she added, "Bear in mind that Martin is the campaign press officer. Normally he organises interviews. He probably thought that if the possibility ever came up, he could steer you away from any chance of seeing me here. In any case, Marcus mostly gives interviews in a hotel suite down the road, not in the office."

He looked searchingly at her. He couldn't see any hint of evasion or subterfuge in her face; but then, he'd never doubted her when she'd come visiting in Hampshire, and he'd been wrong about that.

He said, "Why did you agree to do this?"

"It was good money. Six hundred pounds plus expenses – in cash. I don't get anything like that kind of money where I work." She paused. "And no harm done."

"Except that you wasted my time on a fake interview." He looked at her steadily. "And you deceived me."

"I know. I'm sorry."

He let her reflect on that for a moment, then said, "So where *do* you work normally?"

"In a bar in Richmond."

* * *

To his surprise, she offered to buy another round of drinks. "I'm still rich from that fee," she said with irony.

When she returned from the bar he asked her, "Won't they miss you back at the office?"

"I doubt it. We come and go as we please. The whole setup is a bit too sloppy if you ask me, but I'm not complaining."

"Is this man Frankl there tonight?"

"I don't think so. He doesn't usually work in the evenings. I wouldn't have sneaked out here to meet you if I thought he would be watching."

"What do you actually do at that place?"

"I compile statistics. I find situations where leaving the EU will make the country worse off – that kind of thing. The idea is to build a dossier of properly documented reasons why leaving is such a mistake." Her voice abruptly rose in pitch. "And it *is* a mistake, trust me. It's a Big Fucking Mistake."

Her sudden vehemence surprised him. "So you're committed to the cause?"

"Damned right I am!"

He found himself half-smiling. "I wouldn't have taken you for such a zealot."

She bridled at this. "What, you think I'm too young to have convictions? Or too female, maybe? Where is that coming from?"

"Sorry, I have a habit of speaking before thinking."

She stared at him for a moment, then shrugged. "Apology accepted. I'm hardly in a position to complain at you."

Unexpectedly, he realised he wanted more than reluctant acquiescence from her. Searching for something that would paint him in a more favourable light, he said, "The referendum age barrier was wrong. Sixteen-year-olds should have been allowed to vote."

She gave him a look of curiosity, perhaps wondering if he was speaking from the heart, then nodded. "Hallelujah to that." She sipped her wine. "Anyway, I'm not that young. I realise half the volunteers at that place are students, but you shouldn't assume we all are."

"How old are you then?"

"Twenty-seven, if you must know."

He looked at her more carefully. In place of the ponytail she'd worn in Hampshire, her hair now dangled past her shoulders: reddish-gold in colour and slightly wavy, with indeterminate highlights threading through it. Her features were even, and seemed to settle in a natural smile. He couldn't have begun to guess her age.

They chatted for a while in less combative mode, but eventually he checked his watch. "I'd better go. I need to catch a train back to Hampshire." He stood up. "What's your real job, when you're not bartending? What are you trained for?"

"What's wrong with bartending?"

He waited.

"OK, I went to drama college. I act."

"Why does that not surprise me?"

She watched in silence as he picked up his walking stick, then asked, "How's your leg injury?"

"Still improving, thanks."

"Glad to hear it."

"Are you going back to your office?"

"No, I think I'll give it a miss now. They'll manage without me."

"Sorry I disrupted your evening."

"So are we square? I don't want you to think of me as an enemy."

He looked curiously at her. There was something discordant in that comment – something beyond what the situation demanded. He said, "We're square, but I still want to know why your guy sent you to interview me."

"He's not my guy."

"Whatever. I want to understand what was behind it. It feels like a threat of some kind. You wouldn't like it if it happened to you."

"I can see that." She seemed to debate with herself for a moment. "Look, if I find out anything more about this, I could let you know."

He gave her a disbelieving look.

She said, "Truly." She pulled out her phone. "Let's swap numbers."

"Why would you do that? It's a bit of change of allegiance."

She hesitated, assessing. "I didn't know you when I agreed to that scam. I do know you now."

As they parted company he said, "I meant to ask you – do you know a man named Neil Bradwell? He used to work for the campaign."

"I've heard of him. I might even have met him once. But I think he left the same week I started working here." She lowered her voice. "I'm glad I didn't know him. Someone told me he killed himself."

Chapter 17

Tom's train back to Winchester had been cancelled. He stood amid the ebb and flow of passengers on the concourse at Waterloo station, wondering what to do. Seemingly there was a signalling fault on his line, and it was unclear when or if another train would be leaving.

There was a simple solution. He could go to the flat that Jan rented in south London and stay the night there. He usually kept a change of clothes on hand for such contingencies. He hobbled out to the taxi rank.

The flat was on the top floor of a tall Victorian mansion block just off Brixton Road. Jan had been right; the stairs would have been tricky on crutches. As things were, he managed the ascent without any problem, though reaching the top floor – up a narrow carpeted staircase with two turns – was tricky.

Something was wrong. He couldn't slot his key into the lock. He tried repeatedly, then checked his key ring in case he'd picked the wrong one. No, he'd got it right. He tried for a final time. No luck.

Had Jan changed the lock for some reason? He pulled out his phone to ask her, but the call went to voicemail. Now what? Irritated, he turned to head back down the stairs. He could try picking up a train at Clapham Junction, or else look for a hotel for the night.

Footsteps sounded on the stairs below. Someone was coming up to the top level. There was only one flat on this floor, so whoever it was must be on their way here. Suddenly Tom felt cornered.

He waited as the steps rounded the first corner, then the second. A figure in a raincoat came into view: a stout white man, somewhere in his late twenties, with a round face and a light growth of beard. He stopped when he saw Tom, then continued more slowly, saying, "Is there something I can do for you?"

"I can't get into my flat. Do you know anything about it?"

"If you mean flat five, I think you must have the wrong flat, or the wrong building. You did want number fourteen, did you?" The man completed his ascent and stood next to Tom in the narrow space next to the front door.

"I should know my own flat. This is it. Can I ask who you are?"

"I live here." The man frowned, then rummaged in his pocket and pulled out a pouch of keys. He opened it and selected one. "See – here's my front door key." He reached out and made a show of slotting it into the lock. It turned without resistance and he pushed the door open slightly.

Tom said, "I don't understand. This is our flat." He tried to peer inside, but the man was blocking his view.

"You seem to be mistaken."

Tom stared at him in disbelief. "How long have you lived here?"

"A few months – not that it's any of your business."

"But I'm telling you, it's our flat – or at least, it used to be."

"Clearly it's not now."

Floundering, Tom said, "Can I ask who you're renting from? Do you know my other half, Jan Carrington?"

"I'm renting through an agency. If I were you, I would take it up with them. Frattons."

The man was sounding increasingly testy. Tom decided he'd better cut his losses. He muttered, "Sorry to have troubled you," and made his way back down to the street.

He took out his phone and tried calling Jan a second time, but once again the call went to voicemail. Jan had said she would be at home this evening, so where was she?

He limped back to the main road to hail another taxi, scrolling through the browser on his phone. If the trains still weren't running, he would need to find a hotel for the night.

*   *   *

It was mid-morning when he got back to the house. He'd stayed the night in a hotel in Wandsworth, and had texted Jan to report that he wouldn't be back until the next day. She hadn't replied.

Jan would have left for work hours before. He checked the house a little cautiously, but everything seemed in order. He settled on the sofa in the lounge and embarked on a session of internet research for his article. The job eventually filled the rest of the day. He was relieved when he heard Jan's car pull into the drive at the usual time, but he was also nervous. How would she explain the presence of that man in the flat?

"You got back from London all right," she said breezily as she walked into the lounge.

"Not before making a complete fool of myself, trying get into the flat and offending a man who says he lives there."

"Ah, that." She put down her bag and shrugged off her jacket. "I meant to tell you about that." She was avoiding his gaze.

"Tell me what?"

"I've put in a tenant on a sublet." She turned to the door, clearly keen to make light of it.

He said, "Why?"

She turned back, still not looking directly at him. "We needed the money. The renovations on this house weren't cheap. I thought of the flat. We don't use it much. I thought we might as well make some money out of it."

"But you said the work on the house cost less than you expected."

"Relatively speaking, yes. But it was still bloody expensive."

"What about the pile of money you've been earning all these years? Couldn't you have dipped into that?"

In fact Jan had always been cagey about her income. She made it sound a lot, but she kept it stashed away, well clear of their joint bank account. He'd felt it would be intrusive to press her about it.

"All my savings are tied up in investment trusts and bonds – that kind of thing. I couldn't have messed around with them to pay for this." She gestured vaguely round the room. "There would have been forfeits, loss of interest, break penalties."

"OK, I see that." He was thinking fast. "But when I suggested staying over at the flat a few weeks ago, you never said you'd rented it out. In fact you said I wouldn't be able to get up the stairs. You made it sound as if that was the only obstacle."

"Did I?" She gave him a vague look. "That was probably just habit. I'd probably forgotten I'd rented it out."

"But why didn't you tell me all this in the first place – when I was in hospital, or when I moved in here?"

She shrugged. "I don't know. We were focusing on your recovery. It probably didn't seem relevant."

It sounded lame. He was ready to challenge her further, but reminded himself at the last moment that this wasn't supposed to be an interrogation. If he continued, it could explode into a full-blown row. Was he ready for that? What would it achieve?

As a parting shot, he said, "It's a pity you didn't mention it. You would have saved me an unnecessary taxi ride and a load of embarrassment."

"I'm sorry, Tom. *Mea culpa*. Can we just leave it at that?"

He nodded, and she headed off to take a shower. It was only then that he realised he hadn't asked her why she'd ignored his calls and texts last night.

Chapter 18

What should he do about the fake insurance interview? The following morning he sat staring out the window, mulling this over. It felt like something he couldn't ignore.

He should probably take his concerns to the police. After all, impersonating an insurance agent must surely constitute a crime of some sort? But that would mean betraying Emily Sanders' trust, and although he barely knew her, he was reluctant to go back on his agreement to protect her identity.

Alternatively he could confront Martin Frankl, the man who had apparently instigated the bogus interview. Or he could try to make contact with Marcus Headington direct, and raise concerns about Frankl with him. But these remedies, too, would mean betraying Emily. She'd managed to tie his hands remarkably effectively.

He googled Martin Frankl, and discovered that as Emily had speculated, he was a fourth-generation immigrant of German stock. Previously he'd worked for one of the big international public relations firms, and before that he'd been in the army. He seemed to have a reputation as a good-natured hustler: ideal, no doubt, for Marcus Headington's anti-Brexit campaign.

But why would the campaign's head of press relations care about Tom's loss of memory? It seemed utterly bizarre. Until Tom's visit to talk to Headington he'd had virtually no contact with the organisation – apart, that was, from his attendance at that Brexit conference. He'd spoken to Headington there, and also to some of his aides, including Neil Bradwell. Perhaps the clue to Frankl's interest lay there.

He picked up his phone and scrolled to the number he'd been given for Bradwell. He'd failed in his previous attempts to check it with Headington's PA Sue, so he still didn't know if it was correct. He tried calling it again. As on all previous occasions, it was unobtainable.

He opened his laptop and sent Sue another email message. Then he tried googling Bradwell's name again, this time adding the word "suicide" to the search criteria. As before, nothing relevant came up.

Flicking back to the email window, he found that Sue had finally replied to his enquiry. "Yes, the phone number I gave you for Neil Bradwell is definitely the one we have on file."

So much for that. Almost every time he tried to unpick the events of the week before his accident he ended up with a blank.

* * *

He decided the only way to reach a conclusion about the insurance scam was to talk to Emily Sanders again. Another conversation might reassure him of her good will. But as he picked up his phone that evening he wondered about the soundness of this logic. She was a trained actor, so could he rely on anything she said?

She answered quickly, but sounded wary. "Hang on. I'm at the Stay and Prosper office. I don't want anyone to know I'm talking to you." There was a long pause, then she said, "OK, I'm in the kitchen area."

"I could call you another time if this is a bad idea."

"No, it's OK. What did you want?"

"I wondered if you'd found out any more about why Martin Frankl wanted you to come and see me."

"No, sorry, I haven't seen him since you were here."

"Oh, right."

This looked like being a short conversation, but then she said, "I did find out about Neil Bradwell. One of the other girls said she was pretty sure he'd committed suicide. But she didn't know any details."

Neither of them spoke for a moment. He was about to wind up the conversation when she said, "You were here that night when someone threw a fake bomb through the window, weren't you?"

"I was. I didn't see you there though."

"I was working in the bar that night. Anyway, I thought you might be interested to know the latest. They think it was the done by that pressure group, Right Thinking."

"You mean the police think that?"

"That's the buzz in the office."

"OK. That's interesting."

"I'd better go. I was in the middle of something when you called."

"Thanks for your help."

*   *   *

Next morning he decided to phone Christine in Winchester. He wanted to talk to her again, and he didn't want to leave it to chance that he would meet her in the street.

She took the call, but it didn't go as he'd expected.

"It might be better if we didn't meet for a while," she said.

"But I told you the other day that I'm not avoiding you. I don't remember anything about any email that I sent you."

"It's not that, Tom. David and I had a long talk the other day, and we're going to have a shot at a reconciliation."

He wasn't ready for this. He felt an illogical sense of disappointment. Picking his words with care, he said, "After five years? Do you really think that can work?"

"It's six years. But he wants to make an effort, and I don't want to put obstacles in his way."

"I thought he had a new girlfriend."

She hesitated, perhaps wondering how far she wanted to continue in this vein. "Not any more."

"It seems a bit too convenient, don't you think?"

Had he really just said that? He felt at sea in this conversation. He seemed unable to strike a note that corresponded properly with their relationship – whatever that was.

She said, "Convenient for him, you mean? I know that. But I want to do what's right for everyone. For my family. This is for the best."

Quickly he said, "Sorry. I understand. I hope things work out for you – honestly."

"Well, thank you."

"I just want to find out what happened that week when I had the accident."

She gave a sigh of impatience. "Can't you let sleeping dogs lie? You know David has never liked me talking to you. I don't see any point in raking this up – especially now."

"Raking *what* up?"

Quietly she said, "Be your age, Tom. Work it out. I have things to do before David gets here."

Chapter 19

"Concussion and two fractured ribs," Bernard said. "They don't know why I was out cold for so long, but they say I'm OK now."

He beckoned Tom over towards the sofa without rising to greet him. He looked fit but gaunt. On the coffee table in front of him was an open laptop computer.

Marie had sounded delighted when Tom phoned to suggest visiting them. "He'll be so glad to see you. He's going mad, sitting around all day doing nothing."

Bernard patted the seat next to him. "This is how I'm spending my time at the moment." He indicated the screen.

Tom sat down carefully and looked at it. The browser was open on a retail website.

"I didn't know you were into all that."

"Keeps me busy," Bernard said dryly. "I'm becoming the world's most acquisitive home shopper. Being inactive is costing me a small fortune."

Tom looked at him more closely. He was the same old Bernard – and yet there was a frailty about him that had never been evident before.

"So how are you really?"

"I'm all right. I feel as if I've had the stuffing knocked out of me, if you want to know."

"I'm not surprised. Have they found out anything more about the man who did this to you?"

"I think you and I both identified the same man from the police photographs – that man we met in the pub. But they don't seem to have any other proof that it was him."

"I'm so sorry I put you in that situation in the first place. You were just doing me a favour, driving me up there."

Bernard waved away his words. "I brought it on myself. I know that. I should learn to keep my opinions to myself."

"Nothing entitles anyone to do what they did to you."

"Maybe not. But all's well that ends well."

"I'm glad you're willing to see it that way."

"I don't have much option." Bernard brightened. "Anyway, how are you? You seem a lot more mobile now. And you're driving again."

"They're telling me my leg is healing well."

"I'm glad to hear it." He adopted a more confidential tone. "I heard on the grapevine that you might be going back to work for Felix full-time."

"Not if I can think of something better."

"Can't say I blame you."

"What about you? Will you go back to your courier job?"

"I'm not sure. I'm giving it a few weeks. Felix can manage without me." He shuffled himself into a different position. "I just wish there was more I could do here."

Tom was thinking fast. "I tell you what, since you're such a computer whiz, do you fancy doing some research for me?"

"What – for that article you're writing?"

"Not exactly, no. This is something else. But it does involve someone I met in connection with the article."

"Tell me more."

Tom told him about Neil Bradwell, and explained how difficult he was proving to find. "I can't see how anyone can go about their lives these days without having a presence on the internet, yet I can't dig up anything on him. It's as if he never existed."

"Leave it with me," Bernard said.

* * *

That afternoon he had a call from Malcolm Drew, his friend at the news website. "Remind me who you've talked to for your article," Malcolm said.

Tom threw him a handful of names, including those of Marcus Headington and Kenneth Moir.

"So you haven't talked to anyone from the Far Right?"

"No – and I don't think I want to. A friend of mine was beaten up by a right-wing bigot the other day."

"I don't mean the violent fringe – I just mean people with a heavy nationalist bias. People well to the right of the UK Independence Party."

"Such as?"

"Well, there's that pressure group, Right Thinking. They would fit the bill. Maybe you could have a word with them?"

Tom had heard that name somewhere recently. Of course – Emily Sanders had told him the police thought the group might be responsible for the fake petrol bomb incident. He said, "From what I've heard, they're not above a bit of violence if it suits their agenda."

"Well, if you talk to someone there you can make up your own mind."

So he googled Right Thinking, and found that it was a loose association of like-minded people with no formal spokesperson and no premises of its own. However, he soon discovered its *de facto* leader was a man named Adrian Dowdeswell, who ran a food processing company in north London.

Tom thought about it for a while. Did he want to speak to these people? Not really, but presumably it would do no harm. He might even get a sense of whether they really could have been behind the bomb threat.

He dialled the number of the factory. The receptionist transferred him to a department manager, who transferred him to Dowdeswell's personal assistant. Finally he was able to arrange a meeting for the following week.

*   *   *

Tom's next call took a bit more thinking about. Since he was going to London again, he could try to orchestrate a meeting with Martin Frankl, the man who was apparently behind the bogus insurance visit. If he succeeded, he could test Frankl out, and with luck find out what lay behind his strange deception. The question was whether or not he had the nerve to go through with it.

On the upside, he had a ready-made excuse to visit the Stay and Prosper offices again. He'd neglected to reschedule the aborted meeting with Victor Rudge, but there was nothing to stop him suggesting it now.

The gods were on his side. He reached Rudge with his first call.

"So you haven't finished that article you were working on?" Rudge asked him.

"No, it was always going to be a long-term project. Completion in a week or ten days."

"In that case a quick word would be very timely."

Chapter 20

Bernard was triumphant when he phoned Tom next day.

"I thought you said the web trawling job you gave me was going to be difficult."

"And it wasn't?"

"Piece of cake."

"What have you found out?"

"OK, well Neil Bradwell was thirty-two years old and single. He grew up in Muswell Hill in north London, but for the last few years he lived on the south coast in Kemptown, a district of Brighton. He joined the Stay and Prosper campaign towards the end of 2016, but he was fired a few months later."

"You're putting all this in the past tense."

"That's right. He committed suicide early this year – just after he was fired by Stay and Prosper, in fact."

Confirmation, then, of the reason why Tom had failed in his efforts to contact him. He asked, "When precisely did this happen?"

"It was the day after your accident."

Tom was silent for a moment as he tried to take in the implications of this. Finally he said, "That's a hell of a coincidence."

"It is."

"And do we know why he committed suicide?"

"No idea, I'm afraid. There's nothing about that in the press reports. But they do say he was a bit of a loner, so that might be a clue."

"What were the circumstances of his death exactly? Do you have any details?"

"Believe it or not, he jumped off a cliff." Bernard gave a bleak laugh. "It sounds ridiculous, doesn't it? But apparently it's true. There are plenty of cliffs to choose from in that part of the world."

"How bizarre."

"But not uncommon, unfortunately."

"So there was nothing suspicious about it?"

"Nothing was reported. I don't know what the police think."

Tom was silent for a moment. There seemed to be some significance in what he was being told, but he couldn't piece the elements together.

Bernard said, "D'you want to know why you never found him on the internet?"

"Go on."

"He didn't go by the name Neil, except officially. His nickname was Ben. It was based on his initials – Bryan Neil. His death was reported online and in the local press under the name Ben Bradwell. That was also the name of his Facebook account and all that."

"Huh!" Tom thought about this. "But the people at that Stay and Prosper place called him Neil."

"Maybe he was reinventing himself." Bernard put verbal quote marks round the phrase.

Tom said, "You might mock the idea, but it's not unknown."

"Anyway, if you think the date of his death is a coincidence, how about this? Before he joined Stay and Prosper he worked in administration at a courier firm in Brighton. And guess which firm that was?"

"Not Carswells?"

"You've got it."

"Bloody hell! I wonder what that means."

"I suppose it means he might have met you at some point."

"Maybe."

Bernard said, "If you don't mind me asking, what is this guy to you, exactly?"

"I met him about a week before my accident, but I'm still trying to piece together the details. And I wondered if he was the person in that weird call on my answering machine."

"Right. Well that's certainly something to think about."

Tom thanked Bernard for his work, and prepared to wind up the conversation, but Bernard hadn't finished. He said, "I could try to find out the police view of this guy's suicide if you want. No promises, but I might come up with something."

"How would you do that?"

"A mate of mine is a retired detective inspector. Joe Henderson. He still has contacts on the force."

"Well, great. No harm in asking the question."

"Consider it done."

*   *   *

An envelope dropped through the letterbox just after lunch – a new piece of correspondence from Tom's personal accident insurers. The sheaf of paperwork included a copy of the form D700 that the contact centre agent had mentioned. He glanced through it, noting phrases such as "multiple tibial fractures" and "event-specific retrograde amnesia". At the top, someone had scribbled, "Home visit – not required."

The gist of it seemed to be that the company was finally preparing to pay out the insurance money. Three cheers for that. There was even a guarded note of apology for the length of the delay, which the company blamed on complications that had arisen while the extent of Tom's injuries were being established.

Perhaps if he succeeded in meeting Martin Frankl, this whole insurance saga might provide a way into the subject. Something else he could bring up in that conversation was the subject of Neil Bradwell and his untimely death. Or would any mention of it antagonise Frankl? He would have to play that by ear.

He wondered again if Bradwell was the person in the phone conversation he'd inadvertently recorded in Winchester. It would help if he could find another recording of Bradwell's voice to compare it to, but where would he look for such a thing?

Bernard might be able to help him with this. He picked up his phone.

"How do you fancy a bit more web research?"

"Bring it on, Maestro."

"I'm wondering if you could try to find a voice recording of that man Bradwell. He might have left something out there on the web somewhere. It's a bit of a long shot, but it's worth a look."

"You want it for comparison with that recording on your answer machine?"

"On the nail."

"OK, leave it with me. And by the way, I've asked my ex-police mate the question about his suicide – whether it was an open-and-shut case or not."

"Already? That was fast work."

Bernard chuckled. "He's like me – doesn't like to leave things dangling."

"Did you have to explain why you wanted to know?"

"Not really. He trusts me not to waste his time. But you need to be ready to step forward if you stir anything up."

"Fair enough."

"I'll let you know what he says. It might take a few days."

"That's fine. Just let me know when you hear something."

Chapter 21

Getting to London was much easier now that Tom could drive himself to the station in Winchester and leave the rental car there. His main concern was that the repeated trips were becoming expensive, and he wasn't clear how much of the cost he could charge against the article he was writing. He would have to raise it with Malcolm.

His meeting with Victor Rudge was at eleven am. He arrived on the dot, and was shown upstairs to a modest office facing the yard at the back of the building. Rudge was seated behind a rosewood desk, leaning back and talking earnestly on the phone.

He was much as Tom remembered him: a slim man of around fifty with short-cropped dark hair and a look that seemed to bore right through him. As last time they'd met, he was dressed all in black. Was this his trademark look? He gestured to a visitor's chair and continued his phone call.

Finally he disconnected. "Good of you to come, Tom. How are you?"

The show of interest seemed out of character, but there was no warmth behind it. If anything, Rudge was looking at him suspiciously.

Tom said, "You mean my injuries? I'm getting over them, thanks."

"Marcus said you had no memory of the accident you were in?"

"That's right. I seem to have lost an entire week of my life. They say I might never remember it."

"Really?" Rudge continued to watch him with probing brown eyes.

A little awkwardly Tom said, "I'm still not sure why you wanted to see me."

"Ah, yes." Rudge steepled his hands for a moment, then leaned forward. "You were telling me on the phone that you haven't actually written up the article you were researching when you met Marcus recently."

"No, I'll be doing that over the next week."

"Right. Well I just wanted to make the point that Marcus was a little … shall we say over-casual in what he told you when the two of you met. Normally we have people on hand to make sure that the message is on song."

"He gave you a run-down of the whole conversation?"

"No, no, just the gist. In particular, I believe he told you he wasn't sure if Britain would leave the EU or not."

"I think he was just emphasising the uncertainty of the situation."

"Well we're not uncertain here. We know Britain won't be leaving. That's our core belief, and that's the message we want to get across."

"Don't you think a little uncertainty makes Marcus sound more plausible?"

"We live in a world of soundbites. These days people think thoughts that will fit into the length a tweet. Look at the US President – he's got it down to a fine art. There's no room for subtlety any more. What you call 'a little uncertainty' doesn't play well with social media. Anything that isn't definite sounds like vacillation and doubt."

Tom looked at Rudge for a moment without responding. He was thinking back to his time as a rookie journalist. Much of what he'd written in those days had been influenced by the advertising potential behind it, yet despite that, the diehard journalists on the paper had drilled into him the sanctity of editorial independence. Had the world changed since then?

He said, "Should I take it that you're telling me how to report Marcus's comments?"

"I'm just encouraging you to accentuate the positive. I'm asking you to write what he actually meant, as opposed to quoting the specific words that he might have used. Don't forget, he was speaking off the cuff." He gave a curt smile. "We like to give ongoing access to writers who enter into the spirit of our enterprise."

This sounded like a vague threat combined with a bribe. Tom said, "I should tell you I'm not opposed to your campaign's objectives. If anything, I'm on your side."

"Good to know, Tom." Rudge stood up abruptly. "I think we understand each other then. Thanks for coming in."

* * *

Tom's plan had been to find Martin Frankl after he'd finished with Victor Rudge, but now that he was here, he was unsure how to proceed. However, luck was on his side. As he was heading for the staircase he heard someone talking in one of the rooms. The door was open, and inside he could see a man standing near a desk, immersed in a phone conversation. He recognised Frankl from pictures on the campaign's website, and gave a discreet knock.

Frankl looked up, and even across the room Tom recognised a succession of fleeting emotions: surprise, annoyance, even alarm. Frankl ended the phone call abruptly, and his expression slid into one of studied perplexity.

"Can I help you?"

"It's Martin Frankl, isn't it? Sorry to interrupt you, but I was passing and I thought it would be an opportunity to say hello. I'm Tom Anthony, and I'm writing an article about Brexit for *Seismic Scene*.

Apparently recovering, Frankl said, "Right. Sorry. It's just a surprise to see a stranger wandering around the building unaccompanied."

"I've been in a meeting with Victor Rudge. I'm on my way out."

Frankl was a good-looking man in his late thirties. He had light coloured hair, and was wearing an open-neck shirt, fawn business trousers and a matching waistcoat with a double row of buttons. He said, "Come on in for a minute." His accent was middle-class, perhaps with an American tinge to it.

Unlike Rudge's office, Frankl's had a sunny aspect on the street side of the block. He said, "Have a seat, have a seat," and pointed to a sofa set against one of the walls. He leaned back against his desk and said, "I'm the press officer around here, but I seem to have been missing out on my duty. First you arrange a meeting with Marcus all on your own, now you schedule a meeting with Victor, and I'm not in on that one either."

Tom said, "I didn't mean to sideline you. I didn't even know you existed when I first contacted Marcus, and it was Victor Rudge who approached me to talk to him."

"Fair enough. Our mission is to achieve exposure for our cause. I suppose I shouldn't cavil about how we get it." He gave a quick smile.

Tom watched him with interest. He was making a fair job of conveying brisk self-confidence, though behind his eyes there was still a hint of alarm. He kept glancing over towards the open door, as though fearful of someone who might walk past.

Tom said, "I don't think Victor would entirely agree that anything goes. He just told me in so many words how to report what Marcus said to me."

Frankl raised his eyebrows. "Oh, that's what he wanted with you, was it? I wouldn't worry too much about that. Victor comes from a world where people try to control information very tightly – not that they always succeed."

"What world is that?"

"Finance. He was a trader, and head of a private equity firm. Still is, in fact. He has a lot of fingers in a lot of pies. I would have thought you would know that."

"I'm a new boy to this. I used to be a journalist in the distant past, but I've had nearly ten years out of it. I'm feeling my way back."

"Well, Victor brings fiscal rigour to our campaign message, just as Marcus brings the benefit of his business insight."

Tom waited for more, but Frankl appeared to have had his say. The meeting was ending, yet so far Tom had failed to bring up the matter of the fake insurance visit. Could he do it at this late stage? Then Frankl gave him an opening.

"How did you get the leg injury, if you don't mind me asking?"

If Frankl really had been behind the fake insurance interview, he must already know about the accident, but Tom had to play along. He said, "I was in a car smash last winter. It's been a slow recovery process, but I'm getting there."

"What happened?"

"Ah, that's a good question. I don't remember anything about the accident, or any of the week leading up to it. Apparently I simply drove off the road and into a field. But I'm told I might remember more as time goes on."

Frankl's expression was impossible to read. He said, "That must be reassuring."

"It depends what I got up to during that week. If I robbed a bank, I'd rather not know." He risked a smile. "At any rate, my insurance company is satisfied that it's genuine retrograde amnesia."

Tom was watching Frankl carefully as he said this. Was that a fleeting slip in the composed mask? It was hard to call.

As they stood up, Tom said, "Any more news about that petrol bomb incident?"

"Ah, of course – you're the journalist who was here at the time. That was a neat little piece you wrote on that website with the inside story."

Tom shrugged. "I hope it gave the right impression."

"No complaint from me."

"And the police still don't know who was behind it?"

"They have their suspicions, but they don't have any proof yet. We may never know."

Frankl came down to the foyer with Tom. Conversationally he said, "Where are you off to now?"

"As it happens, I'm going to see a man named Dowdeswell, the head of Right Thinking."

Frankl gave an ironic laugh. "That'll be nice for you. In the political balance he's off the scale."

Chapter 22

Adrian Dowdeswell, *de facto* head of the Right Thinking group, was a slightly-built man in his mid-forties. He had a full face and thinning mouse-coloured hair, and he was wearing a grey lambs' wool jersey over his business shirt. His features had an angry set to them.

"Tell me again who you represent," he said as Tom was ushered into his office at the food processing factory. He didn't stand up to shake Tom's hand or invite him to sit down. There was a visitor's chair near the desk, so Tom nodded towards it with eyebrows raised. Dowdeswell said, "By all means have a seat."

"I'm writing the article about Brexit for *Seismic Scene*, the online news service."

"And what do you want from me exactly?"

Measuring his words carefully, Tom said, "I hope I've got this right. I'm assuming that Right Thinking means 'right leaning', so I'm hoping you can give me a perspective on Brexit from that point of view."

"A perspective? What does that mean?"

Tom hesitated. "Do you mind if I record this?" He pulled out his phone.

"I'd rather you didn't."

If Dowdeswell's intent was to intimidate before they'd even started, it was working. Tom put his phone away and took out a notepad and pen. He said, "I was hoping you might comment on the progress of Brexit negotiations so far, and give me some idea of how confident you are that things will work out for the best in the end."

"If you mean will we get the result we need, then yes, things will work out for the best, as you put it. Britain will be free of its European ties. We'll be able to dictate our own destiny again."

"But?"

"But so far the Government has made a total dog's dinner of the exit negotiations. No wonder the Europeans think the Brits are a bunch of tossers."

"But you wouldn't want another general election, surely?"

"Not now. When the time is right."

Tom sat back, wondering whether he should risk antagonising this man. Cautiously, he said, "Don't you think there's a bit of a contradiction here? Since the referendum we've already had one general election, and now you're saying you wouldn't mind if we had another. Yet when anyone suggests having a second referendum, your group treats the idea with contempt. What's the difference?"

"It's a ridiculous analogy. The cases bear no comparison."

"Why not? Why are people allowed to change their mind about who they want for Prime Minister, yet they can't change their mind about whether they want to be in the EU?"

"The terms of the referendum were completely different. People were asked to make a once-and-for-all choice."

"But that was just at a moment in time. Did people really know what they were committing themselves to? Were they given the true facts? Is it fair to hold them to it?"

Dowdeswell stared at him. "I assume that's a rhetorical question."

Trying one last jibe, Tom said, "The vote wasn't a mandate, it was just an expression of opinion. Legally speaking it was advisory."

Dowdeswell swivelled one way and then the other in his chair, staring at Tom. Finally he said, "I'd like to see you run that past the man in the street. If there's serious talk about rewinding the referendum, it'll end up in riots."

"I thought your group was opposed to direct action?"

"I'm not saying we would tell people to riot, I'm saying they would do it of their own accord."

"But you wouldn't rush to stop it?"

Dowdeswell said nothing. They were getting into deep water. Tom needed to lighten the tone. He said, "So if you were handling the negotiations, what would you do differently?"

"Pay the Europeans whatever they want and simply walk away. There's nothing to be gained by offending them and skulking off under a cloud. We might be leaving their cosy coterie, but they'll still be there across the Channel. We can't change geography."

"Then why leave in the first place?"

Dowdeswell glared at him again. "I assume you don't expect me to give you a serious answer to that. Don't get me going on the petty regulation, the red tape, the vested interests, the creeping Europeanisation, the loss of sovereignty. I wouldn't know where to start."

Deciding he'd better change his line of attack again, Tom said, "Where do you stand on immigration?"

"Where do I stand?" Another contemptuous frown. "You're not going to get me saying anything inflammatory about immigrants. Half the people working in this factory are first-generation or second-generation immigrants. More than half. We couldn't function without them."

"But you think Brexit will bring immigration under control?"

"Of course it will. At the moment immigration is completely out of hand. It's been mismanaged for decades. The EU's insistence on freedom of movement between countries has made a bad situation worse. We've simply been stacking up racial tensions and social unrest. Well, now that can stop."

The conversation stuttered along in a similar vein for another twenty minutes. Dowdeswell's answers were always unpredictable, sometimes reasonable, sometimes not. Eventually he started glancing at his watch.

Tom closed his notepad and sat back. "What's your opinion of the Stay and Prosper campaign? They're convinced Brexit will never happen."

"They're pissing in the wind. The only people they're convincing are themselves."

"If they don't pose a threat to Brexit, why did someone throw a fake bomb through their window?"

For the first time in the entire interview, Dowdeswell smiled. It was an unnerving smile – gleeful, yet at the same time ironic.

"There will always be gullible fools and fanatics out there," he said, "but I doubt whether any organised group was behind that fake bomb.

It certainly wasn't any of our people, if that's what you're thinking. The police came here asking me about it, but they agreed with me." He fixed Tom with his stare. "We deplore violence. Make sure you tell your readers that."

* * *

As Dowdeswell ushered Tom out he handed him a business card. "My mobile number is on there," he said. "Ring me any time if you want to talk more."

Surprised, Tom thanked him and slipped it into his pocket. He found it hard to imagine ever wanting to contact Dowdeswell again, but turning down potential contact details went against the grain.

He was led back to the reception area by a young male assistant. They paused in front of a large picture window that looked out on to the factory floor, where dairy products were being created for sale to supermarkets. "Adrian's father started this business in his garage," the assistant said.

"How long has Adrian been in charge?"

"About five years." The man gestured towards the giant metal vats. "We've nearly doubled in size in that time."

To Tom's further surprise, a car had been organised to take him to the nearest rail station. As they drove off, he reflected that Dowdeswell was an unfathomable contradiction: immovable in his defence of Brexit, unrepentant in his veiled racism, yet strangely pragmatic in other respects. His barely contained anger made him seem fearsome, but Tom had seen nothing to suggest that his anger might spill over into direct action. His repudiation of the bomb threat had sounded entirely convincing.

Chapter 23

Tom needed a new car. He'd been studying the rental agreement for the car he'd hired, and the figures made unpleasant reading. He'd already driven hundreds of miles in that car, and had it for many days. The bill was going to be steep.

His car insurers still hadn't paid out on the car he'd written off, but he now knew they were about to. The latest piece of correspondence from them had promised payment "within days". However, their cover didn't include the cost of a replacement hire car.

In the meantime, if he wanted to buy a car he would have to find enough money from his own funds to tide him over until the insurers paid out. He opened his laptop and called up the details of his and Jan's joint bank account. They'd opened it as a token of their strengthening relationship, and later he'd paid ten thousand pounds into it – his contribution to the cost of a new kitchen and bathroom that they'd planned, but never actually bought. He hadn't known then that he would soon be losing his job.

He was surprised to find that the balance was now just under one thousand. How could that be? He checked his private account. Had he moved some of the cash there? No, that was nearly empty too. He flicked back to the joint account and scanned through the transaction list more closely. There it was – a single outgoing payment of eight thousand pounds, which had been transferred into one of Jan's accounts. It had been made while he was in hospital.

How was he to deal with this? In theory Jan had as much right as he had to draw money out of the account, but it was supposed to be used for joint expenditure. What shared costs of this magnitude had she encountered while he was in hospital?

While they were both preparing their supper that evening he said casually, "I was thinking of buying a new car, but there's not much cash in our joint account at the moment."

Without looking round, she said, "Why not use your own account?"

"I paid ten thousand into the joint account last year. I thought I would use some of that."

"We're supposed to pay in agreed amounts."

He looked at her in frustration. "The point is, there's hardly any money in the account now. I don't understand where it's gone."

"Why don't you just wait for the insurance payment?"

"Jan." He put down the knife he'd been using. "I know the insurance will pay for the car. That's not the point. I just wanted to borrow the money for a week or two, until the insurance money comes in. But most of it has been paid out into your account."

She turned round. "Well sorry, but that's what *I* did – I borrowed the money. I needed it to go towards the bills on the refurbishment. As soon as the house is rented out, we'll be getting the money back with interest. Then I can repay what I took out."

He gave her a long look. "OK, fair point, but I thought that was why you sub-let the London flat – to help cover the refurbishment costs?"

"It was, but that money only comes in dribs and drabs. I needed cash in a single hit, so I just drew it out of the account."

"Couldn't you have told me about this? If I'd borrowed that sort of amount, at least I would have checked with you first."

"For god's sake, Tom, I was more concerned with getting you back on your feet than with giving you bulletins about our bank balances."

There was a moment of brittle silence. A wrong word from either of them would send the conversation spiralling into open hostility. Was this the moment for it? Tom was tempted to let it happen, but somehow managed to swallow his annoyance again just in time. He wasn't ready to challenge Jan's strange behaviour, but he wouldn't forget it either. He shrugged and returned to the lounge without saying any more.

As he sat down, he wondered if he was being unfair to her. She'd put up with a lot over the past year. Her father had died not long before Christmas. She'd dealt with the funeral arrangements, sorted through his belongings, and arranged to have his house refurbished from top to bottom.

Then in January Tom's accident had put him out of action, and for nine days she'd had to contend with the possibility that he might never wake up from his coma. After he had, she'd visited him regularly in hospital, then brought him to her father's house and helped him get back on his feet.

On the face of it, he ought to cut her some slack, but he had an unsettling sense that relationships shouldn't be measured in terms of obligation and debt. If that was the basis of this one, it didn't have much future.

* * *

Next morning he called up his bank website again. He had various accounts set up for different purposes, and he realised that by combining their contents, he could scrape together just enough cash to buy a cheap car outright. The redundancy money from Carswells left him a little to spare, and the various insurance payments would soon top it up.

He drove into Southampton and headed for a district where he knew there were several used-car lots. He was unconcerned what make of car he chose; it simply had to be presentable, convincingly maintained and automatic. And affordable.

Within half an hour he'd found what he wanted – a six-year-old Ford in a fetching shade of grey. They said they could have it ready for him by tomorrow.

Chapter 24

"It took me a long time, but I finally found it – a video of Ben Bradwell."
Bernard was exultant.

Tom smiled into the phone. "Excellent. What do you have?"

"It's just a short clip. Someone was going round an outdoor café,
doing joke interviews with the people sitting there. They stuck a camera
in Bradwell's face and asked him some daft questions. His bit only goes
on for a few seconds."

"That should be enough. Where did you find it?"

"It was on the café's website. It's a bar really, in Brighton. I'll send
you the link."

"You did well."

"Something else that might interest you – my police mate got back
to me about his suicide."

"That was quick. What did he say?"

"Well, there are good reasons for thinking it was just a classic suicide.
In particular, Bradwell had recently split up with his partner, a guy from
Shoreham. They think he was depressed, and decided to put an end to
it all."

Tom reflected for a moment. "You say there were good reasons for
thinking it was suicide. Does that mean your mate isn't convinced?"

"He reckons his contacts on the local force were undecided."

"Any particular reason?"

"One reason is the location. Apparently people who want to throw
themselves off a cliff tend to go to the obvious place. In that area
it's Beachy Head, which is twenty miles along the coast. Or else they
go to the nearest point to where they are at the time – which in his
case would be Telscombe Cliffs. That's only a stone's throw from
Brighton."

"And?"

"Bradwell went to a place in between the two – Seven Sisters Country Park. It's that series of seven chalk cliffs, all in a row. He had no known history with the area."

"Interesting."

"It gets more interesting. The actual location is a long way from the nearest road. It's only accessible via cliff paths. And in any case, Bradwell's car wasn't there. They found it parked near his flat in Brighton."

"Could he have gone there by bus?"

"Yes – in fact there's a good bus service along that route. But seemingly they couldn't find any evidence that he did." Bernard paused. "Anyway, can you imagine catching a bus to a place where you want to jump off a cliff, and then walking a mile to get there?"

Tom shuddered. "No, but I can't imagine jumping off a cliff in the first place."

"Fair comment."

"Bernard, you've done an amazingly thorough job. Thanks for all this."

"No worries. To be honest I enjoyed it – piecing all the bits together, building up a picture. Give me another job any time you like."

* * *

Tom watched the video clip several times. Bradwell was seated at a picnic table with a group of other people in their twenties and thirties. The sea was just visible in the distance behind them. The angle was wide, suggesting that the video had been shot with a phone rather than a camera. The voice behind the clip was asking everyone what they thought of the beer, and they were all giving facetious replies.

He immediately recognised Bradwell. When they'd met at the Brexit conference Bradwell had been dressed formally, whereas here he was in a white T-shirt and was wearing a baseball hat back to front, but there was no mistaking the freckles and the slightly upturned nose.

Was that the same voice Tom had heard in the conversation recorded on his answering machine? He couldn't be sure without listening to it again. He fetched the audiotape from his bedroom. It looked like a standard cassette tape.

Jan had told him she'd held on to her father's old hi-fi equipment, which almost certainly included a cassette player. She'd said she'd put this kind of thing in the garage, and hadn't got round to disposing of it yet. He made his way through to the connecting door at the back of the mud room.

The garage floor was cluttered with Jan's parents' belongings – an old CRT television set, the hi-fi system, several old radios, a defunct lawnmower, a built-in coal-effect fire (now not built in), and several cardboard cartons packed with miscellaneous junk.

He half-lifted, half-dragged the hi-fi set into the house and plugged the mains lead into a socket on the kitchen wall, leaving the unit itself on the floor. Then he went back out into the garage to fetch one of its wooden speaker cabinets. He inserted the tape in the tape transport slot, rewound it and pressed the Play button.

The playback was very quiet. He twisted the oversized volume control to its maximum. "There are things you don't know about the Remain campaign," the mystery caller's voice said. Immediately Tom was in no doubt – it was Ben Bradwell.

He sat down on one of the kitchen stools, trying to work through the implications. He already knew that he and Bradwell had connected briefly at that conference. Now he also knew that Bradwell had called him at home, saying he wanted to tell him something important about the Stay and Prosper group. What kind of information could that have been, and did he ever pass it on?

Perhaps more to the point, if he'd been so keen to share this secret with Tom, why had he decided within a week to kill himself?

Tom reminded himself that the two events didn't have to be mutually exclusive. Stay and Prosper might have loomed large in Bradwell's intellectual life, but emotional turmoil might have taken precedence.

All the same, the contradiction was curious.

He took the hi-fi and speaker back to the garage. As he glanced around, ready to switch off the garage light, his eye was caught by a black bag on the floor in the corner, leaning against a work bench. It reminded him of his canvas bag – the one he'd used for taking his laptop computer and notes to meetings. He hadn't seen it since the accident, and he'd assumed it had been destroyed along with the laptop.

He went over to look at it more closely. It *was* his old bag. It had a long tear in the front and scuff marks all over it. Someone must have rescued it, and Jan had shoved it in here.

Then he realised that on the concrete floor behind it was the laptop itself. It was in several pieces. The keyboard was out of position, the screen was completely detached and leaning separately, and disconnected bits of circuit board were visible inside the main unit, which was bent in the middle.

On a whim he picked up the bag and peered into it. Nothing there – but something felt harder than it should have through the soft exterior. He'd never found a use for the small internal compartment, but there was an object in it now. He fumbled for the zip and slid it open. Inside was his old mobile phone. Someone at the accident scene must have shoved it there for safe keeping, but the reports had simply indicated that it had disappeared.

* * *

The phone's screen was cracked and the case was scraped and scuffed, but when Tom connected it to a charger the little red light came on as expected. He checked it an hour later, and found he had a working phone. There was no live connection – the phone's contract had been terminated months ago – but he could access his old contact list and view text messages. He scrolled through them.

Mostly they were mundane: arranging drinks with friends, confirming arrival times at meetings, checking what time Jan expected to be home from work. He felt a wave of nostalgia for the life he'd been living without a shattered leg – when pain was absent, and he could jump up and undertake any task he chose without thinking twice.

Then he found two messages that stopped him in his tracks. One was from Christine across the road. "What time are you coming over? I forget – do you like chilli?"

Utterly banal, yet so revealing. As far as he knew, he hadn't sat down to a meal with her for years – certainly not since their brief fling all that time ago. Yet here was evidence to the contrary. He checked the date stamp. It was part-way through the week leading up to his accident. It was further evidence that during those missing days their relationship had taken a short-lived lurch in a new direction.

The other message was much more cryptic. "Can u make it 10pm not 8?" It was from an unknown number. What hit Tom immediately was the date stamp: mid-afternoon on the day of his accident.

He scrolled through the message list, searching for other messages from the same sender. He found an earlier one: "U ok with 8pm at place we agreed?" It had been sent on the morning of the same day. He had simply replied, "Yes."

He searched for more messages to or from the same number, but found none. There was no clue in the call log either. Nevertheless, this felt like a breakthrough. It was the first clue he'd found about where he might have been going on the night of the accident. It was presumably to meet this person.

He didn't know the sender's identity, but he was already wondering if it had been Ben Bradwell. All the clues seemed to be pointing in that direction. He tapped the number into his new phone and tried calling it. A voice told him, "Number not recognised."

He wondered if the meeting had actually taken place. He'd been told he'd been heading back towards Winchester at the time of the accident, but that didn't prove he'd reached his intended destination or met anyone along the way.

Presumably the only way he could find that out was by remembering of his own accord. At the moment, the week remained stubbornly blank.

Chapter 25

The website article was due within a week. The time for interviews was over; now Tom had to pull the strands together into a coherent whole. Curiously, in a world of soundbites and simplistic arguments, Malcolm had told him the article should be "quite long".

Tom had expressed surprise at this. "Even when I was still in the game, people were saying the era of the long feature article was dead. Readers didn't have the time or the inclination to plough through acres of prose any more."

"That's the beauty of online publishing," Malcolm had said. "It's not like a newspaper. People can only see a screenful of text at a time, so they're not intimidated by length. They'll carry on reading an article for as long as they're interested." He'd paused, then said pointedly, "All the more reason to keep your piece lively and readable."

"No pressure then."

Tom's task for today was to play through his recorded interviews and transcribe them into usable chunks, ready to dip into for the article. It was a lengthy process, and felt rather like reliving the interviews themselves. He knew there were voice transcription apps that could do the job automatically, but he wanted the opportunity to be selective.

Gradually he built up what became an immensely long document of hastily typed notes, in which his own thoughts were interspersed with extracts of the speakers' comments. Now he had to break all this down into logical themes, then connect it all together and knock it into intelligible, authoritative prose.

He leaned back on the sofa and stretched out his injured leg, which was throbbing from the intensity of the work. At least he now felt he could actually write this article and make something useful of it.

He found himself thinking again about those messages on his old phone. Had the sender really been Ben Bradwell? It now occurred to him that he already had a phone number for Bradwell – the one Sue at Stay and Prosper had looked up for him. He pulled out his current phone and scrolled through his emails until he found it, then compared it with the number for the text message on his old phone. They were different.

This proved nothing. Bradwell might have had two phones, or he might have borrowed one to send those texts. Tom had no way of finding this out, but perhaps Bernard's police contact could help him again. He picked up his current phone.

"I have another question for your police mate, if you think he'll look at it."

"Go on."

Tom told Bernard about finding his old phone, along with its cryptic messages. "It would be really interesting to know if they were sent from Bradwell's number."

"Can't you just ring it and see who answers?"

"I tried that. It doesn't work."

Bernard hesitated. "I'll gladly ask the question for you, but you do realise the implications, do you? If that number really is Ben Bradwell's, it connects you and him directly on the day before he died. I don't think the police will sit on that. You'll have to expect them to come knocking on your door."

Tom considered this. "Come to think of it, if that *was* his number, presumably they would already have found out that he'd texted my phone. They would have questioned me about it."

"Not necessarily. If they were satisfied that it was suicide, they might not have seen any reason to follow up that kind of thing."

"So if I raise this now, I'll be stirring things up."

"Exactly."

"But for god's sake, I wouldn't have done Bradwell any harm. I barely even knew him before all this."

"You know that and I know that, but the police have their own way of going about things. They simply follow the evidence. They would want to know why the two of you planned to meet up."

"Well, I can't tell them anything about that because I don't remember anything."

"So are you ready to have your memory loss put under scrutiny?"

Tom thought about this. "You seem to be finding all the downsides to this. Don't you want me to find out what happened to me during that missing week?"

"I know how these things work. Once you make yourself a person of interest, it can be a long time before you cease to be one."

There was authority and knowledge in Bernard's tone. Tom said, "What makes you such an expert in all this?"

"Didn't I tell you? I was once on the force myself."

* * *

"It was a very long time ago," Bernard said. "We were living in Manchester then. I got as far as detective sergeant, but Marie hated the hours and I hated the stress, so I resigned and worked in corporate security for a while. Then I switched to line management, and the rest is history."

"You cagey old bugger."

"It never occurred to me to mention it."

"Of course it didn't."

"Truly!" Bernard chuckled. "It feels like another life now. But you never forget the police mentality – the way they think."

"I suppose not."

"So I'm just giving you a word of advice. If you're right in what you're guessing, this guy Bradwell must have been trying to blow the whistle on that campaign group of yours. But I don't know why, and nor do you, so don't get too excited about it. If you go to the authorities and start questioning how he died, you'll be pointing a finger at some powerful people. Have your story straight before you rattle any cages, otherwise it'll just rebound on you."

Tom put the phone down with a sense of unreality. Not only did Bernard have a history he'd never dreamt of, but he'd also articulated a thought that Tom couldn't ignore: that he was in the middle of something complex and increasingly alarming, and he needed to think carefully how to proceed.

The Stay and Prosper campaign lay at the centre of it. He thought back over his various contacts with the organisation. Marcus Headington had seemed honest, conscientious and committed. It was hard to see any evil intent in him. Victor Rudge was coldly enigmatic, but again had done nothing to suggest he was anything but honest.

Martin Frankl was the unknown quantity. In person he seemed smoothly sociable, yet he'd been quite happy to orchestrate a bizarre subterfuge to investigate Tom's memory loss. That ploy, although unnerving, had initially seemed a curiosity, but now it was acquiring sinister overtones. Bernard's advice to get his story straight before going to the authorities was no doubt sound, but he hadn't told Bernard about the bogus insurance interview. If and when he did, the advice might be different.

Chapter 26

"Is this the man with the wonky leg?" A woman's voice, warmly musical: it was Emily, from the campaign office.

Tom was on his own this evening. Jan had texted an hour earlier to say she would be staying over in London. He'd nearly finished writing his article, but it needed fine-tuning, and he'd had enough for today. He was glad of the excuse for a conversation, and felt himself smiling into the phone.

He said, "Less wonky than it once was. I'm planning on taking up hurdling next week."

"I can just see that."

"To what do I owe the pleasure?"

"It's a pleasure, is it? I'm very glad to hear that." Her words sounded slightly slurred, and from the background noises he decided she'd already spent some time in a pub or bar.

"Let me put it another way. How can I help you?"

"Help me? I don't think you *can* help me. I just thought you might like to know that I've been fired from the Stay and Prosper campaign. My contribution has been terminated. Forthwith. No more need for Emily."

"Fired? Why?"

"They don't have to give you a reason because you're not employed in the first place. They can just tell you to fuck off, and that's it. You're gone. History."

"It doesn't make sense. Surely you're helping them? And you're doing it for nothing."

"I know that! Try telling them."

He said, "I'm really sorry."

"So am I. I thought they were the great hope for the future – the people who could finally close the book on this Brexit insanity. Where do I take my talents now?"

"Do you think it's to do with the insurance scam? Have they blamed you for telling me about it?"

"Ha! You've hit the nail on the head. I'm assuming you dropped me in it, did you?" Curiously, she asked this with resignation rather than rancour.

"What? Of course not."

"It's all right, it's all right – I don't blame you. I would have done the same if it were me."

"But I didn't! No way. If you want to know, I've been bending over backwards to avoid mentioning your name in connection with this."

"Oh." She took a moment to process this. "Is that true?"

"Absolutely!" He lowered the phone, staring around as if for corroboration, then raised it again. "I *like* you. I wouldn't have bothered otherwise."

"You like me? Really?"

He found himself laughing in spite of himself. "For god's sake. Yes!"

"But listen, listen. You were at the Stay and Prosper office this week, weren't you? Whatever you talked about, you stirred things up with Martin. If you didn't tell him about me, he must have decided to dump me anyway, to make sure you didn't meet me next time you swanned in there."

It sounded plausible. He couldn't really argue with her. He said, "I wasn't planning on making regular visits."

"What, not even to see little old me?"

"Not even for that."

She fell silent at last, and he took a moment to think about what she was telling him. He said, "I suppose if you've left the campaign, there's nothing to stop me confronting Frankl about that insurance thing."

"Huh. Good luck with that."

"Why do you say that?"

There was a long silence. Finally, sounding suddenly sober, she said, "He'll deny it. He'll say I've got a history of mental instability, and I made it all up. He's got it covered."

"Is that true?"

Another silence, then: "It depends how you look at it. I had … I had an *episode* when I was twenty. I crashed out of university. Relationship issues, all kinds of crap. I couldn't hack it. I went into therapy. I wouldn't call it mental instability, but he would dress it up that way."

Tom was thinking fast. He said, "But how the hell could he make out that you invented that insurance thing off your own bat? It would have been ridiculous. What could possibly have been in it for you?"

She took a while to answer, but eventually said, "You were at that Brexit conference last winter, weren't you? The one where the campaign had its official launch."

"Yes, I met Marcus Headington there. It was a few days before my accident."

"Right. Well I'd just started working at the campaign that week, and they offered seats in the conference to any of the volunteers who wanted to go. So obviously I went along."

"You were actually there?"

"That's what I'm telling you." A theatrical sigh of impatience. "So I'm sitting there in the audience, watching Marcus and his merry men progressing up the aisle, and all of a sudden he stops in the middle of the gangway and starts talking to this tall thin man. I turn to my mate Sally ..." She tailed off.

"And?"

"OK, and I say ... well, something flattering about this guy."

"This guy being?"

"You, obviously. Keep up!"

"Sorry, sorry."

"All right. But just don't start getting ideas, all right? I'm only telling you this because you forced me to at gunpoint."

"I get it."

"OK. So Sally, she's my mate, was going out with Martin Frankl at the time. Strange taste in men if you ask me, but what can you do?"

"And ..."

"She's seen the error of her ways now. They've broken up, thank god."

"But getting back to the point ..."

"OK, OK. So she must have told Martin what I said about you."

"Which means …"

"Which means Martin has his cover story. Mad girl Emily spots Tom at conference, develops instant crush, can't wait to see him again, but bang – he's in hospital with his leg in traction. So she stalks him on the web, keeps an eye on his progress, then as soon as she's out, she invents an excuse to go and visit him in Hampshire."

"Bloody hell – you've got it all worked out."

"You mean Martin has. He's a sly one, that man."

Thinking aloud, Tom said, "I ought to go to the police about this."

"No!" Suddenly there was panic in her voice. "I would never have told you all this if I thought that's what you would do. I trusted you."

"It's OK, honestly. I won't." He reflected for a moment. "But you haven't done anything terrible. That insurance visit probably wasn't even illegal."

She was silent a moment, then said, "I've got a history. When I went off the rails, I got into some stupid things. Not drugs, just shoplifting, crap like that. I got a suspended sentence, but it's all on my record now. If you go to the law, it'll come back and bite me. I'll probably lose my job in the bar, for a start."

He said, "OK, I hear you. It's just a pity …"

"I know – it's a pity I got myself into the insurance thing in the first place."

"I wasn't going to say that."

"But you'd be right. I only have myself to blame. At the time it seemed harmless enough, but it wasn't really, was it?"

The call had apparently run its course, but she seemed reluctant to end it. The muted background chatter seemed louder now. He said, "Are you at work in the bar?"

"What? No, I'm in a pub in Hammersmith – down the road from where I live. My flatmates are around here somewhere." He imagined her looking round the bar for them. "But I'm going back to evening shifts in Richmond from tomorrow. The pay's better, and my evenings are free now." She gave an ironic laugh.

He said, "Maybe you could carry on doing the Brexit research at home, and feed the results to the campaign anonymously?"

"Fuck 'em. They don't deserve me. Anyway, bar work is much easier. No thinking required."

"What's the name of the place?"

"The Crown and Mitre." A pause. "You should come and visit us some time."

* * *

How was he supposed to feel about all this? He was flattered by Emily's undisguised interest in him, and reassured by her apparent honesty, yet those feelings were drowned out by his mounting alarm over the implications of what she'd been telling him.

He tried to jostle the sequence of events into some sort of order in his head. All this had started when Ben Bradwell had contacted him and suggested meeting up – apparently to tell him something important. Tom had driven off on one night, probably the night of the intended meeting, and he might or might not have gone through with it. Then on the way back he'd crashed his car.

The accident had left him with a shattered leg and traumatic amnesia. He had no recollection of any of these events, and for the next four months he'd been out of action in hospital.

Then as soon as he was back in the community, Emily Sanders had been despatched by Martin Frankl to find out if his memory loss was genuine. She'd already admitted to this when he met her in London, but now he had chapter and verse. Meanwhile, on the day after the accident Bradwell had killed himself by jumping off a cliff.

There were a lot of loose ends here. Tom didn't know for sure that the person he'd been going to meet was in fact Bradwell. If it *was* Bradwell, he didn't know if they'd actually met up, or if so, what Bradwell might have told him. Therefore he didn't know why it would worry Frankl so much.

What could Bradwell know that was so threatening to Frankl? That was impossible to guess at. The most likely answer was something deeply embarrassing. In his cryptic phone call, Bradwell had hinted at a connection with the Stay and Prosper campaign, but probably he'd just meant that whatever it was, it had spilled over into the campaign's affairs.

And now Bradwell was dead. Could that really be a coincidence, or was there something suspicious about it? Frightening though the thought was, Tom simply couldn't discount it.

Frustratingly, little of what he knew was substantial enough to take to the police. The only aspect he could prove was Emily's insurance deception, and rather stupidly, he'd just renewed his commitment not to reveal that.

There was also another reason to be circumspect about going to the police. If Bradwell really was the person he'd met on the night of the accident, and he'd been killed that very same night, Tom would surely be at the top of the suspect list.

Chapter 27

"Bernard, I need to pick your brains again."

After waking in the night, sweating over the implications of what he was learning about Frankl and Bradwell, Tom had decided he needed to do something to inch matters forward.

"Go for it."

"When you were researching Ben Bradwell for me, did you find out the name of his ex-partner?"

"Hang on – let me look." There was a long pause. "Right, I knew I had it. Michael Choat – Mickey to his friends. He lives in Shoreham, just west of Brighton."

"I don't suppose you have a phone number?"

"I doubt it. Let me have a look and get back to you."

Tom stood up stiffly and went over to the window. In the cold light of day, the very idea of murder and cover-up seemed wildly fanciful. It simply didn't happen in his safe, normal world. Yet even as he reflected on this, he realised that living in this house was making him feel uneasy. He was alone all day at the quiet end of a quiet village, isolated and exposed. Maybe not so safe after all.

The phone shocked him by bursting into life in his hand. It was Bernard calling him back.

"I don't have this guy Choat's number, but I've just confirmed something else. He works for Carswells in Brighton. He drives a van for them."

"Ha! That must be how Ben Bradwell knew him. Bradwell worked in their office, didn't he?"

"Correct."

"Maybe I can get the number from somebody there."

After disconnecting he thought back to his time at Carswells. The Brighton branch was bigger than the one at the head office, and was owned by the company itself, rather than being franchised out, like many of them. It was home to the company's information technology department, and Tom had sat in on several liaison meetings when the new computer system was being rolled out.

He phoned the branch and asked for Simon Meredith, the information technology manager. After the initial greetings, Tom said, "You can probably guess there's a reason why I'm calling you."

"It had crossed my mind."

"I'm trying to get hold of a mobile number for one of your drivers, a guy called Mickey Choat. Is that something you could track down for me?"

"Probably. Should I ask why you want it?"

"Can I get back to you on that another time?"

"OK, leave it with me."

Twenty minutes later Simon called back. "I had to sweet-talk Frank in the ops room, but I've got your number for you."

"You're a star." Tom reflected for a moment. "I suppose Ben Bradwell worked with you, did he?"

"Yes, he was my hands-on guy. Very good with computer hardware and integration. Such a shame, what happened to him. Did you know him?"

"Not really, but I came across him somewhere. What was he like?"

"Quiet. A hard worker. Very intense. Amazingly good with computers. He went to work for that anti-Brexit campaign in London. He was a hard man to replace."

* * *

Tom sat for several minutes, trying to imagine how a conversation with Bradwell's ex-partner might go. In the end he decided he'd have to wing it. He dialled the number.

"Yeah?"

"Is that Mickey Choat?"

"That's me. Who is this?" An unplaceable accent, perhaps from the Brighton area. There were humming and clattering noises in the background: machinery of some kind – perhaps a tail-lift being operated on the back of a van.

"Tom Anthony. I don't suppose you'll know me, but I used to work in Carswell's head office, and I knew Ben Bradwell slightly. I was hoping I could talk to you about him."

"How do you mean, talk about him?"

"He made contact with me not long before he died. I'm trying to work out what that was about."

"You mean he hooked up with you?"

"No, no, nothing like that. He phoned me and texted me, but I don't know why."

"What makes you think I can help you?"

How should he answer this without sounding either intrusive or disingenuous? Cautiously, he said, "I'm told you knew him pretty well. It might be that he said something to you … I don't know, some clue."

"About what?

Tom took a deep breath. "It's difficult to explain on the phone."

"What's it to you, anyway?"

Tom swallowed. Warily, he said, "I'm just trying to understand what happened."

There was a pause, then Mickey said, "So am I." And he was gone.

* * *

Jan arrived home early that evening – something she seemed to be doing more often these days. He said, "What's your latest thinking on moving back to Winchester? It seems pointless for us to be hanging on here indefinitely."

As he'd somehow expected, she was resistant. "I told the agency not to put this house up for rent for another month."

"But surely you can change your mind about that? They won't care one way or the other."

"They'll have posted their listings for the month. It's easier to let things ride."

"Shall we aim to go back next month then?"

"We could make that a target."

What was that supposed to mean? He was still mulling over this when his phone buzzed.

"It's Mickey again. From before."

"Good to hear you." He walked through to the lounge and sat down.

"You caught me on the job when you called earlier. I'm a driver. I thought I'd better find out what you wanted."

"I appreciate it." Tom did some fast thinking. "I've been writing an article for a news website about Stay and Prosper, the campaign group where Ben Bradwell worked."

"Fucking Stay and Prosper. They gave him the boot. Not his favourite people."

"There was something he wanted to tell me about them, but he never had the chance."

"Probably that they're a load of wankers."

"But you don't actually know what it was?"

"No idea."

Frustrated, Tom said, "There's more. Would you be willing to meet me?"

"How do I know this is straight up? I don't know anything about you, do I?"

"Ask anyone at Carswells in Eastleigh – they'll vouch for me."

A long pause, then Mickey said, "OK, why not? Can you get over to Brighton from where you are?"

"No problem."

"My last drop tomorrow is at Kemptown. You know where that is? There's a café on a corner. I could meet you there."

* * *

It was a long time since Tom had visited Brighton. He called up a map on his laptop. The eighty-mile route along the south coast was straightforward and mostly fast, though congestion at pinch points might still make it a long eighty miles.

Kemptown looked easy enough to find. Interestingly, it was where

Ben Bradwell had lived, though whether that was why Mickey had chosen it for their meeting was not clear.

As he pored over the map, Tom was struck by the fact that the Twyford Road out of Winchester would fit precisely into this journey. At the Winchester end, the fast route started with two sides of a triangle – around twenty miles in total – and the Twyford road made up the third side: shorter in distance, but no doubt longer in terms of travel time. If there had been some kind of traffic problem on the night of his accident, he could have used it as an alternative route on his way back.

Chapter 28

The journey to Brighton took nearly two hours. Tom had forgotten how many slow sections there were on the route. He skirted a succession of south coast towns – Arundel, Chichester, Worthing – and finally he was driving between steep swathes of greenery into central Brighton.

The extraordinary fluted domes of the Royal Pavilion rose to the right across the strip of public gardens approaching the city centre, and he looked out for a left turn into Kemptown. The district stretched along the coast just east of the central area: undulating parallel streets of white Victorian terraced properties, many of them town houses or apartment buildings, some of them businesses and small hotels.

The café chosen by Mickey Choat was clean and well turned-out, and Mickey was easy to find; he was the only person in it. He was a slight, wiry figure, about thirty years old, with curly black hair and a prominent nose. He was wearing jeans and red T-shirt. He watched as Tom hobbled over.

"What the hell happened to you?"

"I drove my car into a tree. Broke my leg."

"Sorry to hear it."

Tom sat down at the table. Mickey said, "So what's this about?"

Tom had rehearsed this part in the car. He said, "I was researching the Stay and Prosper campaign for an article, and Ben approached me. He said there was something I should know about the campaign – something they wouldn't tell me themselves."

"And you're still trying to pick his brains after all this time?" Mickey gave him a hostile frown.

"No, of course not." Tom reflected on this. "Well, yes, in a way." He tried a smile, but Mickey merely continued to stare. "But not for the article. I'm trying to piece my own life together."

"How do you mean?"

"It's complicated." Tom drew a breath. "I believe I was supposed to meet Ben to talk about this, but I had the car accident, and I don't know if I ever did."

"You don't know?"

"After the accident I suffered traumatic memory loss. That's what they call it. I don't remember anything at all from the week leading up to the accident. So I don't know if I ever met Ben or not."

"Where were you supposed to meet him?"

"I don't know. I live near Winchester, and I think I drove over this way, but I don't know how far I got." He paused. "Is there anywhere that Ben would have picked as an obvious place to meet – somewhere between here and Winchester?"

"Not that I know of." He was still frowning.

Tom had to get the conversation on to a more positive footing. He said, "Does what I'm telling you make sense to you? Does it sound like the kind of thing Ben would have done?"

Mickey seemed to relax slightly and gave an empty laugh. "Yeah, it's Ben all over. Why do you think he joined that campaign? He wanted to do the right thing – that's what he said. He wanted to make a difference. So if he found something suss about those people, you can bet your life he would have wanted to blow the whistle on them. I called him the quiet crusader."

"But he didn't tell you anything about it?"

Mickey shook his head.

A waitress came over, and Tom ordered coffee. When she'd left them he said, "Were you surprised that Ben killed himself?"

"Yeah. *Very* surprised. He always said life was for living, and you only get one chance. He was that kind of person."

"Could it have been an accident?"

"Nah! Not in a million years. People who live in this area know about cliffs. You'd have to be a total fucking lunatic to fall over one."

"So do you really think he jumped?"

"Well, that's what the cops said. What else am I supposed to think?"

"The press said he was grieving because of busting up with you."

"That's none of your business." He gave Tom an indignant stare.

"Sorry, I didn't mean to be intrusive. I'm just trying to understand this."

Mickey said, "We were still mates. Those reports were a load of ignorant crap."

"So he wouldn't have killed himself over your relationship?"

"Not a chance."

"What about other issues? Debts?"

"Nothing like that. All Ben ever did was work."

"Could he have been depressed because of being fired by the Stay and Prosper people?"

"He *was* depressed! He called me the night he was dumped. He was completely pissed off. Wouldn't you be? He helped to get them going. How else should he feel? But he wouldn't kill himself over it. No way."

"Do you know why he was fired?"

"No idea. Differences of opinion – some bollocks like that."

Tom nodded. He was running out of questions. He said. "Right. So there's no logical reason why he would kill himself."

Mickey sat back, now watching him attentively. "You're saying someone pushed him over that cliff edge. Is that it?"

"I don't know. It's a possibility."

"Why would they?"

"Maybe to stop him telling me whatever he was going to tell me."

"Telling *you*? Why? What's so important about you?"

"Nothing. It's just that I was writing an article. I think he assumed I had the right contacts in the press.

"But you don't know if he ever did tell you."

"That's about it."

"Huh." Mickey sat back emphatically in his chair. It scraped noisily on the tiled floor.

For a moment neither of them spoke. Eventually Mickey said, "You reckon these people who you say killed Ben know about you?"

"Yep."

"So why haven't they done away with you as well? You got some kind of charmed life?"

"No, but I don't remember anything from that week. Maybe they don't think I matter."

"Huh! You're an optimist."

"That's why I'm talking to you. If I can find out what was really going on in Ben's mind, I can take this to the police before it goes any further."

"But now you've dragged me into it as well. According to you, I must be a target too." Mickey's eyes suddenly darted to the café entrance. "Could they be out there now, watching us?"

Tom followed his look in alarm, then realised Mickey was winding him up. A little irritably he said, "Look, I know this is all pretty far-fetched, but you have to admit there's a kind of logic to it."

"Far-fetched is right! My mate kills himself, and you come along months later, making some kind of Pulp Fiction plot out of it. What do you expect me to think?"

Tom sighed. "I'm just trying to work out what's going on."

* * *

Mickey glanced at his watch. "I've got to go. I need to get my van back to Shoreham." He stood up and looked down at Tom, who had stayed in place.

Perhaps it was Tom's disconsolate expression that won Mickey over, but something suddenly seemed to click behind his eyes. He said, "Ben lived just round the corner from here. I don't know if you knew that. I'm going over there now to collect some of my stuff." He pushed his chair under the table. "You can come with me if you like. See if you can find any *clues*."

He gave ironic emphasis to the last word, but Tom merely said, "That would be good. Thanks."

"Are you OK to walk a couple of blocks?"

"I'll manage." He limped off in pursuit.

A couple of minutes later Mickey paused at the front door. "It's up two flights of stairs."

"I've got this far – I think I'll make it."

The flat was small but well furnished in minimalist modern style.

"Ben's mum bought this place for him," Mickey said as they walked through to the lounge. "She's rolling in it. She's going to put it on the market now, but I've still got the keys."

He stood in the centre of the main room, looking around. He said, "That's funny."

"What is?"

"I've been coming here every now and then since he died, and his mum told me last week that no one else had been here."

"But?"

"Things have been moved. That chair should be further back. That lamp should be on the floor, not on there." He pointed to a bookshelf. He continued to look around.

"What are you thinking?"

He gave Tom an ironical look. "You reckon your bad guys have been here, turning the place over?"

Tom shrugged.

"She must have had the cleaners in or something." He relaxed. "Sit down if you want to."

He bustled about, picking up odd items of clothing and a handful of books. He went into the bedroom and came out dragging a duvet. He flashed Tom a slightly embarrassed look. "I bought this for Ben. I don't see why it should go to a charity shop." He started to fold it up.

Tom went over to a small desk at the back of the room. It was scattered with paperwork. He leafed through a couple of items. "You don't mind if I look at this stuff?"

"I suppose not."

The A4-sized pages were mostly covered with notes and embellished with scrawls and doodles, but there was little that Tom could understand. Then he spotted a name that he recognised: Victor Rudge. It was heavily underlined, and near it, in a circle, was written "No deal". Other unknown names were written further down the page, with solid or dotted lines linking to them.

He had no idea what this signified, but it seemed important. He took out his phone, leaned over the desk and photographed the page, then glanced over his shoulder, wondering if Mickey would protest.

In fact, there had been silence in the room for some moments. Turning, he saw that Mickey had sat down on a chair in the corner and was staring bleakly across the room, oblivious to Tom's actions.

"You wouldn't know it," Mickey said, "but this is all so Ben. It's as if he's about to walk in any minute."

"I can imagine."

"No offence, but would you mind fucking off now?"

"Of course. Great to meet you. Thank you for your help."

Chapter 29

Back in his car, Tom glanced at his watch. It was late afternoon, but the sun was bright, and there was plenty of daylight left. It occurred to him that while he was in the Brighton area he could visit the place where Ben Bradwell had died.

He picked up his old printed atlas and flicked to the relevant page. The Seven Sisters cliffs stretched for several miles along the south coast, ending just short of Beachy Head and Eastbourne. He should be able to drive there in well under an hour, but he needed the exact location. He opened a browser on his phone and searched for reports of Bradwell's suicide.

There weren't many, and those that came up were mostly brief and repetitious, but finally he managed to find a slightly different version, which actually gave the name of the spot where Ben had been found: Brass Point. He drove off along the coast road.

His choice of route soon proved a bad one. Much of the journey was a slow grind through urban sprawl – Rottingdean, Saltdean, Telscombe, Peacehaven, Newhaven. The styles ranged from urban chic to modest low-rise, probably from the 1960s, with Victorian townships scattered along the way. Finally he emerged into undulating countryside. Now he needed to look out for the correct turnoff towards the cliffs.

He decided he'd found it when he reached a sign for the village of Friston, at the top of a steep wooded ascent. He turned right on a narrow local road and continued for half a mile until it ended in a rudimentary car park. A footpath continued in the direction of the sea, and a private road offered the opportunity for anyone determined enough to drive further towards the shore line.

He got out of his car and looked around at the terrain. Beyond the end of the road, grassy downland sloped gently upwards, then presumably down again towards the cliffs. It was an unremarkable landscape, but in the early evening sun it had a charm about it, and the sea air felt invigorating. There were a few other cars in the car park, but the only living things in sight were sheep.

He checked the map again. It looked as though he could be nearly a mile from the nearest cliff. Disappointed, he realised he wasn't going to be able to walk there in his present state. It was too far, and he would also have to walk all the way back.

He'd already learned something, though. Ben Bradwell would have had to be very determined to make his way here by public transport, then walk a mile to the cliff tops before throwing himself off it. Maybe the place had some personal resonance for him? But if so, why had he not driven here in his own car?

On the other hand, it was a nicely obscure location for someone with murderous intent. Admittedly, on a benign summer evening like this there would be a strong risk of encountering passers-by – tourists, hikers, dog-walkers. But on a winter night, in the dark, there would be little chance of any interruption. Or witnesses.

* * *

Next morning Tom called Bernard and told him about his trip to Brighton. "I still don't know for sure whether I met Ben Bradwell or not, but I seriously doubt now that he killed himself."

"Go on."

He described his conversation with Mickey Choat and his thoughts on the suicide location. "There was nothing in Bradwell's life to suggest he would kill himself, and it's a ridiculous place for him to have gone to jump off a cliff. But it would have been a good place for someone else to throw him off."

"I thought I was the detective around here."

"You told me you'd given that up."

Bernard chuckled. "I did. Many years ago."

"What I need to decide is whether or not I should go to the police with this."

"I can't tell you what to do, Tom. I can only tell you how it would most likely go down."

"And?"

"Well, if they took you seriously, the first thing they would probably do is check closed-circuit TV cameras to see if your car was seen somewhere near where this happened, or along the way."

"And if it was?"

"That would suggest that you really did meet Bradwell – and that's not good for you."

"Why not? It would confirm what I'm saying."

"In your eyes, maybe. But in their eyes it would put you in the frame for having killed him."

"But why would I step forward to tell them all this if I was the guilty party?"

"It's what criminals do, Tom. Suppose you really had done away with Bradwell, but the coroner had ruled it suicide? You might feel frustrated that your clever work was going unnoticed. You might want to get the police jumping around again by taking this story to them."

"But what possible motive would I have for killing Bradwell?"

"None, obviously. Eventually they would come to that conclusion themselves. But they might give you a lot of grief on the way."

Tom was silent for a moment. "Maybe I'll have to take that chance."

Bernard said, "Presumably no one has come after you, trying to do away with you? That would be logical if they thought Bradwell had told you something they wanted to keep quiet."

"No, nothing like that."

"So maybe there's nothing in this."

"But in that case, why did that guy at the Stay and Prosper group send someone to check out my memory loss? It seems to fit in, doesn't it?"

"Sorry, you've lost me there. What guy is this?"

Tom realised he'd been holding back this piece of information, reluctant to admit to being a victim to the insurance scam. Was it to keep Emily Sanders' name out of it, or to avoid revealing his failure to check her credentials more carefully? Either way, he'd have to own up now.

"Someone from the pro-Remain campaign was sent to interview me about my accident, and pretended to be from my insurance company. They seemed to be especially interested in whether my memory loss was genuine. I'm wondering now if it was to check whether I remembered what Bradwell told me."

"Bloody hell, Tom. How did you find out about this?"

"From the woman who did the interview. I also know who was behind it: the campaign press officer, a man named Martin Frankl."

"So have you confronted him about it?"

"Not yet."

"Why not?"

"I promised the woman that I wouldn't."

"What! Why?"

Tom hesitated. "I don't know. I like her. I don't want to cause her trouble."

"You *like* her?"

"Don't tell me off. I don't need it."

Bernard said nothing for a moment, then, "You can guess my opinion."

"Anyway, don't you think it's likely that this was connected to Bradwell and what happened to him?"

"You've got me there. It's a weird one." Bernard paused to think. "But it's not in the same league as murder, is it? Killers don't wait around to psychoanalyse their victims. They just get on with it. No, I think this must have been about something else."

"So I should be relieved about that?"

"Probably."

"I'm not so sure."

Bernard said, "Look, if you were telling me about something that made me think you were in serious danger, I would be giving you different advice."

"So what would you do?"

"Keep your eyes and ears open. See what else you can find out. But don't go treading on the toes of anyone who might be behind this."

Chapter 30

"Harry's getting married." Jan hovered in the lounge doorway.

Tom looked up. "Really? When?"

"In a couple of months' time. He's just emailed me about it."

Harry, Jan's brother, lived outside New York City. Neither Tom nor Jan had met his girlfriend, but he knew they'd been together for some time.

He took a deep breath. "Are we going?"

"Well, I'll need to, but you don't have to. You'd probably find the long flight a bit of an ordeal."

It was a reasonable comment, but he knew there was a subtext. During the time he'd been recuperating in this house, the cracks in their relationship had been left in abeyance – unmentioned and unresolved. Living here had a kind of other-worldliness about it. But the issues hadn't gone away, and it was hard to imagine moving forward until they'd been addressed. That was surely what Jan meant. Agreeing to go on a trip together would mean embracing a future that hadn't yet been mapped out.

He said, "Maybe I should wait and see how I feel closer to the time."

"You won't get such a good deal on the air fare if you book it late."

"I'll have to live with that."

She nodded.

He said, "What sort of event will it be?"

"Just a small civil ceremony. But he'll bring a few of his mates over from the UK. It's a pity my father didn't live to see it."

* * *

Malcolm Drew liked the article. His opening gambit when he called next morning was, "Anyone would think you'd been writing this kind of stuff all your life."

Tom breathed a sigh of relief. "I assure you I haven't."

"Well, this proves you made the wrong career choice."

Tom sensed that there was an agenda behind the praise. He said, "Why do I think you want something?"

"Ah, well. I was wondering if you'd like to do more of this kind of thing for us?"

In the back of his mind Tom had suspected that this question might come up, but he had no response prepared. Temporising, he said, "I'm flattered to be asked, but I don't know if I could afford it."

"How do you mean?"

"Well, I was only able to do all that research because I have no other job. It took much more time than the fee justified. It was a labour of love, really."

"You would soon get the hang of how much preparation to do."

Tom sighed. "There's another aspect. I don't have the media contacts or sources to set up as a freelance. I've been out of it for too long. I would only be working for you, and there wouldn't be a living in it."

Malcolm wasn't put off. He said, "There might be a way round that."

"Oh yes?"

He hesitated. "Would you be able to come up to London for a chat? Maybe we could thrash out something that would work for both of us. Tell you what – come on Friday and stay over. Sophie's taking the kids to visit her mother for the weekend, but I get a bye this time. I'd enjoy the company." A pause. "You and Jan, of course."

Tom smiled ironically to himself. That last comment parsed as "Don't bring Jan". Malcolm had never warmed to her, and she seemed to find him tedious. He said, "I'd love to come. Jan might be doing something else, but I can ask."

"Just one thing," Malcolm said. "I've read your article three times, and I still don't know which side of the Brexit divide you're on. Are you a Remainer or a Leaver? I've never read such an even-handed piece about the subject before. It must be some kind of record."

Tom chuckled. "That's for me to know and for you to find out."

* * *

Could he change horses a second time, and revert permanently from management to journalism? Last time he'd switched career, he'd vowed to himself that he would never look back. The press had felt a narrow world, circumscribed by the need to flatter advertisers – to provide unchallenging words to drape round their promotions. He'd found much greater satisfaction in the focus of a management job.

Since then the world had changed, and not for the better. The kind of printed publication he'd worked for seemed to be in terminal decline. To some extent it was being replaced by online media, but the quality of information hadn't improved. Far too many websites seemed happy to recycle news and publish it without evaluation. Readers had always tended to seek out newspapers that played to their prejudices, but nowadays that need for affirmation seemed to go further, prompting people to filter out news they didn't like, or to conclude that it was untrue.

Sadly, they were often right about that. Was this a battleground he wanted to embrace?

Yet there were responsible online news sources that did have integrity – Malcolm's website being one of them. Perhaps he should feel grateful to be invited to have a bigger role in it all.

He was turning this over in his mind when a call came in. It was Emily Sanders.

He said, "Good to hear from you again."

"Seriously? I was a total embarrassment when I called you the other day. Don't deny it." He could hear clattering behind her: perhaps the sound of a kitchen or a bar.

"Not at all."

"I was completely off my head. I was celebrating my release from the clutches of those arseholes in Kensington."

"They haven't asked you back yet, then?"

"No way. I wouldn't go if they did."

"Don't you feel sorry for Marcus Headington?"

"Yes I do. He's a good guy. The volunteers are good people too. It's the management team I couldn't get on with."

"I can understand that."

Tentatively, she said, "Did you ever find out why Martin Frankl sent me to talk to you?"

"Not really. I can't exactly ask him, can I? Do you have any more ideas?"

"No." She paused. "But I did find out something else. You know that guy Neil Bradwell – the one you were asking about? If you're interested, I found out from my friend Sally why he was fired."

Now she had Tom's full attention. He said, "Go on."

Immediately she interrupted herself. "Ah, sorry – I'll need to call you back to explain properly. I'm on my break, but I've just been told I have to go back to work. I'll call you later if I can."

"OK, fair enough."

Did she really have something she wanted to communicate to him, or was she just playing with him? He couldn't decide.

He kept the phone at his side for the rest of the evening. No call came.

Chapter 31

Malcolm Drew and his wife Sophie lived in a comfortable Victorian terraced house in Putney, half a mile from the Thames: high ceilings, polished wooden floors, a hint of stained glass in the frieze above the front door.

Malcolm suggested that Tom meet up with him at the house, rather than going to the office in Shepherds Bush first. Tom was more than happy; he was able to take a train there directly from Waterloo, arriving in the middle of the afternoon.

"What I'm thinking," Malcolm said as they settled in his lounge, "is that you could write a regular piece for us – a bit of in-depth research combined with some opinionated stuff."

Tom smiled at Malcolm, marvelling at his goodwill. Malcolm's actions always seemed meticulous and considered, and his appearance reflected his character surprisingly well: neatly groomed and immaculately dressed, even when he was off duty. His willingness to embrace Tom's more impulsive personality and lifestyle had often struck him as a generous concession.

"As a freelance?"

Malcolm ran a hand over his closely cropped beard. "Possibly, or we could pay you a retainer. It wouldn't be a living, but it would be a decent part of one."

"What would the articles be about?"

"Well, in the long run whatever was topical – preferably with a bit of a political angle."

"I don't know anything about politics."

"You would pick up the basics quickly enough."

"But do I want to?"

Malcolm had nothing to say to that, so Tom asked, "Why this particular brief? What has happened at your end to make it necessary?"

"One of our best writers is leaving – going to work for a Sunday paper, if you can believe that. From digital back to print. We're not looking for a direct replacement, but we want someone who can do some of the same stuff."

It was flattering to be put in the same bracket as "one of our best writers", but it also felt like an enormous challenge. Writing the article for Malcolm had offered a stimulating change from Tom's recent life, but could he really put himself through the same kind of research process over and over again?

He said, "I appreciate your confidence, but I need to think about this."

"You mean you need Jan to think about it?"

"No! Why do you say that?"

"She always seems to be extra-keen on safeguarding your earning power."

From anyone else, this kind of criticism would have seemed offensive, but Tom had enough history with Malcolm to take it in his stride.

"It may look like that from where you're standing," he said, "but why would she need to worry? She's doing well enough for herself at the trading house where she works."

"I can't say I've ever seen much evidence of this massive wealth of hers."

It was a strange thing to hear. Tom knew Malcolm had never liked Jan much, but he wasn't used to hearing her portrayed in this machiavellian light. Despite their recent difficulties, he felt a need to defend her. "That's because she's canny," he said. "She makes her money work for her. She always has an eye to the future."

"But she shouldn't be able to dictate what kind of job you want."

"She doesn't. I wouldn't let that happen."

* * *

Malcolm made tea and brought it through to the lounge with an array of biscuits laid out on a plate. "Sophie made me promise to put on a good show," he said.

Without thinking, Tom asked, "Do you ever hear anything of Guy Freeman?"

Immediately he regretted mentioning the name. Guy had been the third member of their triumvirate at college. Sophie had been going out with him when they'd all started their course, but half-way through their second year she'd switched her allegiance to Malcolm, and eventually she'd married him. Guy hadn't taken it well.

"Not for a long time."

Tom said, "I wonder what he's doing nowadays?"

"I don't know. I bumped into him once on a station platform on the District line. He told me he was a civil servant, but he was quite cagey when I asked him what he actually did. I had a feeling he must be involved in something hush-hush."

"Did you feel you'd finally made your peace with him?"

"Yeah, he didn't seem to bear any grudge. He told me he was married and living somewhere in south London. In fact we swapped contact details. We were all going to meet up." He shrugged. "It never happened."

Memories trickled into Tom's head of a bright, patient young man – one who seemed to cast a measured, assessing eye on the world, but always made light of what he saw. His strongest image was of Guy's sense of humour.

He said, "I should have kept in touch with him. We were good mates. But I stayed friends with you, and he wasn't having it."

"More fool him."

"Did you keep his contact details? It would be great to get back in touch."

Malcolm shook his head. "I doubt it. All this was years ago. He's probably moved on by now."

Tom smiled reflectively. "So out of the three of us, you're the only one who actually became a journalist."

"Well, you gave it a decent shot, didn't you? And if you take this job I'm offering you, you'll soon get back into the swing of it."

The evening was approaching, and Malcolm suggested eating out. An idea came to Tom.

"We're not far from Richmond here, are we?"

"Far? That's an existential question. It all depends on how fast the traffic is moving through Sheen. Why?"

"I'd like to try a pub there."

"Any special reason?"

"Wait and see."

Chapter 32

The Crown and Mitre was in the centre of Richmond. Malcolm had to drive twice round the little town's one-way system before he found somewhere to park.

The pub was Victorian, but inside it was decked out in retro chic, and the place was heaving with Friday night drinkers. As Tom edged their way towards the bar he peered behind it. Would Emily be here?

There was no sign of her. He was disappointed. After her interrupted phone call he'd heard nothing more from her. He still wanted to know what she'd intended to tell him about Ben Bradwell, and he now also realised he'd simply been looking forward to seeing her.

Then as the barman pulled their pints, she came into the serving area from somewhere at the back. She was wearing black jeans and a green T-shirt with the pub's brand embroidered on it. She spotted him immediately, and he thought he saw a faint smile cross her face. However, she headed for the side of the L-shaped bar with barely an acknowledgement and started serving a customer there.

As Tom paid for their drinks she turned and called over her shoulder, "I never expected to see you here."

"We were in the area."

"I see." She turned back to her customer.

He watched her as she completed the sale, tapping in the details on the electronic display and taking the customer's money. She had a small white flower in her hair – a plastic one, presumably worn as a joke, but under the pub lights it gave her a red-headed gypsy look.

Malcolm leaned towards him confidentially. "You know that girl?"

"Sort of."

"Did you know she would be here?"

"I hoped she might be."

Malcolm gave him a knowing look. "You must have loosened

up a bit since I last saw you."

Tom frowned. "Don't jump to conclusions."

They were being edged away from the counter by other customers. Tom shuffled his way round to the side of the bar and called to Emily over the shoulders of waiting customers, "Might you have five minutes to spare while we're here?"

She gestured broadly round the bar and shrugged. "It's pretty mad here tonight."

"We'll be around for a while."

"I'll have to see how it goes."

They stood at a tall circular table. Tom said, "That girl used to work at Stay and Prosper, the Remain campaign run by Marcus Headington. She was a volunteer researcher."

"Was?"

"They parted company. It's a long story."

"You seem to know a lot about her."

Tom shrugged. "Not really."

Malcolm gave him an assessing look. "You're into her, aren't you? I can read you like a book."

"Bollocks!"

A table came free in a corner. As they sat chatting, Tom kept glancing over towards the bar. Occasionally he glimpsed Emily through the crowd, but he wasn't able to catch her eye. He'd already decided he liked her, and he now had to admit to himself that Malcolm was right – he was also attracted to her. He'd merely avoided acknowledging it to himself. That was partly why he'd wanted to come here. And she'd more or less confessed on the phone that she was attracted to him. It was a potent mix.

Eventually Malcolm suggested going to look for a restaurant, but Tom protested. "Let's have another round first."

"What, so you can talk to your friend?"

"Well, yes, if you must know."

Malcolm smiled his knowing smile.

Twenty minutes later she materialised beside their table. "I've got two minutes," she said. "They don't like bar staff wasting time talking to customers – not when we're as busy as this."

Tom pushed a spare chair out and she slid into it, saying, "How come you're here? You live near Winchester, don't you?"

"Malcolm is a college mate. He lives in Putney."

She glanced at Malcolm for the first time, nodding to him.

Tom said, "It's not always as busy as this here, is it?"

"God, no. I couldn't keep this pace up every night."

Malcolm said, "I bet you could."

She looked sharply at him, but he merely smiled benignly.

She turned back to Tom. "You wanted to know about Neil Bradwell."

He gave her a look of mock reproof. "You were supposed to be calling me back about him."

She smiled apologetically. "Sorry, things were a bit hectic. I would have got round to it in the end."

"Well, I'm here now."

"OK, I found out why he was fired. I assumed you would want to know. The official story is that it was over a policy disagreement with Victor Rudge."

"About what?"

"There was a sub-group on the research team, compiling a database of economic developments that would benefit from Brexit."

"But surely they would undermine the campaign position? What was the point of that?"

"Simple. It was to be prepared. The idea was to make sure our spokespeople would have their counter-arguments ready in advance. They didn't want to seem like idiots who were ignoring the theoretical advantages of leaving the EU."

"Sounds logical."

"But then Victor decided to shut that project down. He just wanted to leave one person on that job, and only part-time. He said there was no point in digging up ammunition that would be useful to the pro-Leave camp."

"Where did Ben Bradwell come in?"

"He challenged Victor about it one day. It was just before I joined. Apparently they had a blazing row in the foyer, in front of other people. He reckoned that dropping the counter-research would make the campaign seem more doctrinaire and less credible."

"How do you know all this?"

"My friend Sally was there. She saw the whole thing. She said it was quite heated."

He said, "Arguing with Rudge doesn't sound like a sacking offence."

"He wasn't fired at the time. He was allowed to go to that conference where I saw you. But I think he was a dead man walking by then. He was dumped just after the conference."

Tom cringed inwardly at the "dead man" image. "You said that was the official story. What did you mean by that?"

"That's what they told us after he left. But Sally said there was more to the argument than that. She overheard Neil accusing Victor of losing the plot, whatever that meant. He said he was going to the media over it."

"Really? But you don't know what he meant?"

"Sorry, no."

For a moment the three of them sat in silence. Emily glanced over her shoulder. "I'd better get back to work."

"It's quieter now."

"Try telling that to my boss." She glanced round again.

Tom said, "What was Ben Bradwell's job at Stay and Prosper?"

"I think his official role was IT manager. He put in their computer system and ran their website – that kind of thing."

"So he wasn't involved directly in policy?"

"Not as far as I know, but Sally says he had a hand in almost everything."

She started to get up. He said, "I'm sorry that all I've done tonight is pick your brains about Stay and Prosper."

"It's all right. I don't know if what I've told you is any use, though."

"Nor do I, but it's food for thought."

She looked down at him and smiled faintly. "Come again some other time, when it's quieter."

"Maybe I will."

She started to walk away, then paused to reach down and pick up his empty glass. "Might as well do my job."

*   *   *

"She's gorgeous," Malcolm commented as Emily headed back towards the bar. "Mind you, I shouldn't say that."

"How do you mean?"

"Our policy on the website is to stick to gender-neutral, non-judgemental terminology wherever possible. I don't even know if I could say 'highly attractive'. It's a challenging limitation sometimes." He drained his glass. "Shall we get going?"

Tom watched as Emily disappeared behind the bar. "She *is* 'highly attractive' as far as I'm concerned. No argument there."

"So what was all this about, if you don't mind me asking?"

Tom looked at Malcolm cautiously. What Emily had told him about Bradwell's dispute with Rudge was interesting, but barely sensational; yet he felt it had helped to build up an overall picture. He simply didn't know what that picture showed.

He said, "There might be a story in this eventually. In fact if there is, I'd like to write it for you, whether I'm working regularly for you or not."

"I should hope so."

"Good." He gave Malcolm an assessing look. "In the meantime, could you manage to forget the conversation we've just had?"

"Just so long as we're getting the story in the end."

Chapter 33

On Sunday morning Malcolm decided he needed to work. Tom took the hint and headed home a day earlier than he'd planned. He arrived back at Storton just after lunchtime, expecting to find Jan there, but her car was missing and there was no sign of her in the house.

He sat down heavily on the sofa, wondering what to do next. He'd finished the Brexit article, so that particular diversion had come to an end. He could continue to dig into the life and death of Ben Bradwell, but he was beginning to wonder whether there was any point. The charade of Emily Sanders' strange insurance visit remained a mystery, but nothing bad had come of it so far. Perhaps he should leave well alone and simply await developments. Perhaps there would never be any.

What he should really be doing was deciding where his life was going. He needed a permanent job, and if he didn't take up Malcolm's offer to become a regular writer for the website, he would need to think of something else. One option was to sound out Felix Schaefer about working for him at Carswells again, but he was reluctant to do that. It would seem a backward step.

He also needed to resolve the situation with Jan. Did they have a future together or not? She'd certainly been supportive over his injuries, helping him in numerous ways through the recovery process; yet the lack of warmth in her manner towards him was becoming more and more evident. Had the decline in their relationship passed the point of no return? He had to face up to that possibility.

It could explain why she was so reluctant to return to their old life in Winchester. Perhaps she was marking time, calculating that eventually he would insist on going back. She could then opt to stay on here, translating their implicit separation into a fact.

Yet he couldn't imagine her continuing to live here in the village.

She was far too much a party animal – happier in the company of others than on her own. She had a circle of friends in Winchester, and others connected to her job in London. Perhaps once he left the house she would rent it out as she'd suggested, and go and live somewhere else. Or she might simply sell it and make a new start. Maybe her insistence on staying here was just her way of bringing matters between them to a head.

These were details. Whatever the reality, it wasn't looking good.

He stood up and stared out of the window. His innate optimism was under pressure, yet he still felt there had to be a way forward. If that meant a future without Jan, he'd better start adjusting to the idea.

* * *

Unaccountably, he found himself thinking about his old computer. It was sitting on the floor of the garage – a prey to any whim on Jan's part to consign it to the dump, along with all the other junk stored there. He decided to retrieve it and move it into his own space.

He went through to the garage and lifted up the separate pieces of the laptop, placing them on the workbench. As Jan had said, they looked beyond repair, but still he was reluctant to throw them away. He picked up his damaged canvas bag, piled them into it and turned to the door.

The sight of the old hi-fi system reminded him that he'd left the audio tape from his answering machine in its built-in cassette player. He put down the bag, stooped in front of the hi-fi unit and opened the cassette lid.

No tape.

Had he taken it out himself after he'd carried the unit back into the garage? He didn't remember doing that. He glanced around, wondering if he'd absent-mindedly put it down on top of the junk pile in the centre of the floor. No sign of it. He poked among open cardboard cartons in case it had fallen inside one of them. Nothing. Nor was it on the floor, nor on any of the shelves at the back of the garage.

He picked up the canvas bag and limped back into the house. Pausing in the kitchen, he checked counter-tops and drawers in case he'd brought the tape back in here. No luck. Then he did the same thing in his bedroom, checking cupboards, drawers and bookshelves. Still nothing.

He would ask Jan about it when she returned. Then something else occurred to him. His old phone was nowhere in evidence. He went through to the lounge, looking on every surface and around the area where he usually sat. No sign of that either.

The apparent disappearance of both the cassette tape and the phone seemed more than a coincidence. Could Jan have taken possession of them? Why would she do that?

He made his way upstairs for the first time since his accident and peered into Jan's room. It was the master bedroom, and he couldn't help but feel impressed by the decoration and furnishings – a tasteful combination of blacks and greys. No wonder the refurbishment bill had been high.

He made a quick check of available surfaces, then warily opened the drawers of the dressing table, one by one. Presumably he would hear Jan's car if she returned from wherever she'd gone, but all the same he was nervous. The two of them might have shared a bedroom for over three years, yet here he felt he was intruding.

He found no sign of the phone or the cassette tape, but his eye was caught by a message pad next to her brush and comb set. A one-line message was scribbled on it in Jan's hand: "DM, Sun 2pm." Who or what was DM? Probably some friend of Jan's in Winchester.

He straightened and turned towards the door, and then froze. He'd heard the unmistakable sound of someone inserting a key in the front door lock. Jan must have come back, and somehow she'd arrived silently.

He mustn't let her find him here. He wasn't quite sure why, but he was immediately convinced that nothing good would come of it. He moved quickly to the bedroom door and out to the landing. What should he do? Hide in one of the other upstairs bedrooms? It seemed ridiculous, but how would he explain his presence up here?

Too late – he heard her footsteps cross the hall floor and start up the stairs. The only thing he could do was to appear to be on his way down. He approached the top of the staircase, calling, "This is a surprise!"

She stopped in her tracks with a cry of surprise, then continued more slowly to the top and stood staring at him. She was wearing her light skirt and russet top: one of the outfits she chose when she was dressing to impress.

She said, "My god, you gave me a shock."

"Didn't you notice my car in the drive?"

"I was in a rush. I wasn't thinking." Her look turned into one of annoyance. "Anyway, what the hell are you doing here?"

"I was bored. I thought I'd explore the house."

"No, I mean I thought you were staying over at Malcolm's until tomorrow."

"He had to work, so I came back."

Abruptly she said, "Christ!" and pulled out her phone. She tapped in a short-dial number and retreated down the stairs, speaking quietly into it. He couldn't make out what she was saying.

How had she arrived back at the house without making a sound? He opened the door to one of the other bedrooms and went over to the window. There was no sign of her car in the driveway. This didn't make sense.

He went back downstairs. She was standing in the kitchen doorway, finishing her phone call.

He said, "How did you get here without your car?"

"Oh." She lowered the phone. "I was visiting Debbie in Winchester, and my bloody car wouldn't start. But I didn't have my AA card with me to call them out, so I came back here to fetch it." She was doing her best to sound insouciant, but he wasn't convinced.

"How did you get here? How are you getting back to Winchester?"

"Debbie dropped me off. She's just gone to the shop to buy some cigarettes." She slid the phone into her pocket. "I'd better go and find my card. I think it's upstairs in my other bag." She brushed past him and hurried up the stairs.

A minute later she was back down again. "Got it! I'd better go outside and wait for Debbie in the street." She turned to him at the front door. "I might be late back tonight."

He walked over to the lounge window and watched her. She turned left out of the gateway, disappearing behind the hedge.

What was all that about? Everything she'd said was plausible – except that she'd acted like someone caught in a lie. And why had she made that urgent outgoing call almost as soon as she'd seen him?

He wondered about her explanation that she'd left her AA card behind. Was it even necessary to have one these days in order to summon help? Surely all she had to do was prove who she was? Or perhaps he was wrong about that. He'd have to research it some time.

* * *

It was after eleven o'clock that night when she made a reappearance, this time arriving in her car. He was watching the end of a film on TV. Leaning round the door, she said, "I'm sorry I was all over the place earlier. You gave me a start when you suddenly loomed at the top of the stairs."

"I should probably be apologising myself."

"We're even, then."

"What happened with the car?"

"False alarm. I tried it again, and it fired first time. What a waste of an afternoon."

They chatted for a moment, and he asked, "As a matter of interest, have you seen my old phone? The one I discovered in the garage?"

"I don't think so."

"I've also lost an old cassette tape. You haven't seen that, have you?"

"No again, sorry."

Both her replies seemed completely innocent, but after her strange behaviour earlier, he was beginning to wonder how far he could trust anything she said.

On the other hand, if the phone and the tape really were missing and Jan knew nothing about it, what had happened to them?

Chapter 34

Investment plan scrapped over Brexit
Thousands of potential jobs lost

American-based international pharmaceuticals giant Monck Chervil has announced that it will not after all be bringing new jobs and investment to the UK, as previously promised. A spokesman blamed the decision on what he described as "the debilitating uncertainty arising from Britain's unresolved post-Brexit trading arrangements with the rest of the European Union".

The company revealed earlier this year that it planned to open a major new research facility in the East Midlands, along with a new factory in South Wales. Between them these two plants would eventually have employed up to three thousand people.

Now the company says the threat of future EU tariffs and other financial and administrative obstacles has made the project too risky.

The exact trigger for this unexpected about-turn is unclear, but it is rumoured that the British Government has withdrawn a subsidy package that was originally offered to the company to secure its commitment to the UK.

Ironically, the reason for the Government's change of mind is thought to be the need to abide by EU competition law. Until the UK finally leaves the EU, it is still required to respect its rules and regulations. Government ministers were originally advised that the proposed subsidy was in line with EU requirements, but we understand that this advice has now been rescinded.

The senior advisor to the Government, Mr Donald Finch, was not available for comment, and the Monck Chervil spokesman denied that the subsidy had been a material factor in its decision to cancel the scheme. "Our investment plan was never dependent on subsidy," he said.

At any other time this story on the *Seismic Scene* website would barely have impinged on Tom's consciousness, but in the wake of his article he was intrigued. A few months ago this company had been thoroughly positive about the proposed investment in the UK, despite the uncertain economic outlook, yet now its stance had shifted through 180 degrees.

He was particularly struck by the paradox behind it. Both the Leave and the Remain camps could claim that the cancellation of the project vindicated their position. Economic uncertainty was cited by the company as the decisive factor in the decision to cancel: a win for the Remain camp. Yet withdrawal of the subsidy had also apparently played a part: a win for the Brexiteers. If true, it meant Britain's membership of the EU had wrecked the deal, not its plan to leave.

As he thought this through, Tom realised that something else was nagging at him. The name of the Government advisor, Donald Finch, seemed faintly familiar, but he couldn't think why.

* * *

He called Malcolm Drew.

"I've just read your piece about Monck Chervil backing out of the UK investment deal. It says they might have changed their minds because a subsidy was cancelled, and it blames someone called Donald Finch. Who is he exactly?"

Malcolm chuckled. "It's out there on the internet, Tom. You're not looking in the right place."

Chastened, Tom said, "I'm still a rusty with all this. I know it. Humour me."

"Finch is a senior civil servant – someone in the department that oversees inward investments and grant funding."

Where had Tom seen the name Finch lately? His mind was still racing.

Malcolm was saying, "Is that it?"

Suddenly he knew the answer. The name had been among the scribbled notes on Ben Bradwell's desk in Brighton. He was almost sure of it.

"So I'll get going then," Malcolm said with irony.

"Sorry, sorry." Tom was thinking fast. "Look, there might be a big story here, but I need to get my head round it. There seems to be a connection with the Stay and Prosper campaign, but I don't know what it's about."

"A bit vague, I have to say."

"I know. But if I keep on the case, you'll run with it, will you?"

"I will if it adds up to anything."

"That's all I'm asking."

"Deal." Malcolm chuckled. "You're beginning to sound like the old Tom Anthony – the one I knew at college. Why don't you give some serious consideration to my offer – a regular slot with us, and half an income. If you can't do it, I'll need to appoint someone else who can."

"Understood. I'm thinking about it. If you find you can't wait, so be it."

* * *

Tom put his phone down with a sense of wonder. Up to a point, Malcolm was right; for the first time in many years, he was reminded of the old thrill of the chase.

He picked up his phone again, opened the pictures folder and scrolled to the photograph he'd taken at Ben Bradwell's flat – the one of his page of notes. He zoomed in, and there it was: Donald Finch's name, with a double-ended arrow linking it to that of Victor Rudge.

He felt he'd latched on to something significant. The question was, what?

His mind jumped back to the evening when he'd first met Victor Rudge at the Stay and Prosper offices. The Monck Chervil deal had been in the news at the time, and Rudge had seemed utterly contemptuous of it. Could that contempt have blossomed into active moves to block it?

The idea made more sense if Rudge and this man Donald Finch knew each other, as Bradwell's scribblings suggested. Could Rudge somehow have persuaded or coerced Finch into changing his advice to the Government over the deal? It seemed far-fetched, but why not?

He needed to know more about the two men. He sat down at the coffee table, opened a browser window on his laptop and started trawling the web for details.

They'd had very different careers – Finch in public service, Rudge in high finance – yet he didn't have to look far to find a point where their lives had intersected. They'd both been undergraduates at Cambridge University at the same time.

Admittedly, they'd attended different colleges, and Finch was slightly older, so they had only overlapped by one year. Nevertheless, they could have met there. It fitted in with Ben Bradwell's doodled note.

However, the fact that Tom had learned this so easily was a disappointment. It meant there was no great secret about it. He needed to find out whether they had kept in touch after they'd graduated, and what kind of relationship, if any, they had now.

This proved a tougher challenge. Google searches and social network trawling turned up no mutual activity at all during the thirty-odd years since the two men had left university. If they'd stayed in contact, it was completely under the radar.

Chapter 35

Next morning Tom had an unexpected call from Christine in Winchester.

"I wasn't sure whether or not to bother you about this, but I thought I saw someone going into your house last night, around ten o'clock. You weren't here in town, were you?"

His heart gave an instant thump. "No, definitely not! We're still living in Storton. What did this person look like?"

"I'm sorry, I didn't pay much attention. I was drawing the curtains in the front bedroom, and it was quite dark. I would say he was about your height, and he was wearing a jacket like that one of yours. I thought he was going into the house next door to yours, but I'm sure now that it was your house."

"Did he look as if he was breaking in?"

"No, I think he was using a key."

That sounded bizarre. Tom did some fast thinking. "Would you mind going over to the house now to see if it looks OK?"

"Well … all right."

He heard sounds of her front door opening and a car driving past. There was a brief pause, then she said, "Your front door is still locked, and your front room looks OK through the window. Not ransacked, anyway." She attempted a laugh.

"I'd better phone Mary next door. She has a key, so she can go and look inside."

"Sounds a good idea."

He heard the faint sound of her footsteps, then of her front door closing again. Before she had a chance to end the call he said, "How are things with you?"

She gave an audible sigh. "All right, I suppose."

"You don't sound very sure."

"Having David around again takes a bit of getting used to. You know how it is – your life develops a rhythm, then suddenly there's someone else around."

"But you're getting on all right together, are you?"

"He's making an effort – I've got to give him credit. And Joanna loves having him back."

"It would be nice for us all to get together when we're back in Winchester." But even as he said this, Tom was aware of just now unlikely it was. The way things were developing between him and Jan, they might never go back there as a couple. Even if they did, he had a sense that David wouldn't welcome them.

She said, "I don't know if that would work, Tom."

"It was just a thought."

She said nothing.

He asked her, "How come you're at home. I thought you were out at work in the mornings?"

"I've cut down my work load since David came back. I'm only doing three days a week now."

"Was that his idea or yours?"

Another sigh. "I don't want to get into that, Tom. It suits us both."

After they ended the call he phoned his next-door neighbour Mary, but the call went to voicemail. She was probably busy at work or out shopping. He made a decision. He would drive to Winchester and have a look at the house for himself.

* * *

At first sight everything in the house appeared normal. It was so long since Tom had lived here that he couldn't be sure how it was supposed to look, but nothing showed obvious signs of having been disturbed. He checked the kitchen and the other main rooms, then made his way upstairs. Situation normal.

He looked again at his desk. The last time he'd come here it had been strewn with paperwork, and it was still covered with paperwork now, but it looked somehow more orderly than when he'd last seen it. Or was it just his imagination?

He glanced around uneasily. Could someone really have been poking about in here? Why? Burglars didn't generally have keys to the houses they selected, so if someone had been in here, it must have been a considered break-in. Had the intruder found what he wanted? If not, would he be coming back?

He couldn't put out of his mind the possibility that this had something to do with Ben Bradwell. He kept finding oddities connected with the man: his cryptic phone call during the week of the accident, his texts on the day itself, then the disappearance of the cassette tape and the phone – both of which contained evidence that he'd made contact.

Meanwhile, Mickey Choat thought someone might have broken into Bradwell's flat in Brighton, and now someone seemed to have broken in here. On both occasions they'd left almost no evidence. It felt like a pattern.

Should Tom contact the police? He was dubious. If the intruder really had opened the front door with a key, there would be no evidence of it. The police would presumably find nothing – but as Bernard had warned, they might start to take an unhealthy interest in Tom himself.

Instead, he called Bernard's number. "Would it be convenient to drop in on you this afternoon? I'm in Winchester, so I'm half-way there already."

Bernard laughed. "Guess what – I'm in Winchester too. Marie took it into her head to come shopping here. We're just walking through the market. D'you want to meet in a café or something? I'm sure Marie will be happy to go off on her own." He broke off to confer with her. "Yes, she says that's fine. Come and join me."

*   *   *

Half an hour later Tom had found a parking place, and was making his way through the narrow streets of Winchester's picturesque city centre towards the market area. He found Bernard sitting in a corner of the café he'd suggested, staring abstractedly towards the window. His face lit up as Tom walked over.

"A life saver! Now I don't have to trek around the town all day."

Tom sat down. "How are you?"

"Better than last time you saw me."

"You look brighter."

"Glad to hear it." Bernard gave a quick smile. "So what is it that you wanted to talk to me about so urgently?"

"I wanted to run something past you." He told Bernard about the possible break-in at his house. "I don't know if it really happened or not, but I doubt if Christine would be wrong about something like that."

"So what are you thinking?"

Tom paused to gather his thoughts. "Did you pick up the news yesterday about Monck Chervil, the American company that was going to create three thousand jobs in the UK? They've backed out of the deal."

"I might have heard something about it."

"I'm wondering if this might be connected with that guy Ben Bradwell in Brighton – the one who supposedly committed suicide. He worked at the Stay and Prosper campaign in London. Suppose he unearthed a scheme by someone at the campaign to derail the investment?"

"What makes you think that?"

Tom recounted his visit to see Mickey Choat, Bradwell's former partner. "There were notes on Bradwell's desk that suggested a connection between a man called Rudge at the campaign and the civil servant who was advising on the subsidy package."

"Quite the detective, aren't we?" Bernard said. He sat back and gave Tom an assessing look. "So you're saying there could have been some kind of collusion between these two people to torpedo the deal?"

"Something like that. I don't know exactly what Bradwell found out, but to put it bluntly, could it have got him killed? And could the same people be worried about what I might know?"

Bernard laughed dryly. "If it was anyone else saying this, I would conclude that they had an overactive imagination."

"But given that it's me ...?"

"Well, I think I follow what you're saying, but let's be analytical about this. Why would cancelling that deal favour these campaign people?"

"It would demonstrate that leaving the EU was a disaster for inward investment."

"But you don't seem to believe that explanation."

Tom shrugged. "If this civil servant really did interfere, the way he did it was by using EU rules to cancel the subsidy package. That's what finally bounced the company into pulling out."

"So in practice, his actions could work against these Remain people, not for them? Their opponents could argue that EU bureaucracy scuppered the deal, not economic uncertainty."

"Exactly."

Bernard thought about this. "It seems to me that you've already made the case against the idea of some plot. Your Stay and Prosper people couldn't have known for sure what kind of fallout there would be."

"Point taken."

"Even forgetting that aspect, it looks a bit thin to me. A scheme to derail an investment project is hardly the basis for your average murder conspiracy, is it?"

"I don't know. You're the expert."

"It seems a bit drastic."

Reluctantly Tom said, "I suppose you're right." Having made that concession, he then added, "There's something else, though. Mickey Choat thought someone might have broken into Bradwell's flat. But if they did, why did they leave his notes about Finch on the desk? Surely they would have taken them?"

"There you are then. False alarm."

Tom let the subject drop for a while, and they talked about other things. Bernard said he was considering going back to part-time courier work for Carswells. "But Marie says I'm mad. She'd rather have me at her beck and call the whole time."

Eventually Tom brought the conversation back to the campaign issue. He said, "I wondered about your ex-police mate."

"What about him?"

"If I talked to him confidentially, would he have a good handle on the police perspective? Would he know who to approach? Would he know how they would respond if I went to them and told them what I know?"

"He would know better than me, but he might not want to get dragged into this. I could ask."

"That's all I was thinking."

Bernard gave him a stern look. "It would be a help if you could find out why that other guy at the campaign office sent that woman to your house to interrogate you. But you insist you want to protect her."

Tom shuffled awkwardly. "I know it seems daft, but I gave her my word." He cleared his throat. "Besides, it doesn't seem to be connected to this Bradwell thing."

Bernard put his cup down and stared at Tom. "What if that girl is running rings round you? What if she told you a load of bullshit? You might be missing the truth when it's staring you in the face."

Chapter 36

Bernard told Tom he had arranged to meet his wife near the cathedral. On their way out of the café they found their path blocked by a woman negotiating her way in with a baby buggy. Tom recognised her round face and sculpted blond hair.

"Debbie. What a nice surprise."

"Tom! How are you doing? You're looking much better than last time I saw you." That was the day when she'd visited him in hospital with Jan.

"Much better, thanks. They're saying I can dump the leg brace within a week or two."

"That's wonderful."

Tom had known Debbie since Jan had moved in at Winchester, but not well. He smiled politely, trying to think of something else to say. "Jan gave you a real run-around at the weekend, didn't she? With the false alarm over the car, I mean."

She gave him a puzzled look. "Sorry, I'm not with you. Don and I were away at the weekend."

Had he inadvertently caught Jan out in a lie? He said, "I mean when her car wouldn't start. I thought she said you drove her out to Storton to pick up her AA card?"

Cautiously she said, "You mean this last weekend? Sorry, I thought you were talking about the one before."

"Yes, this weekend. Didn't she spend Sunday with you? I'm sure that's what she said."

"Of course, sorry, I was getting confused."

Tom was about to pursue this further, but more customers were trying to come into the café, and their way was being blocked. Debbie said, "Look, I mustn't keep you standing here. Look forward to seeing you another time." She slid past him, heading for an empty table, and moments later he and Bernard were out on the street.

* * *

Driving back to the village, Tom thought over his exchange with Debbie. She'd ended up supporting Jan's account of the weekend, but she'd clearly been flustered. It had felt as though she had no idea what he'd been talking about, and had merely been picking up on the cues he'd given her. Had Jan invented the whole episode?

The more he thought about this, the more convinced of it he became. Although Jan had told him Debbie had driven her to the village to fetch her AA card, he hadn't actually seen her. It could have been anyone.

He now thought about the urgent phone call Jan had made as soon as she'd realised he was in the house. Could she have been calling the person driving the car – warning him or her not to pull up outside the gate, in full view of the window? That would mean it definitely wasn't Debbie, but was someone Jan didn't want him to know about: someone she was having an affair with, for instance.

It was all conjecture, of course. Presumably if Jan's account had been a fabrication, Debbie must have phoned her by now so that they could get their stories straight. The only way he would find out the truth of the matter was by confronting Jan, and he didn't have the evidence to support him.

He smiled grimly to himself at this idea. Had their relationship really degenerated to the point where he was thinking in terms of evidence? If so, then there really was no future for them. Things couldn't go on like this.

He was waiting for her in the lounge when she arrived home that evening. She leaned round the door as usual to say hello, and he said, "Can we talk?"

He sensed that she wanted to avoid the kind of conversation he was implying, but she seemed to realise she had no option. "OK, give me five minutes."

She returned in a pullover and jeans – a look she knew he'd always found attractive. Was this a ploy to deflect him from whatever he planned to say? He resolved to press on regardless. He said, "What's happening to us, Jan?"

"This sounds serious."

"I feel as if we're treading water. You've been wonderful in helping me get over my accident, but there are moments when I feel – " he raised his hands helplessly – "I feel you'd rather be somewhere else. Or you'd rather I was somewhere else. We don't seem to connect any more."

"Of course we do." She half-sat on the arm of the sofa. "This has been a strange experience for both of us. You nearly died in that crash, and you weren't yourself for weeks afterwards. At times I wondered if you ever would be."

"Really?" He felt it was the first time he'd heard this. "How do you mean?"

"You didn't remember anything at first. They thought there might have been brain damage. You might worry that you don't remember the week of the accident, but to begin with you didn't remember anything at all. It was a long slow recovery process."

He stared at her, thinking back. His memory of the early weeks after the accident was vague. Mostly he remembered the pain, the immobility and the series of operations. He said, "Am I back to normal now?"

She gave a terse laugh. "Pretty much, I would say."

"And yet this isn't the life we used to live, is it? We're like a crabby old married couple – sleeping apart, saying hello over meals, going through the motions. Surely you can't be enjoying this any more than I am?"

"We can't just jump up and pretend none of this happened. I need time."

"Time for what?"

"I don't know. Time to adjust. Time to get back on track."

"But are you sure you want to?" He shuffled round to face her. "We're both adults. Nobody is forcing us to do anything we don't want to do. I don't want to put pressure on you if this simply isn't working any more."

"Of course it is." She slid off the arm on to the sofa, pressing briefly against him as she settled. The implication of this was unmistakable, and in the past he would have responded in kind, but today he was unprepared. Surreptitiously he moved away.

He said, "I just don't want you to think you have an obligation to me. I can stand on my own two feet now – literally. You're a free agent. Nothing is forcing us to stay together."

She reached over and rested her hand lightly on his thigh for a moment. "I think you're making something out of nothing." She lifted her hand away. "Let's not make any rash decisions."

They had a long supper in the kitchen that night, working their way through nearly two bottles of red wine. Some of Jan's old sparkle seemed to have returned. At the end of the evening, as Tom prepared to retire to his bedroom, she said, "Why don't you come and give the upstairs bed a try? It's much more comfortable than that one of yours."

Did this really mean what it appeared to? Seemingly yes. He followed her upstairs, and a little nervously at first, they embarked on their first-ever session of lovemaking in this house. For a while it seemed that they'd gone back not six months, but three years. There was familiarity, but also a strange novelty about it.

It was only afterwards that Tom sensed something was amiss. As he lifted his head from the pillow, he caught Jan staring at the ceiling with a bleak look on her face and a hint of tears in her eyes.

He whispered, "Are you OK?"

"I'm fine. I just need some sleep." She rolled over and faced away from him.

Chapter 37

Two days later Felix Schaefer phoned. Without preamble he said, "Our AGM is coming up next week."

Tom instantly sensed a manoeuvre to draw him back into the Carswell fold. He said, "What about it?"

"How would you fancy giving a presentation?"

He did some fast thinking. The Carswell AGM was a major landmark in the company's calendar: not so much an annual general meeting, more a combined conference and social gathering. Managers from branches round the country converged to discuss strategy, commiserate over disappointments and gloat over triumphs. Speakers from outside the company were usually booked to give the event more gravitas. Did Tom want to be one of them? He said, "What would I be talking about?"

"The company structure – the benefit of buying into our systems and policies. All the kind stuff you used to know so well. Nobody could do the job better."

"It's very short notice."

"I know. We had a drop-out." At least he was being open about it.

"Where is it happening?" Tom had memories of long journeys to the Midlands and Blackpool to attend previous AGMs.

"It's in London this year – our first time there."

"Would there be any payment?"

"A token fee, plus expenses of course."

"Two nights in London?"

"If that's what it takes."

Decision time. "OK. Send me the details."

"And you'll be welcome to join us at the dinner dance, of course. I'll get a couple of tickets emailed to you."

* * *

He told Jan about the AGM that evening. "We're invited to the dinner at the end of the conference if we want to go. Do you fancy a night on the town?"

Jan had accompanied him to two of Carswell's previous AGM dinners, though she'd cried off a third, pleading pressure of work. She said, "I thought we'd seen the last of those things when you were made redundant."

"Consider this a swan song if you like."

"What date did you say it was?" She was scrolling on her phone. "No, I've got a heavy meeting scheduled for that day. It might run late. I'd better say no."

Somehow he'd expected nothing else. She'd been difficult to read since their night together – more relaxed in some ways, yet also more wary. They'd spent the following night separately again, and that looked like being the continuing arrangement.

He should have been ready for her response, yet felt a wave of disappointment sweep over him. She kept insisting she wanted to repair their relationship, yet she was no longer prepared to take up opportunities like this to buy into his life. Before he could stop himself he said, "You didn't mind spending the whole of a Sunday with Debbie."

"That was completely different! It was a girls' get-together on a weekend. And I didn't even know you'd be back from London."

He said, "Mind you, when I mentioned your AA escapade to Debbie in Winchester the other day, she seemed pretty vague about it."

"What?" Her glance combined hostility with a hint of furtiveness. Quickly she said, "That's typical of Debbie. She never knows what day of the week it is."

"I suppose so."

She continued to watch him warily. After a moment he said, "Anyway, I'm going to the dinner. Might as well do a bit of networking while I have the chance."

"Good for you."

* * *

Tom's resentment towards Jan hadn't abated by next morning. Which version of her feelings towards him was he supposed to accept? The conciliatory one she'd presented to him the other night, which in retrospect had seemed altogether too calculated, or the frosty one that now seemed to have reasserted itself? More to the point, how much longer was he supposed to put up with this uncertainty?

While he was still in rebellious mood, an outrageous idea occurred to him. What if he invited Emily Sanders to the dinner in place of Jan? It wouldn't in fact be unheard-of. Jan had sometimes attended social events in London with partners from her workplace, and in the year Jan had ducked out of the Carswell dinner, he'd paired up with the wife of a colleague at the last minute. Her husband had flu, so it suited them both.

This time would be different, of course. Jan wouldn't know. Still, he felt that the precedent had been set. But would Emily take him up on the idea? That was hard to gauge, but the spark of interest she'd shown in him suggested she might be. A kind of recklessness was flooding through him, and he decided he was ready to chance it. He grabbed his phone.

He had to wait for ten rings, and was about to cancel the call when she answered. "You woke me up. What time do you call this?"

"Ten-thirty. And you're not up?"

"You weren't slaving in a bar till past midnight."

"Ah. I never thought of that. Shall I call back?"

She cleared her throat. "No, it's fine."

He hesitated, suddenly nervous. "Um, you can say no if you like, but I wondered if you would fancy going to a social event next Tuesday night? With me, I mean. I realise you'd have to skip a shift at the bar. Tell me if it's out of the question."

"You mean on a *date*? With you?"

"Not exactly a date. It's a formal dinner." He hesitated. "And a dance. A dinner dance."

"A 'dinner dance'? How quaint."

"Huh! I never thought of it that way."

She seemed to be thinking it over. "Where is this 'dinner dance' happening? In your village hall in the wilds of Hampshire?"

"No! It's in a hotel in London. With several hundred guests, I should think."

"Oh, right." Another pause. "Man with broken leg – dancing – no compute."

"I can watch." Did that sound risqué? "I mean we can sit it out. The dinner is the main thing. The dancing is an optional extra."

"What about your wife, partner, whatever? What will she think?"

It now occurred to him that if Jan was still in contact with anyone from Carswells, she might eventually hear from them about Emily's presence at this dinner. How would that go down? Then the reckless impulse fought back, telling him he didn't care. If she did find out, perhaps it would bring matters to a head. In fact he had more than a suspicion that they would already have gone beyond that point by then.

"My partner doesn't want to go. You would be a life-saver. You would keep up my street cred."

Emily said, "There's my boyfriend to consider, of course."

He hadn't thought of this. "Oh, sorry, I don't want to cause problems for you."

"I'm just winding you up. We split up weeks ago."

"Oh, right." She seemed to have him on the back foot at every turn. "What about your shift at the bar? Could you square it with your boss?"

"Maybe. But I have to warn you, I'm not very good in that kind of company." She was exaggerating her Lancashire accent. "I might upset your posh friends."

"They're not posh, they're just working people like me. And they're not friends, just business colleagues."

"Bit of a bore, then."

"I told you, you can say no if you like."

"Is it party frocks? I need to know what I'm getting into."

He laughed. "That kind of thing."

"I'll have to consult my extensive wardrobe."

"Does that mean you'll come?"

"I'll think about it."

Chapter 38

Tom's talk seemed to go down well.

He'd checked in at the west London hotel on the afternoon before the event, and run through his speech twice in his bedroom. It seemed to hold together, and his Powerpoint slides made adequate sense. He'd become something of an expert on Carswell's company structure, and after being made redundant he'd wondered who would take over the reins. The answer appeared to have been no one. Hence, no doubt, Felix Schaefer's keenness to have him speak about it at this event.

Emily had kept him waiting for the answer to her invitation, but had finally phoned him two nights before to declare her intention of coming. After the formal presentations he went up to his room to shower and change, then made his way down to the hotel's ballroom to wait for her. He sat at the bar amid a gathering throng of men in their best suits and women in evening regalia.

He didn't recognise her at first. She was wearing a simple purple dress – a vivid counterpoint to her reddish gold hair. By comparison, other women in her vicinity looked overdressed.

He swivelled off his stool and went over to greet her.

"Wow! You found a frock then?"

She smiled in apparent relief as he approached. "Oh, just some old rag from the back of the wardrobe."

"So I see." He stepped away to admire it.

"Get me a drink, quick. I can't handle this kind of thing stone cold sober."

He led the way over to the bar. "I would have thought your job in the pub gave you plenty of practice at dealing with people."

"Ah, but I have a role there. I don't have to prove anything. Same thing with acting. I can hide behind the character I'm playing."

"You don't have to prove anything here. Just be yourself."

"Whatever that is."

He ordered a glass of wine for her, and they stood against a wall, resting their drinks on a shelf.

"You go to a lot of events like this, do you?" she asked.

"Not really. This is an annual dinner. It's being held by the company I used to work for. They made me redundant at the start of the year."

"But you love them so much that you simply can't bear to tear yourself away?"

He laughed. "I think the boss regrets firing me. He hasn't found anyone else who can do the job I was doing. He asked me to come and give a talk to these good people this morning."

"Does that mean you'll go back to working for him full-time?"

Tom shook his head. "I don't know. I might, but I think I've had enough of the company. I used to be a journalist long ago, and I've been trying my hand at getting back into that. Did I tell you that?"

"I knew you were writing something about Brexit, but I didn't get how that fitted into your life."

He looked at her for a long moment. He detected curiosity, amusement, irony, and a hint of self-consciousness. She seemed ready to enjoy the occasion, yet she was uncertain what to make of it.

His stare eventually unsettled her, and she laughed awkwardly. "You'll know me next time."

"I know you this time."

"You wish!"

He said, "How much acting do you do?"

"Not enough. My agent is worse than useless. He hasn't got me a single audition for months, and the last one was just for a TV commercial."

"Did you get the job?"

"I'll give you one guess."

He gave her an assessing look. "How good are you?"

"Bloody brilliant, obviously. Wrong question."

The hubbub around them was rising in volume. It was becoming increasingly difficult to hear what Emily was saying, and he had to lean in each time she spoke. He was very conscious of her large eyes and attentive look, and of the cascade of wavy hair that framed her face.

She was asking him something, but he'd tuned her words out for a moment. He said, "Sorry, can you repeat that?"

"I was saying you surprised me when you asked me along tonight. You seem a very straight guy. I know your partner isn't available, but you don't seem like someone who looks for stand-ins."

"You're not a stand-in."

"Oh no? What am I, then?"

He hesitated, trying to work out an answer that would be both truthful and witty, and then froze. Through the crowd milling round the bar area, he thought he'd glimpsed Jan.

* * *

"Christ!" He stood up straighter and peered past Emily.

"What's the matter?"

"I thought I saw my partner, Jan." He shook his head in disbelief. "It can't be her. She definitely isn't coming tonight." He attempted a laugh. "I must be getting paranoid in my old age."

"I hope so." She chuckled lightly.

Then he caught another glimpse of the woman he'd seen. She was wearing a long green dress – very like one of Jan's. Finally the throng parted long enough for him to see her properly. It *was* Jan. She was peering around, presumably looking for him.

"Oh god," he said. "It really is her. This is terrible. I don't know what to say."

She managed to chuckle again. "This has the makings of a monumental cock-up."

"I'm so sorry. I never imagined in my wildest dreams that this would happen."

"Nightmares, more like."

Jan had spotted him, and was making her way slowly over.

"Surprise, surprise! My meeting ended early. I brought my glad rags with me to work this morning, just in case."

"It's certainly a surprise."

She glanced expectantly between him and Emily. "Are you going to introduce us?"

He said, "Jan, this is Emily Sanders. She works at the Stay and Prosper campaign office. At least she did until she was fired."

"Jan Carrington. Nice to meet you."

Emily shook her hand briefly, then turned to Tom. "I'd better go and find that man of mine. I don't know where he's hiding." She shot him a quick and indecipherable glance and slid away into the crowd.

Jan watched her go, then turned and gave him a curt smile. "You could look a bit more pleased to see me."

"Sorry, sorry. It's great that you've gone to all this trouble to get here."

"So are you going to get me a drink?"

He glanced around, still feeling wrong-footed. "Could you brave the queue on your own for a minute? I need to take a quick bathroom break."

Before she had time to protest he strode off in the direction Emily had taken. Once clear of the crowd he trotted up a flight of stairs towards the foyer and spotted her heading for the cloakroom.

He called after her, "Emily, this is terrible! I've never felt so humiliated in my life."

She turned. "It's OK, honestly. I'll head off. I've just read the menu, so at least I know what I'm missing." She flashed him an ironic smile.

"I'm so sorry. Jan should be the one who's leaving, not you."

"That's not going to work though, is it?"

"I suppose not." He shook his head. "I can't believe this. What a disaster."

"Don't worry about it."

"It was amazingly quick-thinking of you, the way you ducked out of that conversation. If it had been me, I would have caved in and confessed everything."

"You partner might notice in the end that I'm nowhere to be seen."

"Too bad."

They looked at each other for a moment. He said, "I should have faced her out, shouldn't I? I bottled it."

"I don't think that would have helped. You were never going to send her back to Hampshire on her own, were you? I would have done the same thing in your shoes."

"It's good of you to say so."

She said, "I'd better go. And you'd better get back." She started to turn, then hesitated. "Well, bye."

"I owe you. Big time"

She shrugged, then headed off to fetch her coat. Tom turned with a sigh and made his way back down towards the ballroom.

Chapter 39

The dinner passed in a blur. Tom did his best to seem upbeat and to appear grateful for Jan's presence, but he was strongly aware of the hypocrisy of his actions. He would have preferred to have Emily here, and that told him a lot.

But she'd been right, of course. This would have been no place for a showdown with Jan, and it would have been irresponsible to draw Emily into one. Yet the disloyalty of letting her back out nagged at him. She'd been remarkably gracious about it, but it should never have been necessary in the first place.

The meal ended and a five-piece band struck up, mixing ancient and modern rock with dance classics. A few diehards took to the floor at the end of the room, but most of the guests started mingling among the tables, networking with friends and associates. The Carswell branch manager on Tom's right disappeared as soon as the music started.

A middle-aged man ambled over and sat down in the now-empty chair. "Dan Hollis of Dingle Deliveries in Sleaford." He held out his hand.

"Dan, of course. How are you doing? How is the fifty per cent working out for you?"

"You mean having half our fleet in Carswell livery? It's an improvement on two thirds." He chuckled. "I shouldn't knock Felix Schaefer. He's done wonders with his company, and we've earned a lot from being part of it." He waved his hand broadly at his surroundings. "It focuses the mind when you see all these people here in one place. A common purpose and all that. We could never compete with this on our own."

"I think he wants me to go back to working for him full-time, but I'm not decided yet."

"You could do worse."

They sat in silence for a moment, then Hollis said, "Did the police ever take any action after your friend was attacked?"

"Not as far as I know."

Hollis leaned forward. "Confidentially, I heard there was a bit of a puzzle about that."

Tom eyed him curiously. "Puzzle?"

"They knew the man you talked to in the pub, but they reckon the guys who attacked you were different people."

"Really? That's very bizarre." Hs shuffled round to face Hollis more directly. "How do you know this, if you don't mind me asking?"

"A friend of mine has connections in the force."

"Small world."

"Small community, anyway. No great surprise."

"So what did he tell you?"

Hollis leaned in further. "Promise me you won't repeat this? He said they found some CCTV images of the guys who attacked you. The image quality was bad, but they were pretty sure it wasn't the same people. Plus, the guy in the pub had a cast-iron alibi, so it couldn't have been him."

Tom thought about this. "But the men who attacked us actually quoted the words of the man in the pub. It must have been them."

Hollis shrugged.

"You surely aren't saying they went off and hired a couple of rent-a-thugs to do their dirty work – and set it up in the space of about an hour?"

"I'm only repeating what I heard."

Tom nodded. "Of course. I appreciate you telling me this."

Hollis wandered off, and Tom turned towards Jan. She was deep in conversation with a woman on her other side – a Carswell branch manager from somewhere in the north. He watched her as she chatted. She seemed animated, and looked happy enough to be here. As usual, she was a contradiction, and impossible for him to read. At one point she turned to him and raised her eyes in complicity over what the woman next to her was saying. It reminded him of the way their relationship used to be.

Felix Schaefer planted himself in the chair beside Tom – a neat figure whose commanding presence always seemed to belie his modest frame. "Enjoying the party?"

"The best yet."

"I agree. And holding this event in London makes us seem more of a national player."

"You don't have anything to prove."

"Oh yes we do. Always." Felix sipped his drink. "That was a good presentation this morning, Tom. Thank you for stepping in."

Tom waited. He could feel another request looming.

"Look, I know you don't want your job back, but would you consider doing me another favour? For a fee, of course."

"Go on."

Felix sighed. "We're having trouble with another of our members – Rackhams in Nottingham. This time it's not just a case of griping over details, they want to quit the network altogether."

"And?"

Irritably, Felix said, "I'm not having it! They're one of our best-performing members." He sipped his drink again, then in calmer tone said, "I'm going to see them next week, before it's too late. I'd appreciate it if you came along and helped me sweet-talk them into staying with us."

"Surely that's someone else's job?"

"That someone else has just left the company. He got a better offer."

Tom glanced round the ballroom. "Are the Rackhams people here tonight? You could introduce me."

"No, they decided not to come. It doesn't look good, does it?"

"I see what you mean."

"I'll be driving there. I could pick you up from where you're living on the way."

Tom waited a moment, then said, "OK, I'll come."

Felix nodded and started to rise. "I'll email you the details." He strode off, opening his arms in generous greeting to the people on the adjacent table.

Tom turned back to Jan. The conversation on her other side seemed to have run out of steam, and she was staring vacantly across the table. She became aware of Tom and focused on him. "Who was that woman you were talking to when I came in?"

Feeling suddenly caught out, he said, "I told you – Emily Sanders. I met her at the Stay and Prosper offices in Kensington." He attempted an innocent frown.

"What's she doing here?"

He was reluctant to tell a lie, yet this seemed hardly the time for the truth. He said, "Don't ask me." No outright lies up to this point, but how far was she going to press it?

"You looked pretty thick with her to me. How well do you know her?"

"Not that well." He attempted a laugh. "What is this – the third degree?"

"Of course not, but since Danni – well, I suppose I'm over-sensitive."

The name came as a sudden jolt. For the past eighteen months he'd tried to forget it. By tacit agreement it was never mentioned in their household. He was unprepared.

Danni had been an administrative assistant at Carswells, and by coincidence had also been one of the Winchester set with whom Jan mixed. She'd been a friend of Debbie's. Tom had been drawn to her, and in another life their friendship might have blossomed into something more.

* * *

He'd found himself thrown into Danni's company on a project they were both working on. Nothing had come of it, but he'd enjoyed her company, and her liking for him must have been obvious enough for her friends to notice. Somehow it had been reported to Jan.

It hadn't occurred to him at the time, but Jan's attitude to him even before this had turned strangely inconsistent. One day she would seem inexplicably aloof, the next day overly fond. He'd never fully understood why, but perhaps Danni's steady and undemanding good nature had seemed a welcome counterpoint to Jan's unpredictability.

Once Jan knew about Danni, he'd had to withstand night after night of her reproaches and her stinging silences. Eventually he'd asked for Danni to be taken off the project they were working on.

Then one day he'd come home from work to find Jan already back from London, sitting weeping in the kitchen of their Winchester house. She'd looked up and said, "I'm a cow, aren't I? Banging on at you over Danni. What right do I have to complain at you?"

It was as near as she ever came to an apology for her own mercurial behaviour, and afterwards their relationship seemed to revive.

He looked at her now, unable to decide how to react to hearing Danni's name after all this time. Finally he said, "What on earth makes you bring her up?"

"Oh, I don't know. Once bitten, twice shy?"

She looked unhappy rather than accusing, and he felt unexpectedly guilty. He said, "Don't worry, there's nothing for you to be concerned about."

Part of him wished it were true.

Chapter 40

Felix Schaefer had a red Ferrari, but he drove it like a mid-range family car.

"It's not new," he told Tom, "but I always promised myself I'd buy one when I could afford it. Call it vanity."

Tom's injured leg had nearly buckled as he stooped to climb in, and he was finding the ride unremittingly hard, but he said nothing. Felix added, "Of course, the van drivers think I'm just flaunting my money. But you know what? It's their problem, not mine."

Tom said, "I suppose it's a success symbol."

"Exactly."

Felix had arrived in the village at half past eight that morning to pick up Tom for their 150-mile journey to Nottingham. Now they were crawling northwards in heavy traffic on the M3. Felix said, "Do you know what you want to say to these Rackham people?"

"I'll take my lead from you."

"You'd better not. I'm bound to piss them off in the first five minutes."

"Tell me about them, then."

"You probably know all you need to know already. They're our biggest member-company. They've been with us nine years. They have three depots – Nottingham, Leicester and Rugby. They've picked up some good contracts in the last year or two."

"I never met their CEO."

"Darren Wright. Difficult bastard, but he knows how to run a tight ship."

"What have you done to upset him, then?"

Felix cast Tom a sheepish glance. "They put a list of proposals to me – ideas for changing membership rules, streamlining the network, that kind of thing. I got Martha to knock together a reply." He hesitated.

"Mostly I had to say no to what they wanted. It felt like the tail wagging the dog."

"You should have emailed the list to me in advance."

"I wanted you to come to this with fresh eyes."

"Huh." Tom thought about this. "Can you back down on some of their proposals, and let them have their way?"

"I may have to."

* * *

The introductions were over quickly, and before Tom knew it, Rackham's chief executive, Darren Wright, was staring at Felix truculently across the boardroom table. He was in his fifties and heavily overweight, but his face was unlined and looked like that of a man ten years younger.

"I appreciate that you've driven a long way this morning," Wright said, "but I have to tell you now that you're unlikely to change our minds about leaving the network."

Felix said, "At least let's have the conversation before we get to the outcome."

Wright stared at Felix, tapping his pen on a manila folder in front of him. "So what are you offering that's new?"

"A listening ear?" Felix attempted a grin.

Tom said, "Tell me the things that you would most like to change."

Wright swivelled round to face him. "OK, well one is having to use Carswell procedures and IT systems when we're dealing with our own non-Carswell customers."

Tom turned to Felix. "What's the purpose of that?"

Felix shrugged. "Harmonisation? Streamlining? We've found over the years that when we don't apply that rule, people get muddled and things go haywire."

Wright said, "You don't have to impose rules on efficient members just to cater for the ones who get things wrong."

"It doesn't make sense to have one rule for one member and another rule for the rest."

"But circumstances differ. Your rigid rules have never taken account of that."

Felix nodded glumly. "I hear you."

"And here's another thing. If a driver from another Carswell branch somewhere else in the country comes here and applies to work for us, we're supposed to take him on without question as soon as we have a vacancy, even if there are drivers in our own area looking for work. What's the point of that?"

"It's supposed to give staff confidence in staying with us – to make them feel part of something bigger."

Tom said, "I always thought that was a pretty contentious rule."

Felix sighed. "We can look at it again."

Tom said, "What about money? I assume we wouldn't be having this conversation unless there was a financial dimension."

Wright drew a long breath. "The 'financial dimension', as you call it, is that we pay a hell of a lot into Carswell's central fund for services rendered, yet we don't get adequate recompense for the revenue we generate. Never have."

Felix put in, "Basically, you want a reduction in the commission you pay?"

"We want to change the sliding scale, so that we don't get so much taken off high-value contracts. We want a bit more fairness." He opened the folder in front of him, pulled out a sheet of paper and slid it across the table. "We need a hedge against future uncertainty."

Felix studied the page, saying nothing.

Tom sat back, suddenly amused. This felt like a Brexit discussion in miniature. Rackhams were threatening to leave the union, and Carswells didn't want to let them go. There were freedom of movement issues, and there was a disagreement over contributions to the central budget. Presumably there might also be an argument about divorce terms. Would this situation end any more happily than Brexit seemed likely to?

Felix looked up at Darren Wright from the proposal document, frowning. "I can't give you this kind of deal. You must know that. What kind of message would it send to the rest of the membership?"

"Then I don't see any point in having this conversation."

"Hold on, hold on, I didn't say we couldn't shift our ground a bit. Let me think about this. I'll need to talk to our full board, and see what we can come up with."

"We're not going to move far from those figures."

Tom was thinking fast. Something Wright had just said didn't quite gel. He said, "What did you mean just now about wanting a hedge against uncertainty? What uncertainty?"

Wright looked slightly uncomfortable. "Economic forecasts are all over the place. You know that. We need a bit more security going forward."

Tom was unconvinced. It was only intuition, but he felt Wright's concern was more specific than he was admitting.

Chapter 41

The meeting broke up with no agreement. The Rackham team had made very few concessions, and Felix had merely agreed to "review" the various points they'd raised.

They hovered in the open-plan general office. Darren Wright went off to attend to a phone call, and Felix disappeared into one of the cubicles to confer with the operations manager. As Tom waited, he was approached by a woman in her forties.

"Tom! Fancy seeing you here."

She had tight greying curls and pronounced freckles – a distinctive look, yet for a moment he struggled to place her. Then it clicked; she'd worked in administration at Carswells during his first couple of years there. They'd got on well, but then she'd left, and he'd never seen or heard of her since.

"Julie, what a nice surprise."

"We moved back from Southampton to Nottingham. It's my husband's home town. I got a job at Rackhams straight away because of the reciprocal employment policy."

"And was it a good move for you?"

"Very good." She hesitated. "I'm not exactly Darren Wright's biggest fan, but everyone else here is great."

"I'm glad to hear it."

She moved closer to him. "I assume you came here this morning to talk about Rackham's plan to break away from the Carswell network, did you?"

"Something like that."

Quietly, she said, "I probably shouldn't be speaking out of turn, but there's more to it than meets the eye."

"Sorry, what do you mean?"

She glanced around nervously. "People like Darren Wright are ambitious. They want to be more than just a cog in a wheel. He's done wonders with Rackhams, but he could do more. He keeps telling the other directors that Rackhams can stand on its own two feet, and I think at least one of them agrees. They think they don't need Carswells any more."

"That's a fairly understandable viewpoint."

"But that's not the whole story." She lowered her voice. "I've kept in touch with Jacqueline in Southampton. She thinks someone from Carswells has been telling Darren that Felix Schaefer is going to sell the company, and the new owners will break up the network. They'll insist on buying up the franchised members, and they'll dump any who don't want to sell. They'll just set up their own branches instead."

"Where would that leave Rackhams?"

"They would never sell to Felix. They're far too independent-minded. They would go it alone. So Darren wants to get ahead of the game – to break away now, before the shit hits the proverbial."

"And is this stuff about Carswells true?"

"You should know better than me. You're there at head office all the time."

"No I'm not. I was made redundant months ago. I'm here today as a favour."

"Oh, I didn't know that." She looked at him awkwardly. "Perhaps you should ask Felix about it."

He looked at her for a moment, thinking fast. "I don't see why Darren hasn't challenged Felix over this."

"Ah, well he wouldn't, would he? There are some big courier contracts in the pipeline. If the network falls apart, they'll be up for grabs. Darren wants to keep his powder dry, and be ready to snatch them away from Carswells and take them for himself. He would gradually go national as an independent. That would be his aim, anyway."

Did Tom want to get embroiled in these company politics? He looked uneasily at Julie, who was waiting for some sort of comment. He said, "Why are you telling me this?"

"I always thought you were a very straight person. I thought you might know what to do for the best." She leaned forward. "Also I want to keep my job here. If the network breaks up, the employment pact will go out the window. I've heard they're thinking of making cuts, and Darren wouldn't be sorry to see me go."

* * *

Felix invited Darren Wright and two of his colleagues out to lunch, but they pointedly declined, blaming pressure of work. As the little group hovered in the reception area Tom noticed a van in the forecourt with lettering for Monck Chervil. He turned to Wright.

"I'd forgotten you worked for them."

Wright turned to him with a patronising look. "Nottingham has always been a centre for pharma and the life sciences. Monck's have had a big factory here for years. We've got a fleet of delivery vans out on long-term hire to them. It's our biggest single operation." He glanced at Felix. "It's a Rackhams operation, of course – nothing to do with the Carswell business. It just involves us and them"

"You must have been disappointed when they pulled out of this new UK investment project?"

"Yeah, they were proposing a big new production facility. But that would have been in South Wales, not Nottingham. That's way out of our territory. Up here they were going to build a new research base. Not so much call for transport in that."

"But the Carswell group might have got involved in the South Wales development."

"I suppose so."

As they walked over to the exit, Tom pointed across the yard to a line of bright yellow and green vans parked against the wall. "What are they for?"

Wright said, "They're the latest vans for the Monck Chervil operation. They're going into service at the end of the month."

Back on the road, Felix turned to Tom. "Darren seemed very cool about the Monck Chervil investment programme going tits-up, don't you think? He didn't seem to care whether Carswells would have picked up the South Wales business or not."

"I suppose if he's thinking of leaving the network, it wouldn't have affected him one way or the other."

"I thought he changed the subject too quickly. I wonder what scheme he had going on in his head?"

"Well, now that the investment has been cancelled, we'll probably never know."

They drove on in silence for a while, then Felix said, "So what do you think? Do we stand any chance of keeping Rackhams in the Carswell fold?"

"I wouldn't say you can bank on it."

"Precisely my thought."

Tom hesitated. Would he be breaking a confidence if he reported what Julie had told him? Choosing his words carefully, he said, "Are you planning on selling Carswells? I'm picking up rumours about that."

"Are you indeed?" Felix was immediately indignant.

Tom pressed on, "If people believe it, they might think the network is under threat. What if the new owners want to go one hundred per cent in-house, and end the franchise operation?"

Now Felix was angry. "Utter bollocks! There's no truth in that whatsoever. I wouldn't do that. Who the hell told you that?"

"Just rumours." Tom waited for a challenge on this, then when none came, added, "But what if someone is putting that idea about? It would make people like Darren Wright nervous, wouldn't it?"

"Are you saying someone *is* doing that? Who? What do you know about it?"

"Nothing! I'm just speculating."

"Are you indeed."

Felix remained silent for several minutes, then glanced at Tom more propitiatingly. "Can I trust you on something?"

"I would like to think so."

"All right. Well I *am* talking to a potential new investor in Carswells – an American logistics group. But they support the franchise model. They wouldn't dump it. And in any case, I don't want an outright sale, just a partnership. I would remain the majority shareholder. So if someone *has* got wind of this, they're twisting it for their own ends."

"Fair enough. If it comes up in conversation, I'll try to put people right."

"Don't say anything about what I'm telling you. Just calm things down if you can."

Chapter 42

Four days later Felix was back on the phone.

"Thank you for your support in Nottingham."

From Felix this comment was effusive. Tom paused to savour the moment, then asked him, "What's happening with Rackhams?"

"Nothing so far. I've drafted a new set of proposals to meet some of their complaints. Now we'll have to see what Darren Wright has to say about them." Felix paused. "I've done some checking. I think you were right that someone here has been putting out misleading stories about a sell-out and what it would mean for the franchised network. I'm bloody annoyed."

"But you don't know who it is?"

"Not yet, but I'm going to find out."

Tom said nothing, and there was another pause. Then Felix said, "Listen, I know you don't want to come back to the company full-time, and I understand that, but how would you feel about a six-month contract? If any more members are going to get jumpy, I could do with having someone around with your knowledge to trouble-shoot."

"I appreciate your confidence."

"You don't seem to have a lot else going on. Why not earn some money until you get yourself sorted?"

Tom hesitated. "Can I sleep on it?"

"If you're on board, I can copy you in on things like this Rackham situation automatically."

"Fair enough."

"I'll put some figures together and email you."

"It would need to be a flexible arrangement, not a nine to five job."

"I can live with that."

"OK, I'll have a think about it."

Tom hung up indecisively. He'd been reluctant to be drawn back to

Carswells, but he was nowhere further forward with the article he'd proposed to Malcolm Drew, and his big idea of switching back to the world of journalism was beginning to feel like a damp squib. If that was the case, he needed a proper job. The contract with Felix would be a good compromise.

* * *

Tom had barely ended the call with Felix when Mickey Choat rang him. "I've been doing some thinking," he said without preamble. "You've got me wondering about what happened to Ben."

"What do you mean?"

"Remember that day you came over to Brighton? After you left, I wanted to check something on Ben's laptop, but it wasn't there. Vanished into thin air."

"Could his mother have taken it?"

"No, I asked her. She lives up in the north, and she's only been to the flat once since he died. She's going to sell the place, but she hasn't had the agents round yet, or anybody else."

"So when did you last see it?"

"I don't know, that's the problem. I've been going round there every now and then to make sure everything's OK, but I've never looked for the laptop. For all I know, it went missing the day Ben died."

Tom was thinking fast. "Why has this made you rethink Ben's death?"

Mickey seemed to be debating with himself. Finally he said, "I had a break-in at my place in Shoreham. The bastards took my own laptop."

"Right."

"Well, it's a fucking coincidence, wouldn't you say?"

"I suppose it is."

"And they didn't damage anything getting in. It's as if they had a key."

"That *is* weird."

There was another long pause. Tom waited.

"The thing is, Ben had another laptop – a brand new one. Top of the range. He'd only had it a few weeks."

"So has that gone missing as well?"

"No, that's not what I'm getting at." Mickey cleared his throat. "Look, this is in confidence, right?"

"Absolutely."

"OK. Well, I decided I'd have the new laptop for myself." He paused, then in an indignant tone added, "What was his mother going to do with it? She would probably just have put it in a drawer and left it there forever. Such a waste. And if she wanted one to use, well, his old one wasn't that old. It was a good little machine. He just wanted something faster."

"Except that someone stole it."

"Yeah, but I didn't know that, did I?"

"So have the burglars stolen the new one from your place as well?"

"No, that's the thing. I gave it to my sister."

"You gave it to your sister."

Mickey said, "She sells children's clothes online. She built her own website – she's really into all that stuff. Ben helped her. But she's a single parent with no money. She could never afford a decent laptop – nothing like Ben's."

"And does she still have it?"

"Yeah, yeah, no one has bothered her about it."

Tom was thinking fast. He said, "Look, if these people really were looking for Ben's new computer, and they knew enough about his life to come looking for it at your place, they might work out that you gave it to your sister."

"I wondered about that."

"You can't ignore the possibility. They might go after her."

"So what would you do if you were me?"

"Go to the police and tell them what you know. If they take it seriously, they might look again at Ben's death."

"You mean go and tell them I stole his computer? I don't think so."

"You could say you borrowed it."

"What, borrowed it and gave it to my sister? Hardly."

"Or maybe it was a gift from Ben to you?"

"Yeah, I'm sure they'll believe that." He was apparently thinking again. "I was a bit wild when I was young. The cops know me."

Tom said, "Do you know what might be on the computer? I mean, why do these people want it?"

"No idea."

"Would you be willing to let me take a look at it?"

"I suppose so."

"I could check it over, and then put it somewhere safe. In a bank or something."

"Or I could do that."

"There might be some clue about what really happened to Ben, and I might recognise it more easily than you."

"My sister will love me for this."

"I think you need to find a way to square it with her. This is more important than her feelings about it."

He grunted his assent. "I suppose so."

"How about if I came over there and picked it up from you? I would keep you in the picture about it, and in the end maybe we could work out a way to get it to the police without getting into a mess over it."

"These people might still break into my sister's, though. They wouldn't know I'd taken it away from her, would they?"

"Maybe you could get her to call the police and tell them she's seen someone suspicious hanging around. They would probably go and give her place a once-over, and they might get their patrols to keep an eye out around her area."

"Yeah, I suppose she could do that."

"And you could still report the theft of Ben's old computer to the police."

"His mother's already done that. The fucking cops came round here the day after I told her about it, wanting to know if I nicked it." He gave an indignant groan. "You can see what I'm up against."

"So when would suit you to meet up?"

Mickey thought for a moment. "My sister lives in Littlehampton. I'll be going over that way the day after tomorrow, so I could pick up the laptop from her and meet you somewhere around there."

"Sounds good to me."

As soon as he lowered his phone Tom felt a rush of anxiety. He'd already failed to report Emily Sanders' bogus insurance visit to the police; now he was complicit in helping Mickey Choat to avoid reporting something potentially more concerning. If there was evidence about Ben's death in any of this, he might eventually be accused of perverting the course of justice.

And why? In both cases it was to prevent someone else from getting into trouble. Honourable, maybe. Wise, probably not.

Chapter 43

Mickey had suggested meeting at a large service area between Littlehampton and Arundel – nearer to Brighton than to Winchester. It took Tom an hour and a half to drive there through early afternoon traffic.

He looked around curiously as he entered the service area. Could this have been the place where he'd arranged to meet Ben Bradwell all those months ago? He'd found a reference to it in the notes he'd left on his desk in Winchester before his accident, and now that he was here, the place seemed tantalisingly familiar, yet he couldn't swear to it.

He spotted Mickey's box van at the back of the lorry park and walked over to it. It was larger than most of the vans in the Carswell fleet. Mickey jumped down from the cab holding a black canvas computer case, and handed it to Tom. He said, "The charger's inside, and the password is just 'bradwell123', with a lower-case B. If I were you I'd get shot of this as soon as you can. Stow it somewhere safe."

"Thanks for bringing it.

"Do you really think there are people out there looking for this?"

"I honestly don't know. But I can talk to someone who might have a better idea than me."

"Not the law?" Mickey was suddenly nervous.

"Not exactly. Someone who knows how these things go."

Mickey gave him a long look. "What's all this about? Do you have any idea?"

"Not really. I'll tell you if I find out anything."

"OK."

"How's your sister? All well with her?"

"Yeah, no sign of trouble up to now." He chuckled grimly. "She's disappointed to be going back to her old laptop, though." He started to climb back into his cab. "Best not to hang around here, eh?"

* * *

It was nearly six o'clock when Tom arrived back at the village. Before doing anything else, he decided to contact Bernard again. He'd told Mickey he 'knew someone'. This seemed a good moment to find out how true that was. He took out his phone.

"How are you doing, Tom?"

"Sorry I haven't been in touch lately. I've been busy."

"So have I. I've done two courier runs for Carswells this week. One of them was this morning. Only local, thank god."

"I'm glad you're back in the saddle."

Bernard chuckled. "What can I do for you?"

"I wondered about that ex-police mate of yours. Were you able to find out if he would talk to me off the record?"

"Yes, he says he doesn't mind having a conversation. But you need to realise he's a copper through and through. He's only recently come out of the force – he's not like me. If you told him you'd latched on to something illegal, he couldn't ignore it, even if it involved your lady friend."

"She's not my lady friend."

"You know what I mean."

"What if I made it hypothetical?"

"You'd have to play it by ear."

"Can you set up a meeting, then?"

"Best do it over a pint one evening, I think."

"Whatever works for him."

He put his phone down and unpacked the computer, a gleaming metallic model. He set it on the dining room table, then plugged the charger into a wall socket for good measure. It booted quickly, and he typed in the password. Now what? He started rummaging through the files on it.

Mickey's sister had separated her work from Ben's via a different login account, but happily the same password worked for both. Her own account contained various recent documents about children's clothes, presumably created in connection with her business, but Ben's material appeared to be intact. Soon Tom was looking at his emails and notes about the Stay and Prosper campaign.

It all looked interesting, but nothing jumped out at him as embarrassing or controversial. Clearly it would take him time to go through all this in more detail.

He continued to scroll around, and spotted some large video files. This seemed potentially interesting. What video had Ben decided to save in the short time he'd had this computer?

He heard the front door open and close quietly. Jan had told him this morning that she was planning to stay over in London for the night. She must have changed her mind. Absently he called, "Hi!"

There was no response, but a moment later the dining room door swung open and a man stepped in. Tom had never seen him before.

"Hi," he said.

*   *   *

The man was somewhere in his late thirties. He had close-cropped greyish hair, a lean physique and an amiable face. He was wearing a grey jersey with heavy vertical ribbing, along with casual grey trousers and grey trainers. It was something of a military look. He was also wearing thin leather gloves.

Tom felt a prickling sensation shooting across his shoulders and down his back. He said, "Who the hell are you! How did you get in here?"

The man smiled genially. "No need for any of that. I won't keep you long." So far he'd said and done nothing threatening, yet he was radiating an aura of unmistakable menace, somehow reinforced by his calm demeanour and air of utter self-confidence.

Tom pushed back his chair as if in preparation for a fight. The man said, "Relax, please." He pulled out the chair opposite and sat down. "I just want a quick chat."

Tom stared at him. "Fuck that!"

The man watched him with an expression of steely amusement. "You don't have to say anything. Just listen."

"Why the hell should I?"

Patiently, the man said, "Because you have no option." He offered this almost as a question, but it was also an assertion that would brook no dispute.

Tom stared at him. Helpless fury was pounding in his head, rendering him almost speechless. Finally he managed to say, "OK, what do you want?"

"You've been meddling with things that don't concern you. I'm here to tell you to stop." He looked calmly at Tom, waiting.

"That's it?"

"That's it."

"And what if I don't?"

"We'll kill you."

That statement conveyed so little, and yet so much. The man had said it firmly but unsensationally, as if the intent behind it was beyond dispute. Tom swallowed and said, "You'll kill me."

"I will, or one of my colleagues will." He scratched his nose. "I could do it now if you like." His stare remained steady and unflinching.

Tom looked at him for a moment, then gave a nervous laugh. "No thanks."

"Just kidding." But there was no humour in that stare.

"I'm glad to hear it."

"But this is not a joke. You know that. If you keep stepping out of line, you'll be gone, and no one will know what happened. You understand that, don't you? You're out of your depth here, so we're doing you a favour. Step back. Understood?"

Tom swallowed again. "Can I ask something?"

"Ask away."

"What things have I been meddling in that you want me to drop?"

"You'll have to work that out."

"Great."

"You'll manage it."

"Are you from the Stay and Prosper campaign?"

A blank smile. "Who are they?"

"And if I do as I'm told, you'll leave me alone?"

"So long as you do what I'm telling you."

Moments passed. Tom could hear the clock ticking across the room. He said, "I don't believe this."

"I think you do. And bear in mind that we'll be watching you. We'll know if you step out of line." The man pushed his chair back. "So we're clear now, are we?"

Tom shrugged.

With sudden firmness the man said, "I need to hear you say it. NOW!"

"We're clear."

"Right." He stood up and leaned over the table. Tom flinched instinctively, but the man merely unplugged the mains lead from the back of the laptop and snapped the lid shut. "Will you pull that plug out from the wall please, and give it to me?"

Mutely Tom obeyed.

The man tucked the machine under his arm and started coiling the cable. "I'll be going now. You can stay there where you are."

Seconds later he was gone.

Chapter 44

Tom sat motionless for a long time. The evening sunlight flickered in through the windows.

He was stunned. He felt as if he'd been physically assaulted. Despite the lack of overt aggression, his visitor's ascendancy had been total. Tom had never for a moment doubted the man's ability to carry out his threats, and this awareness had left him angry and humiliated. Part of him wanted to weep.

What kind of people were these? They must have been watching him, and had known he'd taken possession of Ben Bradwell's computer. They also had the ability to open locked doors without apparent impediment. What else could they do?

Tom had watched his share of paranoia films – tales of plucky individuals pitched against the state, the mob, the machine. He knew the way the bad guys seemed to have limitless power to monitor people's movements, to eavesdrop on their conversations, to intercept their phone calls, to inspect their bank accounts … and to exterminate them with impunity. He'd always assumed that while some of this must be fact, a lot of it was fiction. But how was he to know which was which?

Eventually he stood up and walked through to the kitchen. He pulled the whisky bottle from its unofficial home in the cereal cupboard and poured himself a healthy measure. The liquid was stinging, but the initial effect was limited. It couldn't banish what had just happened.

He tried to think things through rationally. These people couldn't know everything, and couldn't monitor everything. That had to be his starting point. Part of their strength lay in the power of suggestion, and it was up to him to resist it. The tricky part was working out how to do that.

He went out into the hall and opened and shut the front door. There was no sign of damage. Clearly the ability to open locked doors was indeed part of these people's skill set.

He wandered into the lounge and slumped down on the sofa. His first instinct was to report the intrusion to someone in authority, but for the time being he couldn't begin to think how that would work out. His second instinct was to call up Bernard again, but something also warned him against that. Telephone monitoring probably wasn't rocket science for a specialist, and these people were obviously specialists.

But if he really had offended people who had this kind of resource base, what on earth were they up to? What nefarious activity had he threatened to expose? It was looking increasingly as if Ben Bradwell really had paid for his knowledge with his life, but Tom still had only the vaguest idea of what that knowledge was. And now it was going to be far more dangerous to find out.

*   *   *

His phone buzzed on the dining room table. He limped through and sat down again. It was Bernard.

"I've had a word with my mate Joe. He's happy to talk to you. Can you get yourself down here to Southampton tomorrow evening?"

Suddenly Tom felt cornered. Were these mysterious people listening to this call? Would they know he was about to air his suspicions? Awkwardly he said, "Oh, I see."

"So can you make it? We can switch it to another day if tomorrow's no good."

"No, it's not that. I'm not so sure this is such a good idea after all."

"You seemed pretty sure an hour ago. What's changed?"

Tom glanced round the safe, mundane dining room. Was the world outside really as frightening as it suddenly seemed? "I don't think I'm quite ready to talk about this, that's all. I don't think this is the time."

"Are you all right, Tom? You sound strange."

"I've just had a shock. I'm probably not thinking straight."

"A shock? What kind of shock?"

"It's nothing. I'm fine. Can I call you back about this?"

Clearly bemused, Bernard said, "OK, let me know when you're ready to talk."

"Will you apologise to your mate for me?"

"That's all right – I can still meet up with him. I think we'll manage all right without you."

* * *

Tom stared at the blank space on the table in front of him where he'd placed Ben Bradwell's computer. It was hard to take in the fact that he'd had it in his possession, and now it was gone. It might have provided the key to what was going on. The irony was that if he hadn't suggested taking it from Mickey Choat's sister, she might still have it.

He wondered if the sister had looked at those video files, or examined any of Bradwell's documents and emails. It was a long shot, but perhaps he should ask her.

Then it occurred to him that this was exactly what his visitor had told him not to do. If he did, and if the visitor was to be believed, "they" would kill him. It seemed too far-fetched for words, yet that threat had felt utterly convincing.

He thought again about Mickey Choat's sister. He didn't know her name, but presumably he could find it out. But how would he contact her? If his phone calls really were being intercepted, that would be the most basic of mistakes. And he couldn't call Mickey to ask. It would amount to the same thing.

Supposing he found out her address? Could he go there? If they were watching him, the answer was probably no.

He stood up and started pacing around the room, ignoring the protests from his injured leg. Surely he was exaggerating the risks in all this? If he was as much of a threat to these people as that man had implied, then being brutally honest, surely they would simply have gone ahead and killed him? On a strictly practical level, mounting a twenty-four hour surveillance on him would be absurdly expensive and labour-intensive. Whoever they were, they must have better things to concern themselves with than Tom Anthony and what he might or might not know.

The fact that they hadn't already disposed of him seemed to suggest that they weren't about to, providing he played his cards carefully.

All he had to do was convince himself of that.

Chapter 45

The next morning things seemed much simpler. Tom sat at the kitchen table, working through the logic of his situation.

His big mistake, it seemed to him, had been promising Emily Sanders not to tell anyone about her part in the bogus insurance visit. She was worried that it would come back to haunt her, but it seemed a small thing in the light of what had happened since then. If he could work round that obstacle, it would clear the way for him to go to the police.

That still left the problem of Mickey Choat. Tom had promised not to reveal that he'd stolen Ben Bradwell's computer. But surely death threats and some kind of sinister plot took precedence over petty theft?

He wasn't clear what to do about Mickey, but he felt he must be able to resolve things with Emily. He glanced at his watch: just after ten o'clock. He called her number.

She answered immediately. "Thank you for a lovely dinner."

He screwed his face up in embarrassment. He'd sent her two apologetic texts the day after the dinner, but she hadn't replied to either of them. He hadn't been able to bring himself to speak to her.

He decided to keep the tone light. He said, "You're up already, then."

"Last night was my night off, so no need for a lie-in this morning. Things to do, places to go."

"You're still speaking to me, then?"

"Course I am! Why shouldn't I? You've given me an awesome story to tell. I've never been double-booked on a date before." She chuckled. "Airlines do that with seats, but this was something else."

He groaned. "I don't know what got into Jan. She never changes her mind like that – and she hates those dinners. This was completely out of character."

"So you sneak behind her back quite a lot, do you?"

"No, no, no!" He was surprised at his own vehemence.

"This was just a one-off, was it?"

"It wasn't anything. I just … I thought it would be nice."

"It's all right, I'm just giving you a hard time."

The conversation was meandering away from its original objective, yet Tom was reluctant to redirect it. If he told her point blank that he was going to reveal her insurance ruse to the police, he had a strong sense that there would be no more conversations like this.

Instead he said, "Maybe I could make amends."

"What did you have in mind?"

He cast around for inspiration. If he could persuade her to meet up again, perhaps he could ease her into the idea that he was going to the police. A little wildly he said, "A proper dinner. In London. Somewhere nice."

"La Gavroche? Bibendum? I come expensive."

"Better let me check my bank account."

Another laugh. "It's all right, I'm just messing with you."

"I'm serious! I'd like to do it. But I'll need to work out how to swing it." Immediately he regretted saying that. It made the whole idea sound furtive and tawdry. He added, "Ah, did I just shoot myself in the foot?"

She said nothing for a moment, then, "What's the situation with you and her? Are you getting married soon or what?"

"God, no!"

She chuckled. "Sounds like I touched a raw nerve."

There was a moment's silence, then he said, "Thanks for cheering me up."

"I didn't know I had."

"I had a horrible experience yesterday. I really needed the lift."

"What sort of experience?"

"Best if you don't ask."

"Well, we're here to oblige."

* * *

Jan was unusually friendly when she bustled in that evening. "Did you miss me last night?"

"I survived."

"Fillet steaks tonight. I'm starving."

Fillet steaks had a special resonance for them. They tended to imply red wine, a long evening and a longer night together. A few weeks ago Tom would have been pleased; it would have been evidence that Jan was ready to rebuild their relationship. He would have reciprocated. Now, however, things had moved on, and it was hard to see how they could ever go back. All the same, he felt more than a pang of guilt over his phone call to Emily.

He sautéed the potatoes and prepared the salad and the dressing, then hovered as Jan grilled the steaks. She was smiling in that rare and mysterious way of hers, radiating warmth and indeterminate promise. He'd seen little enough of it in recent weeks, and he should have been pleased and relieved. Yet as he watched her, he found himself reflecting that he still didn't really know her. They'd lunged into their relationship, sharing early confidences with abandon, but somewhere along the line her revelations had come to an end, and in retrospect he realised he'd learned little more about her since then.

He owed it to her to bring this situation to an end. Two-timing went against his nature, and it surprised him that he'd allowed his dalliance with Emily to develop as far as it had. It might not lead anywhere, but if there was any future with Jan, it shouldn't be happening at all. And if there was no future, he should make that clear.

Yet this seemed hardly the time to rock the boat. Yesterday's death threat was worrying enough. He couldn't bring himself to throw his personal life into turmoil as well, especially when Jan seemed to be making such an effort.

All the same, he wasn't sorry when she turned to him at the end of the evening, saying, "I'm beat. Do you mind if we call it a day?"

He retreated to his room with a sense of guilty relief.

Chapter 46

Marcus Headington phoned out of the blue next morning. Tom was surprised. It was many weeks since they'd met, and he hadn't expected to remain on Headington's radar.

"Tom, you made a nice job of writing up that interview you did with me – and I liked your roundup on the fake bomb."

"Did you ever find out who was responsible for that?"

"No we didn't. The latest is that the police think it was some lone zealot, trying to make a point. We're keeping an open mind."

"So what can I do for you?"

"We're holding a seminar on Thursday – a talking shop for thought leaders and the press. We've booked a hotel suite in the West End. Very short notice, but I thought you might like to come along."

"I'd love to." Tom hesitated. "I'm surprised that you're phoning round yourself."

"It's a last-minute thing." Headington gave a sigh. "We're short-handed today, so I said I would roll up my sleeves. We want to make sure we get a good cross-section of interested parties."

"I'll look forward to seeing you there."

He ended the call with a sense of bemusement. One minute his life seemed to be drawing him back towards transport management, the next minute he was being nudged in the direction of mainstream journalism. The only problem was he had no specific commission to cover this event. Would Malcolm Drew have someone on hand at the seminar? He phoned him to ask.

"I've got a freelance covering it," Malcolm said, "but if you can come up with a background 'think' piece, we can probably make room for that as well. I can't pay you a lot for it, though."

It was enough. It validated the visit, and gave him a solid reason for going to London again. That meant he could meet up with Emily, and he wasn't about to ignore the opportunity. He googled restaurants in west London in search of something both affordable and adequately impressive, and settled on one in the King's Road.

He checked his watch: eleven in the morning. He called Emily's number, and she answered promptly. He said, "Could you get a night off work this Thursday? I'm ready to book a table."

"That was quick. I thought you were bluffing about the dinner."

"I never bluff about food."

She laughed. "Depends if I can swap shifts tomorrow. Where did you have in mind?"

He told her the name of the restaurant.

"That'll do nicely. I hope you've checked your bank account."

Crossing his fingers, he turned back to his laptop and booked himself into a hotel in Chiswick for the night. He'd just logged off when Emily phoned him back.

"I've arranged to do the lunchtime shift instead of the evening, so I'm clear for Thursday. What time do I turn up – and how many other women will I be fighting off when I get there?"

*　*　*

The seminar delivered little that was new. Tom listened attentively and made copious notes, but he had to wait until the first coffee break before he heard anything that had him pricking up his ears. That was when he found himself in conversation with a journalist from one of the daily newspapers, who said, "Did you hear that Victor Rudge was thinking of shifting his financial empire to Frankfurt?" The journalist was speaking *sotto voce*.

"Seriously? That would be a bit of a betrayal, wouldn't it?"

"If it's true, it just shows he's got his head screwed on. He might be making a fuss about leaving the EU, but he's got his Plan B in place for when we go."

"*If* we go."

"I wouldn't build on the idea of any doubt, if I were you."

"But you don't have a real source for this?"

The journalist gave him an ironic smile. "It's just a rumour. If there were a proper story in it, I wouldn't be telling you about it."

"So you don't give any credence to it?"

"Not really. It's typical of the misinformation that's washing round this subject. You can bet your life some mischief-maker has been putting it about."

The journalist drifted away, and Tom went over to the coffee table in search of something to eat. He became aware of Marcus Headington standing next to him.

"Useful event?" Headington asked.

"Fascinating. It's remarkable the way you're keeping this debate alive."

"Someone has to." Headington poured himself a coffee from one of the urns. "Have you seen this morning's news headline? Supposedly I'm one of Britain's ten top traitors. Why? Simply because I dare to question the wisdom of leaving the EU."

"I don't know how you put up with that kind of thing."

"You think that's bad? What about the tweets I get every day, saying I should be exterminated from the face of the earth?" He shook his head grimly. "And we're supposed to be living in a democracy."

He picked up his coffee and half-turned to leave, then said, "The internet is responsible for a lot of the misinformation out there. We keep hearing about transparency and openness, yet actually it's providing a gift for the manipulative and the devious."

"It serves both sides, of course."

"So you think it comes down to which side uses it most unscrupulously?"

"Maybe."

"It makes you despair, doesn't it?"

Headington started to move away, then turned back. "We're putting on another big conference in November. You must come along. We're not going to be silenced by defeatism and media spin."

"Thanks – I'll look forward to it."

Chapter 47

Tom smiled across the table at Emily, who was tackling her guinea fowl with vigour. She seemed to have a remarkable appetite for someone so slim. He said, "Do you think Victor Rudge could be planning on transferring his financial organisation to Germany when we leave the EU? One or two people were whispering that today."

She looked up. "I very much doubt it, given his history."

"How do you mean?"

"I thought you would know. He's from German Jewish stock. His grandparents fled the country just before the second world war and came over to England. I don't think he would be very keen on relocating to the old country."

"Rudge doesn't sound a very German name."

"I think he took his mother's maiden name."

He nodded, filing away this information for future reference.

Emily was wearing the same purple dress she'd chosen for their aborted dinner arrangement. "Since we're having a re-run, I thought I'd stick to the same props," she'd told him as he greeted her.

There was a lively buzz about the restaurant. They were seated next to a long row of windows. A lantern flame was flickering outside. It was a romantic setting, but he wondered how romantic the evening would seem by the end.

She said, "Any exciting bits of news at your seminar today?"

"I got the sense that there's a disagreement between Victor Rudge and Marcus Headington. Marcus wants the final decision on leaving the EU to be thrashed out in a parliamentary vote, whereas Victor still wants a second referendum."

"I see you're tuning up your reporter's instincts. You almost sound like a proper journalist."

"Who says I'm not a proper journalist?"

"You don't seem to think you are."

He was both annoyed and intrigued to realise that her opinion mattered to him. A little defensively he said, "I'm trying to refocus my career. It's a difficult call."

"You're lucky to have two jobs to juggle with. I'm only just hanging on to one."

This wasn't something he wanted to hear. If he was injudicious in the way he told the police about the death threat and his suspicions about Martin Frankl, Emily's one job could be in jeopardy.

She said, "I suppose all of us in the campaign wanted a second referendum at the beginning. The trouble is, these days it's a precarious bet."

"I thought you'd left the campaign."

"Not in my heart."

Her words touched him. She was looking at him with an expression that mingled enthusiasm and regret, and for a moment he was lost for words.

To lighten the mood, he said, "You sound more like a politician than an actress."

"Actor."

"Actor, sorry."

She grinned at him. "I'll forgive you that." She sipped her wine. "I got into politics at college, but in the end I decided acting was more fun. The only trouble is, I never get to do any."

"You'll get your break in the end."

"Yeah, a lot of people have told me that. I'm still waiting."

He sat back and smiled at her, marvelling at the way she managed to project such a complex mix of self-deprecating humour and commitment to the things she believed in. And on top of that, she was attractive – strikingly attractive. It was strange that he hadn't been more aware of it the first time he met her. Her smooth complexion was broken only by laughter lines at the sides of her mouth. Her hair was its usual dark golden colour, but she'd added extra highlights since he last saw her.

She smiled back at him. "What?"

"Nothing. It's strange how things work out, isn't it?"

* * *

Over coffee he brought up the subject of Mickey Choat and Ben Bradwell's computer. He described the visit by the man who had issued the death threat. She listened with mounting amazement.

"My god, Tom, this is unbelievable! What does it mean?"

"I don't know. I'm assuming Ben found out something that could be seriously harmful to somebody, and that person is determined to keep it quiet."

"And you think it has something to do with the Stay and Prosper campaign?"

"I'm pretty sure of it, but I don't have any proof."

"Have you talked to the police?"

"Not yet."

"Why not? This is terrible! People can't just barge into your home and threaten to kill you, and get away with it."

"There's a problem."

"What?" She was watching him closely, and enlightenment slowly spread across her face. "I get it. You want to tell them about me coming to see you and pretending to be an insurance agent."

"I don't see how I can avoid it."

"But *why*?"

He toyed with a spare knife on the table. "I need to tie these threats up with everything else that's been happening to me." He looked up at her. "If I don't mention you and Martin Frankl, I'll only be telling them half the story."

"But a death threat is a death threat. Surely it's up to the police to work out what's going on? It's not your job. It might have nothing to do with Martin."

"You have to admit that the insurance thing was extremely weird. Have you ever heard anything like it before?"

"No, but it was pretty harmless, wasn't it?"

"I don't know. I don't have the first idea what it was all about. Do you?"

Abruptly she pushed her chair back. "Is that what this is all about? Are you telling me you brought me here just to butter me up? What did you expect me to say? Yes, yes, by all means report me to the police?"

He shook his head vehemently. "I asked you here to make up for the balls-up at the dinner dance."

She merely stared at him.

"And I asked you so that I could explain what's happening."

She started to get up. "You mean you wanted to break it to me that you're shafting me."

"That's not it at all." But he knew that to a large extent she was right.

Her chair made a scraping sound as she pushed it fully back. "You're perfectly right, of course. You have every right to go to the police. So go ahead – do it. What did I expect? It won't be the first time I've been out of a job." She picked up her jacket from the back of her chair. "I'm so fucking *stupid*!"

"No you're not." He was floundering now. "It's just a pity you went through with that insurance scam in the first place."

"I *know* I shouldn't have done it, and I'm VERY SORRY. How many times do I have to say it?" The table pressed against him as she squeezed out into the gangway. "Thank you for the dinner. I assume you're paying?"

"Of course."

"Fine. Bye then." She started on her way to the exit, then turned back. "You know what's ironical about this? If I hadn't come down to your house in Hampshire, I wouldn't know you in the first place. We're only having this conversation because I did. Talk about going round in circles."

Chapter 48

"I'm going to spend a week in Winchester."

Tom looked at Jan expectantly. He was awaiting some indignant riposte, but she said nothing.

"I might make it a fortnight. In fact I'll probably just stay there for good."

"You know my brother's wedding is coming up in a few weeks' time?"

"That's OK. It won't affect what I do, will it?"

"Can't you wait a few more weeks? Then we can go back to Winchester together."

"Why?"

She seemed to falter, then said, "The contractors have been on to me. There's some problem with the new wiring here. It doesn't meet Building Regulations or something. They need to reinstall it, but they can't start for a couple of weeks."

"More cost?"

"No, it's their mistake, so they'll pay. But they need to do work in most of the rooms, and then make good again. Someone needs to be here."

"Well why don't you work from home, or get Dennis from next door to keep an eye on things?"

"But you're here all the time."

"Not necessarily. I'm still talking to Felix about signing up with him again for six months. I'll probably have a lot of travelling to do – maybe some nights away. It makes sense for me to be based in Winchester. It's nearer the office and the motorway."

"It's hardly ideal timing, Tom. And what about the arrangement with Dr Melcombe? Don't you have a catch-up appointment fixed with him next week?"

"I can contact the surgery in Winchester and tell them I want to go back to the old arrangement."

She looked ready to protest, but in the end said nothing.

He said, "I need to get my life sorted out, Jan. I need to move on. Staying here – " he gestured round the room – "I'm in a backwater. I'm not getting anywhere."

What he meant was that their relationship was in a backwater. Although he had alienated Emily last night, the fact that he'd become interested in her at all was telling him something. The unresolved situation with Jan couldn't continue. He'd decided he needed to force the issue, and he'd confronted her as she arrived home that evening.

But now Jan seemed to relent. "I see what you're saying. Maybe it does make sense for you to go back to Winchester. I can hold the fort here until the work is done."

He should have made this a conversation about their relationship, not about the mechanics of where they lived. Now she'd taken away the initiative. In a rearguard move, he said, "Are you sure you want to come back to Winchester at all?"

"Of course I do. Why wouldn't I?"

He couldn't adjust quickly enough. He wasn't primed for a weighty conversation about their life together. She gave him a quick smile and bustled off to shower and change.

He sat down with a sigh, and turned his mind to the other question that had been nagging at him all day. Should he contact Bernard again, and re-schedule the meeting with his policeman friend?

In theory, if he put aside his curiosity about Ben Bradwell and stopped trying to find out what had happened to him during the missing week of his accident, there would be no need for the meeting. He could simply continue with his life. The people making threats against him would go away, and he wouldn't need to report Emily's scam to the police. Subject closed.

Yet he knew it wasn't true. He couldn't simply assume that those people would let him alone. They might decide that whatever he knew or might find out, it was too risky for them to leave to chance. They might come after him anyway. The thought seemed almost laughably melodramatic, but he simply couldn't dismiss it.

He reached for his phone.

* * *

"Let's just run though this again in the correct chronological order."
Bernard's friend Joe gave Tom a penetrating look.

They'd met up in a pub along the road from Bernard's house on the
outskirts of Southampton. Joe was somewhere in his sixties – trim in
build, with a heavily lined face and a full head of fine dark hair streaked
with grey.

Tom said, "Do you want me to go back to the beginning?"

"No, I'll give you my take, and you can correct me if I get
anything wrong."

"Fair enough."

"OK, so first off, you go to this conference in London, and you come
across this guy Bradwell – someone you might have met at Carswells in
the past, only you don't remember."

Tom nodded.

"Then he leaves a message on your voicemail machine about
meeting you, only you don't have the tape any more. And he texts you
to confirm the meet, but you don't have the phone in question either.
So you shoot off somewhere in your car – maybe to meet him, but you
don't know for sure. And on the way back you hit a tree and end up in
hospital, with no memory of the preceding week"

"You're making this sound like a load of nothing."

"I'm just going through the sequence of events as you explained
them to me."

"OK, OK."

"Meanwhile, Bradwell ends up at the bottom of a cliff, but there are
no witnesses to his death, and there's nothing to suggest it wasn't suicide.

"So there you are recuperating, and this man ... Frankl? ... from the
Remain campaign office sends a minion to check out your memory loss.
She tells him it's a hundred per cent kosher. But that's the end of that
story, so far as we know."

"Correct."

"Then you contact this man Bradwell's ex-partner, and he reckons someone might have broken into Bradwell's flat. Later on, he works out that Bradwell's old computer is missing. But never mind, he's already stolen his mate's shiny new one. Then someone breaks into his own flat, presumably looking for it, but that's OK because now he's given it to his sister."

Tom nodded again.

"So you persuade him to let you take this computer home with you. But before you get a proper look at what's on it, a bad man comes along and takes it away from you. Oh, I think I forgot to mention that someone has already broken into your house and stolen that message tape and the phone." He sat back. "Have I missed anything?"

"The death threat," Tom said a flat voice. "Let's not forget that."

Joe lifted his pint from the table. "Don't get me wrong, Tom, I believe everything you've told me. But unfortunately it doesn't add up to much."

"Death threats? Not much?" Tom frowned at him.

Joe wiped his mouth with the back of his hand and put his glass down. "There's no evidence of all this, is there? No one reported any of these break-ins, and your phone and tape are gone."

"Ben Bradwell's mother must have reported that his old computer was missing."

"She may well have done, but she was hundreds of miles away at the time, and she only had his mate's word that it ever even existed. And the mate didn't notice it was missing until weeks later, by which time the trail would have gone cold, assuming there was one."

"It *did* go missing. I'm certain Mickey Choat wasn't lying."

"I'm not saying he was. What I'm saying is that whoever these people are, they're professionals. They know how to break and enter without leaving a single clue, and from what you say about your visitor, they're supremely confident."

"Doesn't my word count for anything? I was there when this guy rocked up. I had to sit there being humiliated."

"Of course it counts for something, but there's no independent corroboration. And what are we supposed to think this is all about?

According to you, it has something to do with these pro-Remain people, but you don't actually have any evidence for that, do you?"

"That man told me to keep my mouth shut and stop interfering."

"But he didn't actually specify what he meant by that, did he?"

Reluctantly Tom said, "I suppose not. He seemed to think it was obvious."

"But strictly speaking, it's just guesswork."

Tom had another thought. "Ben Bradwell wrote some names down in his notes. That must mean something, doesn't it? I still have a picture of them on my phone."

Joe looked at him reproachfully. "I don't think anyone's going to build a Federal case on the back of some doodling."

Tom glanced at Bernard, who smiled encouragingly.

Joe said, "As far as I can see, the only thing anyone could actually investigate here is the way that woman tricked you into believing she was from your insurance company. But you say you want to keep her name out of it – and in any case, there's nothing concrete to link her visit with all this other stuff you're telling me. We don't know what it was about."

"Don't you see some sort of pattern here?"

"Oh yes, I see a pattern." He smiled grimly, which Tom took to be mildly encouraging. "The trouble is, this is armchair detective work. If you want the police to allocate real-world money and resources to investigating this, you need to give them somewhere to start. You don't have much to offer."

Bernard said, "And I keep telling Tom, if he reports all this, they'll start off by investigating *him*. They'll only take him seriously when they've got past that point."

Joe said to Tom, "They'll get there in the end, but we already know you, whereas they don't. They won't take your word for anything – they'll do things by the book."

Tom sat pensively for several moments, glancing between the two men. Finally he said, "What would you do if you were me?"

Joe said, "I'd go to the cops – but then, I would say that, wouldn't I?" He thought for a moment. "I suppose you might consider whether you could offer them better evidence – something more convincing."

"But that's not much good if these people find out that I'm meddling again, and decide to kill me before I have the chance to report it." He gave an indignant half-laugh.

"You'd certainly be well advised not to do anything stupid."

"Can't you use your influence with your ex-mates to fast-track this with them? Surely they'll listen to you?"

Joe looked at him carefully before replying. "Convince me, and I'll do my best to convince them."

"I thought you already believed me?"

"I just need something I can work with."

Chapter 49

Tom was conscious that he'd kept Felix Schaefer waiting too long over his job offer. He'd been putting off responding, but he had to make a decision some time. He called him the day after he returned to Winchester. His old life seemed to be pulling him back in more ways than one.

"If the contract offer is still on the table, the answer is yes."

"Excellent!" Felix sounded genuinely pleased. "I already have a job for you. I'm putting put together a proper document for new members to explain the Carswell network, and I need a section on our latest computer system. Not a technical manual – a plain man's guide to the benefits. I want you to go and talk to my IT man in Brighton, Simon Meredith. Get him to describe it all to you, then rewrite it in words I can understand."

As Tom finished the call, he realised he now had a tailor-made opportunity to catch Mickey Choat in person. He'd been worried about phoning him since hearing the intruder's warning: "We'll be watching you." Would these people really be monitoring his phone calls? Could they? Did that apply to Mickey's calls as well as his own? He was in no mood to put all this to the test.

He drove over to Brighton two days later, and spent a useful couple of hours with Simon Meredith, a genial man with thick-lensed spectacles and a strangely unblinking gaze. Simon gave him a patient account of the company's computer system – how it worked and why it worked well – and Tom made extensive notes, hoping he would be able to interpret them properly when he read them over.

Simon only offered one comment of protest. "I don't know why Felix didn't just ask me to write this up," he said. "I could have done it."

"Don't forget I was a journalist once. He wants a simplistic version, and he thinks that's what I'll come up with."

"And is he right?"

Tom laughed philosophically. "Probably."

The meeting ended in the middle of the afternoon. Tom said, "You must miss having Ben Bradwell on your team."

Simon nodded. "He was a real asset. In fact one of his last jobs for me last winter was rolling out the new IT system in Nottingham. We were having trouble integrating it with Rackham's old system, and their man on the spot was useless."

"I didn't know Ben had a roving brief."

"He didn't really, but I needed to have someone trustworthy up there to sort things out."

"And did he?"

"Oh yes, in the end everything was working like a charm." He paused. "Such a shame about what happened to him."

As Tom returned to his car he kept an eye out for Mickey Choat. He was in luck. He spotted him over in a corner of the yard, steam-cleaning his van. His curly hair and beaked nose were immediately recognisable through the swirling clouds of mist. Mickey turned and lifted a hand in greeting as he walked over. "Hello, mate."

"How's it going?"

"All right. How are you doing with Ben's laptop?"

"Not so well."

Mickey switched off the steam cleaner and put down the hose.

"What's the matter?"

Tom described how the computer had been taken from him. Mickey listened with growing alarm. "Bloody hell," he said at the end of it. "This isn't funny."

"I know. That's why I wanted to tell you this in person. I didn't want to phone you in case these people have some way of listening in."

"Are you for real about that?"

Tom squinted at him. "I don't know. Maybe not. We can't be that important to them. If they wanted to get rid of us, they would have done it already."

"Charming." Mickey started peeling off the heavy orange gloves he'd been using for the cleaning job. "I suppose you think we should tell the cops about this." He gave Tom a disconsolate frown.

"I know you don't want to, but if we don't, we'll be letting these people do what they like and get away with it. I don't think the cops would worry about you taking Ben's laptop. This looks much bigger to me."

"Maybe." He still seemed dubious. "What are you doing here, anyway?"

"I'm doing some work for the company."

"I thought you'd left Carswells a long time ago."

"It's a favour to the boss."

Mickey nodded absently. "But you're not going to the cops?"

"That's what we ought to do."

"Just let me think about it for a day or to." He put his rubber gloves back on, then stooped and picked up the steam cleaning hose.

* * *

The conversation with Mickey had been frustrating. Tom had wanted a clear consensus that they should take their concerns to the police, but he'd failed to establish one. If he convinced Joe he had solid evidence of what was happening, he would be on his own.

He decided to call Mickey and try one more time to square things with him, but he was still nervous about being overheard. Then a remedy occurred to him. The following morning he went in search of the nearest phone shop, and bought himself a cheap pay-as-you-go phone. Presumably it would take these shadowy people a while to cotton on to its existence.

Ironically, that evening Mickey phoned him. He was calling on Tom's main phone, but instinct told Tom there was no point in protesting. Mickey sounded as if he'd just come back from the pub. "I've been thinking," he started ponderously. "You're not going to the cops about all this stuff, are you?"

"That's what we ought to do."

"All I can say is, if you drag me into it, I'll deny everything. I don't want any part of it."

"Don't you want to know what happened to Ben?"

"Of course I do!" Mickey suddenly sounded angrier than Tom had ever known him. "Don't treat me like a fucking idiot. But if somebody killed him and got away with it, and now they've nicked his computer, what else might they do? I don't want to be next in line, and I don't want Amy involved in this." He paused. "You need to stop acting like a one-man police force, mate. Look where it's got us."

"I know. I'm sorry. That's why I should go to the real police. I know you don't want me to, but at least we'd get some proper backup."

"You're dead set on making things worse, aren't you?"

"Come on – they're not going to worry about you taking Ben's computer, are they? We could be talking about murder and conspiracy here. This is big league."

There was a very long silence. Finally Mickey said, "I might have nicked some other stuff from time to time. They might haul me up over that."

"What other stuff?"

"Nothing to do with this. Just this and that. But I'm off their radar at the moment. I don't want to put myself back on it."

"Don't Carswells pay you enough?"

Mickey was instantly angry again. "What gives you the right to pass judgement, sitting in your shiny office? You don't know anything about my life."

Quietly, Tom said, "No I don't. But I don't want to be in these people's firing line any more than you do. The police might be our only protection."

"I'm not convinced." He clicked off.

Chapter 50

"Did you hear about Donald Finch, the civil servant? He's just resigned."

It was Malcolm Drew from the *Seismic Scene* website. He'd phoned as Tom was preparing breakfast the following Monday.

Tom felt caught out by the call. He'd accepted the six-month contract with Carswells without telling Malcolm he couldn't take on the journalist's job. He hadn't even made any progress with his promised follow-up article for the site.

Sliding into automatic mode, he said, "Why did he resign?"

"A parliamentary question was asked about the Monck Chervil investment. Someone wanted to know why the Government subsidy was waved through and then suddenly cancelled."

"And?"

"The junior minister who was involved in the project said he'd been acting in good faith. He blamed the civil service. He said he was given wrong advice, and then it was rescinded. And of course Donald Finch was the man who provided it."

"Was it a resigning issue for the minister?"

"Not necessarily, but the Opposition always jumps on anything that looks bad for the Government. My guess is that the minister needed a scapegoat. Somehow he persuaded Finch to resign so that he wouldn't have to."

"What's the name of this junior minister?"

"Elias Wallington. He's the MP for some rural constituency in the Midlands."

Tom considered this. "I'm guessing you're looking to me to write something about this."

"I just thought it might fit in with the new article you're already working on. You *are* working on it, are you?"

"Yes, but it's been on the back burner, I'm afraid."

"Maybe you should shift it to the front burner." Malcolm paused. "I had to make a decision about filling our editorial vacancy. I assumed you didn't want the regular job with us."

"I should have got back to you about that. Life has been … complicated."

"Well, I can uncomplicate that part for you. I've got an ex-*Times* journalist on board now, so you're off the hook."

"I'm sorry I didn't let you know."

"But if you're up for writing the follow-up piece, we'll still run it. You made it sound pretty heady stuff."

"It should be, but there's a way to go before I can complete anything."

"OK. Well have a look into this Finch thing. It might fit in."

Tom hung up feeling annoyed and disappointed with himself. Malcolm's writing job had seemed potent with promise, yet he'd passed it up through his own inertia, and gone back to what he was doing before. This simply wasn't like him. He was put in mind of the famous advice from Arthur Ransome, the children's novelist: "Grab a chance and you won't be sorry for a might-have-been."

He'd always tried to live up to that aspiration, but in this case clearly he'd failed.

* * *

Glancing out of the window, Tom spotted Christine sweeping autumn leaves from her pathway. Her long dark hair was bobbing behind her. He hadn't seen her since his return to Winchester. He went outside and called over to her.

She looked up and smiled. "Hello stranger."

He could tell she was in a good mood. It was as if a benign bubble was hovering round her. He crossed the road. "How are things going with David?"

"Not badly. He's given up his flat in Southampton."

"So it's pretty permanent."

"I think so."

"I'm glad for you."

"How's the leg?"

"Mending well. Thanks for asking."

She leaned her brush on the wall, wiped her hands together and folded her arms. "So are you back in Winchester for good?"

"Probably. I've had enough of the country life."

"I don't see any sign of Jan."

"She's coming back eventually. There are things she needs to sort out at the house in Storton."

"So you really did patch things up?"

She'd asked him something like this before. He wondered why she kept coming back to it. He said, "What exactly did I say to you? You seem pretty convinced things were going downhill between us."

She wrinkled her nose. "You mean you really don't remember?"

"Apparently not."

She seemed to weigh her words for a moment. "You told me you were splitting up. You said you'd had a big bust-up, and you'd told her you'd had enough. After you'd calmed down, the two of you talked it through, and she decided she was going to leave. I think she was going to stay in her dad's place until she decided what to do."

This should be a bombshell, yet immediately it seemed to fit in with all that had been happening. Nevertheless, Tom heard himself saying, "Seriously?"

She gave an edgy laugh. "You don't think I'm making this up, do you?"

"No, no, of course not. But she hasn't said a single thing to me about this. It's as if it never happened."

"It was quite sudden. You said you'd been trying to work things out with her, but then … you found out something."

"What kind of something?"

She gave him an awkward look. "You decided she was having an affair."

He said nothing for a moment. She was watching him warily, perhaps fearing an indignant riposte. Finally he said, "That's an interesting choice of words. Do you really mean I decided this, or I knew it for a fact?"

She shrugged. "I don't know, Tom. It wasn't a long conversation. I think you just had suspicions."

"Did I confront her about it?"

"I don't know. I suppose so."

"And did I say who the other person was?"

"No. I don't think you knew."

He breathed in deeply. "I'm glad you've told me this."

"I wanted to talk about it before, but you wrote me that email saying you didn't want anything more to do with me."

"If I said that, I don't know what the hell I was on about. It seems so ridiculous."

"You might think that now, but you sounded deadly serious at the time. I nearly didn't say anything today."

"But honestly – one minute I'm leaving Jan, the next minute I'm falling out with you. It doesn't make any sense." He shook his head. "Did I say I'd changed my mind about splitting up with Jan?"

"No, nothing like that. Your email was just a few lines long."

"I wish you still had it."

She shrugged. "Anyway, I'm glad we're still speaking." She looked down for a moment, then back up at him. "I hope I've done the right thing, telling you about all this."

"Of course you have. I'll probably remember it myself in the end. There's no need to feel you have to take responsibility."

"Does it change things? I mean, Jan seems to have been very good to you all this time – helping you get over your injuries. She probably wants things to go back to the way they were before."

"Maybe you're right." He looked at her without speaking for a moment. "Thanks for being straight with me. I need to go away and think about this. Can we talk again?"

"Of course. Any time."

*   *   *

He walked back stiffly across the road, feeling foolish. As he reached the house he heard Christine's front door shut. It seemed symbolic.

She'd shared her information; now it was down to him to deal with it.

He ran his mind over what he'd just learned. Apparently he'd told Jan he was splitting up with her, and she'd accepted it. Yet when she realised he'd lost his memory of that week, she must have decided not to remind him what had passed between them. It was a massive omission.

What was she thinking? Was she hoping he would never recover his memory? Or was she simply assuming that he would regret his decision to split up if he ever did?

Either way, she must have been living on tenterhooks, especially while he was in hospital and when he first moved to the village. It probably explained why she'd been so distant a lot of the time. At any moment, he might have remembered everything. Their domestic arrangements might have fallen apart at a stroke.

He couldn't decide how he should feel towards her. Since he'd returned to Winchester his overriding sense had been one of relief. They might not have formalised their separation, but that was what this seemed to amount to. He'd been feeling it was probably for the best.

Now he was perplexed. Whatever Jan's motivations, she'd made a massive effort to keep him on side. She seemed determined to stay with him despite everything.

Yet if that were the case, where was the warmth he should have expected? It was there in small doses, but most of the time since the accident she'd seemed remote and edgy – so remote, in fact, that he'd gradually become interested in another woman.

Should he conclude that she really was having an affair? His mind jumped to the time when he'd become friendly with Danni at his office. Now that he thought about it, Jan had been acting in much the same mercurial way back then. Could the explanation have been the same?

Chapter 51

"Tom, it's Marcus. I hope you don't mind. I wanted to pick your brains."

Tom smiled in wonder. He'd been surprised when Headington had phoned him to invite him to the seminar in London, but he'd done that because his team was short-handed. To be phoned by the great man and asked for advice was something else. What advice could Tom possibly have to offer?

This was one of his free days. Twice a week he was now driving down to the Carswell offices in Eastleigh. Sometimes he visited Carswell branches, mostly on his own. The rest of the time he was free to do as he pleased. Felix seemed happy enough with this arrangement.

He told Headington, "I'm flattered that you keep remembering me."

"Of course I do." The affable, confiding manner was coming through strongly. "You were with us on the night of the bomb scare. That gives you a special place in our history."

Tom chuckled. "I'm not sure it's something I want to be remembered for."

"Look, the reason for my call – we're canvassing a few of our contacts for inspiration. We've got this major conference coming up, and we're still organising speakers. I'll be frank with you – we were hoping to get Gordon Brown to give an address, but we couldn't pull it off."

The former Prime Minister was a noted Remain advocate. To have booked him for the conference would have been a major coup for the campaign. Tom said, "That's a shame."

"Yes, but now we're re-thinking how to play it. Instead of replacing him with another big name, we're taking a different approach. We want to bring in fresh blood – to let rank and file Remainers put their case. We're looking for two or three good speakers to talk for around ten minutes each – younger people, preferably. We're open to ideas."

"Surely you have a ready-made resource on your doorstep –

your own volunteers? I'd have thought they would jump at it."

"We've already looked at that, and one of our guys is going to do it – a young man of nineteen. He's future ministerial material, in my book. But the others aren't keen. They see themselves as back-room people. They don't want to stick themselves in front of an audience."

An idea sprang into Tom's mind. He said, "Do you know Emily Sanders? She used to be on your research team."

"Yes, I think so. Striking young woman – good sense of humour. She left us a while back, if I remember rightly."

"She was asked to leave by Martin Frankl."

"Was she indeed? I don't think I knew that. You're still in touch with her, are you?"

"In a manner of speaking."

"A bright and articulate lady." Headington was warming to the thought. "Very committed. I should have thought of her in the first place."

"But I don't suppose you would want to get into conflict with Martin over this."

"That would depend on why she left. Do you know?"

Now Tom was moving into murky waters. He said, "I think it was personal."

"Well, that's up to her and Martin. We wouldn't be asking her to work for us again – just to do a one-off presentation. I'll give her a call."

Quickly Tom said, "If you don't mind, would you let me have a word with her first? It's a long story, but I feel this would work better coming from me."

"Fine. Will you do that for me? But I need an answer within a day or so at the latest. You know where to reach us."

* * *

Tom put the phone down and sat back in sudden panic. What had he just done? If this conversation got back to Martin Frankl, which it surely would, he would know for certain that Tom had been in contact with Emily. That would inevitably tell him that Tom had discovered the truth about the fake insurance visit. Given that knowledge, what would Frankl do?

The best-case scenario was nothing. After all, Tom had never challenged him on the visit, so why should Frankl think he would do so now? Frankl himself would presumably be the last person to expose Emily's part in the ruse, since it would reveal his own involvement. Therefore no harm should come to her from this new development. On the face of it, the episode had faded into history.

But what if it was connected to the mystery surrounding Ben Bradwell's death? If so, then putting Emily in the limelight would be a red rag to a bull.

Tom shut his eyes as he tried to juggle the events of recent months into some kind of coherence. The key question was simple enough: was Emily's visit connected to Ben Bradwell's death or not?

Instinct told him no. The whole insurance affair had an amateurish, improvised quality about it. It had been cleverly executed, but it had never been watertight. There had always been a possibility that Tom might discover the truth by accident – which was exactly what had happened. By contrast, the people who had stolen Ben Bradwell's computer and data seemed consummate professionals. They would never have left so much to chance.

Tom opened his eyes again, feeling moderately reassured. There was no need for him to unpick anything. He could still contact Emily and put the idea of the conference presentation to her – or he could do nothing, and allow the whole notion to lapse.

He smiled grimly to himself. He was assuming a lot in thinking Emily would even speak to him. And given her history with Frankl, it must be doubtful that she would consider giving a presentation at this event. Yet something told him she would be reluctant to pass it up, and he wanted to give her the chance. And if he was honest, he could see that it might be a way to win back her good will.

Chapter 52

Emily had gone to ground.

Tom phoned her mobile three times, but was transferred to voicemail each time. On the first attempt he simply asked her to call him back. The second time, he told her he hadn't gone to the police about the insurance visit, and might not have to. The final time, he said he'd come up with an opportunity for her to give a talk on the merits of staying in the EU. He didn't say where.

Nothing seemed to work.

He phoned the pub in Richmond and asked to speak to her. They told him she'd quit her job and gone to work somewhere nearer home. Did they know where? No they didn't.

He sent her a long and elaborate text message. She didn't reply. He sent a short one. Same result. He looked up her Facebook page, thinking he would send her a private message, then he abandoned the idea. Even if he got the message through, she wasn't going to read it.

He was stuck. He didn't know her home address, and couldn't think what to try next. Then he remembered her friend Sally at the Stay and Prosper office. Would she speak to him? It must be worth a try. However, he also remembered Emily telling him that Sally and Martin Frankl had once been an item. She'd said they'd broken up, but could he rely on that?

His determination to move things forward got the better of his doubts. That evening he phoned the campaign office and asked to speak to Sally. After a moment he was connected.

"This is Tom Anthony. We don't know each other, but I'm a friend of Emily Sanders."

"I know who you are." Her accent was upper middle class, her tone coolly noncommittal.

"Great. Well I'm trying to contact her, only she's not taking my calls. I wondered if you could help? It's quite urgent."

"If she doesn't want to speak to you, I don't think I should interfere."

"I just need to give her some news."

"What kind of news?"

Presumably Sally already knew about the presentation opportunity, and might even have asked to be considered for it herself, but she wouldn't necessarily have thought of telling Emily about it. He could ask her to pass on the information now – but what if she relayed the message to Frankl instead? It would be better for him to talk directly to Emily.

He said, "It's personal. I'd rather not go into it now, but she'll understand when I tell her about it."

Abruptly she said, "I'm sorry, I have to go. I have to be taught how to use the new computer system." A small sigh. "I thought I'd ducked out of it by now. I should have known they'd get me in the end."

Her switch to this conspiratorial tone seemed encouraging. He said, "I'm only asking you to give Emily a message."

"I don't know …"

"You'll be doing me a really big favour, and I bet she'll thank you for it."

"If you know Emily at all, you'll know she won't do anything just because I say so."

Another idea came to him. "What if you just tell me where she's working now?"

A pause, then she said, "It's the Old Goat in Chiswick High Road."

"Great – thanks." He decided to press his luck. "You don't happen to know what shift she's working this week?"

"Absolutely no idea."

*   *   *

The role of stalker was not a natural one for Tom.

Catching the train to Waterloo next morning was straightforward enough. Travelling to west London on the District line was more unnerving. What if Emily boarded the same train in Hammersmith?

She didn't, but he felt his heart rate speed up as he walked along Chiswick High Road. He could encounter her at any moment.

Traffic bustled past. He peered forward and behind him. The road stretched away in either direction – a long, tree-lined urban thoroughfare, with clusters of upmarket local shops merging into an endless parade.

He felt his pace slowing as the Old Goat came into view. It was an updated Victorian corner pub with a modern grey fascia. He walked gingerly inside. The owners had retained the original panelled interior, but added a gloss of urban chic. It was smaller than the bar in Richmond, and not especially crowded at the moment. He felt conspicuous as soon as the door closed behind him.

With good reason. Emily was there behind the bar, facing the entrance and pulling a pint. She saw him straight away, and froze for a moment with the pump handle half-way down.

Forcing himself not to hesitate, he walked over to the bar and stood next to the man she was serving. She took his money, then turned to Tom.

"What are you doing here?"

"Just passing?"

"Of course you are." She flicked her hair back off her shoulders. He'd forgotten that distinctive gesture.

"I just wanted a word."

"I don't think we have anything to talk about."

"Please."

She squared her shoulders as if in readiness for combat. "What can I get you?"

"A pint please, and a quick chat."

"We don't do chats, but I can do you the pint. Which beer?"

He pointed randomly at one of the pumps. As she filled the glass he said, "Did you pick up my phone messages?"

"No, I deleted them. I'm not into special pleading."

"Well thanks a lot. If you'd listened to them, you'd know I haven't gone to the police."

She looked at him curiously. "But you still might."

"Not if I can avoid it."

Three customers arrived at the bar together. She said, "Work to do. If you hang around, I might get the chance to speak to you later."

* * *

He took his pint over to a small table near the front window and sat there as customers came and went. He checked his email on his phone, then called up an e-book he was reading. Time passed.

Finally Emily came over and sat down facing him. "You're a stubborn bugger, aren't you? I thought if I waited long enough you'd get the message and go away."

He tried to read her mood. Was there a glimmer of amusement behind that frown? He said, "I came all the way from Hampshire this morning just for this. I'm not going to turn round and go back without giving it my best shot."

"Well three cheers for you."

"Why don't you just listen to what I have to say?"

"OK, try me."

"Right, here's what it is. Marcus Headington is looking for someone to give a ten-minute talk at the campaign's national conference in Manchester next month – a man in the street's view of Brexit. Or a woman in the street's view. I suggested you."

Her face broke into an ironic smile. "Oh, *you* suggested me? You and Marcus are just like that, are you?" She linked fingers to demonstrate. "Since when is this?"

"Of course we're not 'just like that'. I hardly know him. But I'm on his contact list. I was one of the people he called for inspiration."

"They've got a whole building full of volunteers who would jump at the chance to do a conference presentation."

"Apparently not. One of their guys is doing it, but they're still trying to find two more contenders."

"But I was fired. Why would they want me to do it?"

"You weren't fired. Martin Frankl simply told you to sod off. Marcus didn't know anything about it. He thinks you would be a good choice for this."

"I thought you said you didn't know him? Where are you getting all this from?"

"I'm just adding up two and two."

She thought about it. "But if you've recommended me, Martin will get to hear about it, won't he? He'll know we've been talking to each other. He'll know you found out about the insurance thing."

"But what can he do? So long as nobody accuses him of it or calls in the law, it might as well never have happened. He's not going to own up to it of his own accord, is he?"

"Yeah, but even if Marcus decides to use me, Martin will simply veto it."

Tom sat back. "Look, other things being equal, would you like to do it?"

"Yes!" She was looking animated for the first time today. "What exactly do they want me to talk about?"

"I think you're just supposed to describe what the EU means to you – why you think staying in it is such a good idea. I don't know the detail, but they'll probably let you cover whatever ground you like."

She was nodding absently, perhaps already thinking about what she would say. Then she focused on him again. "So how do we swing this?"

"I can get back to Marcus and try to head off Martin Frankl at the gulch."

"You and Marcus again?" A faint grin.

"I can give it my best shot."

She sat for a moment without speaking. He said, "You don't feel offended, only being offered a ten-minute talk?"

"God, no. Why should I?"

"Well, you're wise enough and confident enough to give a full-length presentation. Don't you feel a ten-minute slot is a bit demeaning? You could argue that they're treating you like a twelve-year-old."

"You're wise and confident enough too, but they're not giving you a slot at all, are they?" She shook her head. "No, it's a good offer. I'm grateful for whatever I can get."

He picked up his beer and drank the rest of it. She was looking at him curiously. She said, "Are you telling me you came all the way to London today just to have this conversation? That must have cost you a bit."

"If you will insist on not answering my messages …"

"All the same. Above and beyond, some people would call it." She gave him a deadpan look. "I suppose you want me to thank you for this?"

"Up to you. I just don't like people thinking badly of me."

She straightened. "I'd better get back to work. The managers here are all right, but it's not fair to the other staff if I sit around too long."

"I'll let you know what Marcus says."

Chapter 53

"How would you fancy a trip to the USA? In a couple of weeks' time?" Felix had clearly crafted the question to sound casual, but Tom guessed he'd posed it with care.

They were sitting in Felix's office the following morning. Tom looked at Felix cautiously. "To do what?"

"To hold my hand." Felix gave his version of a complicit smile. Actually it looked furtive rather than engaging, but after all these years Tom understood the intent. In his mind Felix would always be a kind of overgrown ferret. He had a ferret's agility and tenacity, but interpersonal skills had never been his strong point.

"Why are you going there?"

Felix glanced over at the door to ensure it was closed. "We're talking to Dunleavy Logistics about selling them a stake in Carswells. I told you about it a while ago. This trip is to tie up the deal."

"But why do you need me? I don't even work here full time."

Felix gave an impatient sigh. "I won't be telling them that." He glanced out of the window, then back at Tom. "I need your calming influence, that's what it is. I'm already taking Frank with me, but he's just a bean counter. He'll think he can bore them into submission. I need someone else there as well – someone with a lighter touch."

"Where is Dunleavy Logistics based?"

"Philadelphia."

"Well, I'm flattered to be asked.

"So you'll come?"

"Let me check the dates." He took out his phone and scrolled to his calendar app. Felix's American trip would come a couple of weeks before the Stay and Prosper conference, so there was no conflict.

"Looks as if I'm clear."

"Excellent. I'll get Martha to arrange it."

As Tom was walking out of the office his phone sounded. Glancing at the screen, he saw that it was Marcus Headington. As usual, he experienced a jolt of surprise at being called directly by the great man.

"Tom, Marcus here. Sorry to hassle you, but is that lady Emily Sanders willing to do the presentation for us? If not, I've found someone else who could take it on."

"Absolutely. I talked to her yesterday, and she'd love to do it. She'd be really disappointed to lose the opportunity at this stage."

"Excellent. I think she would be more suitable than this other person."

"There's just one thing." Tom hesitated. "May I speak frankly?"

"Go ahead."

"She agrees with me that Martin Frankl will put objections in the way. He might tell you she's unsuitable or untrustworthy or something."

"What's his problem with her? Were they in some kind of relationship?"

"No, nothing like that. I think they just rubbed each other up the wrong way. Maybe that's why he fired her. She's given me her word that she'll play it down the line."

"All right, I hear what you're saying. Thanks for following this up, Tom. We'll get in touch with her and see what we can organise."

* * *

As Tom drove home that afternoon he remembered Jan's brother's wedding. It must be happening around the time he'd just agreed to go to Philadelphia. Maybe this trip would enable him to go to it after all.

He tossed the idea around in his mind. If he went, it would demonstrate to Jan that he was still willing to make an effort to rescue their relationship. In theory, it would be a shrewd move. But did he want to make it? Was there enough left in their relationship to rescue?

As soon as he'd parked he pulled out his phone to check the dates. Yes, the wedding fell on the day after Felix's meeting, and New York City was only a couple of hours up the coast from Philadelphia. It was too good an opportunity to miss. He could go to it – and Felix Schaefer would be paying the air fare.

He composed a text to Jan. "Guess what – I can come to the wedding. Felix will foot the bill. I'll be travelling to NY from Philadelphia. Can you let me have the details?"

He was sitting at his laptop later that evening when Jan called him back.

"Tom, it's great that you want to come to the wedding, but I told Harry you definitely wouldn't be there. It's only a small affair."

"But surely he could squeeze in one extra person? It's not as if I'm demanding bed and board or a free flight."

"I just don't like to mess him around."

Tom leaned over his laptop. An email had come in from Harry a couple of weeks ago, encouraging Tom to come to the wedding. He found the message and read it to himself while Jan was speaking. It said, "Sorry you can't be here on the big day. If you change your mind, let me know. I've told Celia all about you, and she's dying to meet you."

He and Harry had always liked each other. The running joke between them had been that with a Tom and a Harry in the mix, all they needed was a friend called Dick to complete the set. He said to Jan, "You sound as if you don't want me to come. Harry seems happy enough about it."

"It's not that. I'm just being practical."

He felt a sudden burst of anger. Whilst giving the impression of clinging to their ongoing relationship, Jan was denying him this practical opportunity to pick up the threads of it. He said, "Maybe I'll just sneak in at the back and keep quiet. No one will even know I'm there."

She gave a sigh. "You're impossible when you're like this."

Like what? She seemed to have let her guard down for once, allowing an unfamiliar hint of hostility to show through.

He said, "I'll give it some thought," and disconnected before she could reply.

With his pulse still racing he tapped out a text message to Harry. "I'll be in Philadelphia the day before your wedding, so I should be able to make it after all. Can you confirm the time and place?"

Chapter 54

Tom was packing for his American trip a couple of weeks later when a call came in from an unfamiliar number. A well-spoken woman's voice asked, "Is that Tom Anthony of Carswell Group?"

"Speaking."

"My name is Dorothy Bradwell. I hope you won't mind me contacting you. It's about my son Neil." She sounded middle-aged or older. Despite her tentative opening, she seemed composed and confident.

A range of reactions shot through Tom, but chief among them was concern that the call might be monitored. Quickly he said, "I'd be delighted to speak to you, but could I call you back in two minutes?"

"Oh, all right, fine."

He disconnected, fetched out his cheap phone and tapped in her number, reading it off his main phone's display.

"Sorry about that. My battery was running low."

"That's all right." Now she hesitated. "I understand you knew Neil."

"Yes, but only slightly. We met briefly a couple of times."

"Oh. I had the impression he knew you fairly well." He heard her take a deep breath. "Perhaps I'd better explain. I live at Morecambe in Lancashire. Just before my son's … accident, I had a letter from him, with one of those plug-in computer memory things enclosed."

He had a feeling she was being deliberately vague, and knew exactly what she meant. Perhaps it suited her image of herself. He said, "A USB flash drive?"

"Yes, that's it."

"What's on it?"

"I don't know. To be honest, after what happened to Neil I couldn't bring myself to do anything with it. I thought it might have photographs on it – something like that. Anyway, a couple of days ago I put it in my laptop to have a look at it. I thought it was time."

"And?"

"It has some very big files on it, but I can't open them, so I phoned Michael Choat and asked him if he had any ideas." She spoke the name with a hint of distaste. "I assume you know him, do you?"

"Yes I do."

"I have nothing against his orientation – I just don't like the man." She cleared her throat. "However, I must say he's been very helpful acting as my feet on the ground in Brighton."

"What did he say?"

"He said he didn't want anything to do with this. He suggested I talk to you, and gave me your number."

Tom's mind was in overdrive. Could these files be further backups of whatever had been on Ben's laptop? He said, "Are you willing to let me have that drive? I'm sure I could find out what's on it for you."

"I suppose so, providing you promise to return it. Shall I post it to you?"

"Well, could you send it to the Carswell office in Brighton, not to my private address?"

"Whatever is best for you."

"Let me give you the address."

"I already know it."

He said, "I'm sorry about what happened to Neil. It must be dreadful for you."

"Thank you for saying that. I'm still trying to come to terms with it."

He left that comment hanging in the air for a moment, then said, "I hope you won't mind, but I need to ask you a favour. Could you possibly post that dongle today? I think it might be quite important."

"Oh." He could tell that she was puzzled, but she said, "Well, yes, I suppose so."

"Could you send it Special Delivery, and address it to Simon Meredith? He's the head of IT at Carswells."

"I know him. I spoke to him when Neil was there."

As soon as the call ended, Tom phoned Simon. "Could I ask you small favour?"

"Go on."

"Someone is going to send me a letter via your office, and it will be addressed to you. Could you get your receptionist to look out for it, and give it to you as soon as it arrives?"

"I suppose so. What am I supposed to do with it?"

"It should contain a USB flash drive. Could you put it in your safe or whatever you have there? Then we could look at it together next time I'm over there."

"What the hell is on it?"

"I don't actually know, but it could be seriously sensitive. I'm not joking."

"You don't mean hardcore porn? I don't think we should be party to that kind of thing."

"No, no, nothing like that. It's more likely to be political scandal – something like that."

"OK, I'll look out for it."

* * *

That evening Bernard phoned Tom. He said, "You've been keeping a very low profile lately."

"You know I'm working for Felix again on contract. He's been keeping me pretty busy."

"I thought it might be that you didn't want to follow up that conversation with Joe about this stuff that's been happening in your life."

"No, not at all. It was really helpful. I just didn't have anything to add."

"So you haven't found out any more about Ben Bradwell?"

Suddenly Tom realised he was having this conversation on his main phone. He wasn't about to take any chances. He said, "Let me call you back." He fetched the cheap phone and returned the call.

"Sorry about that. I don't like talking about Bradwell on my old phone. I don't know if I'm being overheard."

"You really are taking this seriously then."

"You're not going to tell me I'm imagining it all?"

"No, on the contrary, I have some news for you. According to my mate Joe, the police are looking again at Ben Bradwell's death.

"You're kidding!"

"Not at all. Apparently some witness has come forward, claiming he saw Bradwell on the cliff path with two other guys."

"Bloody hell. That's pretty conclusive, isn't it? He didn't jump – he was pushed."

"Well, no. It was dark, and this witness couldn't make out any faces. He just saw someone being walked along between two other men. He thought the man in the middle must be drunk, but it could also mean he was being dragged."

"So they're reopening the case, are they?"

"I'm not sure they've taken it that far. I think they're just looking at it." He paused. "But this might be a good time for you to tell them what you know. They have something to work on now."

"Let me think about this. I'm off to America tomorrow for a few days, with Felix."

"That'll be fun for you."

"I'll let you know."

"Happy landings, then."

"I'll call you when I'm back in GB."

Chapter 55

The flight from Heathrow left almost on time. Tom dozed for most of the journey, waking at intervals to listen to Felix talking strategy. Actually the strategy was simple: talk up the company for all it was worth, and hope the people from Dunleavy Logistics were convinced.

Frank, the finance director and third member of the team, was a quiet man in his early fifties. He toyed with a spreadsheet on his laptop for much of the time, occasionally interrupting Felix to correct him on some point of detail.

Felix had made the trip before, and once they'd cleared customs at Philadelphia International Airport he led the way confidently to the Transportation Authority rail station. "Quicker than a cab," he declared, "and a fraction of the cost." In barely half an hour they'd been whisked through the suburbs, and emerged in the smoked-glass skyscraper canyon of Market Street, one of the main thoroughfares running across the Center City area.

Felix had avoided arranging a meeting on the day they arrived. The five-hour time difference might have allowed it, but he argued that they would have turned up exhausted and jet-lagged, and not sharp enough for negotiation. Instead, they checked in at a big downtown hotel.

After dinner they wandered through to the bar, but presently Tom made his excuses and left them. Back in his room he tried phoning Jan to report his arrival in America, but the call went to voicemail. He wasn't unhappy. They hadn't spoken since he'd told her he planned to come to the wedding, and her reaction had scarcely been enthusiastic. He would just turn up, and she could make what she liked of it. He sent her a short text instead.

It was only as he sat down on his bed that a new thought crystallised in his mind. He wanted to hear a friendly voice, and the voice he was thinking of was Emily's.

The last time they'd been in touch was on the day of his visit to Chiswick. He'd assumed she would call him back to report on her conversation with Marcus Headington about the conference opportunity, but she hadn't. Well, to hell with it. He would call her anyway. He glanced at his watch: ten o'clock in the evening local time, five o'clock in London. He scrolled down to her number.

"Hello?" He heard surprise and mischievous pleasure in that husky voice.

"It's Tom."

"I know who you are."

"Are you working today?"

"No, you're in luck – it's my day off."

"So did you get the job?"

"The conference gig? Yup, all sorted. Ten minutes to set the world to rights."

"I'm glad."

"I know I should have thanked you for putting me up for it."

"It's your call."

"No need to be huffy. I was waiting to pick my moment."

He laughed. "I see."

"I had to go to the Stay and Prosper office last week, to give them an outline of what I would say. Martin Frankl was looking daggers at me."

"But you managed to beat him off?"

"Yeah, I made sure I wasn't left alone in the same room as him. I didn't want him jumping down my throat."

He said, "I'm calling you from Philadelphia."

"Seriously? You mean Philadelphia PA, not Philadelphia Tyne and Wear?"

"I didn't know there was one."

"It's a mining village outside Newcastle. You should get yourself an education."

"Well, this is the one in the USA. I'm here with the head of the company I used to work for."

"You just can't let it go, can you?"

He laughed again. "I'm here as backup in some negotiations. He worries that he'll antagonise people unless he's held in check."

"And you're the man to do it, of course."

"He thinks I am."

"So how is good old America?"

"It's OK so far. I haven't seen much of it yet. But after the meeting I'm going to a wedding in New York."

"What – just anyone's wedding, or did you find one in advance?"

"Oh, I did a Google search, and chose one I liked the look of."

The banter continued for some minutes. Eventually Emily said, "I'd better go – shopping to do. I'm cooking for my flatmates tonight. Mexican."

"Sounds delicious."

"You should come to London again."

*   *   *

Dunleavy Logistics' head office was on the thirteenth floor of an office building on John F Kennedy Boulevard in downtown Philadelphia. They could have walked there from the hotel, but Felix insisted on taking a cab. "I don't want someone to catch sight of us arriving on foot. It makes us look like cheapskates."

After the hassle of getting to Philadelphia to attend the meeting, the event itself was an anticlimax. The Dunleavy team were friendly and well informed, and seemed to know exactly what they were buying into. They confirmed Felix's claim that they supported the franchised network approach – "but if any branches want to sell out, we would advocate buying them," the CEO said.

They did however seem to know that some Carswell branches had been angling to leave the network. Felix started to respond to this defensively, and Tom spotted a need to chime in. "It happens from time to time with this kind of transport network," he said. "If people are determined to leave, sometimes it's best to let them go. But we know the score, and we've got it in hand."

They broke for a working lunch, and the meeting finally ended around four o'clock. Felix and Frank were staying another night in order to discuss detail the following day, but Tom was due to catch a train to New York City. He walked to 30th Street Station and found a window seat in the train. Then for much of the next hour and a half he watched the endless ribbon of urban development streaming past.

In the thronging underground concourse at Pennsylvania Station he was surprised to see a man holding up a card showing his name and the name of his hotel. He didn't remember telling anyone exactly when he planned to arrive. The man was finding it hard to hold his own against the torrent of commuters. He looked faintly Indian or Middle Eastern, but greeted Tom in an American accent. "Courtesy hotel transit for Mr Tom Anthony."

"I'm amazed that you found me."

"All part of the service."

Bemused, Tom was led up escalators and along passages until finally the two of them emerged into the street lights. The man peered along the street, and after a few moments a black multi-purpose vehicle pulled up and the passenger door slid open. "Please," the man said, gesturing towards it. Still mystified, Tom climbed in and the man followed.

The vehicle accelerated away sharply, but Tom soon realised it wasn't on its way to the hotel.

Chapter 56

There was a second man inside the car, so Tom was captive between him and the one who had fetched him from the station. The new man was solidly built and wore round spectacles and a light-coloured coat. He looked like a stressed businessman.

Tom glanced between the two of them. "Where are we going? What's this about?"

"Don't worry," the man in the coat said tersely. "We'll be there soon."

"You're *kidnapping* me?"

"You're our guest."

"In that case I'd like you to drop me off, please."

The man gave him a look of studied patience. "Don't be ridiculous."

Tom turned to the other man and made a sudden move to lean across him. The vehicle was crawling along in dense traffic, and he was hoping he could open the door and lunge out. The man pushed him back into position with apparent effortlessness.

"Please – just bear with us."

"Why should I?"

"You'll find out."

The windows were tinted and it was dark outside. Lights slid past as they slowly progressed. Eventually they turned right on to a more open stretch of divided road and sped up. The two men exchanged glances, then the business type leaned over abruptly and pinned Tom's arms to his sides. He struggled, but the man's strength was immense.

"Don't resist," he said. "You'll find this arrangement much more pleasant than the alternative."

"What arrangement?"

In answer, the other man pulled an elasticated eye mask over Tom's head.

"If I let you go, will you promise not to take off the mask?"

Tom swallowed, feeling helpless and humiliated. "All right."

"And another thing." Abruptly Tom felt a pair of earphones with large padded ear pieces being pulled on to his head. Dance music was pounding out from the speakers. He heard the man shouting, "Best if you don't hear any sounds from outside."

After travelling at speed for a few minutes they slowed down again, evidently contending with traffic lights and commuters. They made multiple turns, and Tom lost all sense of direction. Finally they turned on to some kind of rough track and bumped to a halt.

"Get out please."

Tom did as instructed, and heard the MPV pulling away. There was a chill in the air, and he could smell the river not far away. After two minutes he was just able to hear another vehicle drawing up, and he was ushered inside. It felt much like the previous one.

"Not far now."

The journey resumed, and took them back into the city streets. Altogether they were on the move for about forty-five minutes, then they were descending a spiral ramp, presumably entering an underground car park. As they drew to a halt, Tom could hear the squeal of tyres over the music.

They took off the headphones but not the mask, and led him across an expanse of concrete and into an elevator. It was difficult to tell whether it was going up or down, but it was on the move for some seconds before he heard the doors slide open. Then he was marched along a corridor and round a corner. He heard a hinged door open and he was pushed sideways. He could tell from the more muted sounds that he was now in a small room. The door clanged shut.

"Hold still." His mask was pulled off.

Harsh strip lighting hurt his eyes, but gradually he took in his surroundings. The room had metal walls, and looked something like a cross between a cell and a pharmaceutical clean room. There was a table in the middle with a grey laminate surface. Three hard metal chairs were tucked under it. The Indian-looking man had disappeared, and he was alone with the business type.

"Sit down and wait here."

The door slammed shut behind him, and Tom heard the sound of an electrical lock engaging. With a sigh, he slid out a chair and sat down.

* * *

He stared around him, still shaken. Part of his mind was telling him this was all a dream, and in reality he was striding along West 34th Street, heading for his hotel.

The room was about twelve feet square and almost completely featureless, apart from the table and a bench with a grey blanket on it. Glancing up, he saw a video camera mounted in the corner of the ceiling above the door.

His captors had taken his suitcase from him, but he still had his phone. He reached into his jacket pocket and pulled it out. No signal.

Long minutes passed. He stood up, stretched, walked all the way round the table and sat down again. Then he noticed what looked like a small door set into the far wall. Behind it was a small cubicle, and inside was a built-in metallic toilet.

It didn't take him long to gravitate to the bench. Its thin padded covering proved considerably more comfortable than the chair. He sat on it for a while, then swivelled round and lay back on it with his hands behind his head, staring disconsolately up at the ceiling.

His best guess was that all this must have to do with Ben Bradwell's death, and about his continued efforts to understand what had brought it about. He found it hard to imagine how these Americans could possibly have had anything to do with that, but no other explanation made sense.

Nothing else happened for an hour or so, then the door opened again and the man with spectacles came in carrying a tray. "Room service," he muttered without any sign of humour. He retreated without saying more.

Tom swung himself into a sitting position and went over to the table. The tray held a microwaved instant meal, lukewarm and still in its plastic container, along with a Styrofoam cup of water. A plastic fork had been provided. He realised for the first time that he was ravenously hungry. He sat down and wolfed down the entire meal in minutes.

That was the last excitement of the day. No one came back to retrieve the tray. Monotonous hours passed. He stood up. He walked around. He sat on the chair. He lay back on the bench. The minutes dragged.

At ten o'clock the lights abruptly dimmed. He was being told it was bedtime. He made use of the toilet, then tried to fashion the blanket into a cover. Although the room was warm, the blanket was scarcely thick enough. He shivered for a while, then draped his jacket on top of it, and eventually slid into a shallow sleep.

Chapter 57

Breakfast was a re-run of last night's ritual. The man came in with a tray containing cereal, toast and a sad-looking muffin, and took the previous tray away. After Tom had eaten, the man took the second tray away, replacing it with a plastic bowl of water, presumably intended to allow Tom a rudimentary wash. Then he returned to remove that. Each time he waved away Tom's attempts to engage him in conversation.

Several hours passed. It struck Tom that he would miss Harry's wedding. Too bad; that was the least of his concerns. At the moment he was busy trying to keep claustrophobia at bay. He'd never been good with confined spaces, and he was desperately trying to avoid the spiral of panic that would lead him down that path.

Lunchtime came round. This time a store-wrapped sandwich was on the menu. As before, he ate it eagerly.

More time passed.

It was around 4 pm when the door clunked open again and a new figure came in – a man of around forty with short sandy hair and gold-rimmed spectacles.

He looked at Tom with interest. "So you're the man we're all wondering about," he said genially.

"I don't know – am I?"

"Usually we don't waste time like this. You should be grateful."

"Well forgive me if I don't look it."

"My colleagues were all for dumping you in the East River." His ironic look indicated that Tom was not supposed to take this literally.

Tom folded his arms involuntarily. "Is that supposed to be funny?"

"Not entirely." The man's look hardened.

"So what makes you take a different view?"

"Change of plan. You know how it is. Factions."

Tom unfolded his arms slowly. "So can I leave please?"

The man looked thoughtfully at Tom for a long moment, then pulled a small device from his pocket and pointed it up at the CCTV camera. The red light on the front of it went out. Turning back to Tom, he said, "I think a little privacy is in order."

Tom said nothing. The man walked round the table and sat down facing him. He tilted his chair back and clasped his hands behind his head. "I'm agnostic about this, but it seems you have a fairy godmother. You should consider yourself lucky."

"What does that mean?"

"We brought you here because some friends of ours asked us to. But now that you're here, we find that someone we listen to is rooting for you. I hope he's right."

He said, "Are you police? The FBI? Homeland Security?"

"You don't need to know who we are. We need to know who *you* are. If you get your head round that, we can hurry this up."

Tom shuffled himself into a more comfortable position in his chair. He said, "What do you want me to say?"

"It's very simple. When you leave here you need to contemplate a simple question – and we don't often give people that option."

"What question?"

"Are you going to keep on interfering and causing committed people grief, or will you back off for the greater good?

Tom stared at him. "The greater good? What the hell is that?"

Back in benign mode, the man said, "You asked who we are." He tilted his chair forward. "You could call us the agents of last resort." He smiled to himself. "The ALR. I just made that up, but it has a nice ring, doesn't it?"

"What does it mean?"

The man mused on that for a moment. Choosing his words carefully, he said, "A lot people are frightened of the way society is heading in this country – the reversion to right-wing values, the tendency to turn inward. A lot people think we need a change of direction. Most people don't know how they could achieve that." He left a dramatic pause. "Some of us don't see any problem."

"I don't know what you're talking about."

"Yes you do. And people in your country have problems of your own. Sometimes we help each other. You're just refusing to connect the dots."

Tom stared at the man, but concluded after a moment that he was not about to learn anything more. He said, "So can I leave?"

The man put his hands on the table decisively. "Yes, you can leave, my friend, but you need to take a lesson away with you. Consider what's in your own best interests before you rush to interfere, and keep in mind that you won't get off so lightly next time." He frowned. "We can find you wherever you are – and we can also find people who are important to you."

Tom merely stared at him.

In a much louder voice, the man said, "Are you hearing me? I really really need to know."

He nodded reluctantly.

"Good." He stood up and looked down at Tom. "If it weren't for your fairy godmother, we wouldn't even be having this conversation."

"Who *is* my fairy godmother?"

"If you don't know, it's not up to me to tell you."

*   *   *

Tom was returned to Midtown Manhattan in the same way he'd been taken. He was handed his suitcase and dropped off in an alley next to some garbage bins – presumably out of sight of surveillance cameras.

His instructions were simple: check into his original hotel for the second of the two nights he'd reserved, then proceed directly to JFK next day and catch his planned flight back to Heathrow. Speak to no one.

He did as he was told: took the train to JFK, caught his flight to Heathrow, made his way to the long-term car park, retrieved his car and drove back to Winchester. The whole journey passed in a blur. He arrived home in the middle of the following night, jet-lagged and battered by the travel, and scarcely able to believe what had just happened.

Initially he'd been tempted to go to the police in New York, but he'd soon dismissed the idea. How would they react to some strange Brit with an outlandish story about kidnapping, abduction and vague threats?

Not well, he suspected. He would no doubt have faced disbelief and probably long interrogation, yet the only certain result would have been to antagonise his captors.

He could now go to the British authorities, but he had a feeling the whole episode would seem too distant for them to pursue – not to mention too far-fetched.

From the secure haven of his familiar lounge in Winchester, the entire experience seemed like a dream, but he was all too aware that the threat to his life was still hanging over him. Whoever those Americans were, they must surely be connected somehow to the people who were hounding him in Britain, and their message was plain enough. Do nothing, and he should be safe. Continue to meddle, and that safety was not guaranteed.

Chapter 58

Tom's plan to do nothing was immediately compromised next morning. He had a call from Simon Meredith in Brighton.

"That package you said would be sent to me with a flash drive in it – it hasn't come yet. I just wondered if I'd misunderstood what you told me?"

During the trip to America Tom had lost his sense of time. He counted the days back to his conversation with Ben Bradwell's mother. If she'd mailed the drive by Special Delivery as promised, it should have reached Brighton two days ago.

He told Simon, "I'll look into it. Thanks for letting me know."

As he ended the call he realised he'd been talking on his normal mobile phone. If these people were monitoring it, he'd just put himself straight back in their firing line.

He sat holding the phone and looking at it thoughtfully. Just how extensive was these people's reach? Was it really possible for them to intercept calls made to and from mobile phones, or was he ascribing fictional powers to them?

Then a much simpler thought came to him. What if this house was bugged? What if the house in Storton had been bugged too? Could that mysterious black multi-purpose vehicle in the village have been part of a surveillance operation? He knew nothing of these things, but he knew that bugging was an old, low-tech science. Why the hell had he never thought of this before?

He glanced round the room. Where would he look for a bug? Slowly at first, but with increasing urgency, he looked under tables, behind pictures – everywhere he'd seen bugs placed on TV and in films. Within ten minutes he'd found it: a small circular device with a trailing wire, hidden behind the books on one of the bookshelves.

"Unbelievable!" He snatched up the device before even thinking, carried it through to the back yard and dropped it in the bin. Were there more bugs in other rooms? He would do a full search later. First, he wanted to phone Ben Bradwell's mother and ask what had happened to the USB drive. He fetched out his cheap pay-as-you-go phone and went outside into the front garden. Although he'd just dumped the bug, he still felt vulnerable.

The call rang out repeatedly. He was on the point of hanging up when a woman's voice answered tentatively, "Hello?"

"Is this Dorothy Bradwell?"

"I'm sorry, no, it's her sister Ellen here. She can't use her phone at the moment. Who is speaking?"

"Tom Anthony. I knew her son Ben ... Neil, I mean. Is something wrong?"

"Well, yes, I'm afraid she's been in an accident. I'm speaking from the hospital."

"Oh no. Is it serious?"

"She's in an induced coma at the moment." There was a break in her voice. "They think she'll be all right when they wake her up, but they won't know for sure until they do."

"I'm so sorry." He wondered how far he could press her. "Do you mind me asking what happened?"

"She was knocked down by a car near her house. They think she was going to the shops."

"Well when she wakes up, please give her my best."

He ended the call and glanced up and down the safe, normal street. Had Dorothy Bradwell been intercepted on her way to send off the flash drive? Like everything else that had been happening lately, it seemed far-fetched, yet now that he'd met the people behind all this and heard about their capabilities, he couldn't dismiss the idea. Yet again, some kind of evidence gathered by Ben Bradwell had been suppressed before it reached him. The implications were chilling.

A voice was calling his name. He looked up to see Christine emerging from her house across the street. She came over. "How are you doing?"

"I've just been to Philadelphia and New York."

"Sounds exciting."

"You wouldn't believe it if I told you."

She looked questioningly at him, but he added nothing. She said, "I saw Jan here a few days ago."

"I didn't know she was coming over. What was she doing?"

She flashed him an ironic smile. "We didn't speak. Was I supposed to ask?" Then she relented. "She seemed to be collecting some of her stuff. She had her car parked outside your house on the yellow line, and I think she was bundling some clothes into it."

"Was she indeed?"

* * *

As soon as he was back inside the house a call came in on his other mobile. It was Felix.

"How was the wedding?"

"Ah." Immediately Tom was floundering. "It was a complete balls-up, if you want to know. I got the day wrong, so I completely missed it."

"What? I thought you were more organised than that." Felix chuckled humourlessly. "And here's me paying extra so that you can fly back from New York instead of Philadelphia."

"Send me the bill for the difference."

"No need to be tetchy. I'm just kidding you."

"I'm sorry. It's been a difficult couple of days." Tom rubbed the back of his head, wondering how to rescue the conversation. "Did you tie up the deal with Dunleavy Logistics in the end?"

"Pretty much. I can work with these people. There's just one thing. They're unhappy with the Rackham situation. In the long term they don't care if Rackhams stay in our network or leave, but short-term, they don't want an expensive fuck-up as soon as they're on board."

"So ...?"

"Can you get yourself up to Nottingham again and find out what it will take to bring Rackhams back into the fold? I don't think there's any point in me going, but you might just pull something out of the bag."

* * *

Driving up the M1 was a welcome relief after the events in New York. Tom kept the car radio turned up loudly for much of the way, hoping to drown out thoughts of the American trip.

While he was waiting in the open-plan office for Darren Wright to appear he was approached by Julie, the administrative manager who had transferred to Nottingham from Carswells in Southampton.

"Tom, I'm glad you're here. I was going to contact you again. I wanted a private word."

"What did you have in mind?"

She glanced around nervously. "Darren has an appointment at lunchtime, so he won't be asking you out. Maybe we could slip round the corner to the pub?"

"OK, I'll come and find you when we've finished."

Darren Wright was in a marginally better mood this time than he'd been when Tom visited him with Felix. "We might be able to sort out something with Carswells," he told Tom as they wound up the meeting. "There are benefits to being a member as well as drawbacks."

"So you can't decide whether you're Leavers or Remainers?"

Wright glanced at him suspiciously, then gave a deadpan smile. "You could look at it like that. We've had our frustrations with Felix's network, but I can't deny the pluses. It's a matter of striking the right balance."

Chapter 59

Julie was waiting for Tom when he left Wright's office. They went out to his car, and she directed him to a modern pub in a housing estate not far from the depot. Once they were settled at a table she leaned towards him confidentially. He was very conscious of her freckled face and troubled frown. "I probably shouldn't be telling you this, but someone ought to know."

"Know what?"

"I assume you know that Carswell's computer man Ben Bradwell was here for a week late last year? He was integrating our new computers with the Carswell IT system."

"Yes, I picked that up."

"Well, a few days ago I was doing some routine work on our computer system, and I found a secure area that Ben had set up. I thought I should check to see if it was something that could safely be deleted."

"How did you know the login?"

She chuckled. "I was in the room when he was setting it up. He actually turned round and asked me to suggest a password. He must have used it for a laugh, and meant to change it, but he never did."

"Right."

"It seemed to be full of emails that he'd saved – emails to and from the management team here at Rackams. He must have hacked into their mailboxes on the server and copied them." She reached into her bag and pulled out a tablet computer. "I copied some of the messages on here so that I could look at them outside the office."

He leaned over and read the opening paragraph of the first.

To: Elias Wallington
From: Darren Wright

Re our conversation the other day, it now seems MC will definitely

*close Nottingham once they're live in SW. Can we stop this? A lot of
your constituents will lose their jobs, and so will a bunch of my drivers
and warehouse staff – and we'll lose one of our biggest contracts. It's
not a proper investment – it's just robbing Peter to pay Paul.*

He looked up. He'd heard the recipient's name somewhere recently,
but he couldn't place it. "Remind me, who is Elias Wallington?"

"He's a local MP for a constituency up in this part of the world, and
he's a junior minister in the Government, looking after grant aid for
business investment and that kind of thing."

"So this email is Darren Wright telling Wallington that Monck
Chervil is going to close down its Nottingham operation once the South
Wales factory is ready?"

"Yes, and it would have been a fast-track project – on stream within
a year. All their jobs here would have gone to South Wales, and
Rackhams would have lost their top money-earner."

"How did Darren know this?"

"Oh, it'll be through contacts at Moncks. These people talk to
each other."

"Couldn't Rackhams have opened a new branch in Wales to run the
contract from there?"

"No, because Monck already has a relationship with a carrier in
Swansea – one of our biggest rivals. All the new work would have gone
to them, including the part that would have been transferred down there
from here."

Tom sat back and looked at Julie with a mix of wonder and
admiration. "You've been doing an impressive spying job."

She shrugged. "Not really."

"What happened in response to this?"

"Darren got the brush-off. Elias Wallington replied that the project
wasn't robbing Peter to pay Paul because the overall value of Monck's
commitment to the UK would be far higher afterwards. It was more than
his life's worth to block any inward investment – especially with Brexit
looming. His Government responsibility outweighed his loyalty to his
constituents in the East Midlands, etcetera etcetera." She held out the
tablet. "You can read the email if you like."

He shook his head. "I get the drift, but I have the sense that there's more?"

"Well, Elias Wallington also said, 'If the official advice I was given had been less emphatic, that might have helped.' I think that was a coded message."

"How come?"

"Because then there was this." She scrolled on her tablet, then held it up to show him a further email.

To: Vic
From: Darren

Good to see you last week. Picking up what you said, something has come up already. Monck Chervil is about to announce a major new UK investment, with a big bribe from the Government. This fucks up your claim that Brexit has put the brakes on this kind of thing, doesn't it? You might think I would be pleased, but it's bad news for me too. We'll lose out in Nottingham because they plan to switch all their production to Wales.

The minister in charge, Elias Wallington, says he won't change his mind over this, even if his constituents up here lose their jobs. But I have an idea. I found out that the civil servant who advises him on this is none other than Donnie from Cambridge. You knew him better than I did. Do you think a bit of persuasion might help change his mind?

Tom looked up. "Vic?" he said.

"Victor Rudge. He works for an anti-Brexit campaign in London."

"What! You won't believe this, but I actually know him."

"Oh." She gave him a surprised glance. "So you'll know the kind of person he is."

"Evidently he's someone who doesn't shy away from 'persuasion', whatever that is."

"And you can guess who Donnie is. The name of that civil servant is Donald Finch."

Tom looked at her in wonder. "It worked, didn't it? The advice was changed and the project was cancelled. In the end Donald Finch resigned."

* * *

As they walked out to the pub car park Tom said, "What you've just told me is pretty incendiary stuff."

"That's what I thought." She stopped and looked at him. "What do you think we should do about it?"

"I honestly don't know. If it got into the press it could be a resigning matter for that MP, and it could do serious harm to Rackhams. It could even rebound on Carswells."

"Exactly." She watched him uneasily.

He was reflecting that if Victor Rudge really was involved, it could also do massive damage to the Stay and Prosper campaign. He could already see the headline: *"Remain group sabotages inward investment to block boost for Brexiteers."*

He said, "I think we should keep a lid on this until we have time to think. And don't under any circumstances tell anyone else about it."

She nodded. "Fine by me. I don't want to undermine the company I work for. I just thought someone else besides me should know what's been going on."

"I'm glad you chose me."

As they drove back into Rackham's yard Tom said, "Don't put anything in writing to me about this for the time being, and don't talk about it on the phone unless I tell you it's a secure line."

She gave him a wide-eyed look. "You really think we need to keep our heads down?"

"It's safer. I'll definitely get back to you about it."

"OK, agreed."

* * *

So Victor Rudge somehow knew Darren Wright of Rackhams. How? Back at home, Tom sat down at his laptop to find out.

The answer wasn't hard to come by. They'd both been students at the same Cambridge college at the same time. He hadn't spotted this when he was researching Rudge's connection to Finch because Wright hadn't been on his radar.

So all three of them knew each other – and apparently Rudge and Wright knew something compromising about Finch, and had planned to threaten him over it. He wondered briefly what it was, but then realised that in practical terms the detail was irrelevant. What mattered was that they had all been implicated in a scheme to derail the investment – and apparently it had worked.

Could this have been the focus of the shadowy American group's interest, or was that too simplistic an interpretation? In some ways there was a convoluted logic to the idea. Perhaps their objective had been to keep Monck Chervil's spending programme within the United States – to "put America first", which was the current protectionist rallying cry. Clearly Rudge had initiated the plot, but perhaps these Americans had somehow taken ownership of it.

It sounded plausible, but there was a flaw. The group Tom had brushed with in New York seemed to be driven by a kind of rational liberalism, which ran counter to such an inward-looking philosophy.

There was a more obvious flaw, too. According to the press, Monck Chervil had never denied an alternative plan to split the investment between France and the Netherlands. The Americans would have gained nothing from the cancellation.

They must have had some other agenda.

Chapter 60

Emily phoned next morning. "Bet you didn't expect to hear from me again so soon."

"I live in hopes."

"I believe you. So how was your American wedding? Did it meet your expectations?"

"I never got there. Very long story. If you promise not to ask, I'll promise to tell you when I can."

"Oh." She took a moment to process this. "And you're back in GB now, are you?"

"Yup. It was a flying visit."

"The reason I called – I was hoping for a word of advice."

"Seriously?"

She sighed. "Shall I go on or not?"

"Please."

"Martin Frankl has demanded full sight of my presentation for the conference. He wants to vet every single word in advance.

"I see."

"Not that I give a flying fuck, you understand, but there's a point of principle here. This wasn't the deal Marcus Headington put to me. He said I could talk about anything I liked." She paused. "But when I repeated that to Martin, he threatened me."

"Threatened you? What did he say?"

"He said I should make sure I have my insurance in place, ha ha. It was obvious what he meant."

"That's ridiculous."

"So what would you do if you were me?"

Something odd about this was nagging at the edge of Tom's consciousness. He said, "Why do you think Martin is so worried about what you say in your presentation? I know he's a died-in-the-wool marketing man, but this seems a bit extreme. What does he care?"

"I think Victor must have some sort of hold over him. He's a master of manipulation, that man. I used to think he had a hand up Marcus Headington's back, but on the whole I might have done Marcus an injustice. He's his own man. But Martin is just a fly in the wind."

Until now, Tom hadn't considered the possibility of collusion between Rudge and Frankl. This was something he would have to think about. He said, "That's very interesting."

"It's just my opinion."

"Can you let me think about this for a bit?"

"All right, but I'm supposed to submit my presentation within a week."

"I'll get back to you."

* * *

After hanging up, Tom found himself wondering again about Rudge and his apparent hold over Finch. Finding out the detail was academic in some ways, yet he felt compelled to pursue it. He phoned Malcolm Drew at *Seismic Scene*.

"I need a favour. I know it's unprofessional to ask, but I'm looking for some backup. I don't have political or media contacts. I don't have sources. I've been out of the game too long."

"OK, try me."

"It's to do with the follow-up article I promised you. I need to do some research on it, but I don't know where I would begin."

"Research into what?"

"It's about that man Donald Finch – the civil servant who advised on the Monck Chervil grant funding package."

"Go on."

Tom explained his theory about a blackmail scheme. Initially Malcolm was sceptical. "You're saying he was blackmailed into changing EU rules?"

"Huh! No, if only it were that easy. No, I'm just thinking that these decisions can hang on interpretation, can't they? Someone could have forced him to consult different legal counsel, or give one rule precedence over another."

"And why am I chasing this up for you?"

Tom hesitated. "As a favour, nothing more. I know I shouldn't ask."

"Why is it so important?"

"If I ever get to write this story, you'll see." He paused. "But there's a caveat. If I decide I don't want to go public with this, you have to agree to bin the whole thing. I need your assurance on that."

"You strike a hard bargain."

Tom laughed grimly. "If I do write it, I think you'll be impressed."

* * *

Tom phoned Jan that evening. If there was any future left with her, he needed to know. But was there? In theory they were still together, but they hadn't met in person for several weeks. These calls felt like a last-ditch way of keeping the relationship alive.

Her greeting was unpromising. "I still can't believe you missed the wedding after going all that way."

He'd already called her to make his peace with her. He'd admitted to arriving in the United States, but claimed that his meeting had run into a second day, and he couldn't duck out of it.

"I told you – the timing went haywire. There was nothing I could do."

"Whatever."

To change the subject he said, "I hear you were over here at the house the other day."

"Huh. Nothing gets past that Christine woman, does it?"

He should have known it was unwise to raise this. "She just happened to see you."

"And she just happened to report it to you."

"I bumped into her in the street, that's all."

She said nothing.

"What were you doing here, if you don't mind me asking?"

"I was just picking up some more of my clothes. I'm fed up with the stuff I've been wearing all this time."

"Ah, I see. I don't blame you."

"I should hope not!" She gave a short laugh to take some of the sting out of her words.

Trying to sound more cheerful, he said, "How's the work progressing?"

"What work?"

"The rewiring. You said it would take a couple of weeks."

"Oh, right. Of course. It's nearly finished. It took longer than I expected."

"So when it's all done, are you thinking of coming back to Winchester? It would be nice to know."

"That's still the plan, isn't it? What were you expecting?"

"Well, it's been a strange time. Sometimes it feels as if we've drifted off into parallel lives."

"We can work things through when I get back there. It shouldn't be too much longer. Truly."

Despite her combative opening, she was sounding surprisingly positive. He hadn't expected it, and he was left more uncertain than when he'd picked up the phone. Every time he braced himself to make a clean break with her, she seemed to have a knack of heading him off. In some ways it was reassuring, in other ways merely confusing.

Chapter 61

The following morning Tom had a flash of inspiration. He was thinking back over his conversation with Julie in Nottingham when a new idea came to him. If Ben Bradwell had used Rackham's computer system as a private repository for his own material, perhaps he'd done the same thing elsewhere. What if he'd set up a similar secure area on the Carswell IT network?

The more Tom thought about the idea, the more plausible it seemed. In effect, Ben would have been hiding sensitive content in plain sight, but in a place where no one would think to look for it.

He explored the various angles in his head. Whatever these files contained, Bradwell might have assembled them after resigning from Carswells to work at the Stay and Prosper campaign. However, he could have left himself a way to access the Carswell computers. It was the kind of thing computer experts did.

What about the mysterious people who had been searching for the files? Wouldn't they have thought of this? Not necessarily. They weren't infallible. They'd probably checked to see if Ben was backing up his files to a Cloud server somewhere in the world, but this was something they might have overlooked.

He glanced at his watch: there was plenty of time to catch Simon Meredith at Brighton. He grabbed his cheap phone.

Simon grumbled, "Not more phantom files for me to open?"

"Not exactly. I don't think you'll ever be seeing the USB flash drive that I was expecting."

"What then?"

Tom explained what he was thinking, and Simon reluctantly agreed to look into it. "But I can't let Jake allocate a lot of time to this. He's tied up integrating our IT system with two new member-companies."

"I understand. Whatever you can do."

"I'll let you know if we find anything."

* * *

Tom assumed he would have to wait days for an answer, but in fact Simon Meredith called him back that afternoon.

"Am I using the right phone?" He seemed unable to keep the irony out of his voice.

"Yes, but bear with me a minute." Tom stood up and crossed to the front door. He went out though the front garden and walked a few paces down the street. No harm in taking extra precautions. "OK, go ahead."

"You're not going to believe this, but it looks as though you were right about Ben leaving a private cache on our server. We found it quite quickly, and thanks to my man Jake we cracked the password pretty easily."

"That's amazing. So what's in it?"

"A bunch of very large files."

"What are they?"

"We don't know. They're encrypted."

"Any chance … ?"

Simon cut in, "Before you ask, the answer is no. I don't know how the encryption was done, but what I do know is that it's not something we could crack here in a few minutes, if at all."

"But could Jake do it?"

"It's not fair to ask him, Tom. I've already got him working overtime on the integration job. I can't take him off that, and I can't ask him to work in his own time either."

"Not to worry. I'll have a think about that. In the meantime I'll come over and collect those files this afternoon, if that's all right."

* * *

He knew he was being foolish. So long as those files stayed on the Carswell server, no one outside the business would know about them. On the other hand, if he took copies, there was a risk that the shadowy people who were hounding him would find out that they existed. He couldn't quite envisage the consequences, but if they realised the files were encrypted, presumably they would be extremely keen to prevent him or anyone else from decrypting them.

He couldn't help himself. He had to pursue it. He scoured his desk drawers for give-away USB flash drives, and eventually found three. Then he made his way to where his car was parked and headed off in the direction of Brighton.

The journey was no quicker than last time: too many roundabouts; too many pinch points. An hour and three quarters later he pulled into Carswell's yard.

He held up his three USB drives to Simon Meredith. "Will those files fit on these?"

"Let's see what Jake thinks."

Jake, a confident man in his early twenties, glanced at the three non-matching pen drives and shook his head. "Not a chance." He opened a drawer, pulled out a compact external hard disk drive and looked up at Simon. "Can we lend this to Tom?"

Simon gave Tom a long-suffering glance. "You'll bring it back, won't you?"

"Hopefully."

While Jake was doing the copying, Tom asked him, "What kind of files do you think these are?"

"Most likely video. They could be zipped archives full of smaller files, but I think video is more likely."

"Do you think it will be possible to crack the encryption, or is it a lost cause?"

"Never say never – that's my motto. It ought to be possible."

"I appreciate your help."

"I'm sorry I don't have time to do more."

Back in his car, Tom did some fast thinking. Who could he ask to decrypt these files? The best lead he had was Bernard Weatherley. It seemed unlikely that Bernard himself would have any computer-savvy contacts, but his friend Joe might. It was worth a try.

He pulled out his cheap phone to call Bernard, then realised that if his own house was bugged, Bernard's might also be. Was he being fanciful again? The situation seemed too serious to take unnecessary chances. He needed a plan.

He made the call.

"Hello?" Bernard obviously didn't recognise Tom's new number.

"It's me. What are you up to?"

"Hi Tom. The answer is nothing. No courier work until the day after tomorrow."

"Great." He hung up without saying any more.

He drove back along the A27 towards Southampton and made his way to Bernard's house, arriving long after dusk. He parked a few doors down the street, then walked warily back to Bernard's gateway. Instead of ringing the bell he trotted down the side passage and into the back garden. Through the picture window he could see Bernard on the sofa, reading the paper. He went over and tapped on the glass, holding his finger up to his lips. Bernard looked at him in surprise. He pointed to the back door.

When it opened, he beckoned Bernard outside and led him across the garden towards the greenhouse at the far end.

"Sorry about this cloak-and-dagger stuff. It probably seems ridiculous, but I'm in some serious trouble, and I don't want to take unnecessary risks."

Bernard squinted at him. "Serious trouble?"

"I mean it. I'm way out of my depth, and I'm fed up with dealing with it on my own." He meant to say this lightly, but he could hear the plangent tone in his voice. He hadn't realised until now just how isolated his recent experiences had made him feel.

"You mean you've done something you shouldn't have?"

"God, no – nothing illegal. I've shaken a stick at those people I was telling you and Joe about, and they don't like it. I'm pretty sure now that Ben Bradwell was murdered to shut him up about something, and I think I'm close to finding out what it was. But these people are dead set on preventing that from happening."

"What can I do?"

Tom smiled gratefully. "I thought Joe might have some ideas."

"I'll ask him."

"In particular, there are some encrypted files I'd like to open." He held up the portable hard drive. "They may explain a lot about this."

Bernard nodded thoughtfully. "You might be in luck. I have a feeling his nephew works in computer forensics. He might be able to help."

"This would need to be done privately, not through some company."

"I'll see what he says."

"Can you discuss it with him in person, not on the phone? And not anywhere that might be bugged?"

Bernard stared at him. "You think that's necessary?"

"I certainly do. And don't tell me anything about this explicitly on the phone. Just let me know if you get anywhere."

* * *

Bernard called him back next day. "I'm in the garden," he said with irony.

Tom took the hint and went outside. Better safe than sorry. However, he said, "This is like a joke, isn't it?"

"Let's hope it is. Better that than the alternative."

"So what have you got?"

"Can you get yourself to Chichester tomorrow morning? That's where Joe's nephew works."

"You mean he's already been looking at those files?"

"Not only that, he's also opened one of them. He wants you to interpret it."

"That's incredible!"

Bernard hesitated. "There's something you should know, Tom. You'll find that Joe's in on this, and when he puts his mind to it, he moves fast. To cut a long story short, he'll be bringing along someone from the security services."

"Oh."

"It's no good saying, 'Oh.' I told you Joe would escalate this if he thought he had to."

"Don't they care what happens to me?"

"Of course they do. But if national security is at risk, they're not going to look the other way, are they?"

"And that's what he thinks?"

"You'd better ask him."

Chapter 62

Phipps & Butler, the computer forensics company, was based in a period office building in the picturesque centre of Chichester – a city the size of a small market town that lay half-way between Winchester and Brighton. It had taken Tom nearly an hour to get there in heavy traffic.

Despite the building's unassuming period façade, it was all twenty-first century inside. Tom had to run the gauntlet of an airport-style security system, watched closely by two attendants. The woman guiding him smiled apologetically. "Some extremely sensitive material passes through here. We need to keep up our guard."

He was led upstairs to a room facing the street. The cathedral was just in view through the window. A man in a white shirt was sitting in front of a large computer monitor, while two others stood behind him, looking over his shoulder. One was Bernard's ex-policeman friend Joe. Tom didn't recognise the third.

Joe made the introductions. "This is my nephew Adam – " he gestured towards the man at the desk – "and this is Jay. I'll let him introduce himself."

"Tom, I've been hearing a lot about you." The other man was somewhere in his forties, with dark hair and piercing eyes. "Jay Reynolds." He held out his hand.

"How do you fit into this?"

"Let's just say you've skipped the police bit. I'm the man you get when you've been nudged up the security ladder. I'm here to look, listen and evaluate." His manner was affable, but Tom sensed an underlying steeliness.

Tom glanced at Joe. "I thought you told me I'd have to explain myself to the police before I could get anyone else to listen to me?"

Joe said, "I decided to run all this past Jay's team, and something you told me tripped a flag with them."

"How do you know each other?"

"Best not to ask."

Tom nodded, already feeling a long way out of his comfort zone.

Joe said, "I've told Jay everything you told me the other day. I know you won't mind. I thought it would save us going over it all again."

"Evidently I don't have much choice in the matter."

"And Adam has security clearance, so you can speak in confidence here."

"I see."

Jay looked down at Adam. "Can you run the video again?"

"Will do."

They watched as the playback started. It was immediately obvious that it was surveillance camera footage, black and white and grainy, but clear enough to show plenty of detail. It had been shot from a high point in a wood-panelled room, and Tom quickly recognised Victor Rudge's office at the Stay and Prosper headquarters. Rudge himself was half-seated on the edge of his desk. He was staring angrily across the room at Martin Frankl, who looked rattled.

> Rudge: "I still don't understand how that stupid man Bradwell knew anything about it. Do you?"
> Frankl: "Not yet. We underestimated him."
> "That's an understatement if ever there was one."
> Rudge was passing a paperweight from one hand to the other, weighing it each time like a grenade. He said, "And you reckon he decided to spill the beans to this man Tom Anthony. Why?"
> "I heard them talking at the conference. I just have an instinct."
> "But why Anthony?"
> "He used to be a journalist, and Bradwell knew him from the place where they both used to work."
> "But did Bradwell actually tell him about Donald Finch? That's the sixty-four thousand dollar question."
> "I don't know. Since his car crash Tom Anthony has been in a coma. He might never wake up."
> "Let's hope not."

"Come on, Victor, this isn't funny."

"I want you to watch him, Martin. If he wakes up, find out what he knows. I can't afford to have this nagging away at us. We're surrounded by Brexit bollocks from dawn to dusk. We need to save our energies for that, not worry about things like this."

"What if he does know about this?"

"We can take appropriate steps."

* * *

Jay turned to Tom and gestured him towards a spare chair. "I take it you understand all this – am I right?"

"I'm getting the picture."

"This stuff about 'Donald' – do you know what it's about?"

"I imagine that means Donald Finch, the civil servant who knocked that Monck Chervil investment scheme into touch in the summer."

"And this man Victor Rudge was somehow involved in that?"

Tom was doing some fast thinking. If he told them about the emails Julie had discovered in Nottingham, he would be betraying her trust – yet surely the implications eclipsed his concern for her? He took a deep breath. "I think I can explain what's been going on here."

He described the emails and explained what he thought they meant. "Darren Wright of Rackham Road Services planted the idea of blackmailing Finch in Victor Rudge's mind. Presumably that's exactly what Rudge did."

The others listened without comment. Tom concluded, "If you can avoid making Julie's name public, I would be grateful."

"We're not making anything public until we understand exactly what's going on here."

Joe said, "The same applies to your lady friend – the one who came to interview you. We don't care about her either."

Tom turned to him with a reproachful look. "I told you I wanted to keep her out of this."

Jay said, "Joe's right – we're not interested in her. We just want to piece the story together. Working back, we can assume that Martin Frankl sent her to your house in Hampshire to find out if you really had lost your memory. It was his way of following up the instruction that Rudge gave him in that video. I think we can also assume he must have paid someone at the hospital to keep him updated on your progress. He seems to have a knack of improvising."

Tom shook his head in disbelief.

"From what I'm hearing, your lady gave you a platinum rating: absolutely no doubt about your memory loss. That was even better than Rudge was expecting. It meant that even if Bradwell had told you anything about the blackmail plot, you'd forgotten it. So they could push on and get the American investment quashed, and no one would know they were responsible."

"But what if I'd remembered it all later?"

"No doubt they had some fallback plan – something to discredit you." He left a significant pause. "Or worse."

The room was silent for a while. Adam waggled the mouse, clicking randomly on desktop icons. Jay watched the other two men calmly.

Tom said, "What about the rest of the files that Bradwell left? What's in those?"

Adam looked up. "We don't know yet," he said. "They may be corrupt. If not, a different encryption system has been used for each file, but we haven't worked out the algorithm yet. He was very skilled, this man Ben."

A new thought occurred to Tom. He said, "Wait a minute, the video you've just shown me must have been recorded after Ben Bradwell's death. How come?"

Adam glanced at Jay for approval, then said, "We think Ben must have set up the surveillance system to forward the video automatically to Carswells. So even though he was dead, it carried on working. The files just stacked up."

"Surely they would have filled the Carswell system in the end, and someone would have noticed?"

"The CCTV camera was voice-activated, so it only worked when someone was talking. In any case, it doesn't appear to be working now. At some point after Ben died it must have stopped sending."

Tom sat absorbing this for a moment, then asked, "Was the video originally stored on Stay and Prosper's own computer system? Could the files still be hidden somewhere on there?"

"We thought of that." Jay gave him a slightly evasive look. "We have people who can poke around remotely. Nothing doing. If they were there, they've been totally scrubbed. Gone."

Tom looked from one face to another. He had a sense that they were waiting for him to say something. He swivelled idly in his chair, then finally said, "If you'll forgive me asking, how come the security services are involved in this? Surely Martin Frankl's scheme to send someone to interview me was the ultimate in amateurishness? And blackmail isn't a security issue, is it?"

Jay said, "That's a reasonable assumption, but Mr Rudge has come up on our radar in another connection. We're trying to join the dots."

"What other connection?"

"I can't go into the detail."

"Does it have to do with the people who stole Ben Bradwell's computer and warned me to keep out of it? I assume Joe told you about that?"

"He did."

"And you think it's related to something else, not the Monck Chervil thing?"

"What do *you* think?"

Tom looked speculatively at Jay. This was his prompt to introduce the American kidnapping episode. Until now he hadn't been clear about how to find someone who would believe his story and take it seriously. Finally he had an audience who might.

He said, "There's something else I think you need to know."

Chapter 63

Tom recounted his abduction in New York City blow by blow, adding his suspicion that it had been connected to the threats he'd received in the UK. Jay listened with growing fascination. At the end of the narrative he said, "This is remarkable. It's even better than we hoped."

"How so?"

"It fits in precisely with what we suspected."

"Did I play it right by coming straight back to the UK and not reporting this?"

Jay raised his eyebrows. "I suppose that depends on your perspective. From my point of view, I'd say very much yes. I'm sure our American friends would have preferred to hear all this from you first-hand. But being selfish, we'd rather have the information directly from you than get it secondhand from them, or not at all."

"So what's all this about?"

"We've been getting vague reports for a while about the emergence of a shady group like the one you're describing – but no first-hand corroboration. This is a bit of a breakthrough."

Tom sensed a suppressed excitement behind Jay's words. He said, "What do you mean by a shady group? A group doing what exactly?"

Jay seemed to consider the question. "The less you know about it, the better."

Angered, Tom said, "Come on! I'm putting myself out for you here. Can't you tell me what the hell's going on?"

"Let's see how this develops. We may have an opportunity now."

There was another silence. Tom looked round at the others again, then said, "Why do I get the feeling you want something from me?"

Jay hesitated. "You're right to have made the connection with these American people, but whichever side of the water you look, they're extremely good at keeping their heads down. We don't have any proper evidence."

"So …?"

"You've got them rattled. Not only have you been poking around in Ben Bradwell's life, you also have police and press connections. That's presumably why they've been so keen to keep you quiet."

Tom waited.

"All we want you to do is keep on doing what you've been doing. Probe gently into Ben Bradwell and his computer tricks. See what you can turn up. Eventually these people will start to worry, and that's when they'll make a mistake."

"You want me to make myself a target? You must be joking! They told me that if I kept on interfering, they would lose patience."

"We'll be watching your back. You'll be perfectly safe."

"Oh really?" Tom sat back heavily. "I've seen the films, I've read the books. I know how this goes. You people will lose the plot, and suddenly I'll be on my own at the end of a gun, or at the bottom of a ditch."

"You'll just have to trust us."

Tom thought about that for a moment. "So how do I get in touch with you if I need to?"

Jay glanced at his colleagues. "Give Joe here a call, and we'll get back to you."

On cue, Joe reached forward and handed Tom a business card.

Tom turned back to Jay and stared at him for a long moment. "I have two questions for you."

"OK."

"One is, do you think these people are somehow involved with the Stay and Prosper campaign, or is this about something else altogether?"

"It almost certainly has to do with Victor Rudge, but we don't know whether the campaign itself is implicated. Hopefully that's something we'll find out. What was the other question?"

"Why haven't these people got rid of me already? It sounds as if that's what happened to Ben Bradwell, so why not me?"

"To be honest, I'm not exactly clear. At the moment, maybe they think you don't know enough to be a threat to them."

"But if I keep on interfering, they'll change their minds about that, won't they?"

"That's when we'll step in."

He gave Jay a penetrating look. "What if I don't play along with this?"

"Simple. You'll be on your own. Even if you do nothing, these people might still decide you're an unacceptable loose end. Your next car crash might not turn out so well for you as the last one."

This stopped Tom in his tracks. He said, "You really think these bastards were responsible for that?"

Jay shrugged. "I'm not aware of any evidence of it, but we can't rule it out."

"Jesus."

"My point is that that if we're not on the same page with all this, we won't be there to help you."

As Tom left them he turned. "If you do open those other video files, will you tell me what's on them?"

They exchanged mutual glances, then Jay looked back at Tom. "I don't think so. The less you know, the better."

* * *

He headed off along the chocolate-box streets of Chichester in a state of disbelief. He'd arrived this morning with unanswered questions, but felt as if he was leaving as part of a spy movie.

He wandered unseeing past white rendered Georgian façades, then slowed to circumnavigate the extraordinary Market Cross – an elaborate, eight-sided mediaeval stone structure the size of a small house. It looked like part of a church that had been lopped off and dumped in the middle of the crossroads. A group of street musicians were performing in front of one of its arches.

The good news was that Tom had been given the answers he wanted, or some of them. He now knew, for instance, exactly why Emily Sanders had been sent on her fake insurance errand, and he sensed that she was unlikely to face any legal comeback over it. He also knew Martin Frankl had not been acting alone in the scheme, but had constructed it at Victor Rudge's behest.

Tom also had implicit confirmation that Ben Bradwell had been murdered. At any rate, Jay hadn't denied it. Ben had evidently stumbled into something bigger than he expected, and had paid with his life for interfering.

Perhaps above all, Tom had been able to report his New York experience to people who immediately believed it and understood its significance. In some ways it was a massive relief.

On the minus side, he was apparently expected to keep on upsetting some very frightening people, and simply take it on trust that he would be protected if he found himself in difficulty. But how reliable were those who were supposed to look out for him?

He made his way to his car, which was parked near a stretch of preserved city wall. Was he being watched at this very moment? He glanced round the car park. Surely not. Everything looked safely prosaic: shoppers, off-season tourists, business people. He shook his head and unlocked the car.

* * *

Part-way home, he noticed that his fuel gauge was hovering near empty. He pulled into a service area, and on a whim he parked and went over to the catering complex. In the shop he selected some snacks and joined a short queue at the checkout.

After a moment a man in scruffy green overalls sidled up to him. He had a round, reddish face and curly red hair, and looked every inch the off-duty workman, but when he leaned confidentially towards Tom, his voice and tone belied his appearance. He said crisply, "You don't want to mix with our friend Jay. No good will come of it. This will be your very last warning."

Tom took a step back in alarm. "Who the hell are you?"

The man gave a brief nod to underline his message, then turned and walked calmly away. Tom started to follow, but quickly realised he was holding goods he hadn't yet paid for.

He glanced around. Where was the backup Jay had promised? Nowhere in sight. Thinking back later, he realised he could have dropped his purchases and followed the man out, at least to find out what car he was driving. As it was, he watched helplessly as the green overalls disappeared round the corner.

Returning to his own car, he allowed his mind to play over what that man had said. He'd known Jay's name. How could that be? Had the man been keeping a covert watch on the forensics company, and recognised Jay when he arrived?

This was possible, but there could also be a more disturbing explanation. Someone on the inside might have told him Jay would be there. And if someone could find out that, what other influence did they have?

Chapter 64

More than ever, Tom felt the answer to what was going on lay in those video files. Yet it appeared that Jay and his associates weren't going to share the contents with him, even if they succeeded in opening them. He should have made copies of the files before handing them over – though how he would have decrypted them was a different question entirely.

Then he had another flash of inspiration. Jay had told him in so many words that his team had hacked into the Stay and Prosper computer system, and the files weren't on it. But when Tom had been trying to track down Emily a few weeks ago, her friend Sally at the Stay and Prosper office had mentioned something about having a new computer system installed. Could she have meant a new physical computer system – something to replace the cluster of servers Marcus Headington had pointed out all those months ago? What if Jay knew nothing about this? What if Ben's files were still stored on the old one? Was that possible?

Next morning he phoned Emily. She said, "I thought you were going to call me back about showing my conference presentation to Martin Frankl."

"I'm calling you now."

"Just in time."

"Look, I can put your mind at rest. You're completely off the hook as far as the insurance thing goes. No one is interested. So you don't have to show Martin your speech. He has no hold over you."

"You mean you did go to the police after all?"

"Not exactly, no." He hesitated. "I can't really go into it, but the point is that the authorities know about it and they don't care. You're in the clear."

"Seriously?"

"God's honest truth."

"Huh." She was silent for a moment. "I'd like to know what makes you the fount of all knowledge on this subject."

He glanced around for inspiration. "It's all bound up with some stuff I've got into lately."

"Stuff?"

"Some seriously heavy shit."

She exploded into husky laughter. "I can't believe you just said that. It's so not you."

"I don't know how else to describe it."

"OK, heavy shit. I get the picture."

"I'm sure you don't."

She continued to laugh.

He waited a moment, then said, "Look, I wondered if I could beg a favour?"

"Go on. What?"

"I need to know about the Stay and Prosper computer system. Your mate Sally told me they were having a new system installed. I wondered if she meant new hardware, or just a new way of doing things. If it was new hardware, what had happened to the old hardware?"

"This is getting exceedingly geeky."

"I know, but could you ask her?"

"I suppose so. She probably won't know though."

"It's worth a try."

*   *   *

She surprised him by calling back within an hour. "I think I've got your answer. The Stay and Prosper people did put in a new PC server a while back. Sally says they wanted to update the system, but they couldn't understand how Ben Bradwell's computers worked, and they decided the easiest solution was to start all over again."

"Wonderful what you can do if you have the money."

"Yeah, and nearly all of it comes from donations. I wonder what those generous people would think if they knew their cash was going on fancy IT systems?"

"Anyway, what about the old system?"

"Sally says it's still there in the corner of the research office. No one could be bothered to pull it all out, so they just disconnected it."

"That's fantastic!" He paused to think about it. "Do you think it would still work?"

"Don't ask me. I haven't been there for weeks." She paused. "It was a mini-rack server system, if you know what that means."

"Do you think Sally would try running it up and do a search for me?"

"No way. She has computer phobia. You're lucky she found out this much."

"Do you know anyone else there who could do it?"

"Sorry, no."

He sat in silence for a long time. She waited. Finally he said, "What if I found a way to get into the Stay and Prosper offices, and took a look for myself?"

"Are you mad? They put in extra security after that bomb attack. There's no way you could break in there."

"I thought maybe you might have some ideas."

"Me?"

"Well, you worked there for months. You know the layout."

"Why is this computer so important?"

"I'm trying to track down some video files. I think they might be hidden somewhere on it."

"What video?"

He took a deep breath. "Look, this has to do with Victor Rudge. I can't explain it all now, but it could implicate him in some stuff that would be really bad for the credibility of the campaign."

"Let me think about this."

* * *

She phoned him back that evening.

"I'm on my break at the pub, so I'd better not take long, but I think I might know how to do what you want."

"Go on."

"There's a lane at the back of the building, so you could get into the patio from there."

"Surveillance cameras?"

"No idea, but I can find out."

"Then what?

"If you go down some steps, there's a door into the basement with no security on it. It's kept locked, but Sally could unlock it."

"Would she do that?"

"She says yes."

"Really? Why?"

"She's pissed off with Victor and Martin. She reckons their hard-line Remain attitude is losing them popularity. She's happy with any plan that might discredit them."

"What about the computer system? Would it still work?"

"She actually asked the man in charge of the new IT system. He said it probably would. He hasn't pulled it apart or anything. But there's a problem all the same."

"What?"

"There was a fingerprint recognition login system. We all had to check into it before our computers would connect to the network."

"Oh. That sounds pretty advanced for this kind of setup."

"It was quite weird. I think it was Ben Bradwell's idea. Sally says he was into that kind of thing."

"So that fucks up the whole idea."

"Well, Sally reckons I was still listed as a volunteer when they dumped the old system. They never deleted me, and she says my name used to pop up sometimes."

"So … ?"

She waited for a moment. "That's why I'll have to come with you."

Chapter 65

Emily's shared flat was on the top floor of a nondescript 1930s block in a Hammersmith backwater. Neither of her flatmates was at home when Tom arrived late the following evening.

"Home sweet home," she commented, smiling awkwardly at him.

He looked around. The place was friendly but cramped. He looked back at her. There was a strange electricity between them – probably a combination of nerves and latent sexual tension.

She was dressed in what she declared to be her "safe-cracker outfit" – black jeans, a black sweater and a dark jacket. She went over to the dresser and picked up a black woolly hat. "I think my hair might be a give-away without this."

He'd come attired in his own version of the same kit – dark trousers and a black anorak. He said, "I think we'll probably both be arrested for offences against fashion."

She laughed edgily. "Speak for yourself."

"Has Sally definitely unlocked the door?"

"She said she would. We'll have to take her word for it."

"And no surveillance cameras at the back?"

"She doesn't think so, but she couldn't hang around very long to make sure. If there was one, it would have picked her up."

"Huh. Well let's hope. And what about your login? Do we definitely know it will work?"

"That's the unknown quantity. We can only hope." She ran her eyes over him. "You do have your portable disk drive with you?"

He patted an inside pocket. "What do you think?"

They made slightly stilted small talk, waiting for midnight. She'd told him everyone had to leave the office by then. "They like to make sure their grafters get their beauty sleep." Then they headed out to catch one of the night's last Underground trains to Kensington.

The sky was overcast and there was no moon. The alley behind the office was dark and unwelcoming, and every step seemed to bring the risk of triggering security lights and surveillance cameras. They shuffled along, doing their best to keep their heads down.

Tom whispered, "Pity we didn't black up our faces."

"That would have looked good if we'd run into a policeman."

"Maybe we could have said we were Halloween revellers."

"A bit early for that."

After a couple of hundred metres Emily announced, "This is their back entrance."

The wall was about five feet high, and had a solid wooden gate set into the centre. It was locked. Tom looked at it in dismay. It was slightly lower than the wall, but could he climb over it with his compromised leg? He whispered, "How do we get in?"

"I'll give you one guess. Are you going to give me a leg up?"

She proved impressively agile, and quickly wriggled over the top and landed on the other side with a muted thump. Much more warily he hauled himself up, conscious of his left leg banging repeatedly against the timber.

He clung at the top for a moment, doubled over on his stomach, then dragged his right leg over, and finally his left. With the sudden shift of balance he lost his grip and lunged to the ground, trying his best to land on his good side. It almost worked, but there was a stab of pain in his left leg and he overbalanced in a tangle of limbs.

"Are you all right?" Emily hissed.

"Fine." He struggled gingerly to his feet, reassured to find he could still stand without further pain.

They waited for a moment, catching their breath and peering into the darkness. No security light came on, no alarm sounded.

"There's a flight of steps over here." Emily reached out and took his hand. "It's very narrow. Follow me."

Tom accidentally stubbed his toe on something solid and suppressed a grunt of pain. Emily stifled a hysterical giggle. "Sshh!"

The steps led down to a solid timber door. She turned the knob and pushed. It creaked open.

* * *

Emily led Tom through the building to the office where she'd worked. There were no lights on and there was no sound, so she made her way mostly by feel. Once in the room, she switched on a desk light. "No one will see this from outside," she said confidently. Tom kept looking around nervously.

She directed him over to a small desk in a corner. In an alcove behind it, miscellaneous computer cabinets were just visible in the dim light, apparently mounted in a free-standing metal frame. On the desk were a monitor and keyboard. She leaned over the desk and groped inside the edge of the alcove until she found a switch. LED lights burst into life on the front of the computer, and fans hummed into action.

She switched on another light on a nearby desk, then sat down in front of the monitor and waggled the mouse. Tom pulled a chair over and sat down beside her. He said, "Why does an organisation like this need a computer network at all? Doesn't everyone here work on laptops?"

"It makes them feel more professional." He could hear the scepticism in her voice. "To be fair, they pool all their research stuff on the server, so that everyone can access it. It prevents duplication, and everyone can see what's going on."

The fingerprint reader was a separate device attached to the computer. She fiddled with it for a moment, then said, "Right, we're in!"

"I can't believe it's this easy."

"That's just the first part. Now what?"

"I need to find a folder with some very large files in it. They're video files, but they might not look like it."

"A folder. That's a bit vague."

"Let's just look."

So they did look for more than an hour, taking it in turns to sit at the monitor. Occasionally the building creaked. Each time they looked up in panic. The computer revealed nothing that looked remotely relevant.

"I would go and make coffee," Emily said at one point, "but you can bet your life Victor will have alarmed the kettle."

"I think he would alarm anyone and anything."

She chuckled. "Very good."

Finally he turned to her. "Any ideas?"

"Get the fuck out of here ASAP?"

"Very helpful."

"Keep looking, I suppose."

While he was sitting at the keyboard she sat mutely beside him, watching. He found himself drawing uncharitable comparisons with Jan, who would have fretted and tetched, and would finally have got up and wandered away. The shared purpose of this frightening little endeavour was oddly cheering.

Eventually she pointed to a set of folders on the monitor and said, "Why don't you look in there? I think that'll be where the localhost files for our intranet were stored."

"I didn't realise you were such an expert."

"Didn't you know my middle name was Nerd?"

"I didn't know you had a middle name."

She cleared her throat. "It's Victoria, if you want to know."

They spent the next half-hour rummaging through folders and subfolders full of files making up what was essentially an in-house website. Still nothing revealed itself. They had almost given up when against all expectation, they struck lucky. In a sub-sub-sub-folder buried deep inside a system folder, they were presented with a list of very large .mp4 files.

"These are video files," Tom said, "but I don't see how it can be them. They're bound to be encrypted. These don't seem to be."

"Well at least open one and see."

He double-clicked the file at the top of the list, and after a moment a media application launched itself and they were staring down into Victor Rudge's office from that high-mounted surveillance camera.

"Jesus! It's them, and they're not encrypted."

"Right – so get copying, and let's get out of here."

Tom scanned the array of computer hardware beyond the monitor. "I don't know where to plug this hard drive in."

Emily stood up and started pulling the desk away from the alcove.

"There must be a USB socket somewhere. We just need to find it." She looked down at him. "Well help me!"

He stooped awkwardly behind the desk. "I wish we'd brought a torch."

She fumbled her phone into flashlight mode and pointed it at the computer. Immediately they could see a row of USB sockets, side by side. The keyboard was connected to one of them. He plugged his portable hard disk cable into a spare slot while Emily watched the monitor. "That's it! That's worked."

Tom returned to his seat, and more slowly than he would have liked, the progress bar marked the passage of the files on to his external drive.

The job was done. Emily shut down the computer and switched off the lights. They made it half-way across the room.

Then things went wrong.

Chapter 66

Lights came on in several rooms at the same time and a high-pitched screeching started up.

"Fuck!" Emily blinked in the sudden brilliance. "We must have moved too fast or something, and tripped the alarm. Let's go."

She broke into a run across the room. Tom followed her, but just short of the doorway his left leg buckled under him and a jarring pain shot up from his ankle. He crumpled to the floor with a cry.

Emily stopped and turned. "Quick! Get up." She reached down and started to help him stand. Half-way to his feet, he groaned again and slumped out of her grasp. His leg felt like jelly and the pain in his ankle was even sharper. "I can't do it. I'm sorry!"

"You must! You must!" She wrestled with him, trying to drag him upright.

He made a final attempt, but flopped down once again. "Even if I could make it, I could never climb over that gate." He reached into his jacket and pulled out the hard drive. "You go – and take this with you."

She hovered uncertainly. He said. "*Go*! If you stay, we'll both be arrested and all this will have been for nothing."

She still waited. He said, "And hide that disk somewhere really safe. Not in your flat. Somewhere no one would ever look for it."

She looked at him in bafflement. He said, "I mean it! Some bad people might come looking for it."

She stared, apparently trying to process this.

"GO!"

She turned reluctantly and disappeared towards the back of the building. Tom dragged himself over to the wall and sat back against it. His entire leg was throbbing violently, though when he ran his hands over it, it didn't seem as misshapen as it felt. The discovery was moderately reassuring, but not very.

It took some minutes for the police to arrive. Eventually he heard the front door opening and wary footsteps sounding in the foyer. At the same time, the alarm abruptly fell silent. A voice called, "Hello?"

He shouted, "In here!"

Two policemen in high-visibility jackets peered round the door, then came over to him cautiously.

"Can I ask what's happening here?" one of them said, staring impassively down at him.

"I broke my leg badly a few months ago." He gave them the benefit of a largely genuine grimace. "I think I've fucked it again."

"Could you tell me what your connection is with the occupiers of this property?"

"I'm an acquaintance of one of the principals – Marcus Headington."

"And does he know you're here?"

Tom winced. "I very much doubt it." He looked up. "I think I need to go to a hospital. Could we talk on the way?"

The two policemen exchanged glances, and one of them started speaking into his mobile radio. The other said, "We still need to know what's happening here. Do you have permission to be on these premises?"

Tom sighed. "No."

"So why are you here?"

Tom's mind was racing. What was the correct response? He had no suitable experience to draw on. He said, "I choose not to answer any more questions."

"Oh, you do, do you?"

They stared at each other, then a new voice said, "Tom Anthony, what the *hell* do you think you're doing here?"

It was Victor Rudge.

* * *

Rudge explained to the police officers that he lived near the premises, and had been alerted by the alarm system. Throughout the conversation he darted angry glances at Tom. Eventually one of the officers said, "So you know this man, and you don't want to press charges?"

Rudge said, "Can we have a moment alone? I think a quick chat will clarify the matter."

Reluctantly the officers retreated, saying they were going to inspect the rest of the ground floor. Rudge turned to Tom.

"Right, so are you going to tell me what the *fuck* you're doing in my building?"

Tom was thinking fast. If he explained how he and Emily had gained access, Sally might be in trouble. Fatuously he said, "I was meeting a friend."

"I don't think so. In the middle of the night?"

"What better time?"

"If you expect me to believe that, you're deluding yourself. I know you've been meddling and interfering, and now you're doing it again. Who the hell *are* you? Are you some kind of agent for the Brexit brigade?"

"God, no! I'm on your side. Or I thought I was. But I don't know what your side is any more."

"And how did you get in here?"

"No comment."

Rudge stared down at him, chewing the inside of his cheek absently. He said, "You have a choice here. Either you tell me what's going on, or I leave you to those policemen, and you can spend the night in a cell."

Tom stared up at him. He'd been reluctant to reveal his knowledge of Rudge's recent activities, but he now realised he would have to bargain. He said, "I know about Donald Finch."

"What?" He had Rudge's attention now.

"I know about your scheme to head off the Monck Chervil investment. I know how you applied pressure. If you press charges against me, I'll go public with this as soon as I'm bailed, and your campaign will be in tatters."

"Absolute rubbish. The Government aid package broke EU rules, plain and simple. A shame, but there it is. Go and look it up in Hansard if you don't believe me. You don't know what the hell you're talking about."

"So you want the press to write that on your epitaph, do you? 'EU rules sank investment scheme.' That'll do you no end of good."

"They can say what they like. You have no evidence for any of this."

"Oh yes I do." This was partly bluff, but it was true enough for him to be able to say it with conviction. He stared up defiantly.

"What evidence?"

"You'll see soon enough."

Rudge continued to stare at him, then finally said, "You haven't heard the last of this, *Mister* Anthony."

* * *

The police had summoned an ambulance, which took Tom to the nearest hospital. While he was waiting he tried phoning Emily's number several times, but each time the call went to voicemail. He had to settle for sending her a text message reporting that he'd escaped the clutches of the police.

He was seen by a doctor after half an hour, and was told that this counted as fast-tracking. "You're lucky we're quiet tonight," a nurse told him. "Also we need to be sure your injuries aren't severe."

After an X-ray and another much longer wait, Tom learned that he hadn't in fact disturbed his previous leg injuries, he'd merely twisted his ankle, probably though running awkwardly to protect the delicate work of his surgeons. "You're very lucky," he was told again, this time by the doctor who bound up his ankle. "You should be moving about more carefully. Leg injuries like yours can take a long time to settle down."

A porter wheeled Tom to the exit and handed him his left shoe and a basic walking stick, muttering, "Last time we'll ever see this, I suppose."

Tom hobbled over to the empty taxi rank. It was after 4am. He shivered in the night air.

Now what? He'd checked into the same hotel as last time, but he wanted to reassure himself that Emily had escaped undetected. When a taxi eventually appeared, he gave the driver her address.

She buzzed him in with a cry of relief, and he made his way upstairs in the rather spartan lift, grateful that it worked at all. She then kept him waiting a moment before opening her front door. "I was on my way to bed," she explained. "I waited for hours to see if you would show up, and I've been trying to call and text you, but then I realised my phone isn't working. I dropped it on the way over that gate, and I must have buggered it up."

"Well, I'm here now."

She gave him a wry glance. "I'm so pleased you got out of this all right."

"I wouldn't say all right, but at least we achieved what we set out to."

"How's your ankle? It doesn't look good."

"Sprained. Hurts like hell, but I'll live." He looked around vaguely. "Did you hide that disk?"

"I put it in an envelope and bunged it in our mailbox downstairs."

"That's clever."

"I thought so."

They smiled tentatively at each other. He said, "I should go to my hotel. I might still get some sleep."

"Stay here. The couch is really comfortable. Don't put yourself through any more hassle tonight."

"Seriously?"

"I think we can manage something."

As she started to bustle around, he said, "I can't believe you put yourself through this for me."

She glanced over at him. "Don't flatter yourself. It was for Marcus Headington and the campaign."

"Of course. Sorry."

She grinned as she handed him a slightly tired-looking duvet. "The bathroom is in there. If you know what's good for you, don't wake me up before ten."

Chapter 67

He slept badly. The effect of the painkillers gradually wore off, and his ankle throbbed remorselessly. Also the couch was too short, so he had to hunch up his head and shoulders to keep his legs on a level.

In the event, he had to get up early. One of Emily's flatmates emerged from her bedroom at eight o'clock, expressing no more than mild surprise when she discovered Tom on the couch. "You're one of Emily's waifs and strays, I suppose?"

"Something like that."

"I'm Jenny."

He dressed quickly in the bathroom and then watched her preparing breakfast in the tiny kitchen. He explained that he'd sprained his ankle, but she seemed curious rather than compassionate. However, she did make him a cup of coffee.

It felt strange to be plunged into the impermanent world of shared flats – a world he'd known briefly after leaving college. The lounge was randomly furnished but homely, yet he felt out of place here. If he'd been in a relationship with Emily he might have warmed to the bohemian atmosphere and allowed himself to be embraced by it, but while things were unresolved between them he felt like a fish out of water.

He was due to visit a Carswell branch in Bournemouth that afternoon, but he had no chance of getting there. He phoned the manager and postponed the appointment. Once he'd completed that task he sat fretting. He wanted to examine the video files, but needed Emily to retrieve the disk drive.

At ten past ten she wandered into the sitting room, bleary-eyed. "You slept well, I hope?" she asked.

"Not really, but I can't blame you for that."

She went downstairs to fetch the disk drive. "Good to know our precautions weren't necessary," she commented as she handed it to him.

He shrugged. "I didn't know what to expect."

She booted up her laptop and handed it to him. "Hopefully you can play back those videos on this."

With trepidation he opened the first file – the one they'd viewed at the office. It showed a short and insignificant phone conversation between Victor Rudge and someone in the media.

The second file wouldn't open. Nor would any of the others he tried.

"I don't believe this!" He showed her the error messages. "This is turning into a joke. Every time I nearly find out what's in these files, something gets in the way."

She looked at the screen over his shoulder. "What's wrong with them?"

"I think they're encrypted. Obviously the first one wasn't. It must have been a trial, or a mistake that slipped through."

She continued to look at the screen, then said, "I might have an idea."

"Seriously?"

"There's a guy who works in the greengrocer's shop round the corner – he was done for hacking. He reckons he's a world expert at this kind of thing. Maybe he would know what to do."

She went down to enquire, then came back twenty minutes later with a smile on her face. "He'll have a look on his break after lunch."

"You're a genius!"

"Let's wait and see."

He spent the morning seated on Emily's sofa, browsing the internet on her laptop. At one point she sat down beside him and mutely handed him a photograph album. It contained pictures of her from her childhood, mostly depicting her dressed up in antique clothes and putting on some kind of show. "Acting was in my blood right from the start."

"It's a shame you don't get to do more of it."

At lunchtime she made sandwiches for them both. Finally it was time to go down to see her friend in the greengrocer's. She shoved her laptop into a plastic bag and offered Tom her arm as they walked along to the lift. He took it gratefully, conscious that this was the first time their contact had extended beyond a handshake.

Billy was a youth of nineteen or twenty with a shaven head and a cheery manner. He gave an enquiring glance at an older man serving behind the counter, presumably his boss, then led them through to a back room. "I'm not supposed to go within ten feet of an internet connection," he commented. "So this didn't happen, right?"

He sat down at a table and fired up the laptop, then plugged in a flash drive of his own, followed by Tom's hard disk. Tom and Emily watched. After a few moments he said, "OK, these aren't actually .mp4 files." Then he corrected himself. "Maybe they have .mp4 files inside them, but they're just containers. Whoever created them probably renamed them just to add confusion."

"Can you open them?"

"I should think so. I just need some time. Do you want to come back later?"

* * *

At half-past four Billy phoned Tom's mobile. "Job done."

"You've opened all the files?"

"Yup. Not a problem."

"That's fantastic!"

"You owe me fifty quid. Twenty-five for me, twenty-five for my boss, for taking me off my work."

"Sounds fair to me."

"Make it sixty."

He had just enough cash in his wallet. He handed it to Emily, who went down to fetch the disk drive. As she came back she said, "I need to go to work at the pub. What will you do?"

"My overnight bag is still at the hotel. I need to fetch it." He grimaced. "I could do with some clean clothes."

"Stay another night here. I can pick it up for you tomorrow."

Despite the shortcomings of the couch, the offer was tempting. He said, "OK, thanks."

"You'll find some instant meals in the freezer. Help yourself." And she was gone.

He phoned the hotel to explain that he would retrieve his bag next day. Then he settled in front of the laptop and prepared to examine the video files.

The first file still showed Victor Rudge on his phone, apparently talking to a journalist. The timecode showed a date some weeks before Tom's accident. He moved on to the next file – the first one Billy had decrypted. This time Rudge was sitting on the edge of his desk, talking to someone on the phone about a TV appearance.

The next one showed two people. Rudge was seated behind his desk, issuing instructions to a woman who appeared to be part of the campaign's media department. In the next one he was on the phone again, walking round the room and talking strategy with someone at his finance company. In the next he was back on the edge of his desk, ordering a Chinese take-away.

Tom sat back and looked at the folder on the screen. There were dozens of files – probably hundreds. He opened one or two more at random. From the timecodes, they seemed to be listed in correct date order. How long was it going to take him to look through them all? Hours, clearly. All he could do was plough through them, hoping he wouldn't miss anything significant. He went back to the files he'd already viewed and started with the next one.

He was still unclear why Ben Bradwell had installed the webcam in the first place. He might never find out, but the evidence suggested that Ben must have been innately cynical, and also remarkably attentive to what was going on around him. Up in Nottingham, his suspicious nature had led him to monitor Darren Wright's emails, and down here at Stay and Prosper, something must have prompted him to turn the spotlight on Victor Rudge. But what? Hopefully these video clips would provide the answer.

Emily's flatmate Jenny arrived back at seven in the evening and heated up a meal for him from the freezer. She told him she worked in an office near Holborn. She said Kim, their other flatmate, was away for a week. "I'd let you sleep in her room, but it's not really my place."

"Don't worry about it. The couch is fine."

She went off to bed shortly after eleven, but Tom waited up for Emily and continued to work his way through the video files. He found he was assessing each conversation from the way it started – guessing whether anything significant seemed likely to follow, and skipping to the next as soon as the answer seemed to be no. It was a crude approach, but he was aware that if he played through every conversation, the task could take days.

For a long time nothing striking came up, though he gradually formed a clearer picture of the man himself. For the most part Rudge came over as driven, impatient, critical and manipulative. He seemed to have a wide array of friends and associates, yet Tom found it hard to imagine how anyone could actually like him.

Then came a clip that had him leaning forward over the laptop. The timecode at the bottom of the image showed a date not long before Tom's accident. Rudge was sitting on the edge of his desk, talking to Martin Frankl, who was standing facing him, clearly uneasy.

> Rudge: "This Monck Chervil investment plan is bad news. We should block it if we can."
>
> Frankl: "It may never happen. At the moment it's just gossip. It probably depends on whether or not the company gets Government funding."
>
> "But if it does happen, it'll be a gift for the pro-Leave people. They'll be shouting, 'Business as usual! Brexit is good for Britain – here's the proof!' I'm not having it, Martin."
>
> "I don't see what we can do about it."
>
> "I know the man who looks after Government support for this kind of thing – a nasty bit of work called Donnie Finch. If he approves a funding package, I can persuade him to think again."
>
> "How the hell do you make that out?"
>
> "I know things. I know where to apply pressure." A calculating smile.
>
> "Why are you telling me this?"
>
> "I want you on side, Martin. We're in this together. I need you to be my flanker in the field."

There it was: an admission of Rudge's plan to blackmail Donald Finch. Paired with the video he'd already seen – the one where Rudge ordered Frankl to put a watch on Tom – it must surely be enough for someone to start building a case against him.

* * *

It was well after midnight when Emily came in. "You're still up," she said softly.

"Of course."

She had a glow about her. Tom sensed that she might have been sampling the product she was serving. She came over and took the laptop from him, then sat down beside him on the sofa and looked searchingly at him. He was very aware of the closeness of her body and the cascade of reddish-gold hair down her back.

She said, "Just to be clear, you do fancy me, do you?"

In a dry voice he replied, "What do you think?"

She leaned slowly towards him and put her hands on his shoulders, and he leaned over to meet her. The kiss was long, gentle and eloquent. He reached forward and ran his hands through her hair.

She pulled away and gave him a brief smile. "I'm off to bed. I hope you enjoy the couch. Usually it's better the second night, or so I've been told."

Chapter 68

Emily slept in even later next morning than the last. Tom was already on his second coffee by the time she appeared, and he'd inspected dozens more video files. He'd slept badly again, but not as badly as the previous night, and the pain in his ankle had subsided to a persistent ache. Today the painkillers seemed to be doing their job.

"Any luck?" she asked.

"One interesting clip so far, but I think there must be more."

"What are you expecting to find?"

"I won't know it until I see it."

He searched on. It was some time after eleven thirty in the morning when he arrived at another video that caught his attention. The date was shortly before Tom's accident. Rudge was sitting in his familiar position on the edge of his desk, talking on his phone. He said, "Of *course* it's scrambled. What do you take me for?"

Tom pricked up his ears and watched closely as the clip played through.

> Rudge: "No, no, there's no point in targeting extreme right-wingers. Nobody loves them, not even the most ardent pro-Leave supporters …"
>
> "Exactly. The real enemy is the 'reasonable brigade' – people who paint a convincing picture of little Britain sailing into a prosperous new dawn …"
>
> "Well, it could be a moderate Brexiteer or revisionist Remainer – someone who has renounced the cause …"
>
> "I can suggest some obvious candidates straight off the top of my head …" He reeled off half a dozen names, all of them prominent politicians and business people.
>
> "All the blame has to go to the hard Brexit people. If there's even a chance of your man being caught, the whole point will be lost …"
>
> "Yes, it needs to be dramatic – to have resonance. Ideally it would be at a public event of some kind – a rally, a conference …"

"No, not now!" A burst of anger. *"Some time towards the end of the
          year. By then people will know more about the mess they're getting
          into …"*

*"Yes, exactly. That's why we need to pick the right target. If it's
          someone who sounds convincing, it'll look as though the hard-liners
          are worried about getting a 'soft' exit after all …"*

*"What I'm saying is stand down now, but keep in touch. We need to
          be ready when the time is right."*

A pause. "We need to decide just how radical we can afford to be …"

*"Yes, that's what I'm thinking. It would make the point, wouldn't
          it? …*

"I realise we're talking high stakes here …"

*"Look, if we want to get the nation on side, maybe we should strike at
          the heart of the movement…"*

"All right, well let's see how things play out over the coming months …"

Tom played the video through twice. What did Rudge mean by
"targeting"? Was he talking about a smear campaign – an attack on
some individual's business or private life? Or was he talking about
making the person a literal target? All explanations seemed sinister,
but the mention of a specific event seemed to point to something
dramatic.

He resumed his trawl through the video files, dismissing numerous
mundane conversations about the management of the campaign. The
only other clip of interest he found was one showing a very short phone
conversation in which Rudge left a terse voicemail message. He said,
"Darren, this is just to let you know the MC project won't be happening.
Our friend Donnie got the message."

It was probably as near as anyone would ever get to extracting an
admission from Rudge that he had coerced Donald Finch into cancelling
the Monck Chervil grant funding.

*   *   *

Emily went off as promised to retrieve his overnight bag from his hotel,
and came back with shop-bought sandwiches for lunch. After last night's

embrace, the level of tension between them had risen a notch. Another night on the couch was hard to imagine. He should head back to Winchester.

She seemed reluctant to let him go. As they ate, she said, "Why not stay until tomorrow? Then you can focus on those videos without any interruption." She spoke lightly, but the subtext was difficult to ignore.

At least his bag had given him a change of clothes. He said, "Let's see how it goes."

She demurred. "I have to go in to work early this afternoon. I need to know if you'll be here when I get back."

He smiled. "OK, I'll be here."

"Fine. Just so long as we're clear."

After she'd left, Tom picked up the laptop and resumed his search through the videos. He had to force himself to concentrate as clip after clip unfolded the minutiae of the campaign's day-to-day affairs. Hours passed, but he found nothing else of interest.

He sat back, reviewing what he'd learned. Apparently Rudge had been planning what he called "dramatic" action to make a point. He wanted to deliver a very public blow against Brexit moderates, and he aimed to blame it on the hard-liners in order to undermine their position.

Tom wondered about the timeline. It had been early that year when these recordings had been made, and Rudge had talked about taking action "towards the end of the year". That would be around now.

He scribbled down the names of the six people Rudge had mentioned and trawled the internet to see what was being said about them. In particular, he wanted to find out if any of them was likely to appear at some high-visibility event in the near future. They all seemed to lead extremely busy public lives, but it wasn't possible to build an exact diary of their movements.

Then he sat forward with a start. Kenneth Moir, the pro-Leave ex-MP he'd interviewed earlier in the year, was involved in a lecture tour spread over several months, speaking at universities and in other public venues. And the last event of the series was taking place this very day in Colchester, fifty miles north-east of London. *This very day!*

He checked the computer calendar in disbelief. There was no mistake. Moir was due to take to the stage at eight o'clock this evening.

He pushed the computer away from him on his lap, as if he could distance himself from the implications of what he was learning. A plot could be in train to murder Moir in a very public place, and it could be scheduled for tonight. The coincidence of his finding this out hours before the event was mind-bending, but the reality of it was inescapable.

Was he being over-dramatic about this? The words "kill" and "murder" appeared nowhere in those videos. Rudge had been far too careful. And even if that was the plan, there was nothing to indicate that it was scheduled for tonight, or that Kenneth Moir was in fact the target. Those other names could still be potential candidates.

Had Jay Reynolds and his security team decoded these videos themselves? If so, they would surely have reached the same conclusion as Tom had. After all, they must have better resources at their disposal than a nineteen-year-old hacker working in a greengrocer's shop? And if they knew what he knew, presumably they would already have put some of their people on the ground in Colchester, even if just as a precaution.

He couldn't make that assumption. He needed to find out for himself. He grabbed his phone and scrolled to Joe's number. The call went to voicemail. He said, "Joe, I know this will sound mad, but I've seen those videos taken in Victor Rudge's office, and I think he might be planning some kind of disruption at an event *tonight*. Kenneth Moir is due to speak in Colchester. I don't know how serious the threat is, but the answer could be very. *Please* get back to me, and pass this on to Jay Reynolds."

He ended the call. It didn't feel like enough, but he simply wasn't prepared for this sudden crisis, sprung on him out of the blue. All he could do was improvise.

He scrolled to Bernard Weatherley's number and phoned that. Again the call went to voicemail. He left a simpler message, saying he was urgently trying to reach Joe.

Now what? He glanced at his watch. It was just after six in the evening. In mounting panic he called directory enquiries and requested the number of Phipps & Butler, the computer forensics company in Chichester. They seemed to have gone home; all he got was a recorded message listing their opening hours.

He sat back, feeling helpless, and waited for a few minutes to see if anyone would call him back. No one did.

He searched for a website relating to the lecture venue in Colchester, but decided the most relevant number was one for a council office. It seemed too remote from the actual event to be of much use.

Then he remembered he still had Kenneth Moir's mobile number on his phone. The call went to voicemail. Of course. He said, "I don't know if you remember me. It's Tom Anthony here, a journalist. You gave me an interview earlier this year. I'm worried that some sort of terrorist event may be planned for your talk in Colchester tonight. Please call me back as a matter of urgency, or call the police."

He left his phone line clear again for a few minutes. Still no incoming calls.

He was out of options. He took a moment to collect his thoughts, then dialled 999. When the call handler picked up he said, "I believe there may be a bomb at a public event in Colchester tonight."

Chapter 69

The police arrived within minutes. Tom had briefly considered making his phone call anonymously, but then concluded that they would trace his location from his phone, and would probably arrive in force. Emily wouldn't thank him if they barged her door down.

So he buzzed them in when they arrived downstairs, and greeted them at the door to the flat. There were five of them, and they didn't look amused. They told him to grab his jacket, then led him to the lift and down to an anonymous-looking black car with a blue light flashing behind the front grille. A striped police cruiser, also with light flashing, had pulled up behind.

Minutes later they were in a police station. He was led to an interview room and told to sit at a table. The policemen who had brought him in conferred among themselves for a while, then two men in suits entered the room and sat down, and they were left alone.

The one who spoke had a brisk, no-nonsense air and an impatient edge to his tone. He said, "Mr Tom Anthony, correct?"

"Yes."

"So what's this about a bomb?"

"Have you alerted the people at Colchester? It might not be a bomb, it might be a sniper, or a knife, or something else. I just know Kenneth Moir could be in danger."

"Forget about that. What we need from you is to know where you're getting this from. Are you involved?"

"God, no!"

"So?"

Tom looked bleakly between the two of them. How much of this would he have to endure before they let up on him? He said, "I need you to contact a man named Jay Reynolds in the security service. He knows about this, and he'll vouch for me."

"Oh really? And which security service might that be?"

Tom looked at him helplessly. "I don't know. MI5?"

"You don't know." The voice was freighted with disbelief.

"Please. If you can track him down, he can tell you more about all this than I can. I just happened to work out that this plot might be timed to kick off tonight. I don't know if he knows that or not. I couldn't reach him to ask. Somebody ought to tell him. He'll know what to do."

"So you're in touch with someone from MI5, but you know more than he does?"

Tom sighed. "Please. Just chase him up. Then all this will make sense."

"I tell you what – humour us. Tell us what the hell this is about, and leave us to decide what to do about it."

* * *

The two interrogators kept Tom talking for well over an hour. Periodically one of them left the room, presumably to confer with colleagues. Then they both rose and left, and Tom was on his own for at least another hour. He started to worry that they would make a connection with his break-in at the Stay and Prosper office, but it seemed not. When one of them finally came back, he told Tom, "You're lucky. We've tracked down your Mr Reynolds."

"So can I go?"

"For now, yes, but my strong advice to you is to stop sticking your nose in where it's not wanted."

"So he knew about Colchester, did he?"

"I'm not at liberty to say."

"But is Kenneth Moir safe?"

"To the best of our knowledge, yes."

As he stood up, Tom said, "Was there some kind of threat at Colchester? Surely you can tell me that."

"Sorry, I can't give you any more information."

He was driven back to Emily's flat and dropped at the entrance. He had no key, but when he pressed the buzzer she answered in person.

He made his way up to her floor, and managed to smile sheepishly as she opened the door.

She said, "You look as if you've been run over by a bus."

"I feel like it."

"And where's my laptop?"

As he limped past her he looked at the coffee table. The laptop was gone, along with his hard disk drive. He said, "I think the police must have it. Sorry."

"The police?"

"I've been with them most of the evening."

"My god – is this about us breaking in?"

"No, no. It's much more complicated than that."

"Well sit down. You really do looked wrecked."

As he lowered himself on to the sofa she thrust a glass of red wine into his hand. "I'm afraid I don't have anything stronger."

He told her about his discovery of the suspicious videos and his guess about the implications. She listened in silence, then said, "You were assuming a hell of a lot in thinking that guy in Colchester was the target. What if you'd been wrong?"

"I probably *was* wrong. I panicked. But if you'd experienced what I've experienced in the last few weeks, you wouldn't take anything for granted."

"So did the police find anything at Colchester?"

"If they did, they're not telling me."

"I suppose it's hard to know what to make of something that didn't happen."

She went through to the kitchen to make coffee, then leaned round the door. "Do you want something to eat? You must be starving."

He struggled to his feet and hobbled over to her. "Nuts or crisps would be good."

"I expect we can manage that."

He said, "I wasn't sure if you'd be back home this early."

"You're lucky I was. Jenny's out. If I hadn't been here you'd still be standing in the street."

"So how come?"

"Early start. I took up the option to knock off at ten." She looked down, uncharacteristically hesitant. "I didn't know what to think when you weren't here."

He was standing close to her. He reached forward and touched her hair lightly, then lowered his hand. "I'm glad I'm here now."

She lifted her head and seemed to recover her composure. "You must be fed up with the couch by now. Why not sleep in Kim's bed tonight? I'll square it with her when she comes back next week."

"If you're sure."

"Or …" She was hesitant. "Mine's even more comfortable."

A wave of anticipation shot through him, but he heard himself saying, "My ankle might be a problem."

She smiled, suddenly shy. "I wasn't asking you to run a marathon."

* * *

That first night with Emily was tentative, exhilarating, awkward, affirming. When Tom finally slept, it was badly, but he woke with an unfamiliar sense of optimism.

Emily was already up. He could hear her singing softly to herself in the kitchen. Strangely, he felt tears pricking at the backs of his eyes. That simple, unknowing expression of joy was overwhelming, and he was humbled. When had he last experienced anything like it? Perhaps never.

He took out his phone, and realised the police must have turned if off after they'd seized it the previous night. Several unanswered calls had been logged, including one from Joe, and surprisingly, one from Kenneth Moir. Bernard had left a voicemail message. "Sorry Tom, Marie and I were out at the theatre this evening with Joe and his wife. I understand you were trying to call him as well. Let me know when you get this."

He smiled ruefully at Emily as he prepared to leave. "I hope I'll see you soon."

She looked uncertainly at him. "You're coming to Manchester next week to the Stay and Prosper conference, aren't you?"

"Wouldn't miss it."

"I'll see you there then."

He made his way to Waterloo on the Tube, then caught a train to Winchester. His car had collected several parking tickets. He pulled them off the windscreen philosophically. Without those three nights in London his relationship with Emily might never have progressed so far. This was a price he was more than happy to pay.

Chapter 70

In the middle of the afternoon there was a sharp rap at the front door. Tom opened it to find himself looking at Joe's lined face, and beckoned him inside. Joe shook his head and pointed to his car, which he'd parked directly in front of the house. "Come."

Once in the car, Joe said, "You never know who's listening."

Tom shook his head. "I still find it hard to believe all this is real."

"It's real enough, trust me."

"So what's happening?"

"First, I'm sorry I couldn't get back to you last night. I was at the theatre. We all need a life."

"Of course."

"Second, thanks for the alert about Colchester."

"Was there really a threat?"

"I don't think they found anything, but we know these people are clever."

"So as far as the police are concerned, I'm just a mad hoaxer?"

"Don't worry about the police. The people who matter know different."

Tom said nothing.

"Third, you should have come to us when you worked out that there were copies of those video files in the office in London. You were a bloody fool to think you could deal with this on your own."

"The trouble is, I don't know who to trust."

Joe looked at him sharply. "What do you mean by that?"

Tom did some quick thinking. Could he take Joe into his confidence? He made a decision. "On my way back from Chichester, a guy came up to me in a service area, and he knew exactly what was going on. He even knew Jay's name. He said this was my last chance to stop interfering."

"Did he indeed?"

"Do you see what I'm getting at? He seemed to know more than he should."

Joe said nothing for a moment, then, "I need to think about this."

The silence was broken abruptly by a knock on Joe's side window. He buzzed it down, and a large black woman in uniform said, "No parking here." She had a Caribbean accent.

Joe reached into his pocket and held out a wallet containing a laminated card. He said, "Go away please."

She peered over and glanced at it, then stepped back abruptly and retreated without another word.

Joe closed the window and turned to Tom. "I sometimes worry that I'm losing my sense of humour in my old age."

"I thought you were retired?"

"I am." Joe hesitated. "But not entirely."

Tom said, "So you're telling me your people didn't succeed in decrypting their copies of those video files?"

"That's correct. It seems most of them were corrupted. Transmission errors or something."

"But they have my clean copies now."

"They do." A hint of a smile passed over Joe's face. "I have to hand it to you – it was clever, the way you worked out that they would still be on that computer in London."

"Huh."

"I don't suppose you'd like to explain how you decrypted them? We think we know, but it would be good to have corroboration."

"I don't want to cause trouble for someone who has nothing to do with this."

Joe grunted. "I think I'll take that as confirmation."

"So what happens to Victor Rudge? He's the man behind all this. Can you take action against him?"

"Not necessarily. So far we haven't found anything unequivocally incriminating in those videos – and nothing in fact has happened. We can't arrest the man for some future crime that might never be committed."

"I thought that was exactly what you did with terrorists?"

"Have a heart! We still have to follow due process."

"So what happens now?"

"We're gradually closing in on these crazy people. In the meantime you can probably breathe more easily. If we assume they now know that we have these video files, they'll probably lose interest in you."

"So every cloud has a silver lining."

"You could look on it that way."

* * *

Half an hour later a call came in. "Kenneth Moir here. I've been trying to get back to you."

Tom sat up to attention. "It's good of you to call."

"I wanted to thank you for your efforts at keeping me safe."

"I hope I didn't cause you a load of unnecessary grief."

"Well, the lecture was cancelled, which was unfortunate, but staying alive takes precedence over that, wouldn't you say?"

"So the police treated the threat seriously?"

"Very much so. They didn't find anything – or at least if they did, they haven't told me about it. But I could see that they were concerned."

"What a terrible time we're living through."

"I don't suppose you want to tell me how you stumbled into this? I didn't realise you were an investigative journalist."

"I'm not. It's a long story, but I promise I'll fill you in one day if I get the chance."

"Well, they're re-scheduling the lecture for a couple of weeks' time, so perhaps you would like to come along?"

"Thank you – but with the greatest of respect, I should warn you that I don't share your opinions."

Moir laughed dryly. "So you're a determined espouser of lost causes? You need to reconcile yourself to reality, my friend. Brexit's going to happen, and we all need to pull together to make it work."

* * *

Tom sat in his lounge in the gathering dusk, reflecting on recent events. Was Joe right that these mysterious people would leave him alone now that those videos had been found? It would be reassuring to think so, but only time would reveal whether or not that was true.

Would the police or the security services track down these people, or was the trail too indistinct? Would they be able to take legal action against Victor Rudge, or did they lack sufficient evidence? Would the facts ever come out and undermine the Stay and Prosper campaign? Could it survive if they did?

He wanted to work through the logic of what had happened, but instead he kept finding himself thinking about Emily. She was by far the best thing to have come out of all this. In the past few days their obvious mutual attraction seemed to have settled into something more solid, and perhaps more durable. But could he adapt to her bohemian lifestyle, her ironic personality, her strongly-held beliefs? Would she become bored by his more conventional world? In sheer practical terms, how would an ongoing involvement with her actually work?

He chided himself. He was assuming too much on the basis of far too little. All he could do was push their relationship forward one step at a time.

One factor, of course, represented a major obstacle to any of this – his ongoing involvement with Jan. But as soon as he thought about her, his feelings seemed to crystallise. His life with her was over. If he'd been honest with himself, he would have recognised that it had been over since before his accident.

Partly, he'd banished the thought because he'd needed her after the accident, and she'd been there. According to Christine, they'd decided to separate just before it happened, yet she'd stood by him in spite of that – apparently hoping the break-up had been expunged from his memory. It seemed to indicate extraordinary loyalty on her part, and he found this hard to dismiss from the reckoning. Yet it shouldn't blind him to the retreat of warmth from their relationship. It merely made her strange tenacity harder to understand.

It couldn't go on. He wanted to try to push things further with Emily, but his conscience wouldn't let him. He needed to clear the air, to persuade Jan to accept the reality of their situation.

He needed to talk to her.

She answered his call quickly, but sounded distracted. "Tom, you've caught me in the middle of packing. I'm off to a finance conference in Oslo in the morning."

"Oh, right. I was hoping we could get together and talk."

"I know. I've been busy. We can catch up when I'm back."

"We really do need to talk. We can't carry on like this."

"Like what? What are you saying?"

"I feel as if we've split up without actually saying so. I think it's time to face up to it."

"No we haven't!" There was surprise and indignation in her voice. "Let's not get into this now. We can talk when I get back."

He disconnected with a sense of frustration. Every time he broached the subject of their relationship, Jan seemed to find some reason to postpone the conversation. Now they probably wouldn't have the chance to talk it through before the conference in Manchester next week.

Maybe he would simply have to proceed as if they had.

Chapter 71

In the morning he was phoned by Julie, the ex-colleague who worked at Rackhams in Nottingham. She jumped straight to the point.

"Tom, I found out the name of the man who's stirring things up in Carswell's courier network."

He tried to stifle a sigh. This corporate in-fighting seemed trivial compared with the international plotting he'd tangled with. He had to remind himself that for the people involved, these things were important. He said, "Go on."

"According to my friend Jacqueline at Carswells, the person we're talking about is Gerry Keane, the network liaison assistant at Eastleigh."

"I know him," Tom said. "I deal with him on network issues."

"But you probably don't know where he worked before he joined Carswells. He was at Rackhams, here in Nottingham."

"Are you saying he's some kind of spy for Rackhams?"

"Precisely." She lowered her voice. "And here's the thing. I've realised that Ben Bradwell's computer setup is still active. It's still intercepting email messages between Darren Wright and some of his contacts. I was looking at it again yesterday, and there are some new messages that weren't there before."

"Such as what?"

"Well, I'm calling you because I've just found one to Darren from Gerry. Can I read it out?"

"Go ahead."

"He says: 'Dover branch should be a pushover. Gloucester is already talking to another group, so we need to move fast with them. Bradford is willing to listen. Hull looks a good prospect too. The new network should be ready to go when you are.'"

These branches were spread widely across the country. If they all joined Rackhams in creating a rival network, its coverage would look promising right from the start – and Carswell's coverage would be greatly depleted. He said, "That seems pretty conclusive. Someone needs to report all this to Felix."

"Well I can't, and nor can Jacqueline."

"Why not?"

"Her son works for Rackhams in Rugby. It's a long story, but they did him a big favour by giving him the job. She doesn't want him to lose it." She paused. "And I don't want to lose mine."

Tom reflected on all this for a moment, then asked, "What's the story with Darren Wright? Did he found Rackhams himself?"

"No, he was recruited from the industry a few years ago when old man Rackham died. No one else in the family was available to take over. He's done a lot of good for the company. He's built it into a substantial business."

"But do the other directors want to defect from the Carswell network? What do the family think?"

"I don't know, Tom – I'm not privy to that kind of thing."

"You must have some idea though."

She took a moment to consider this. "I think one director would definitely go along with Darren, but the others are probably more relaxed about it, and the family shareholders just want an easy life."

"So without Darren, this whole defection scheme might go away?"

"Well, that's making a lot of assumptions." She pondered for another moment. "I think it would depend if someone could put a good case to the other directors for staying."

"OK, look, can you send me that email about the network – and also the most revealing one about the Monck Chervil business?"

* * *

He should do something. He wasn't sure what, but he had the glimmerings of an idea. He phoned Felix Schaefer.

"These Rackham people," he said. "Just how important are they to the Carswell network?"

"I thought you were getting them back on side?"

"I know. I'm just trying to get the big picture into my head."

"Well, no member is indispensable, but some are more indispensable than others. Our biggest single revenue stream comes through Rackhams, and they cover three different territories for us. There are no other companies like them in that area, so we'd be hard pressed to replace them like for like."

"And can they really leave the network if they want to?"

"You know the score, Tom. We have a contract with them, so if they do leave, theoretically we can sue them, but think of the mire that would get us into. Think of the ill will and the distraction from the job. We can't make them like us if they don't."

"What if they refuse to pay their dues for services rendered, or to clear their forward commitment to the group?"

Felix gave a sigh. "We'll have to negotiate. It could be painful, but there's no point in screwing them for every penny they have. At the end of the day, if they're determined to leave, they will – and we might want to trade with them in the future."

"Just hypothetically, what if other network members left at the same time as Rackhams, and joined forces to set up a rival network?"

"That would be a very different matter." Suddenly Felix sounded hostile. "We might have to get the lawyers involved if that happened. Why? Do you know something I don't?"

"I'm picking up hints, but I might know how to deal with this."

"Hints? What does that mean? Hints? I want to hear about them. I'm not having this."

"Give me a few days, and I'll get back to you."

"You'd better know what you're doing, Tom. This isn't the kind of situation for a one-man crusade."

"Just bear with me."

* * *

Tom now had hard evidence that Darren Wright was planning to break his contract with Carswells and build a rival courier network. In addition, he had the evidence of Wright's involvement in quashing the Monck Chervil investment scheme.

What should he do with this information? He could present it to Felix Schaefer and leave him to confront Darren Wright, but he had a sense that this might throw unwanted light on the Stay and Prosper campaign. The revelations could ricochet off in any number of directions, and he would have no control of where they ended up.

Alternatively, he could take matters into his own hands. The only question was whether he had it in him to act the hard man and sound credible. It went against his every instinct.

It took him long minutes to brace himself to make the call. He asked for Darren Wright, and after a moment he was connected.

"Darren, it's Tom Anthony of Carswells."

"What can I do for you?"

"I wondered if you'd come to a decision yet about sticking with the Carswell network?"

"No I haven't, and it won't help Felix's case if you keep hassling me about it."

Any trace of hesitancy flew from Tom's mind. He was pleased to have the chance to bring this arrogant man down a notch. Taking a deep breath, he said, "It's a shame that thousands of jobs won't come to Britain because of Monck Chervil's decision to cancel its expansion plan."

"What of it?"

"I don't suppose you would be very popular if people found out that you'd personally helped to prevent it from happening."

There was a very long silence. Finally Wright cleared his throat. "You'd better tell me what you want."

Chapter 72

"I'm not here as an apologist for the Europeans." Marcus Headington glanced down at his notes, then looked up from the lectern and treated the audience to one of his most disarming smiles.

The Stay and Prosper conference was under way at last – the big event at which the organisation hoped to re-galvanise the Remain campaign. Tom had driven up to Manchester the previous evening and checked into a hotel not far from the conference complex.

Behind Headington, a giant image of his face flickered on the screen. Strictly speaking, the conference hall wasn't big enough to make this necessary; even those at the back of the auditorium could probably see his face clearly enough. But it added a gloss of professionalism to the proceedings, and probably conveyed a subliminal impression that the speakers were larger than life.

"Some member-states are plagued with xenophobia and rampant nationalism," Headington said, "and some of our continental friends have been obstinate and intractable over EU negotiations."

"Hear, hear!" a voice called from towards the back.

Headington peered out into the auditorium, blinking under the lights. "I'm glad to know we're agreed on that."

He looked down at his notes, then up again. "But even married couples argue. Relationships require negotiation and compromise. Usually common sense prevails. Strong, enduring partnerships don't end in divorce."

Tom, seated half a dozen rows from the front, glanced around at the packed audience. It was mostly made up of campaign supporters and members of the public who had paid for tickets, but there was a significant smattering of major donors and dignitaries, and even a handful of MPs. There was an extensive press gallery at the back.

"The EU relationship *is* strong," Headington was saying. "It provides a voice that can't be ignored on the world stage. It's helped with the refugee crisis, with Middle East policy, with harmony in international trade. And there have been no wars between member-nations since the project was inaugurated sixty years ago."

Tom scanned the auditorium for Victor Rudge. According to the conference programme he was supposed to be the opening speaker, but Marcus Headington had taken his place without explanation. Eventually Tom spotted him in the front row, watching attentively.

Tom glanced along his row. Emily was sitting at the far end with her parents. He'd spoken to her briefly in the foyer, but the tickets were numbered, so he'd had to sit where he was allocated.

He'd only contacted her once since leaving her flat in London. She'd told him she was in purdah, working on her presentation. During the conference she was staying with her family in Oldham, out to the east of Manchester.

Headington was saying, "How can it be right to silence people who have the temerity to question Brexit? Yet they're instantly shouted down, vilified, accused of treachery. They even receive death threats.

"Riding roughshod over freely expressed opinion is a step on the road to oppression." He paused, then glared towards the press gallery. "Politicians and journalists who fail to deplore every move to trample on dissenting opinion should be ashamed of themselves."

He raised his hands in a theatrical gesture of despair. "A single referendum vote doesn't end freedom of speech. That's the doctrine of the one-party state."

He leaned forward again on the lectern. "Freedom means allowing people the right to disagree."

The largely pro-EU audience burst into enthusiastic applause.

* * *

In the coffee break Tom wandered out into the foyer. The sun was shining, and he found himself drawn to the open air. He made his way to the top of the short flight of steps leading up to the building, and stood there surrounded by delegates talking on their phones, composing text messages or smoking as if their lives depended on it.

In front of the conference centre was a bunch of pro-Brexit protesters – probably fifty or sixty in total. There were men and women of all ages, but mostly they were youngish and middle-aged men. Some were wearing close-fitting woollen hats that hid most of their faces and gave them a sinister look. A good scattering of police stood discreetly to the sides of the group, evidently ready to make a move if the gathering looked like becoming unruly.

Many of the protesters were holding banners or placards opposing the Remain campaign. Glancing around, Tom recognised an insignia on some of them that he now knew belonged to the Right Thinking group. It hadn't occurred to him before that they were as proactive as this.

Back in the conference hall, a succession of speakers took to the stage – business leaders, academics, financial experts – all explaining why Brexit would be bad for Britain. True to its aim, the campaign had picked people with reasonable opinions, not single-minded zealots. There was much quoting of statistics to back up the pro-EU message.

There was a buffet lunch, but he saw no sign of Emily. However, he caught up with her father Derek, a shortish man in his fifties with a world-weary look. "Emily is doing some last-minute fine-tuning of her presentation," he said.

Tom settled back in the auditorium for the afternoon session, and listened patiently as more speakers had their say. Finally it was Emily's turn. She strode confidently on to the stage, wearing a sage-coloured jacket and skirt and a cream blouse. She put her notes down on the lectern, raised her head and looked out into the auditorium.

Chapter 73

"I want to tell you about my dad." Emily peered out into the audience, shading her eyes with one hand. "He's here somewhere today, and I know he won't mind me talking about him."

She straightened. "He's a salesman for a company that makes electrical machinery. He travels all over Europe, talking to customers and making sales. He's been doing it for years. He's visited more than two thirds of the twenty-eight EU countries, and it's given him a good living.

"My dad has never been to India. He's never set foot in Africa, or been to the Far East or South America. He doesn't know anybody in those places. Yet the people who support Brexit keep telling him it's going to open up new markets for him. It's going to usher in a better, fairer world for him and everyone like him, with new opportunities for growth."

She paused dramatically. "Rubbish! Brexit is pulling the rug from under my dad's feet. If we leave the Single Market and the Customs Union, he'll probably have to chat up new customers in those faraway places, fight for new contacts, travel ten times as far, stay away from home for longer, and probably sell less product for less money. And when he manages to make a sale, he'll be paying far higher shipping charges to get his machines delivered. Yet all this is supposed to benefit new trading partners across the world – people who already have perfectly good suppliers on their doorstep."

Another pause. "And my dad's supposed to be thankful for this bountiful gift!

"I keep hearing that after Brexit, Britain will be free to set up new trade deals with countries around the world. Well, maybe it will, but that could take years. And let me tell you something about trade deals. They're not *contracts*. A trade deal doesn't bring one penny of new revenue to anyone. It's just a set of agreements on tariffs and terms.

People like my dad still have to graft like everyone else to sell their products under those terms. Trade deals are a smokescreen to make British people think it will be easy to replace the business we're going to lose from the EU."

Tom watched her with fascination. He could see the performer in her, acting out the role of the rhetorician, but he also recognised the conviction shining through.

"Here's what I think. Brexit is a desperate attempt by older men and women to put the 'Great' back in Britain, just like the people across the water who think they can make America great again. But how do they expect to do that in isolation? The rest of the world will still be there."

She ended, "I think most of us here today share a common belief: this craziness is never going to happen. I'm privileged to stand here at the heart of the movement that's helping people understand that it doesn't have to."

The audience responded with vigorous applause. She smiled for a moment as if surprised, then walked back to her seat on the stage.

As Tom watched her, that closing comment of hers played over in his mind: "I stand here at the heart of the movement." He'd heard something like it somewhere else recently, in a context that had felt unsettling. Where the hell had it been?

* * *

During the afternoon tea break Tom wandered back out to the foyer. He looked in vain for Emily, then found out from an attendant that presenters were being entertained in a private room.

Raised voices could be heard in the street. He drifted over to the entrance, where the pro-Brexit protesters had raised their game. They seemed to have increased in number, and some were now shouting and chanting as they waved their placards. The police were watching them uneasily.

Tom glanced around at the protesters' faces, surprised by the anger they radiated. "Traitors!" some of them were yelling. "The nation has spoken!" He was relieved to make his way back to his seat.

The final session opened in a low key with technical presentations and economic forecasts. Tom found himself tuning out as he waited for Headington's closing speech. His mind was still on the protesters outside the building. Something about them had struck him as odd, but he couldn't think what it was.

Then he realised what he'd noticed. It was one of those faces in the street. He couldn't say he *knew* the man – he hadn't been able to see enough of his face. But he knew what was in the man's soul, and it wasn't anger over Brexit. The man had been shouting and remonstrating with his fellows, but his actions had been at odds with his eyes, which had been coolly calculating.

It was the same look Tom had seen in the eyes of the man who had entered the house in the village and taken Ben Bradwell's computer from him. This might not be the same man, but if not, they were like two peas in a pod. This man didn't belong with those protesters. He had another agenda. But what agenda? Tom was still confused.

Marcus Headington took the stage for the closing address. The other speakers from the afternoon's sessions were seated in a row behind him, ready to answer questions from the floor.

"I'd like to talk about the referendum," he began. Laughter rippled round the auditorium. The referendum had been constantly on the speakers' lips all day. Headington smiled along with his audience.

"I just want to clarify a few facts." He glanced down at his notes. "The referendum was carried by roughly fifty-two per cent of the vote to forty-eight. That's almost fifty-fifty. Usually polls involving major legislative upheaval require a far higher majority. In the United States, for instance, a constitutional change requires a two thirds majority in Congress.

"The referendum was modelled on Britain's first-past-the-post electoral system. In other words, the team with the most votes wins." He grimaced in a show of distaste. "You know what Winston Churchill said about that system in nineteen hundred and nine?" He glanced down, reading. "'The results produced are not fair to any party, nor to any section of the community.'"

He looked up again. "This electoral system is used almost nowhere else in the world. It only works at all here because next time round, the public can change its mind."

He paused and straightened his back. "Yet this referendum, which legally speaking was only advisory, is *forever*. There won't be a 'next time round'. It's a pity some of the 'protest voters' didn't realise that."

He looked around, perhaps waiting for someone to challenge him. When no one did, he seemed to decide to underline his point. "Just consider this. Eventually the Scots will be offered a second independence referendum, yet no one is even allowed to breathe the words 'second EU referendum'. How come? Why are we permitted to have as many referenda as we like while the answer is no, but then never again once it's yes? Every time anyone suggests it, they're treated with the kind of contempt we usually save for child molesters."

Tom tried hard to listen, but he was still thinking about the man he'd seen outside among the Brexit protesters, and wondering about his intentions. Then his mind flashed back to Emily's speech. Could her words offer a clue? "I stand at the heart of the movement." It echoed a comment Victor Rudge had made in one of those videoed phone conversations. "We should strike at the very heart of the movement." *This* was the heart of the Stay and Prosper movement – this gathering here today.

Tom shuffled in his seat as he tried to understand what this meant. Would Victor Rudge really arrange to strike a blow against his own campaign? Why? It seemed unthinkable. Yet the more Tom thought about it, the more plausible it seemed. It would be an extraordinary bid for public sympathy – a desperate attempt to drum up contempt for the Leave advocates and gain a new voice for the Remainers. "It needs to be dramatic," he'd said in the video. "It needs to have resonance." What better way to deliver a dramatic gesture than to aim it at his own campaign, and blame the opposition? It was as elegant as it was deplorable.

But what were these people planning? A violent protest? A shooting? A bomb? He had no idea.

He could feel the sweat breaking out on his face. This could be real, and it could be now. What should he do?

Chapter 74

Tom's first instinct was to jump to his feet and shout out a warning. But what was the threat? How could he justify himself? He'd managed to get away with disrupting Kenneth Moir's public lecture in Colchester, but how would he fare if he tried the same thing again here? He glanced around wildly, paralysed by that peculiarly British inhibition about making a fuss.

Perhaps he should simply yell, "Fire!" But would the situation justify the panic he might cause? Would he even be believed, sitting mid-row in an auditorium where there was plainly no fire to be seen?

Maybe he should shuffle out to the aisle, find a policeman and sound a warning? But what warning? Nothing had happened so far. The police were already keeping a close eye on the protesters outside. What more could he ask them to do?

He pulled out his phone without thinking and scrolled wildly through his contact list. Should he call Joe and try to make contact with Jay Reynolds? No – far too convoluted. He needed to act now.

His eye fell on the phone entry he'd set up for Adrian Dowdeswell, the unofficial head of the Right Thinking group. Maybe this man could intervene in some way. Before Tom knew it he'd initiated the call.

"Dowdeswell." Clearly he didn't recognise Tom's number, but at least he'd picked up, which seemed a minor miracle in itself.

In a low voice Tom said, "It's Tom Anthony, the journalist. I'm at the Stay and Prosper conference in Manchester."

Several people behind him hissed, "Sshh!"

"Bully for you," came Dowdeswell's voice from the phone.

Raising his own voice slightly, Tom said, "I'm trying to do you a favour. A bunch of your followers are protesting outside the conference hall. I have good reason to believe an infiltrator is about to cause some kind of violent mayhem in the conference, and blame your people for it. If you have any pull around here, you'll get them to back off NOW."

"Shut up," someone called from behind. Tom turned and glared at a middle-aged woman.

Dowdeswell was silent for a moment, then said, "Got you," and hung up.

Tom turned back to the stage. Headington was saying, "Brexit is the biggest self-inflicted wound this country has ever imposed on itself, and it's *not necessary*!" He paused and stared round at the audience. "The good news is this madness is not irreversible. We can still stop it. We owe it to ourselves and our children to do it."

There were muffled shouts from somewhere outside the auditorium. Headington hesitated briefly, then seemed to dismiss the interruption and continued to speak. Tom, however, was paying more attention. Those voices could belong to protesters who had fought their way past the police and invaded the conference hall. There was a direct passage between the front entrance and one of the sets of double doors into the auditorium. Anyone determined enough would have no trouble finding their way inside.

He could no longer put off taking action. He rose to his feet, hardly hearing a muttered "Sit down, for god's sake!" from someone in a seat behind him. He shouted, "Marcus, look out! I think we're being invaded!"

Headington broke off mid-sentence and stared over at Tom, clearly taken aback.

"I mean it! For god's sake get off the stage! NOW!"

Murmurs of disquiet rippled round the auditorium. Headington glanced about him wildly, as if seeking corroboration of Tom's warning. The other speakers were less hesitant; they were already rising to their feet. One or two started making their way towards the side of the stage.

More muffled shouts outside. Again Tom shouted, "Marcus! Get GOING!"

Headington stepped away reluctantly from the lectern, apparently realising as he did so that his colleagues were already leaving. At that moment the doors at the back of the auditorium burst open. Hundreds of heads turned, and Tom saw three or four men wearing heavy black woollen masks come in.

They seemed to hesitate as they entered, taking their bearings before deciding on their next move. One of them, however, clearly had a plan already. He stood still, raised some kind of firearm, steadied the barrel across his forearm and fired two or three rapid shots towards the stage. What sounded like a cry of pain was clearly audible.

The explosive sounds seemed to stun the audience into silence for a moment. There were a few isolated screams, then the whole auditorium erupted in anguished cries.

As Tom watched, the gunman turned to his right and walked calmly along a gangway between rows of seats, heading for an emergency exit that led off to the side. Within moments he had disappeared.

* * *

The audience surged towards the exits, engulfing the remaining protesters, who simply merged with them. Tom was swept along in a crush reminiscent of a ride in the tightest-packed Tube train. The atmosphere was one of contained hysteria; the cries of anxiety and fear were very real, but remarkably, no one fell or was trampled underfoot. The overriding sense was one of unrelenting pressure. It seemed to squeeze the very air out of Tom's body. And agonisingly, people trod several times on his injured foot.

It seemed to go on for endless minutes, but finally he reached the exit doors and was plunged into the foyer. Then he was swept up in another surge towards the main entrance, and finally he was disgorged on the front steps. He allowed the crowd to nudge him down into the street.

Hundreds of people were milling around outside the complex – many of them talking earnestly on mobile phones. Police sirens blared and yellow-jacketed police officers scurried about. Tom knew he was likely to be detained and questioned, but in the mêlée no one had so far pointed him out as the one who had shouted the warning. He wanted to go back and ask what had happened to Emily, but as soon as all the delegates were clear of the building, policemen closed the doors and took up defensive positions outside.

He drifted to the outer edge of the throng and glanced along the street. Not surprisingly, there was no sign of men in balaclavas or black woollen hats. He took out his phone and dialled Emily's number. Her voicemail clicked in.

He was still staring uncertainly down the street when an athletic-looking man in his thirties walked past him, heading away from the conference centre. He was moving casually, not hurrying, but all the same he was covering ground quickly. Something about that contained, self-confident gait was familiar. Before he knew it, Tom had shouted, "Hello again!"

The man broke his stride and half-turned, but only briefly; yet it was enough. Tom was convinced it was the man who had broken into the house in the village and taken Ben Bradwell's computer. He'd been right. This had been the man who had mingled with the protesters, and he must have been the man with the gun. Somehow he'd found his way out of the conference hall, and he was making his escape.

Tom shouted, "There! He's getting away!"

Before any of the police could react, the man turned down a side street and disappeared from view. Instead of following him, the police closed in on Tom. Once again, he would have to explain himself to unsympathetic listeners, and this time his explanation was one they would surely struggle to believe.

Chapter 75

Tom was taken into a building adjacent to the conference hall and led to a private room. He knew he would have to tell the police something convincing, but he quickly decided he would say as little as possible – certainly nothing about plots or Victor Rudge. He would simply claim that he'd felt suspicious about the protesters, and had put two and two together when he heard their shouts in the foyer. In the aftermath, he'd spotted a man outside who reminded him of the gunman.

The questioning seemed interminable. Initially the police seemed to think he might have been part of the attack. Their theory was that he had shouted out in order to cause consternation in the auditorium and help the gunman escape. He commented that the shooting would surely have had that effect on its own. Happily, Marcus Headington was still on the premises. Tom managed to get a message through to him, and eventually the word came back that Headington had vouched for him.

"Mr Headington is probably lucky you were there," one of the officers told him. "We're pretty sure he was the intended target."

Tom asked if anyone had been injured, and was told that one of the afternoon's speakers had been hit – an Oxford professor who was still on the stage at the time. "But the wound isn't life-threatening."

One of the policemen escorted Tom to the main entrance, where other officers were still very much in evidence. Their faces radiated concern and focus, but the tension of the afternoon had now dissipated.

He was cheered to find Emily and her parents standing outside the conference centre. He said, "I'd have thought you would have left hours ago."

"Some hope! I had to give a statement, then we hung around in the annex with the other speakers to find out what was happening."

"And what is?"

"Tomorrow's workshop sessions have been cancelled, but Marcus is still holding the speakers' dinner at his hotel tonight."

Emily's mother, an amiable red-headed woman half a head taller than her husband, seemed intrigued by Tom. She said, "Somehow you managed to save the day."

"Hardly."

"Well, we thought so."

Tom turned back to Emily. "I loved your talk. I thought it was brilliant."

"Thanks." She gave him a brief grin, but quickly modified it to an ironic smile. "It didn't stop you grabbing the limelight, did it? What do I have to do to get myself heard?"

"Don't bad-mouth the man," her father said. "If it wasn't for him, someone might have shot you."

"Maybe so."

He asked Emily why Victor Rudge had been removed from the conference programme and had taken no part in the proceedings.

"There are rumours going round that he was taken to a police station and interviewed two nights ago. They think it has something to do with Donald Finch, the civil servant. So I assume Marcus asked him to stay out of the limelight today."

It made sense. The police would have seen the video in which Rudge discussed the blackmail plot. Now the fallout had begun.

"I wonder how much of a fight Victor put up."

"I don't know, but Marcus is stronger than he sometimes looks."

She said, "I'd better get going if I want to make it to Marcus's dinner." She gave him a meaningful look. "Victor Rudge won't be there."

"I'll see you in London some time, then."

She leaned in towards him and whispered, "You'd better."

* * *

Jay Reynolds phoned Tom at his hotel that night.

"I hear you've been busy again."

Tom did some fast thinking. Could he trust this man? On the whole, he felt the answer was yes. The problem, if there was one, seemed to lie with unidentified colleagues of his.

"I put two and two together," Tom said.

"Lucky you did. These people nearly achieved their objective today."

"Which was what?"

"I think you can work that out."

"It was definitely the same team as before, I assume?"

"We're more or less certain it was. My people are going through the CCTV footage now."

"I can't believe the gunman got away."

"Yes, well, we keep on learning all the time."

"I called Adrian Dowdeswell, the head of the Right Thinking group. I told him he should pull his people out. I don't suppose he had time, though."

"You're wrong there. At least three quarters of them suddenly dropped back. When you look at the CCTV recording, it's quite remarkable. It's as if someone blew a whistle."

"So he managed to call them off?"

"Apparently. An influential man, Mr Dowdeswell."

"But the rest of them still invaded the conference hall."

"That was just the zealots at the front – plus the man who infiltrated them. They were already on the move when the others backed off, and there were enough of them to barge their way inside. They caught the police off their guard. Red faces all round."

Tom's mind was racing through the wider implications. He said, "So the press will still blame the far right for this."

"Probably – but they'll say it was hotheads, not the mainstream Right Thinking group."

"But Victor Rudge and his cronies will still get their way. There will still be a big wave of sympathy for the pro-Europe brigade."

"I'm not a politician. It's not my problem. But a foiled assassination attempt doesn't really have the clout of the real thing, does it? As you've rightly worked out, this was intended to be a dramatic blow to bolster the Remain camp. Thanks to you, it will only be a blip."

"Huh." Tom paused to absorb that thought. "I heard Victor Rudge had been questioned by the police."

"Yes, but those videos you've seen aren't really conclusive. We need something more."

There seemed to be an implied question in his words. Tom said, "Well don't look at me!"

"Just make sure you let me know if you find anything else."

The call seemed about to end. Tom said, "Do you mind if I ask you something?"

"You can try me."

"Do you think Kenneth Moir was ever really a target for these people, or was that just a distraction? Was today the real plan all along?"

"Your guess is as good as mine."

"You must have some idea, though?"

"I think all ideas were probably on the table. There are unanswered questions about some of the people who attended that event in Colchester. They might have planned something, then aborted it at the last moment. On the other hand, it might have been a false trail all along."

"Do you think you're going to nail these people? The ones in this clandestine group, I mean? The people behind today's shooting?"

"We're on the case. That's all I'll say."

* * *

Tom lay on his bed in his characterless hotel room, thinking back over the day. What had happened was still hard to believe, and what he now knew about it was even harder.

Victor Rudge, it seemed, had orchestrated a plot to gun down Marcus Headington, the leader of the Stay and Prosper campaign; and it would have been done in front of hundreds of people at its keynote conference, with ample press and at least one TV station in attendance. He'd actually been prepared to sacrifice the group's own charismatic leader in a drastic attempt to attract public attention and garner sympathy for the anti-Brexit cause.

It seemed deranged, but there was also a horrible logic to it. Thinking back, Tom remembered the outcry after the petrol bomb incident. Multiply that by a hundredfold, and he could see the impact a public execution might have had.

He now found himself wondering if the petrol bomb incident had in fact been set up by Rudge himself. Under the circumstances, it now seemed more than plausible. Yet despite the fact that the security services seemed to acknowledge Rudge's guilt in all this, apparently there was insufficient evidence for them to take action against him. He was still walking free, and despite being sidelined at the conference, in theory he was still Marcus Headington's right-hand man.

Chapter 76

"Mr Anthony, it's Frattons here, the estate agents in Winchester. Could you tell us when you're going to be removing the items from the garage?" It was an unfamiliar man's voice.

The call had come in on the landline just after Tom arrived back in Winchester. The drive down from Manchester had taken more than five hours.

He lowered himself on to the sofa with a sigh. "Sorry, what items? I'm not with you."

"The items occupying most of the garage space at the house in Storton. Ms Carrington didn't leave any instructions about them, and we can't reach her."

"I don't understand what you mean. Why should she leave you instructions? What's your interest?"

"We're the letting agents. We need to clear the property and prepare it for the next occupants."

Enlightenment was slowly dawning. "You mean she's gone ahead and put the house back up for rent? I'm sorry, I didn't know."

"Well, no, she's relinquished the tenancy."

Tom was hearing the words, but they didn't make sense. He said, "How do you mean, relinquished the tenancy? Jan is the sole owner of the house, isn't she?"

"No, not at all. I think there must be some sort of confusion here." There was a pause. "You *are* Mr Tom Anthony, am I right? We have you on record as the alternative contact for matters relating to the property."

"Yes, yes."

"Well can I suggest you pop into our office tomorrow? Hopefully we can sort this out."

Tom glanced at his watch. Half past three. "How about I come in today?"

He put the phone down, pulled out his mobile and called Jan's number. It went to voicemail.

* * *

The property agent at Frattons was a smartly-dressed, smooth-talking man with sandy hair. He ushered Tom to a visitor's chair and sat down behind his minimalist desk.

"The property was rented to Ms Carrington's father Daniel for nine years," he said. "When he died, we came to an understanding with her." He gave a perfunctory laugh. "I suppose it was unusual, but it served both sides. We terminated the rental agreement and renovated the house on the basis that Ms Carrington would have first refusal on a short-term let when it was finished."

Tom was almost speechless. Jan had lied about the house ever since he'd come out of hospital. It was never her house in the first place, and had never been her father's either. This meant that the actual owners must have paid for the refurbishment work that had been done on it, not Jan. She'd merely been a tenant.

He could hardly begin to take in what he was hearing. Foremost in his mind was the question of why she had done this. What possible benefit could it have brought her? Then there was the question of the money she'd kept telling him she needed – money to pay for the renovation work, to tide her over until the rental revenue had accumulated from the flat in south London.

Suddenly he was suspicious about that. He said, "I think you handle another property for us – a flat in south London. We rent it through your company, and recently Jan put in a sub-tenant. Could you look that up for me?"

The man looked dubious. "It won't be on our books here in Winchester," he said. "In any case, with the greatest of respect, if Ms Carrington's name is on the rental agreement, technically speaking you won't be a party to it."

Tom's irritation was mounting. Struggling to control his temper, he said, "Look, Jan Carrington is my other half, and she's deceived me about the house. She led me to believe she owned it. This affects my life in a fundamental way. I want to know if she's been deceiving me about the flat in London as well."

The man seemed to consider this for a moment, then picked up the phone from his desk and looked up a number from a chart. "What's the address of the property?"

He conferred with a colleague for a while, then put the phone down and turned to Tom. "It seems Ms Carrington relinquished her tenancy of the flat some months ago, and has no further involvement with the property. It is now rented out to another gentleman on behalf of the primary owner."

The conversation finally turned to the junk pile that Jan had accumulated in the garage at Storton, but by this time Tom was only half-concentrating. He said, "If she's left it there, I should think you can do what you like with it."

"There are also some other items – bedclothes, pieces of furniture belonging to Ms Carrington, that kind of thing. There could be a disposal charge. We need to know where to direct it."

Tom looked at him with disbelief. "I'm afraid I can't help you with that."

* * *

He wandered away along Winchester High Street in a daze. What the *hell* was Jan's game? All this time, she'd been spinning him a yarn – implying that she'd inherited a house worth well over half a million pounds, when actually it seemed likely that she'd inherited nothing. In fact she'd probably terminated the lease on the London flat to help pay the short-term rental fees on the house. That would also explain why she'd emptied their joint bank account. She couldn't be earning as much as she'd always claimed.

Where had she gone? It appeared that she'd moved out of the house and had no intention of coming back. He called her mobile again, and again it went to voicemail. Had she really gone to Oslo last week, or was that just part of the deception? He no longer knew what to believe.

Back at his house, he phoned Jan's friend Debbie, who told him, "I honestly don't know where she's gone, Tom. If I did, I promise I would tell you." She sounded sincere. There seemed no point in pressing her.

He tried a couple of Jan's other friends, but they came back with the same response. He could hear the bafflement in their voices, and reluctantly he decided he had to accept that they knew no more about this than he did. Jan's disappearance had been a well-kept secret.

A new thought occurred to him. He grabbed his laptop and navigated to his online banking website. He'd topped up their joint account with a further five hundred pounds after he'd found it empty. How much would he find there now? As he feared, it was showing a balance of just ten pounds.

An ominous feeling was creeping through him. He switched to his own online savings account. It should have over twenty thousand pounds of insurance money in it. In fact it was showing a balance of one pound.

He sat back, aghast. He was unsure how Jan had pulled off this trick, but he had a vague memory of once telling her where he kept a written record of his bank login details. "You never know when you might need it," he'd said. How true that had apparently been.

He felt he still wasn't seeing the full picture. Jan had stolen some thousands of pounds from him, and had apparently disappeared. He could understand the sequence of events, but not the logic behind it. That money wouldn't keep her going for very long, and it certainly wouldn't buy her a life of luxury. Would she have gone to all this trouble for such a relatively modest gain?

He lay awake for long hours that night. The turmoil in his mind seemed to have banished all hope of sleep. Finally he slipped into doze, but then he regained full consciousness with a start. He had an unpleasant inkling of what all this might be about.

Chapter 77

By seven next morning Tom was poring over finance news websites on his laptop. He didn't have to search for long. Wherever he looked, he found news items with headings on the lines of "Breakthrough for NSRQ". He focused on one of them.

> ***Bonanza for stakeholders in no-hope oil exploration firm***
> *Sceptics were confounded last night when NSRQ Explore, a little-known UK-based oil exploration company, announced a major new gas find in the North Sea.*
>
> *The under-funded company had been struggling for years with little support from the City or the energy industry, which has always regarded its efforts as misplaced and rated its chances of success at almost zero.*
>
> *Against the odds, NSRQ now says it has confirmed the presence of a gas field with good exploitation potential, which was previously dismissed as inaccessible. Unconfirmed reports put the potential yield at up to 100 billion cubic metres.*
>
> *It is believed that the company initially withheld news of the find, fearing the impact of a "hard Brexit" on the future cost of trade in the energy sector. However, the prospect of an accommodation with the EU over the so-called divorce bill renewed its confidence, and there was concern that the news of the find was already beginning to circulate.*
>
> *Investors will be rubbing their hands in glee at the likelihood of a massive hike in the company's share value, which many had almost written off.*

NSRQ Explore was the company in which Jan had invested a chunk of Tom's money three years ago. When his father had died, he'd decided to place half his inheritance in safe stocks and the other half in something speculative. Jan had told him she had an instinct about NSRQ, so Tom had accepted the advice and invested the money.

Since then the company's share price had declined steadily. Tom had been all for cutting his losses and reinvesting what was left elsewhere, but Jan had persuaded him to hang on. It looked as though she'd been right all along.

Tom launched a new tab in his browser, and with mounting trepidation returned to his banking website. This time he opened his current account, which he hadn't examined when he was online yesterday.

There it was. Two days ago a payment of £121,000 had been made into his account, then a few hours later the same amount had been paid out of it. The recipient was "MC", which meant nothing to him, but the implication was plain enough: Jan had cashed in his shares in NSRQ, then cleaned him out.

He thought back to the time when she'd invested the money. She'd handled the transaction for him and was the signatory to the deal, but he'd insisted that dividends and any other proceeds be paid into his own bank account. That precaution had seemed almost heavy-handed at the time, but ironically, it hadn't been sufficient to protect him.

He sat for a long time feeling numb. He'd sometimes doubted Jan's commitment to their relationship, and recently those doubts had solidified into serious concern, but he'd never taken her for a thief – someone who would exploit their involvement in this cold-blooded way. While he'd been distracted by his work, and then by Britain's crumbling relationship with the European Union, he'd allowed the most important relationship in his personal life to disintegrate in front of his eyes.

Instead of indignation, he felt humiliation and a sense of guilt. This treachery of hers seemed above all to convey contempt for him. Somehow, somewhere along the line, he must have done something to alienate her beyond hope of redemption.

* * *

Could he recover the money? Would the police consider it outright theft? He had no idea, and he wasn't about to do battle with the bank's telephone contact centre in order to find out. He drove into Winchester and made his way to his local bank branch, where he insisted on speaking to someone who could explain his position.

The initial response was unpromising. "We can report this to the police as a theft," he was told, "but in practice the outgoing transaction was made legitimately by someone who had full access to your account. To all intents and purposes, that means it was authorised by you."

He said, "Surely I'm indemnified against this kind of thing?"

"Not necessarily. The issue of negligence arises. You'll need to make a full report, then we'll consider the position. Also you'll need to report this to the police. In the meantime, you should change your online banking logins as a matter of priority. We can do it for you now if you like."

"That seems like closing the barn door after the horse has bolted."

"All the same, you need to do it."

Back out on the street and now seething, Tom tried Jan's mobile number yet again. Still no reply. Should he report the theft to the police? He was tempted to walk round the corner to the police station in Tower Street and do it there and then; yet the idea of accusing a former partner of something so hostile still seemed somehow too extreme.

Instead, he walked to the estate agency and waited to talk to the man he'd seen yesterday. He asked, "Can I get into the house in Storton? Will my key still work?"

"Yes, we haven't changed the locks yet. Normally we would have, but when the place is out in a village, these things sometimes take a little longer."

"So you won't mind if I stick my head in and check that there's nothing of mine still there?"

"I think we can trust you."

Tom smiled ironically to himself. This man wouldn't be saying that if he knew what Jan had been up to. He thanked him and made his way back to his car.

* * *

The house was silent and empty, though it still seemed lived-in. There was food in the kitchen cupboards, and Jan's bed was still made up. But her wardrobe was empty, and her other personal belongings had also disappeared. Tom wandered from room to room, unsure what he was looking for. There was no clue about where she might have gone.

Back downstairs, he made his way through to the garage and glanced at the sprawl of junk on the floor. There was nothing here that he wanted. He went out into the front garden, and through the hedge he noticed movement next door. He walked round to the adjoining driveway, where the next-door neighbour, Dennis, a hearty man in his mid-seventies, was clipping dead wood from the shrubbery.

"Hello, Tom! I haven't seen you around here for a while."

"I moved back to Winchester. I couldn't get used to the pace of village life."

"I haven't seen Jan for a few days either. Has she moved back in with you?"

"No." Tom frowned. "Frankly, I'm not sure where she is. She seems to have disappeared."

Dennis lowered his shears and looked at him in surprise. "I'm sorry to hear that. Are you seriously worried?"

"I'm not worried for her safety, I'm worried that I can't contact her. I don't suppose … you wouldn't have any idea where she's gone, would you?"

Dennis frowned. "The last time I saw her, she was with that ex-doctor chap, Melcombe."

"How do you mean, ex-doctor?"

"Perhaps I shouldn't put it that way." Dennis stooped and placed his shears on the ground, brushing his hands together as he straightened. "He's been under investigation by the General Medical Council, but they may not have come to a conclusion yet." He lowered his voice. "Inappropriate behaviour with a patient, that kind of thing. The story was printed in the local rag here." He shrugged. "It doesn't really make any odds. I think he was giving up his practice anyway. There's a much better GP's surgery in the next village, and everyone around here seems to go there nowadays."

"What was Jan doing when you saw her with Melcombe?"

"I didn't really pay attention, but … come to think of it, I seem to remember they were loading stuff into his Range Rover. Suitcases, plastic bin bags – that kind of thing."

Thanking Dennis, Tom returned to his car. There was no sign of Jan's SUV, but that seemed unsurprising. He knew it was leased. She'd probably returned it – or left it standing somewhere.

Chapter 78

Gradually Tom pieced the story together.

Just before his accident, he'd told Jan he wanted to break up with her. That seemed to be where all this had started. For some reason she must have refused to accept the decision with good grace, and instead had decided to steal what she could of his assets and disappear. Just why she'd been so vindictive he might never know, but that was the reality he now had to face.

Possibly her original plan had been modest: empty his bank accounts and make her getaway. Where to? Maybe somewhere abroad, somewhere beyond the UK's judicial reach. Possibly ex-doctor Melcombe had planned to go with her.

However, the accident had allowed her to fashion a much more elaborate scheme. She must have known from her contacts in the finance world that those shares in NSRQ were on the brink of rocketing in value. All she had to do was keep Tom on side until the company went public with its gas discovery, then sell the shares on his behalf and siphon off the proceeds.

This wouldn't have worked if Tom had remembered breaking up with her, but he'd lost his memory of it in the accident. In fact even when Christine had told him about it, he'd given Jan the benefit of the doubt. How stupid could he have been?

Now that he thought about it, he realised that unknowingly Christine had represented a threat to the entire plan. She knew Tom had broken up with Jan, and in fact it looked as though they'd fallen into each other's arms on the night he'd told her about it.

Somehow Jan had found out about this. It explained why she had made such efforts to persuade Tom to recuperate in the village, away from Christine's watchful eye. A wrong word from Chris would have thrown her whole scheme into jeopardy.

He thought again about the email message he was supposed to have sent to Christine, telling her he wanted nothing more to do with her. Jan must have sent that message shortly after his accident, pretending to be him. Once she knew he'd lost his memory of that missing week, her plan was back on track. It had been a remarkably inventive improvisation, calculated to keep the two of them apart: an extra safeguard to deflect Christine from telling him what she knew.

One thing Tom was still struggling to understand was why Jan had felt all this was necessary. Whatever her reasons, she must have wanted to deliver a punishing blow to him, but her determined drive to steal from him seemed to strike a discordant note. After all, she was a high flyer in the world of financial trading. Surely she had more than enough money of her own? Why did she need even more?

He found out the answer next morning when he phoned her company. She'd kept her work and home life resolutely separate, and he'd seldom spoken to anyone there. He had to go online to find the phone number.

The receptionist who answered his call initially sounded baffled. "I don't have an executive called Jan Carrington on my list, sorry."

"But you must have. She's worked there for years. Can you look again?"

There was a long pause, then she said, "We have a Jan Davey."

Davey had been Jan's married name. He said, "Yes, that's her! She's not there now, by any chance?"

After a pause, the woman said, "Sorry, no. I'm told Jan Davey left the company several months ago."

This was turning from strange to surreal. He said, "What? Are you sure?"

"Absolutely. And by the way, she wasn't an executive here, she was on the administrative staff."

Just another shock to go along with all the others. But as Tom ended the call, he reflected that this explained Jan's desire to steal his money. She probably wasn't wealthy after all. Her stories of owning locked investments and managing a high-yield portfolio must have been invented, either to impress him or simply to bolster her own self-esteem.

She would have understood all these concepts, but had probably been watching from the sidelines while others used them to build up their fortunes. She must have decided she wanted a part of it.

* * *

For more than a day Tom did nothing. He went through the motions of eating and sleeping, but spent long periods simply staring into space, wondering how he could have allowed his relationship with Jan to disintegrate so completely without even noticing. He'd been ready to end things with her, but clearly he hadn't tried to look at their situation through her eyes – to understand the frustration and resentment that must have been building up in her. He couldn't stop blaming himself.

Finally he started to pull himself together. Tentatively, he phoned a few of his closest friends, telling them he'd split up with Jan and asking if they'd heard anything of her. No one had. Bernard was predictably sympathetic, and urged him to go to the police. "This isn't a joke, Tom – it isn't petty theft. It's fraud on a grand scale. Don't let her get away with it."

His old friend Malcolm Drew at *Seismic Scene* was more philosophical. "I could see things were going downhill," he said. "Jan wanted different things. She wanted more excitement than you did, more of a social life. I tried to tell you that, but you closed your eyes to it."

"You're probably right."

"So does this mean you'll be chasing up that red-headed beauty in Richmond? I hope so."

Tom couldn't help smiling. "As a matter of fact, I already am."

"Quite right too. Much better for you."

"And her hair is strawberry blond, if you want to know. I asked her."

After a moment Malcolm added, "You probably won't be interested in hearing this now, but I followed up the query you raised about why that civil servant might have been open to blackmail. Donald Finch – remember?

"God, yes. What did you find out?"

"It's the old story. Seemingly last year Finch was accused by various women colleagues of 'inappropriate behaviour', whatever that is. This was before those big scandals broke in the summer – the ones involving Hollywood actors and members of parliament. It wasn't taken seriously by the authorities, but his card was marked. It made him vulnerable."

"Where did Victor Rudge come in?"

"Well, from what I've picked up, Finch was already a bit of a sexual predator even when he was young. While he was at university a female student in his college accused him of rape. But there was some kind of cover-up. Both of them were able to stay on, and the whole thing was brushed under the carpet. There's no documented evidence that it ever happened."

"But Victor Rudge knew about it?"

"I presume so. He moved in the same literary circles as Finch at Cambridge, so maybe he got it direct from him, or else from friends of his."

"So if Rudge had come forward, Finch would probably have lost his job."

"That's about the size of it."

"You've done well to pick all this up."

"But I have to tell you something else. I looked again at the EU rules on government subsidy and competition law. The Monck Chervil package really would have broken them. It must have taken Finch a lot of creative interpretation to approve the plan in the first place."

Chapter 79

Tom wanted to phone Emily, but couldn't bring himself to make the call. Jan's apparent contempt had knocked a hole in his self-esteem. If a woman he knew well could hate him this much, how would Emily feel when and if she came to know him better? What hidden horrors in his behaviour or personality would she eventually uncover? It now seemed a miracle that his relationship with her had progressed as far as it had.

Then Emily phoned him. The call came in from a mobile number he didn't recognise.

"Tom, what's happening?"

He said, "I'm sorry I haven't contacted you."

"Don't worry about that. I'm calling you on Jenny's phone. Billy insisted. He wants to speak to you."

There was a moment's background chatter, then a young man's voice came on the line. "It's Billy, from the shop downstairs. I didn't want to call you on my own phone, and Em didn't want to use hers either."

"What's up, Billy?"

"I cocked up with those video files you handed me. There were two that I didn't give back to you. I didn't spot them when I copied the rest."

"How come?"

"They were .flv files, not .mp4 files. They got muddled up with some of mine." He paused, then he added, "It's just another video format. It doesn't make any difference to the content."

"So have you decrypted them?"

"Yeah, no problem. I thought you might want to see them. But I had the fuzz round here after I handled the others. I don't want them to know about this."

"Did they find anything they shouldn't have?"

"No way. I'm not stupid."

"Sorry."

"But don't ask me to email these files to you, or get Em to do it."

"What do you suggest then?"

"You're in Winchester, right? My parents live in Portsmouth. It's not a million miles away from there."

"I suppose not."

"I'll be down there this weekend. We could meet somewhere."

"OK, great."

Billy paused to think. "How about Cheesefoot Head? It's a tourist spot near Twyford Down. D'you know it?"

The last time Tom had headed off for a meeting in that direction, he'd ended up spending four months in hospital. However, he merely said, "I know where it is."

"It's a nice run up from Portsmouth. I can give my new bike an outing. Say ten o'clock on Saturday morning?"

Emily's voice came back on the line. "Is this OK with you, Tom?"

"It's fine. Have you seen these videos?"

"Billy played me the start of one on his phone. It shows Victor Rudge talking to some man." She broke off, and he heard her saying, "Yes, cheers Billy. See you later." Back on the phone, "Is everything OK, Tom? You sound strange."

He took a deep breath. "Jan has left, and she's cleaned out my bank accounts. I think she was planning it for a long time. She's taken thousands of pounds, and she's disappeared without trace."

"My god, Tom!" She left a long pause, then in a different tone asked, "Are you sorry she's gone?"

"No way. We were finished long ago. I just hadn't accepted it. To be honest, I feel a bit of a fool."

"I have to say I could see it, even if you couldn't."

He chuckled dryly. "She tells me now."

* * *

When Tom's phone rang an hour later, the last thing on his mind was Carswells and its branch network problems. Felix Schaefer's call was a reminder that despite the recent excitement in his life, the world had kept on turning.

"I don't know what you did to that man Darren Wright at Rackhams," Felix said, "but it was as if you lit a bomb under him."

This must have to do with Tom's threat to Darren Wright to reveal his part in the Donald Finch blackmail scheme. He'd never heard the outcome.

"What is Darren telling you?"

Felix chuckled with delight. "He's given up his plan to take Rackhams out of the network. He's all for staying now. He's even got some new contracts for us in the pipeline. Just tell me how you pulled it off."

"I don't think you want to know. Shall we say I forced the issue?"

"What does that mean?"

"I found out something he'd prefer to keep quiet."

"Should I ask what?"

"Maybe another time."

Felix paused to consider this. "You're no bully, Tom. I'm sorry if I've made you into one."

This was profound for Felix. Tom sighed. "It's not you. I think life must be toughening me up."

"Well, it certainly worked. Not only is Darren back on side, those other wobbly members have also dropped their crackpot scheme to set up a rival network."

"It's not a permanent solution, Felix. Darren might start getting itchy feet again in a year's time. In the long run you can't make groups of people stick together by coercion. Members have to want it."

"Don't worry – I'm going to launch a 'stronger together' drive, to make sure our members are glad to be part of something bigger. We can't have this happening again."

"I think that's a very good idea." Tom laughed ironically. "It's a pity no one did that for the EU before Brexit came along."

"Talking of Brexit, I read about you being involved in the shooting at that conference in Manchester. Hero of the hour, they're calling you."

"It was pure luck. I just jumped up at the right time."

"I can see you've got another life going on there, Tom. I just want to say that if you'd rather not stick to the whole six-month contract with us, I won't hold you to it. I don't want to stifle you if you have other ambitions. You've more than paid for your keep by sorting out the Rackhams situation."

"I appreciate it. Maybe we could work out a looser arrangement?"

"Come and talk to me when you're ready."

Chapter 80

The air was crisp and the sun was shining when Tom drove off for his meet-up with Billy that Saturday morning. He started out in the direction of Twyford village, but just past the motorway he took the road across the downs. He was surrounded by rolling fields – some green, some turned over after the harvest. Dark parallel furrows seemed to stretch away for miles. The landscape was broken by patches of woodland and isolated stands of trees.

Cheesefoot Head was a circular depression – a naturally-occurring amphitheatre near the footpath known as the South Downs Way. It sounded a dramatic place for a hand-over, though the site itself was some distance from the car park. Tom arrived in good time, but there was no sign of Billy. He sat back and waited for him to arrive.

After a while he started to wonder if he'd come to the right place. He got out of the car and walked slowly down the car park towards the entrance. Then a large motorcycle pulled in. The leather-clad rider killed the engine, stretched and pulled off his helmet. It was Billy.

"Sorry I'm late. I got held up." He reached inside his leathers and pulled out a mobile phone. "You can take this. It's just an old scrapper. The videos are on it."

"Thanks."

"Em says to tell you hello."

"Have you kept copies of this stuff?"

"No way! I'm not risking having something crucial like this found on me. What you've got there, that's it."

Tom glanced down at the phone, then back at Billy. "Can I offer you something for this extra trouble?"

"Consider it a bonus." Billy grinned. "It's a nice day for a ride." He pulled his helmet back on, pressed the starter button and roared out on to the road with a flourish.

Tom started back towards his car, then realised with shock that another man had appeared from the trees at the far end of the car park. For a moment Tom ignored him, then he realised the man was heading resolutely in his direction. A second surreptitious glance seemed to confirm what he feared. It was the man from the village – and latterly the gunman from Manchester. Now he was here, and he must want the phone in Tom's hand.

Tom had no hope of reaching his car. He would be cut off before he was half-way there. Trying to look insouciant, he changed direction, quickened his pace as best he could and headed out through the car park entrance on to the main road. Traffic would mean people, observers, witnesses.

The two-lane single carriageway road was dead straight. It was flanked by fields and devoid of features, apart from occasional trees. Randomly he turned right. A car hummed past. He struck off along the verge, but the grass was dense and slowed him down, so he switched to the roadway itself. Glancing back, he saw that the man was following briskly. He couldn't run. He could only pray for rescue of some sort.

Nothing presented itself. The hoped-for traffic was a major disappointment. Another car appeared from nowhere behind him, then there was silence. The man was closing on him. A truck loomed and Tom waved his arms wildly, but the truck driver merely gave him a blast on the air horn. Tom dodged on to the verge as the truck roared past, followed by a trail of cars.

He stepped back on to the road and limped a few paces further. After a moment another car came into view. This time he took half a step out into the roadway and waved again wildly. The driver hooted and the car swerved slightly to avoid him. The sound of its engine quickly died away.

The man called, "You know what I want! Stop this fooling around." His voice sounded calm and reasonable. Tom tried to break into a half-trot, but his ankle protested with a sharp jab of pain.

He'd reached a small wooden signpost that indicated the South Downs Way. Across the road, it seemed little more than a footpath cutting across a ploughed field, but to the right it led over grass in the general direction of Cheesefoot Head itself. Surely there would be people around there, even at this time of year? He turned right and headed off along the path, once again trying to break into a jog.

There were no tourists. The landscape seemed empty of humanity. To his left, the ground rose towards the lip of the amphitheatre. Obliquely left was a small wood, but it was too far away in his compromised state for him to hide in. Coming this way had been a serious mistake.

Tom's pursuer seemed to decide he'd had enough. He caught up effortlessly and they both stopped dead. "Just give me whatever you got from that motorcyclist," the man said. "You can make this easy or you can make it hard."

"Why the fuck should I help you?"

"Just hand it over."

Tom looked at him, braced and menacing. He knew when he was beaten, and slowly raised the phone. But without warning the man lunged forward, and Tom now realised he had a knife in his hand.

In that split second he knew he'd miscalculated. He'd imagined a parlay, a transaction, not a summary execution. It hadn't occurred to him that these people had finally lost patience with him. They didn't just want the files, they also wanted him gone.

Desperately he shouted, "Wait ..."

The knife thrust never found its mark. A gunshot resounded from somewhere in the distance, and the man stopped as if frozen, then dropped to his knees. Still staring at Tom in bewilderment, he folded to the ground and lay still.

Tom sank down next to him. Relief was surging through him, but it was tainted by horror at what had just happened. In an instant, a life had been extinguished in front of him. Reaching for the man's neck, he confirmed that fact for himself. There was no pulse. That single shot had been devastatingly accurate. For a moment Tom simply knelt there shivering.

He rose to his feet. Had anyone witnessed this? His glanced around wildly, blinking in the sun, and scanned the rim of the amphitheatre, then the wood, then other more distant clusters of trees. Whoever had fired the shot had already disappeared, and there was no one else in sight. What was he to do? This man was beyond help, but it seemed callous to leave him lying here. Yet if he stayed, how would he explain what had happened? As it was, he might be seen on his way back to his car, and even if he wasn't, his car would surely be picked up by CCTV cameras as he drove home. He felt trapped and out of control.

His own phone rang in his pocket. Dubiously he pulled it out and swiped his finger over the screen. "Hello?"

"Leave him." The voice was faintly familiar, but he couldn't place it. "Go back to your car. Go home. Don't speak to anyone. Understood?"

Tom stared around him. Was the caller somewhere in sight? He could still see no one. The voice said, "Don't just stand there – move! NOW!" The call clicked off.

He moved. He limped back to the road. Several motorists passed him on the way, and in the car park a family was climbing out of a large SUV. Too bad. There was nothing he could do to hide from them. He slumped gratefully into the driving seat of his car. All he could do was follow the instruction he'd been given.

Chapter 81

Half an hour later Tom was back at the house, still shivering at the memory of what had happened on the downs. He'd just been saved from certain death, yet the method had been utterly horrific.

Presumably whoever had shot that man also had the wherewithal to recover his body, even in an open public place like the South Downs Way. Tom had given up trying to imagine these people's methods and abilities. Either that, or in due time the police would come knocking on his door. He simply had to hope they wouldn't.

Eventually he recovered sufficiently to consider the phone Billy had given him. A man had just lost his life over this. He might as well find out why. He booted it up and navigated to the video files. There they were – no longer .flv files now, but standard .mp4s. He launched the first of them.

Unlike all the others he'd been seeing, this one was in colour, and it hadn't been taken in Rudge's office. The picture showed a patio of some kind, but not the one behind the Stay and Prosper building. This one was neater and more intimate. The foreground was bathed in light from behind the camera, but beyond it was darkness. Once again the footage had been shot in wide angle from a high position.

Facing the lens was Victor Rudge, who was talking to a man just under the camera. Only the back of the other man's head was in view. It was unclear whether there would be a full view of his face.

Rudge: "I thought you were never going to show your face here?"
Man: "I want to look you in the eye. I need to know you really mean what you're asking."
Rudge: "Of course I mean it. We've been through all this already."
Man: "Say it out loud for me."
Rudge: "What – you're recording this conversation?" A hint of panic.

Man: "What do you care? You've said enough to hang yourself already." A sigh of impatience. "I want you to say it to my face."
Rudge: "All right. I'm saying we should deal with Marcus Headington."
Man: "Deal with him?"
Rudge: "You know what I'm saying. Silence him. Take him out, if that's how you want to put it."
Man: "Why?"
Rudge: "Why? Because he's got everything wrong. He's popular, but he's weak. He thinks he'll win people over by being reasonable, but he's missing the point. History, as they say, is littered with good intentions. Marcus will do more for this campaign as a martyr than he's ever done for it as a convincing voice of dissent."
Man: "With friends like you, who needs enemies?"
Rudge: "This is Realpolitik, my friend. It's the world we're living in."
Man: "It's OK. You don't need to convince me. I just wanted to check that we're on the same page."
Rudge: "It needs to be as public as possible. This conference we're planning for November could be the place."
Man: "You're looking a long way ahead."
Rudge: "It's all in the timing, isn't it? Not too soon, not too late. I've thought this through very carefully."
Man: "Here's hoping then, eh?"

It was only towards the end of the clip that Rudge started to walk off screen and the other man swivelled round to track his movements. For a fleeting moment his face was clearly visible. It was the man Tom had just seen shot.

So there it was: Rudge's admission from his own mouth that he had instigated the plot to kill Headington, plus self-confessed collusion from the man who intended to carry it out. Wherever this scene was, Ben Bradwell had presumably planted another webcam there. Perhaps it was at Rudge's home.

Tom launched the second video. It was short and insignificant. It showed the same view of the patio, but the only activity involved a cat. So the first video was the smoking gun – the one piece of indisputable evidence against Victor Rudge.

What should he do with it? The obvious answer was to get it into the hands of Jay Reynolds. His first instinct was to take it to him, but then he changed his mind. Why expose himself to any more risk of being attacked? Let Reynolds come to him. Since being phoned by him in Manchester he'd had a mobile number. He called it.

"I think I've got the evidence you need."

* * *

An hour after Tom had made the call to Jay there was a knock at the front door. Glancing through the window, he saw a police car outside the house, its blue light flashing. Dread flooded through him. The police must have found that man's body, and worked out that Tom had been there. He opened the door with trepidation.

The officer looked him up and down and gave him an deadpan smile. "Mr Anthony? Speedy Parcel Deliveries here. I understand you have a package for Mr Jay Reynolds?"

Tom blinked at him for a moment, then said, "Yes, of course. Hang on." He fetched Billy's phone from the lounge. As he handed it over he said, "Don't …"

"It's all right – you do your job, we'll do ours." He gestured towards the car. "Blue light, sirens. Very Special Delivery."

Back in the lounge, Tom felt an overwhelming sense of anticlimax. Apparently his presence at the killing on the downs had so far gone unnoticed. The most active member of the group who had been hounding him was now dead, and the evidence that the group had been trying to suppress was in the hands of the authorities. Finally, it seemed, he could start to believe he was off the hook.

Yet he still had unanswered questions. How had those people known about his meeting with Billy? He'd ripped out the bug from his lounge, so where else were they getting their information? And who was the gunman who had saved his life on the South Downs Way? He was sure he knew the voice on the phone, but frustratingly, he couldn't place it.

Idly he glanced at a couple of letters he'd picked up from the doormat on his way out. One of them was from his bank, inviting him to provide a detailed description of how Jan had come to appropriate the proceeds of the share sale. He was still unsure what to do about that. He put the letter down on the mantelpiece with a sigh. As he did so, his eyes ran over a line of photographs he'd propped there long ago, and suddenly something clicked in his mind.

He knew who the mystery caller had been.

Could he be right? He sat in wonder for long minutes, working through the logic and examining his theory from every angle. At the end of it, he knew he couldn't be wrong.

Knowledge was power. Now that he had a name, he also had the opportunity to exploit it. This man had already helped him, probably more than once, and now he could help him for one last time. Tom's only challenge was how to contact him.

The answer came in a further flash of inspiration. Suddenly it seemed obvious how those people had picked up on his arrangement to meet Billy. There must be another bug here somewhere – one that he'd missed when he was looking before. For weeks he'd been worried that there might be, but he'd never taken the time to give it serious thought. He should be chiding himself for his sloppiness, but actually he was aware that this might give him a remarkable opportunity.

The lounge seemed the most likely target. Slowly, patiently, he set about searching every inch of it for a second time – the lights, the phone, the dresser, the bookshelves, the houseplants, the ageing CD collection, the pictures, even the curtains. He tipped over chairs and looked underneath them. He unscrewed the bayonet fittings from the table lamps.

Nothing.

He finally found it behind a tiny ventilation grille in the front wall, just below ceiling level. His watchers must have extracted the grille to insert the bug, then somehow glued it back in place. These people were true professionals.

He stood precariously on the arm of a chair near the vent and directed his words towards it.

"Are you listening out there?" He raised his voice to something just less than a shout. "I want to talk to my fairy godmother in person. I know his name, and if I don't hear from him, the authorities will know it too. Tell him I'll give him three days to get back to me."

Chapter 82

Two mornings later Tom was on the train to London. No one had responded to his fairy godmother appeal, but plenty of other things had been happening.

Victor Rudge had been arrested and was being held on remand, facing unspecified charges. Emily had phoned to tell him Marcus Headington had personally invited her to rejoin the volunteer team at Stay and Prosper. Headington had phoned him as well, and had invited him to a meeting in London. "I have a proposition for you," he'd said. "I think you'll find it intriguing."

Bernard had phoned to tell Tom he'd heard on the grapevine that Ben Bradwell's death, already reclassified as "unexplained", was now regarded by the police as an unsolved cold case. It might be the best he would get.

Tom phoned Mickey Choat to relay this news, and tried to sound confident that no action would result from his theft of Ben's computer. Mickey in turn had reported that Ben's mother was recovering from the supposed accident in which she'd been knocked down when she was trying to send Tom those elusive computer files.

Tom sat back in the train and watched the Hampshire countryside rolling past. Wintry sunshine dappled the seat opposite him. Bad things had happened, but he had an irrational sense that better things might be on the horizon. Brexit still weighed heavy on his spirit, but it wasn't over until it was over.

The train hummed along. He found his eyes closing, and barely noticed as it pulled into Basingstoke station. A new passenger slid into the seat opposite him. Suddenly he was wide awake. The passenger was speaking to him.

"Tom, you wanted a chat."

* * *

The man in front of him had changed in the fifteen years since they'd been together at college. Back then, Guy Freeman's slight figure had seemed to reflect his mild personality; he'd been witty, likeable and unchallenging. He was still slim now, but he'd fleshed out, and there was definition to his posture. He looked far more confident than he had back in those days, more at ease with himself. His light-coloured hair had been cropped down to a fine buzz cut, giving his head a clean, sculpted look. He had a sunburned complexion, and there were pronounced laughter lines round his eyes. He was wearing a dark zip-fronted jacket and an open-neck shirt.

Tom said, "Guy, it's good to see you."

"Likewise."

"You didn't stick with journalism, then?"

"Public service seemed a higher calling."

"Secret service, more like."

Faint amusement flitted across Guy's face. "Not exactly."

"But you work alongside people like Jay Reynolds, do you?"

He considered the question. "I might have met the man once or twice."

"And then there's this other life that you seem to have ... this freelance life. What about that?"

Guy said nothing.

They smiled for a moment, weighing each other up. Tom said, "I assume you're the one who's been keeping me out of trouble?"

"Doing my best – but you haven't made it easy."

"I suppose I should thank you for what you've done."

Sunlight flickered on Guy's face, and he continued to smile faintly. "So what is it that you want?"

"Will you answer some questions for me?"

Guy glanced around. The seats to the side of them were unoccupied, and the carriage was only half-full. He seemed satisfied that they could speak without being overheard. He said, "Try me."

Tom hesitated. "Aren't you worried I might be recording this?"

"I know you. You're not."

Tom stared at him, disappointed that he was so easy to read. He said, "I take it you know all about what's been going on?"

"I think I've got my head round it, yes."

"OK." Tom wondered where to start. "Am I right in thinking your people were behind the shooting in Manchester?"

"That would be a reasonable assumption. But I wasn't involved personally. I would never have sanctioned it. When I found out I vetoed it, but some of my colleagues weren't listening. I should have been watching them more closely."

"And none of this was done with official approval?"

"God, no. Officially we don't exist. Even unofficially we don't."

Tom looked at him searchingly, but it seemed he wasn't ready to add more yet. Tom said, "Were these the same people who got rid of Ben Bradwell?"

A faint nod. "I wasn't aware, so I couldn't stop it. They decided to stem the leak before it went anywhere."

"You mean about the shooting they were planning?"

Another nod.

"How did they know Bradwell had found out about it?"

"They were doing an integrity check, and they found a video camera on Victor Rudge's patio." He shrugged. "Stupid bastards. God knows how they missed it the first time around. They must have been shitting themselves."

"So they didn't know about the camera in Rudge's office?"

"Not then. They found out about that later."

"But they had to silence Bradwell straight away?"

Another nod. "I have to say that once he knew the score, he was a real problem. In their eyes, there wasn't much else they could do."

"Who came up with the idea of the shooting in the first place? Was it Victor Rudge or your people?"

"I think Rudge must have suggested it, but my colleagues were receptive. It suited their agenda."

"So how did Rudge make contact with them?"

"It was through his American connections. He put out feelers while he was in New York on business. Eventually the message got through to the right people over there, and they made contact with us."

An ominous thought came to Tom. "What about the beating my friend Bernard was given in Lincolnshire. Were you behind that too?"

Guy sighed. "That also happened before I found out about it."

"Jesus Christ! You're telling me it was all a setup?"

"They weren't sure what Bradwell had told you. They kept their heads down at first, while you were in hospital. They hoped your memory loss would keep them safe. But then they decided they couldn't chance it."

"For fuck's sake!" Tom sat silent for a while as he absorbed this new revelation. "But why did they beat up Bernard and not me?"

"You were lucky. They screwed up."

"Lucky? How do you make that out?"

"They paid a couple of locals to wind you both up in the pub, but they brought in their own hard men to do the beating. Then these guys picked the wrong man. It was supposed to be you – and they weren't supposed to stop at a beating."

"Jesus."

"It's against protocol to bring in outsiders, but you can both be glad they did."

"Huh!"

"Anyway, that was when I stepped in. As soon as I heard about it I made them downgrade your status to surveillance and warnings." He smiled grimly. "Much more bloody expensive. I had my work cut out justifying the cost. And you sure made life hard for me. You kept on sticking your nose in."

Tom was reeling as he tried to keep up with this. He said, "Do I assume you had nothing to do with Martin Frankl sending Emily Sanders to check me out?"

"Nothing at all. That was completely coincidental. It was all about Victor Rudge's weird blackmail scheme."

"So Rudge had some sort of hold over Martin Frankl?"

"I think he must have picked up something embarrassing about Frankl's army past. Theft charges or something. It had nothing to do with our people."

"But clearly you know about it."

"I've been catching up."

"You let me keep the video Billy gave me on the South Downs Way. Why was that?"

"We know what it shows – it's my mate talking himself into a hole. Now he's dead, which rather neatly sews things up. No blame, no foul."

"So you had this mapped out in advance? You more or less executed him?"

Guy shrugged. "There was no plan. We didn't know he would try to kill you. We were just keeping an eye on him."

"But he did – so it played out nicely for you in the end."

"Are you saying we shouldn't have saved you?

"No, of course not."

Guy said, "We had to break the circle somewhere."

Tom braced himself to confront the big question. "I have to ask. Were your mates responsible for my car accident?"

Compassion was evident in Guy's face for the first time. "I'm truly sorry about that. It was another thing they got up to before I heard about it. They shadowed you on your way back from meeting Ben Bradwell, and they must have forced you off the road."

"Do you know the grief I went through after that car smash? The surgery? The pain?"

"I can only imagine."

Tom looked angrily into Guy's eyes. "So did Bradwell actually give me those files? Did he tell me anything worth going through this for? I still don't remember."

Guy shook his head slowly. "We don't know."

Chapter 83

Tom gave Guy Freeman a hostile stare. He said, "What kind of setup do you have if you can't even control your own people?"

Guy sighed deeply. "There are sometimes differences of opinion. It's inevitable. We're cellular, so it takes time for instructions to filter through. As for the madcap plot against Marcus Headington, it should never have got off the ground in the first place. But a small breakaway group decided to go ahead with it, even after I warned them off."

"You make it sound as if you're a big wheel in all this."

"We're supposed to be egalitarian, but someone has to take responsibility."

The train slowed as it approached Farnborough station, and by tacit agreement they suspended their conversation. As it pulled out again a woman started to sit down next to Guy. He said firmly, "Sorry, this seat is taken." She retreated with a resentful frown.

Tom said, "Do I assume you're part of this American group? The people who kidnapped me in New York?"

Guy seemed to ponder. "Let's just say we share a common purpose. My colleagues on this side of the pond decided it would be a neat plan to dispose of you on the other side. No trail to follow, no questions to answer. They were still worried about you, and thought I wouldn't hear about it until it was too late. Luckily for you I did. All the same, I had to work hard to get you out."

"So what's the agenda of these American people?"

Guy glanced around to ensure he was in no danger of being overheard. He leaned forward. "Suppose there were a President who became a supreme liability. Suppose his policies led the country steadily closer to social breakdown, inequality, racial conflict, global instability, economic decline. Suppose he pushed the nation to the brink of nuclear war."

Tom waited.

"Suppose the main political parties were all in agreement that he had to go, but no one knew how or when to make it happen. Impeachment? Prosecution? These things have to go the rounds. They could take months – even years. They might never work. Suppose swift action were essential." He paused. "Definitive, untraceable action."

Tom looked closely at him. "Do you mean what I think you mean?"

Guy said nothing, but there was a flicker in his eyes.

"But what if that President's supporters had legitimate grievances? How can these people justify riding roughshod over them? We don't live in a binary world."

"Sometimes we have to proceed as if we did."

Tom stared at him. "Just who *are* these mysterious people?"

Guy shrugged. "Current and past members of the security services, serving and former police, people in higher education, the media, business, politics, the military. A cross-section of right-minded people. Not right-wing people – centrist people with sound values."

"But who decides what 'right-minded' means?"

Guy spread his hands as if the question demanded no response. He said, "The real work is done by a core of professionals with total deniability – people who can do what needs to be done."

"So you and the Americans work hand in glove?"

"You could say we're united in the cause of common sense."

"Whatever that is."

"I know it when I see it."

Tom shook his head in disbelief. "I don't think I like your organisation."

"Live with it, Tom. If this wasn't us, it would be people like us. We've always been here."

"But these days technology gives you so much power."

"The way I see it, we would be irresponsible if we didn't take advantage of it. The bad people always will."

"And you're not the bad people?"

"Of course not."

"But what makes you people think you have special rights to disregard the democratic process?"

"Democratic process? From what I've read, you've been complaining in the press that the Brexit process was anything *but* democratic, and ought to be halted. Well guess what – you're right. We're not here to disregard democracy, we're here to get it back on the rails." Guy sighed. "People don't always know what's best for them. Sometimes they have to be helped."

"So the Brexit vote was a plot? The last US election was a plot? Is that what you're saying? Come on, everyone's heard those conspiracy theories."

"Not conspiracy theories, Tom. You're not following me."

"What do you mean, then?"

"It was just a bit of misalignment, that's all. Populism was on the rise already. There was economic discontent. Mass migration was destabilising the world. Globalisation was a dirty word. All it took was a judicious nudge by clever and manipulative people, and the protest votes won out. The world lurched off in a new direction."

"Or maybe it was just time for populism to have its day."

Guy gave him a contemptuous look. "Do you really believe that?"

"But your interference makes you as bad as the cyber-criminals and social media hackers from Russia and the Far East, doesn't it? You're as guilty as the people accused of spreading lies and misinformation to influence voting."

"So what do you suggest? Do you *want* Britain to be marginalised in world affairs? Do you *want* America to abandon its role in sustaining the western alliance? Who's going to counter these movements if we don't?"

"I want to counter them honestly. I don't want to kick my opponents in the teeth. They have the same rights as everyone else, for god's sake. That's the whole ethos of the Stay and Prosper campaign."

"Very virtuous. Very noble. All I can say is, next time you see the world going to hell in a handcart, just be glad we're here. Don't be in too much of a rush to wish us away."

For a while neither of them spoke, then Guy said quietly, "There are always reasonable voices pointing out the rational path, and there are always people ready to listen. Sometimes they just need a bit of help to organise themselves."

Tom merely shook his head.

The train rattled over points, and abruptly Guy sat back. "You'll probably get your way with Brexit, anyway. We may have to take a step back from that, for a while at least."

"Aren't you worried about the fallout from the bodged shooting? When it all comes out, surely it'll deliver a fatal blow to the Remain movement?"

"Ah, but it may not come out. There's an in-fight going on in the security services over whether or not to release details of Victor Rudge's plot. At first sight it seems a gift for the pro-Leave camp – it would completely undermine Headington's Remain campaign. But nobody is quite sure what the reaction would be if it were made public, so they may just bury it."

"Seriously?"

"Think of the headline: '*Anti-Brexit group shoots itself in the foot.*' It's so extreme that a lot of people would still think it must be a pro-Brexit plot."

"So Rudge gets away with what he did?"

"They might be able to nail him on something else." He paused. "Not the blackmail plot, though. Insufficient evidence to proceed, or so I hear. The police think they'll have to let that drop too. The Remainers have dodged another bullet there."

"Huh!" Tom paused to take this in. "So why are your people backing off?"

"The security services are on the alert now, so we need to keep our heads down."

"But you people *are* the security services, aren't you?"

Guy gave Tom a humourless smile. "As I said, some of us might be."

"Well then."

A sigh. "To be honest, it may not make much difference what we do. It's beginning to look as though Britain might really leave the EU. There's a limit to what even we can achieve."

* * *

The two men fell silent. More countryside rushed past. Tom said, "There's something I don't understand. Once you knew about all this, why didn't you just contact me direct and tell me to butt out? Why all the subterfuge?"

Guy gave him an assessing look. "Would you really have dropped it all just like that? Wouldn't you have carried on worrying away at it – trying to understand what caused your accident, meddling in Ben Bradwell's death? Would you have just bought into what we're doing and kept your mouth shut?"

"I don't know."

"Well, there you are. We couldn't be sure either. After all these years, I don't know you *that* well." He gave Tom what looked almost an apologetic smile. "Anyway, my colleagues wouldn't have swallowed it. As you might have gathered, I can advise them what to do, but I can't always insist. Even after I stopped them trying to kill you, I had to let them play things their way."

Tom settled back into his seat and said nothing.

The train rattled again as it encountered another set of points. It seemed to signal a change of mood. Guy stretched and said, "When did you work out who I was?"

"I thought I recognised your voice when you phoned me on the South Downs, but it clicked when I got home. There was an old picture of the three of us on the mantelpiece – you, me and Malcolm outside that pub. Sophie took it."

"I remember that day." Guy nodded reflectively. "Malcolm and Sophie."

"They're doing OK. They seem happy."

Guy switched back to business mode. "So why did you ask to speak to me? I get the feeling it wasn't just out of curiosity."

"You're right." Tom gave him a searching look. "Is it true that you people have an almost limitless reach? I mean, can you really hack secure computers, burrow into bank accounts, all that kind of thing? The kind of stuff GCHQ is supposed to get up to?"

"No comment regarding GCHQ, but yes, we can do a lot of that."

"OK, so how about this? My girlfriend Jan has just stolen all my savings – the best part of a hundred and fifty grand – and she's disappeared off the face of the earth. Can you find her and get it back for me?" He corrected himself. "You could tell her I'll let her have a fair share if she'll agree to phone me."

Guy gave him an ironic smile. "I thought you were going to ask something difficult." He hesitated. "But if we do this for you, you'll keep a lid on everything you know. Permanently. Is that agreed?"

Tom looked cautiously at him. Was he about to sell his soul in return for recovering his money, or was he so far out of his depth that none of this mattered anyway? He decided to take the latter view.

Almost imperceptibly he nodded.

Clapham Junction station approached. Guy stood up. "This is where I leave you. We won't be meeting again." He squeezed out into the aisle. "None of this happened, right? You know more than you should, but I'm trusting you." He paused meaningfully. "I won't always be able to protect you."

Chapter 84

"I've been told I have to call you if I want my money back." Jan's tone was flat and her voice was subdued.

Tom was alone in Emily's living room. Emily herself was busy working her last evening shift at the pub. She was about to switch to lunchtimes in order to go back to the Stay and Prosper campaign in the evenings. Her two flatmates were also out.

He said, "Where are you?"

"None of your business."

"It's not your money anyway, it's mine."

"I invested it for you! You never would have made that profit if it wasn't for me."

"That's why I'm willing to talk about it."

"I don't know how the hell you've done this."

"Luckily I had friends in the right places."

He thought he heard her draw breath to protest, but if so, she apparently thought the better of it. She said, "So what do I have to do to get my money back? Am I supposed to beg?"

He hadn't expected this conversation to become so combative so quickly. He said, "I want to know what went so wrong. You seemed so supportive after the accident. You really helped me. Or was the whole thing an act from start to finish? I thought we were sorting things out."

"That's why you went off chasing that tart in London, was it? Was that your idea of sorting things out?"

She hadn't admitted until now that she knew about his growing interest in Emily. Indignantly he said, "She's not a tart! In any case, by then you'd made it pretty plain where you stood. You were just marking time."

"Oh was I? A lot you would notice."

"What does that mean?"

She gave a sigh. "You're always such an optimist, Tom. You just don't see what's in front of you."

"So tell me what I did to offend you so badly."

She was silent for a moment. He wondered what was coming.

"I was never enough for you, was I? That's what got me. You had to keep rushing off to Christine to set the world to rights. And then there was Danni. And how many others that I don't know about? And now this Emily woman. Why couldn't you just be happy with me?"

"I *was* happy! They were friends. There was nothing else between me and them."

"In your mind there was. It's the same thing."

This was unexpectedly profound. For a moment he was lost for words. Finally he said, "I don't see that at all."

"That's precisely your problem, Tom." She paused. "Anyway, I know all about Christine, trust me. I always knew there was something going on there."

"But that was ancient history. It only blew up again when you and I were already at the end of our tether – which you decided to hide from me after the accident, by the way."

"And why were we at the end of our tether, do you think? It was so that you could rush off and start it all up again with Christine, that's why."

"Wrong! You've got it all wrong, Jan. You've got the cause and effect completely back to front. Same thing with Emily."

"Don't start talking to me about her. I don't want to hear it."

"OK, OK."

There was a long pause. Finally she said "You're always so bloody positive about everything – so gung ho. I introduce you to my friends, and in five minutes they're all over you – you're flirting without even knowing it. We discuss our future, but you're the one who decides what we'll do. You never stop to see my point of view." She paused. "I did wonder if I'd have more to do when you were injured, but no – Tom looks after himself, Tom jumps into a car at the first opportunity, Tom heads off into the sunset. Well fuck it."

He was listening in bewilderment. "I always thought *you* were the tough one. You're so on top of everything, so composed. You always seem to know exactly what you're doing."

"I must have been acting the part too well. You weren't seeing me, you were seeing the front I put up."

He shuffled uncomfortably on the sofa. Part of what she was saying seemed like post-rationalisation, but he knew he couldn't dismiss all of it.

He said, "Was this why you pretended to be a financial trader?"

She sighed. "I don't know, Tom. That seems a long time ago now. I made up that lie when we met. I didn't even know what you were like then. But since then I suppose it's made me feel we were more on a level."

"I'm so sorry you felt like that."

"I'm just being honest."

Inconsequentially, he thought about the doctor with whom she'd apparently left the village. "What about this new man of yours? Presumably he's more sympathetic than I was?" He couldn't keep the irony out of his voice.

"There's no need to sound like that. He's a good man. He was condemned by the press before he ever got to put his own case forward. That woman who accused him of assault was a vindictive cow. Everyone in the village knows it."

He had a flash of insight. "You got him to watch me, didn't you? You needed to check that I wasn't getting my memory back. What if I had? Would he have given me a dose of GHB to help me forget again? The odd roofie mixed with cough syrup?"

"Don't be ridiculous." Was that a tiny pause before she denied it? He tried hard to push the thought out of his mind.

"So was it your idea or his to fleece me for everything you could get?"

She was quiet for a long moment. "I couldn't see any other way. His career is finished and his maintenance payments to his wife are ludicrous. He has virtually nothing to his name, and nor do I."

He hadn't meant the conversation to descend into recrimination. For some seconds neither of them spoke. In a more conciliatory tone he said, "I'm sorry you lost your real job."

"Huh! In case you didn't know, that was down to one of those people you kept talking about – Victor Rudge."

Suddenly he was alert. "What do you mean?"

"He's a major shareholder in the company I worked for. He has a contingency plan to shift his trading and hedge fund operations to Frankfurt if Brexit goes ahead, and a load of people in our office were made redundant in advance. I was one of the first to go."

Tom listened to this with amazement. Those rumours had been true. Despite Victor Rudge's near-psychotic determination to derail the Brexit process, evidently he'd been making contingency plans to abandon Britain and earn his money elsewhere in the EU. Perhaps it was prudent, but the hypocrisy was mind-bending.

As if following his train of thought, Jan said, "You're a committed Remainer now, aren't you?"

"Yup."

"Well I'm a Leaver. Think of your money as the divorce bill."

He couldn't stop himself picking her up on this. "If that's the case, it ought to be you paying *me*."

She sighed. "You always have to have the last word, don't you?"

"Look, I've already said I'm willing to talk about the money. Do you want to have that conversation or not?"

More quietly she said. "Go on then."

"I was thinking that I deserve to keep my insurance money from the accident, and also the money you invested for me in the first place. You had no call to take all that. There was also the cash in my bank accounts …"

She said nothing.

"I was thinking I would put all that aside, and then we could halve the profit on the shares. That's what I'm willing to let you have back. I just have to send a one-word text message saying yes."

She said nothing for a moment, then, "I don't have much bargaining room here, do I?"

Somewhat tersely he said, "No you don't."

The conversation had run its course. There was little more to add. He said quietly, "I'm sorry you hated me so much. It's hard to take in."

She sighed again. "I didn't hate you, Tom. Don't think that. I just couldn't keep up."

As he ended the call Tom stared bleakly across the room. He'd wanted explanations, perhaps even an apology, not the character assassination he'd just received. Whilst he'd scarcely recognised a lot of what Jan had said, some aspects rang painfully true.

Before he had the chance to change his mind, he lifted the phone, started a new text message, typed in three characters and pressed Send.

Chapter 85

The next morning Emily took Tom on a walk by the Thames near Hammersmith bridge. The weather was sunny again, but cold. Winter was on the way.

"Might as well make the most of my free day," Emily said.

"Jan phoned last night. I didn't have the energy to tell you when you got back from work."

"You mean you had other things on your mind." She gave him an arch grin.

He laughed awkwardly. "*Touché.*"

"So is she giving you back your money?"

"It's already been paid into my account."

"Hurrah!" She turned to give him a high five. "I call that a result."

"I'm letting her keep some of it. We've come to an agreement."

"You're being too generous to her, if you ask me."

He shrugged. "According to her I'm a terrible person."

She grinned. "It's no good fishing for compliments. I don't know you well enough yet."

His disappointment must have telegraphed itself. She linked arms with him and shook him. "Don't look like that! I'm winding you up."

"Really?"

"Of *course* I am! The verdict is 'so far so good'." She beamed at him. "Anyway, what's so terrible about you, according to her?"

"I'm domineering. I don't listen. I do whatever I want. I keep up old friendships when I ought to drop them."

"I think this must be a different Tom Anthony. I don't see any of that. Or are you just keeping me sweet till we're wed?"

He looked round at her sharply, but she shook him by the arm again, laughing. "Don't worry, you didn't make any rash proposals in your sleep. I'm not sure what I'd have said if you had."

They walked on. He said, "I feel as if I sold my soul to get my money back."

"How do you mean?"

"I called in a favour from a friend – the one I told you about, with the renegade colleagues who organised the shooting in Manchester. He reinstated my money, but the price was not to blow his cover."

"He saved your life on the downs. You were never going to turn him in."

He thought about that for a moment. "I suppose not."

"The bottom line is, what could you do alone against an organisation like that? It seems to me that the answer is not much."

"You're very forgiving."

She punched his arm lightly. "Wrong. I'm simply learning the art of pragmatism."

"So you reckon we have to live with these manipulative people?"

"I think we have to pick the fights we can win. We have to prioritise."

He nodded. If he was looking for absolution, this was probably more than he deserved, and the best he would get.

They walked past riverside pubs. Stalwarts were already sitting at outside tables, braving the morning chill.

She said, "So what did Marcus Headington want with you yesterday?"

"He wants me to work for the campaign. He's been short-handed since Victor Rudge resigned, and now he's sacked Martin Frankl as well. But he doesn't expect me to take on that role. He wants something between a copy writer and a PR man."

"Wow! Will you do it?"

"I might. I think I've had enough of the courier world. Too much of the same old same old."

"You told me you were thinking of working for your journalist friend."

"In the long term, who knows? But for the time being I've shot my bolt there. I told Malcolm I had a juicy Brexit story for him, but I can't write it now. I would be breaking too many confidences."

"Take the campaign job then. You could come and live in London." She squeezed his arm again.

"I think your flat would be a bit crowded."

"So sell your house and buy something here."

He looked at her to see if she was serious. She was difficult to read. He said, "Will you still love me when you're a famous actress and I'm just a lowly hack?"

"Actor."

"OK, actor! But will you?"

"I might decide to go into politics instead." Her eyes twinkled. "Who said anything about love, anyway?"

A couple of rowing eights passed on the river below, and they paused to watch. A trainer was travelling alongside them in a motorboat, shouting instructions through a megaphone. The oars cut cleanly through the water as the boats shot past.

"Such energy," Emily said. "Such commitment."

He turned to her. "Marcus is worried that Brexit might be unstoppable."

"What – with all the unresolved issues, all the opportunities for disagreement?"

"The politicians will fudge a result in the end. People like certainty."

"Marcus isn't giving up, though, is he?"

He shook his head. "Not at all. He still thinks the Brexit deal might fall apart at the final knockings."

"There you are then."

"But don't you worry that all this is beyond the influence of ordinary people like us? Don't you feel the world is out of control?"

She crinkled her face in a smile. "All the time. We can only do our best."

There was a screech from two gulls engaged in an aerial spat. Emily said, "Thank god for this."

"For what?"

She linked hands with him and raised their two arms in triumph. "This! The campaign was taking me over. I'd lost sight of everything else." She let their arms fall. "I still hate what's happening – it's such a terrible waste. But we'll still be here if we leave the EU, won't we? We won't drop off the edge of the world."

They walked on, their voices half drowned out by barked instructions to the rowing crews and the gulls' uncertain cries.

end

If you enjoyed Never Going to Happen, please review it!

Good reviews are like gold dust for authors, so if you enjoyed this book, please take a moment to post an Amazon review of it. Even a single sentence will be invaluable. All reviews carry weight, whether you bought the book, downloaded it free, or read it via Kindle Unlimited. The more reviews a book notches up, the more exposure Amazon will give to it.

UK review page: www.amazon.co.uk/product-reviews/B07B79CSJL/
US review page: www.amazon.com/product-reviews/B07B79CSJL/

Further absorbing mysteries from Topham Publishing

The *Mike Stanhope Mysteries* series by Peter Rowlands

"Have you ever read a book you hoped would never end? This was it!"

"A great representation of the quality of work that is sometimes overlooked or ignored by the publishing world."

"I love this fast-paced mind-bending intellectual thriller."

"A good new author to latch on to."

– Online reader reviews

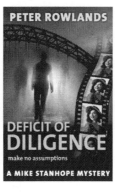
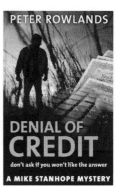

See overleaf for more details on each of these books

Alternative Outcome (Mike Stanhope Mysteries Book 1)

by Peter Rowlands

Mike Stanhope, divorced and disillusioned with his job in journalism, hopes to switch his life to a new tack by self-publishing a mystery novel based on a true story. But someone is after him, and the pressure is mounting.

Could his pursuer be the subject of an investigative article Mike once wrote? Could there be a link to Mike's attempts to track down a girl he knew as a child – the memory of whom he hijacked for his novel? Or might there be some deeper connection to his book?

As Mike struggles to keep his life on an even keel and tries to grasp at the chance of a new relationship, fact and fiction start to intertwine.

www.amazon.com/dp/B01CK1XVHK/

Deficit of Diligence (Mike Stanhope Mysteries Book 2)
by Peter Rowlands

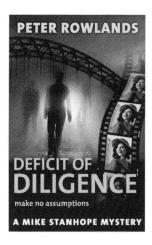

Who was the girl in that ancient film? How does she relate to writer Mike Stanhope? Could she provide a clue to unravelling the increasingly frightening mystery that surrounds him?

Things started so well. Mike is living in a beautiful part of the world, he's in a new relationship, and it seems he's inherited a valuable house. Yet it takes only a few ill-judged decisions and everything starts to fall apart. Despatched north on what looks a simple mission, he soon finds his work and life under threat, and to cap it all, the police seem to view him as a murder suspect.

This taut, pacey roller-coaster of a story works as a stand-alone mystery, but also forms an engrossing sequel to its predecessor, *Alternative Outcome*.

www.amazon.com/dp/B01N0PRFV0/

Denial of Credit (Mike Stanhope Mysteries Book 3)
by Peter Rowlands

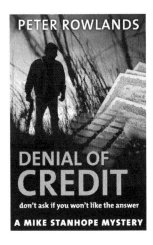

The opportunity to ghost-write an autobiography for a top executive appeals to journalist Mike Stanhope, but his subject, Alan Treadwell, is a tough taskmaster, and soon Mike is wondering if he's bitten off more than he can chew. It doesn't help when he learns things about the great man that he'd rather not know – things, moreover, that someone else also seems determined to keep quiet.

Meanwhile, Mike's personal life reaches a crossroads as the prospect of a new relationship makes him question everything. His life lunges towards a crisis on all fronts as the story approaches its explosive climax.

www.amazon.com/dp/B06ZZ9693L/

Author's note and acknowledgements

At its heart, *Never Going to Happen* is a mystery thriller and a romance. Contrary to what you might think, it was never meant to be a book about Brexit or about the American presidential election. These developments simply provided a useful backdrop.

There *is*, of course, a lot going on behind the main plot. It's a story about the fragility of democracy, and its tendency to take people to places they never expected to go. It's about the persistent belief among bright people of all persuasions that they know better than the majority, and need to reverse what they see as social or political aberrations. It's about the apparently limitless power of the internet and modern media to disrupt and redirect opinion. And it's about the insidious forces that may well be controlling our daily lives, insistent but unseen.

Given the real-world backdrop to this book, I feel I should reiterate that all organisations and characters in it (apart from known public figures) are totally fictitious. No campaign group like Stay and Prosper has ever existed as far as I know, though I sometimes wonder why not. Nor am I aware of any American organisation like ALS. Right Thinking is also entirely fictitious.

Locations, however, are nearly all real, apart from the village of Storton and the various London pubs, all of which I invented.

I owe a massive debt to the people who have encouraged me in my writing, and have tolerated my one-track mindedness whilst I've been doing it. In particular, my thanks go to those friends who have read this book in draft form (sometimes in more than one version) and commented so helpfully on it; and to Cass for her endless patience and encouragement.

About the author

Anders Teller is a pseudonym for an established British writer with several previous mystery dramas to his credit. He has spent most of his career as a specialist journalist, and lives in London.

51137537R00236

Made in the USA
Middletown, DE
30 June 2019